TH
A
SURROU

BY
MEREDITH WEBBER

TAMED BY HER BROODING BOSS

BY
JOANNA NEIL

MILLS &
BOON

Meredith Webber says of herself, 'Once, I read an article which suggested that Mills and Boon were looking for new Medical Romance™ authors. I had one of those "I can do that" moments, and gave it a try. What began as a challenge has become an obsession—though I do temper the "butt on seat" career of writing with dirty but healthy outdoor pursuits, fossicking through the Australian Outback in search of gold or opals. Having had some success in all of these endeavours, I now consider I've found the perfect lifestyle.'

When **Joanna Neil** discovered Mills & Boon®, her lifelong addiction to reading crystallised into an exciting new career writing Mills & Boon® Medical Romance™ . Her characters are probably the outcome of her varied lifestyle, which includes working as a clerk, typist, nurse and infant teacher. She enjoys dressmaking and cooking at her Leicestershire home. Her family includes a husband, son and daughter, an exuberant yellow Labrador and two slightly crazed cockatiels. She currently works with a team of tutors at her local education centre to provide creative writing workshops for people interested in exploring their own writing ambitions.

THE SHEIKH
AND THE
SURROGATE MUM

BY
MEREDITH WEBBER

First published in Great Britain 2012
by Mills & Boon, an imprint of Harlequin (UK) Limited.
Harlequin (UK) Limited, Eton House, 18-24 Paradise Road,
Richmond, Surrey TW9 1SR

© Meredith Webber 2012

ISBN: 978 0 263 89792 0

Harlequin (UK) policy is to use papers that are natural, renewable
and recyclable products and made from wood grown in sustainable
forests. The logging and manufacturing process conform to the
legal environmental regulations of the country of origin.

Printed and bound in Spain
by Blackprint CPI, Barcelona

CHAPTER ONE

'JUST because some bloke with more money than sense has bought the place, we don't need to go into a full-scale meltdown. He's bought the hospital, not our bodies and souls. We have to—'

Dr Elizabeth Jones was addressing her slightly panicked night shift staff outside the special care neonatal unit of Giles Hospital when a deep, slightly accented voice interrupted her.

'This word "bloke"? It means?'

She turned to face the source of the voice and her heart thudded to a halt, flopped around a bit and then went into a gallop rhythm she couldn't recall ever having felt before.

He wasn't drop-dead gorgeous, or even astoundingly good looking—he was just so, well, very *male*!

Arrogantly male!

His bearing, the slight tilt of his head, the imperious look in his near-black eyes, all shouted *leader of the pack*.

'Oh! Um—it's actually nothing. Aussie slang, you know—means a man...'

The words faltered out in dribs and drabs, her brain

too busy cataloguing the stranger's attributes to construct sensible sentences.

Smooth olive skin, the slightest, neatest of clipped beards and moustache emphasising a straight nose and a strong jaw, not to mention framing lips like—well, she couldn't think how to describe the lips, although the words 'eminently kissable' had sneaked into her head.

He wore a dark suit, though the way he wore it—or maybe it was the suit itself—made her wonder if she'd ever really seen a man in a suit before.

'I see!' the lips she'd noticed before the suit mused. 'So the "bloke" who bought the hospital has more money than sense?'

It was the accent making her toes curl in her strappy sandals and sending feathery touches up and down her spine.

It *had* to be!

'It was a stupid thing to say,' Liz added, back in control. Almost. 'It's just that this particular hospital is hardly a money-making concern because part of the original trust that set it up ensures we treat a percentage of non-paying patients, although—'

She stopped before she insulted the man further— if this *was* the man with more money than sense—by assuming he'd change that rule. In fact, from the day the staff had learned the hospital was on the market they had all assumed it *would* be changed. After all, who in their right mind would invest in a business that ran at a loss?

Who would invest in a business that ran at a loss? Khalifa could see the words she didn't say flashing across her face.

An interesting face—arresting. Though maybe it

was nothing more than the black-framed glasses that made it that way. What woman wore glasses with heavy black plastic frames these days? They did emphasise her clear creamy complexion but certainly didn't match her hair, ruthlessly restrained in a tidy knot behind her head, yet still revealing more than a hint of deep red in the darkness of it.

Intriguing, but he was here on business.

'I am the bloke you speak of, but I do not intend to make money from the hospital,' he assured her and the small group of staff who'd been her audience when he'd approached. 'I will continue to run it according to the original charter, but I hope to be able to bring some of the equipment up to date, and perhaps employ more staff.'

He paused. He'd intended outlining his plan to a meeting of the heads of the different departments, and had walked down to look again at the special care unit because it was his main interest. But now he was here, perhaps a less formal approach would be better.

Or did he want to spend more time studying the woman with the black glasses?

'My name is Sheikh Khalifa bin Saif al Zahn. Just Khalifa will suffice. I have bought the hospital in the hope that you, the staff, can help me and that I can, perhaps, offer those of you who wish to take part an interesting and hopefully enjoyable experience.'

The blank looks on the faces of the small group told him his explanation hadn't worked.

'I have built a new hospital in my homeland—an island state called Al Tinine—and it is operating well. My next wish is to set up a special care neonatal unit like this one. I am hoping to bring staff from my hospital to work here to gain an insight into how *you* work, and I would like to think some of the staff at this hospital would enjoy working for short periods in my country.'

He was certain this further explanation had been perfectly clear—perhaps the blank looks were caused by surprise.

Then the woman—he knew from photos she was Dr Elizabeth Jones, the one he wanted most of all—although in the photos she hadn't had the ghastly glasses and hadn't looked quite so—attractive?—stepped forward, knocking a pile of papers from the top of a filing cabinet and muttering under her breath before holding out her hand. One of the other women began gathering the papers, tapping them into a neat pile.

'How do you do, Dr Khalifa?' Dr Jones said formally, adding her name. 'Forgive us for reacting like dumbstruck idiots, but it isn't often anyone takes notice of our small hospital, let alone wanders in and offers us a chance to visit other countries. As for new equipment, we should be dancing with glee and cheering wildly. We make do with what we have and our success rate here in the special care unit in particular is first class, but the money from the trust that set up the hospital has been running out for some years.'

Khalifa heard the words but his brain had stopped working.

The woman he wanted, now she'd stepped out from behind the filing cabinet on which she'd been leaning, was undoubtedly pregnant. Not a huge bump, but pregnant enough to notice.

The shadow of pain, the fiercer thrust of guilt that chased him through each day had registered the bump immediately.

Dr Elizabeth Jones was as pregnant as Zara had been the last time he'd seen her...

Realising he'd dropped the conversational ball, Dr Jones spoke again.

'It sounds a wonderful opportunity for our staff to travel to your country and I'm sure we'd be very happy to welcome staff from your hospital, to learn from them as well as show them how we do things.'

There was a slight frown creasing the creamy skin, as if she wasn't absolutely certain of the truth of her words, but before he could decide, or even thank her for her kindness, a faint bell sounded and the group of women broke away immediately.

'Excuse me,' the doctor said. 'That was an end-of-shift meeting we were having. The new shift is on duty and I'm needed.'

She whisked away from the makeshift office—was one small desk and the filing cabinet in this alcove off the hall all they had?—and entered the glass-walled room where two lines of cribs held tiny babies. Two women—nurses, he assumed—in black and white patterned smocks leant over one of the cribs, straightening as Dr Jones joined them. Uncertain as to the isolation status of the ward, he remained outside, watching through the glass as she bent over the crib, touching the infant's cheek with one finger while reading the monitor beside it.

One of the nurses had wheeled a small trolley laden with drugs and equipment to the side of the crib but in the end Dr Jones straightened and shook her head, writing something on the chart at the end of the crib and stroking the baby's cheek, smiling down at the tiny being, before leaving the unit.

'You're still here!'

She spoke abruptly, obviously distracted by whatever it was that had summoned her to the baby's crib, then she proved his guess correct by adding, 'She has a little periodic apnoea but I don't want to put her back on CPAP.'

'Has she just come off it?' he asked, and the woman frowned at him.

'You understood that? I was really thinking out loud. Very rude, but I suppose if you've built one hospital and bought another, you probably do know a few things about medicine.'

'I know a few,' he said. 'Enough to get me through my medical degree and a follow-up in surgery.'

'I'm sorry,' she said, flashing a smile that almost hid a flush of embarrassment in her cheeks. 'It's just that health care seems to have become big business these days and the business owners don't necessarily know anything about medicine. But I'm holding you up. You'll want to see the rest of the place, and talk to staff in other departments, won't you?'

'Not right now,' he began, uncertain now that the woman's pregnancy had thrown his plans into disarray. 'You see, I'm particularly interested in this special care unit because I *had* hoped to persuade you to come to Al Tinine to set one up. I have heard and read so many good things about the work you do here, running a small unit that offers premature babies surprisingly successful outcomes on a limited budget.'

She studied him, her head tilted slightly to one side, and he wondered what she was seeing.

A foreigner in an expensive suit?

A bloke with more money than sense?

Guilty on both counts!

'So are you looking for something similar in size? Will there be limitations on the budget of the unit you wish to set up?'

Shocked by the assumption, he rushed into speech.

'Of course not—that wasn't what I meant at all. Naturally, we won't be looking at gold-plated cribs, but I would want you to have the very best equipment, and appropriate staffing levels, whatever you deemed necessary for the best possible outcomes for premature infants born in the southern part of my country.'

She smiled again—not much of a smile but enough to light a spark in the wide blue eyes she hid behind the chunky glasses.

'Gold plate would probably be toxic anyway,' she said, then the smile slid away and the little crease of a frown returned. 'My next question would be, are you setting it up as a working, effective unit that will give preemie babies the very best chance of leading normal lives later on, or are you putting it in because you think hospitals should have one?'

The question shocked him even more than the previous assumption had, although would he have considered it if not for Zara's and the baby's deaths?

That thought angered him.

'Are you always this blunt?' he demanded, scowling at her now. 'I expect you to set up a properly organised special care neonatal unit with some facilities for infants who would, in a larger hospital, go into a neonatal intensive care unit. I understand you have such facilities in your unit here at Giles, which is one of the reasons I chose this hospital.'

No need to tell her that the other reason was because

he'd heard and read such impressive reports of *her* work with neonates.

'Fair enough,' she said easily, apparently unperturbed by his scowl and growling reply. 'But when you said "you", did you mean "you" as in someone from the unit or me personally?'

Direct, this woman!

'I did mean you personally,' he told her, equally direct. 'It is you I wanted—or was you.'

'And having seen me, you've changed your mind?' The words were a challenge, one he could see repeated in the blue eyes for all she hid them behind those revolting glasses. 'Too tall? Too thin? Wrong sex, although the Elizabeth part of my name must have been something of a clue?'

'You're pregnant.'

He spoke before he could consider the implication of his statement, and as her face flushed slightly and her eyes darkened with some emotion he couldn't read, he knew he'd made a mistake.

A big mistake!

'So?'

The word was as steely as the thrust of a well-honed sword, but as he struggled to parry the thrust she spoke again.

'Pregnancy is a condition, not an illness, as I'm sure you know. I have worked through the first thirty-two weeks and I intend to continue working until the baby is born, returning to work…'

The fire died out of her and she reached out to support herself on the filing cabinet behind which her 'condition' had originally been hidden. The air in the alcove had thickened somehow, and though he knew you couldn't inhale things like despair and sadness, that was how it tasted.

'Actually—' the word, her voice strong again, brought him back to the present '—a trip away right now might be just what the doctor ordered. I presume if you're setting up a neonatal unit you already have obstetricians and a labour ward so my having the baby there wouldn't be a problem. As far as this unit is concerned, we have visiting paediatricians who are rostered on call, plus there's a new young paediatrician just dying to take over my job, so it would all fit in.'

The steel was back in her voice and he wondered if it came from armour she'd built around herself for some reason. She'd shown no emotion at all when she'd talked about her pregnancy, no softening of her voice, just a statement of facts and enquiries about obstetric services.

Neither did she wear a wedding ring, although handling tiny babies she probably wouldn't...

'Well?'

Liz knew she'd sounded far too abrupt, flinging the word at him like that, but the idea of getting away from the turmoil in her life had come like a lifeline thrown to a drowning sailor. She was slowly learning to live with the grief of Bill's death, but Oliver's continued existence in a coma in this very hospital was a weight too heavy to carry, especially as his parents had banned her from seeing him.

Oliver's state of limbo put her into limbo as well— her and the baby—while the unanswerable questions just kept mounting and mounting.

Would Oliver come out of the coma? Would his brain be functioning if he did? And would he want the baby?

She sighed, then realised that the man had been speaking while she was lost in her misery.

'I'm sorry,' she said, and this time heard him asking about passports and how soon she could leave the country.

'Right now, today!' she responded, then regretted sounding so over-eager. 'To be fair, I'd need a week or so to bring my replacement up to date. She's worked here before, which is why she wanted to come back, so it won't take much. And it's not as if I won't be coming back—you're talking about my setting up the unit and getting it running, not offering a permanent placement, aren't you?'

The man looked bemused, but finally he nodded, though it seemed to her that his face had hardened and the arrogance she'd sensed within him when he'd first spoken had returned.

He didn't like her—not one bit.

'There is no one with whom you should discuss this first?' he asked.

Liz shrugged.

'Not really. Providing I leave the unit in good hands, the hospital hierarchy won't complain, and as you've probably already discussed your idea of staff swapping with them, they won't be surprised. And this first trip shouldn't take long, anyway. It will be a matter of organising space, equipment and staff. It's not as if you'll be taking in babies until those are all in place.'

Now he was frowning. It had to be the pregnancy. He obviously wasn't used to pregnant women working. Well, it was time he got used to it.

The silence stretched, so awkward she was wondering if she should break it, but what could she say to this stranger that wasn't just more chat? And though she certainly hadn't given that impression earlier, she really didn't do chat.

Relief flooded her as he spoke again.

'Very well. I will be in touch later today with a date and time for our departure. I have your details from the HR office. In the meantime, you might make a list of equipment you will require. My hospital is the same size as Giles, and I would anticipate the unit would be similar in size to this one.'

The words were so coldly formal Liz had to resist an impulse to drop a curtsey, but as the man wheeled away from her, she gave in to bad behaviour, poked out her tongue and put her thumbs to her ears, waggling her fingers at him.

'He'd have caught you if he'd turned around,' her friend Gillian said, before taking up what was really worrying her. 'And what on earth are you thinking? Agreeing to traipse off to a place you've never heard of, with a strange man, and pregnant, and with Oliver the way he is, not to mention leaving all of us in the lurch?'

Liz smiled. The sentiments may have been badly expressed but Gillian's concern for her was genuine. Could she explain?

'You know Oliver's family won't let me near him,' she began, 'and Carol is the perfect replacement, and she's available so no one's being left in the lurch. That said, what is it you're most worried about—the pregnancy, the strange man, or that I've never heard of this Al Tinine?'

'It's the decision,' Gilliam told her. 'Making it like that. It's totally out of character for you. You took months mulling over doing the surrogacy thing—could you do it, should you do it, would you get too attached to the baby? You asked yourself a thousand questions. And while I know you've been through hell these last few months, do you really think running away will help?'

Liz shook her head.

'Nothing will help,' she muttered, acknowledging the dark cloud that had enshrouded her since Bill's death, 'but if I'm going to be miserable, I might as well be miserable somewhere new. Besides, setting up a unit from scratch might be the distraction I need. I love this place, would bleed for it, but you know full well the staff could run it without much help from me, so it's hardly a challenge any more.'

'But the baby?'

Gillian's voice was hesitant, and Liz knew why. It was the question everyone had been wanting to ask since the accident that had killed her brother and put his partner in hospital, but the one subject they hadn't dared broach.

Liz shrugged her shoulders, the helplessness she felt about the situation flooding through her.

'I've no idea,' she admitted slowly. 'The accident wasn't exactly part of the plan when I agreed to carry a baby for Bill and Oliver, and with Oliver the way he is and me not being able to even see him, who knows what happens next? Certainly not me! All I can do is keep going.'

She suspected she sounded hard and uncaring, but from the moment she'd agreed to carry a child for her brother and his partner, an agreement made, as Gillian had reminded her, after much soul-searching, she'd steeled herself not to get emotionally involved with a baby that would never be hers. She'd played it music Bill and Oliver loved, told it long stories about its parents, cautious always to remember it was their baby, not hers.

It would never be hers.

Now its future was as uncertain as her own, and she had no idea which way to turn. No wonder the challenge the man had offered had seemed like a lifeline—a tiny chink of light shining through the dark, enveloping cloud.

Then another thought struck her. Had the man said 'our' departure? Did he intend to hang around?

She felt a shiver travel down her spine, and her toes curled again...

Khalifa sat in the hospital's boardroom, listening to his lawyers speaking to their counterparts from the hospital, but his mind was on a woman with heavy-framed glasses, a pregnant woman who seemed totally uninvolved in her own pregnancy. Zara had been transformed by hers, overjoyed by the confirmation, then delighting in every little detail, so wrapped up in the changes happening in her body that any interest she might ever have had in her husband—not much, he had to admit—had disappeared.

To be fair to her, the arranged marriage had suited him as he'd been building the hospital at the time, busy with the thousand details that had always seemed to need his attention, far too busy to be dealing with wooing a woman. Later, Zara's involvement in her pregnancy had freed him from guilt that he spent so little time with her, though in retrospect...

He passed a hand across his face, wiping away any trace of emotion that might have slipped through his guard. Emotion weakened a man and the history of his

tribe, stretching back thousands of years, proved it had
survived because of the strength of its leaders. Now, in
particular, with El Tinine taking its place among its oil-
rich neighbours and moving into a modern world, he,
the leader, had to be particularly strong.

'Of course we will do all we can to assist you in
selecting the equipment you need for the new unit in
your hospital,' the chief medical officer was saying. 'Dr
Jones has updated our unit as and when funds became
available. She knows what works best, particularly in
a small unit where you are combining different levels
of patient need. I'll get my secretary to put together a
list of equipment we've bought recently and the sup-
pliers' brochures. Dr Jones will be able to tell you why
she made the choices she did.'

He hurried out of the room.

Dr Jones… The name echoed in Khalifa's head.

Something about the woman was bothering him,
something that went beyond her apparent disregard for
her pregnancy. Was it because she'd challenged him?

Not something Zara had ever done.

But Zara had been his wife, not his colleague, so it
couldn't be that…

Was it because Dr Jones running from something—
the father of her baby?—that she'd leapt at his offer to
come to Al Tinine? There had been no consultation with
anyone, no consideration of family or friends, just how
soon could she get away.

Yes, she was running from something, it had to be
that, but did it matter? And why was he thinking about
her when he had so much else he hoped to achieve in
this short visit?

It had to be her pregnancy and the memories it had stirred.

The guilt…

He, too, left the room, making his way back to the neonatal ward, telling himself he wanted to inspect it more closely, telling himself it had nothing to do with Dr Jones.

She was bent over the crib she'd been called to earlier and as she straightened he could read the concern on her face. She left the unit, sliding open the door and almost knocking him over in her haste to get to the little alcove.

'Sorry,' she said automatically, then stopped as she realised whom she'd bumped into. 'Oh, it's you! I *am* sorry—I'm a klutz, always knocking things over or running into people. My family said it was because I live in my head, and I suppose that's right at the moment. The baby in that crib was abandoned—found wrapped in newspaper in a park—and the police haven't been able to trace the mother. We call her Alexandra, after the park.'

Liz heard her rush of words and wondered what it was about this man that turned her into a blithering idiot, admitting to her clumsiness, thrusting ancient family history at a total stranger.

'The baby was found in a park?'

Despite the level of disbelief in the man's voice, her toes curled *again*. This was ridiculous. It had to stop. Probably it was hormonal…

'Last week,' she told him, 'and, really, there's nothing much wrong with her—she was a little hypothermic, occasional apnoea, but now…'

'Who will take her?'

Liz sighed.

'That's what's worrying me,' she admitted. 'She'll be taken into care. And while I know the people who care for babies and children are excellent, she won't get a permanent placement because she obviously has a mother somewhere. And right now when she desperately needs to bond with someone, she'll be going somewhere on a temporary basis.'

Why was she telling this stranger her worries? Liz wondered, frowning at the man as if he'd somehow drawn the words from her by...

Osmosis?

Magic?

She had no idea by what. Perhaps it was because he was here that she'd rattled on, because worrying about Alexandra was preferable to worrying about her own problems.

'You think the mother might return to claim her? Is that why the placement is temporary?'

Liz shook her head.

'I doubt she'll return to claim her. If she'd wanted her, why leave her in the first place? But if the authorities find the mother, they will do what they can to help her should she decide to keep the baby. It's a delicate situation but, whatever happens, until little Alexandra is officially given up for adoption, she'll be in limbo.'

Like me, Liz thought, and almost patted her burgeoning belly.

The man was frowning at her.

'You are concerned?' he asked.

'Of course I'm concerned,' Liz told him. 'This is a baby we're talking about. She's already had a rough start, so she deserves the very best.'

It didn't add up, Khalifa decided. This woman's attitude to a stranger's child, and her apparent disregard for her own pregnancy, although perhaps he was reading her wrongly. Perhaps this was her work face, and at home she talked and sang to her unborn child as much as Zara had to hers.

She *and* her partner talked and sang—

'Will the authorities also look for the baby's father?' he asked, and surprised a smile out of her.

'Harder to do, especially without the mother, although Alexandra's plight has been well publicised in local and interstate papers. The father may not have known the mother was pregnant. A man spends the night with a woman, and these days probably takes precautions, but there's no sign that flashes up in the morning, reminding him to check back in a few weeks to see if she's pregnant.'

There was no bitterness in the words and he doubted very much that her pregnancy had resulted from a chance encounter. Klutz she might be, but everything he'd read about her suggested she was very intelligent.

Though klutz?

'What's a klutz?'

Now she laughed, and something shifted in his chest.

Was it because the laughter changed her from a reasonably attractive woman to a beautiful one, lit from within by whatever delight the question had inspired?

Because the blue eyes he was drawn to behind the glasses were sparkling with humour?

He didn't think so. No, it was more the laughter itself—so free and wholesome—so good to hear. Did people laugh out loud less these days or was it just around him they were serious?

'It's a word we use for a clumsy person. I'm forever

dropping things—not babies, of course—or knocking stuff over, or running into people. Hence the really, really horrible glasses. Rimless ones, thin gold frames, fancy plastic—I kill them all. Bumping into a door, or dropping them, or sitting on them, I've broken glasses in ways not yet invented. I tried contact lenses for a while but kept losing them—usually just one, but always the same one. So I had five right eyes and no left, which would have been okay for a five-eyed monster, of course. Anyway, now I go for the heaviest, strongest, thickest frames available. I'm a typical klutz!'

She hesitated, as if waiting for his comment on klutzdom, but he was still considering his reaction to her laughter and before he could murmur some polite assurance that she probably wasn't that bad, she was speaking again.

'Not that you need to worry about my work abilities, I'm always totally focussed when I'm on the job. In fact, that's probably my problem outside it—in my head I'm still in the unit, worrying about one or other of our small charges.'

Yes, he could understand that, but what he couldn't understand was how freely this woman chatted with a virtual stranger. Every instinct told him she wasn't a chatterer, yet here she was, rattling on about her clumsiness and monsters and an abandoned baby.

Was she using words to hide something?

Talking to prevent him asking questions?

He had no idea, but he'd come to see the unit, not concern himself with this particular employee.

Which was why he was surprised to hear himself asking if there was somewhere other than this alcove off the passageway where they could sit down and talk.

'Of course! We've got a canteen in the courtyard, really lovely, but I suppose you've seen it already. I'll just let someone know where I'll be.'

She stepped, carefully, around him and entered the unit, stopping to speak to one of the nurses then peering behind a screen and speaking to someone before joining him outside.

'How much space do you have at this new hospital of yours?' she asked, the little frown back between blue eyes that were now sombre.

He glanced back at the unit, measuring it in his mind.

'I've set aside an area, maybe twice the size of what you have here,' he told her, and was absurdly pleased when the frown disappeared.

'That's great,' she declared, clearly delighted. 'We can have decent, reclining armchairs for the visiting parents and a separate room where mothers can express milk or breastfeed instead of being stuck behind a tatty screen. Beginning breastfeeding is particularly hard for our mothers. The babies have been getting full tummies with absolutely no effort on their part because the milk comes down a tube. Then suddenly they're expected to work for it, and it's frustrating for both parties.'

She was leading him along a corridor, striding along and talking at the same time, her high-heeled strappy sandals making her nearly as tall as he was.

A pregnant woman in high-heeled strappy sandals?

A doctor at work in high-heeled strappy sandals?

Not that her legs didn't look fantastic in them...

What *was* he thinking!

It was the pregnancy thing that had thrown him. Too close to home—too many memories surfacing. If only he'd been more involved with Zara and the pregnancy, if only he'd been home more often, if only…

'Here,' his guide declared, walking into the leafy courtyard hung with glorious flowering orchids. 'This, as you can see, is a special place. Mr Giles, who left the bequest for the hospital, was a passionate orchid grower and these orchids are either survivors from his collection or have been bred from his plants.'

Khalifa looked around, then shook his head.

'I did notice the courtyard on one of my tours of the hospital, but didn't come into it. It's like an oasis of peace and beauty in a place that is very busy and often, I imagine, very sombre. I should have thought of something similar. I have been considering practicality too much.'

His companion smiled at him.

'Just don't take space out of my unit to arrange a courtyard,' she warned. 'Now, would you like tea or coffee, or perhaps a cold drink?'

'Let me get it, Dr Jones,' he said, reaching into his pocket for his wallet. 'You'll have…?'

'I'm limiting myself to one coffee a day so I make it a good one. Coffee, black and strong and two sugars, and it's Liz,' she replied, confusing him once again.

'Liz?' he repeated.

'Short for Elizabeth—Liz, not Dr Jones.'

He turned away to buy the coffees, his mind repeating the short name, while some primitive instinct sprang to life inside him, warning him of something…

But what?

'Two coffees, please. Strong, black and two sugars in both of them.'

He gave his order, and paid the money, but his mind

was trying to grasp at the fleeting sensation that had tapped him on the shoulder.

Because of their nomadic lifestyle in an often hostile country, an instinct for danger was bred into him and all his tribal people, but this woman couldn't represent a danger, so that couldn't be it.

But as he took the coffees from the barista, the sensation came again.

It couldn't be because they drank their coffee the same way! Superstition might be alive and well in his homeland, but he'd never believed in any of the tales his people told of mischievous djinns interfering in people's lives, or of a conflagration of events foretelling disaster. Well, not entirely! And a lot of people probably drank their coffee strong and black with two sugars.

Besides, he only drank it this way when he was away from home. At home, the coffee was already sweet and he'd drink three tiny cups of the thick brew in place of one of these...

CHAPTER TWO

COULD ten days really have flown so quickly?

Of course, deciding on what clothes she should take had consumed a lot of Liz's spare time. Khalifa...could she really call him that? So far she'd avoided using his name directly, but if she was going to be working with him she'd have to use it some time.

Not that she didn't use it in her head, sounding it out, but only in rare moments of weakness, for even saying it started the toe curling—and she had to stretch them as hard as she could to prevent it happening.

Anyway, Khalifa had given her a pile of wonderful information brochures about his country, explaining that the capital, Al Jabaya, was in the north, and that his eldest brother, while he had been the leader, had, over twenty years, built a modern city there. The southern part of Al Tinine, however, was known as the Endless Desert, and the area, although well populated, had been neglected. It was in the south, in the oasis town of Najme, that Khalifa had built his hospital.

For clothes Liz had settled on loose trousers and long shift-like shirts for work, and long loose dresses for casual occasions or lolling around at home, wherever home turned out to be. Wanting to respect the local customs, she'd made sure all the garments were modest, with sleeves and high necklines.

Now here she was, in a long, shapeless black dress—black so it wouldn't show the things she was sure to spill on herself on a flight—waiting outside her apartment block just as the sun was coming up. Gillian, who would house—and cat-sit, waited beside her.

'Your coach approaches, Cinderella,' Gillian said, as a sleek black limousine turned into the street.

'Wrong fairy-tale, Gill,' Liz retorted. 'Mine's the one with Scheherazade telling the Sultan story after story so she didn't get her head chopped off next morning.'

Had she sounded panicked that Gill looked at her with alarm?

'You're not worrying *now* about this trip, are you? Haven't you left it a bit late? What's happened? You've been so, well, not excited but alive again.'

The vehicle pulled up in front of them before Liz could explain that sheer adrenalin had carried her this far, but now she was about to depart, she wasn't having second thoughts but third and fourth and fifth right down to a thousandth.

Better not to worry Gill with that!

'I'm fine,' she said, then felt her toes curl and, yes, he was there, stepping smoothly out of the rear of the monstrous car just as she tripped on the gutter and all but flung herself into his arms.

He was quick, she had to give him that—catching her elbow first then looping an arm around her waist to steady her.

She'd have been better off falling, she decided as her body went into some kind of riotous reaction that was very hard to put down to relief that she *hadn't* fallen!

'You must look where you are going,' he said, but although the words came out as an order, his voice was gruff with what sounded like concern.

For her?

How could she know?

And did it really matter?

The driver, meanwhile, had picked up her small case and deposited it in the cavernous trunk so there was nothing else for Liz to do but give Gill a quick kiss goodbye and step into the vehicle.

In the back.

With Khalifa.

'Wow, look at the space in here. I've never been in a limo!' she said, while her head reminded her that it had been years since she'd talked like a very young teenager. Perhaps she was better saying nothing.

'Would you like a drink? A cold soda of some kind?'

Khalifa had opened a small cabinet, revealing an array of beverages. The sight of them, and the bottles of wine and champagne—this at six-thirty in the morning—delighted Liz so much she relaxed and even found a laugh.

'You're talking to a klutz, remember. I can just imagine the damage a fizzy orange drink could do to this upholstery. Besides, I've just had my coffee fix so I should manage an hour's drive to the airport without needing further refreshment.'

It was the laugh that surprised him every time, Khalifa realised. He hadn't heard it often in the last ten days but every time it caught his attention and he had to stop himself from staring at his new employee, her face transformed to a radiant kind of beauty by her delight in something. Usually something absurd.

'So tell me about Najme,' she said, a smile still lingering on her lips and what sounded like genuine interest in her voice.

He seized the opportunity with both hands. Talking about Najme, his favourite place on earth, was easy.

And it would prevent him thinking about his companion and the way she affected him—especially the way she'd affected him when he'd caught her in his arms...

'Najme means star. It has always been considered the star of the south because of the beauty of the oasis on which it is built. Date palms flourish there, and grass and ferns, while reeds thrive by the water's edge. When oil was discovered, because Al Jabaya was a port from ancient times, used for trading vessels and the pearling fleet, it seemed right that the capital should be built there. So my brother and his advisors laid out plans and the city grew, but it virtually consumed all his time, and the south was not exactly neglected but left behind. Now it is up to me to bring this area into the twenty-first century, but I must do it with caution and sensitivity.'

He looked out the window as the sleek vehicle glided along a motorway, seeing houses, streets, shops and factories flash by. It was the sensitivity that worried him, bringing change without changing the values and heritage of his people.

It was because of the sensitivity he'd married Zara, a young woman of the south, hoping her presence by his side would make his changes more acceptable.

And then he'd let her down...

'Is the hospital your first project there?' his colleague asked. Pleased to be diverted, he explained how his brother had seen to the building of better housing, and schools right across the country, and had provided free medical care at clinics for the people in the south, but he had deemed the hospital in Al Jabaya to be sufficient for the country, even providing medical helicopters to fly people there.

'But the people of Najme, all the people of the south, have always been wary of the northerners. The southern regions were home to tribes of nomads who guarded trade routes and traded with the travellers, providing fresh food and water, while Al Jabaya has always been settled. The Al Jabayans were sailors, pearl divers and also traders, but their trade has been by sea, so they have always been in contact with people of other lands. They are more…worldly, I suppose you would say.'

'And you?'

The question was gentle, as if she sensed the emotion he felt when talking of his people.

'My mother was from the south. My brother's mother was from the north, so when she grew old, my father took a second wife—actually, I think she was the third but that's not talked of often. Anyway, for political reasons he took a wife from a southern tribe, so my ties are to the south. My wife, too, was a southerner…'

He stopped, aware he'd spoken to no one about Zara since her death, and none of his friends had used her name—aware, no doubt, that it was a subject he wouldn't discuss.

'Your wife,' Liz Jones prompted, even gentler now.

'She died in childbirth. The baby was premature, and she, too, died.'

Liz heard the agony in his voice, and nothing on this earth could have prevented her resting her hand on his.

'So of course you want the unit. It will be the very best we can achieve.' She squeezed his fingers, just a comforting pressure. 'I know it won't bring back your wife or child, but I promise you it will be a fitting memorial to them and be something you'll be proud of.'

Then, feeling utterly stupid, she removed her hand and tucked it in her lap lest it be tempted to touch him again.

This time the silence between them went beyond awkward and, aware she'd overstepped a boundary of some kind, Liz had no idea how to ease the tension. She leaned forward, intending to take a drink from the cabinet—but as she'd already pointed out, spilling fizzy orange soda all over the seat and undoubtedly splashing her new boss probably wasn't the answer.

Instead, she pulled one of the information leaflets he'd given her from her capacious handbag and settled back into the corner to read it. If he wanted the silence broken, let him break it.

He didn't, and, determined not to start blithering again, she refused to comment when the car sailed past the wide road that led to the international air terminal. Sailed past the road to the domestic one as well, then turned into another road that led to high wire fences and a gate guarded by a man in a security uniform.

To Liz's surprise, the man at the gate saluted as the gates swung open, and the limo took them out across wide tarmac to stop beside a very large plane, its sleek lines emphasised by the streaks and swirls of black and gold paint on its side. It took her a moment to recognise the decoration as Arabic script and she could be silent no longer.

'What does it say?' she asked, totally enthralled by the flowing lines, the curves and squiggles.

'Najme,' her host replied, and before she could ask

more, he was out of the limo and speaking to some kind of official who waited at the bottom of the steps.

The driver opened the door on Liz's side and she slid out, not as elegantly as her companion had but, thankfully, without falling flat on her face.

'This gentleman will stamp your passport and one of my pilots will check your luggage,' Khalifa told her, all business now. 'It is a precaution he has to take, I'm sure you understand.'

Totally out of her depth, Liz just nodded, grateful really that she had no decisions to make. She handed over her passport, then hovered near the bottom of the steps until a young man came down and invited her inside.

'Khalifa will bring your passport and the pilot will put your luggage on board,' he told her. 'I am Saif, Khalifa's assistant. On flights I act as steward. He prefers not to have strangers around.'

Liz smiled to herself, certain the young man had no idea just how much he'd told her about his master. But there was no time to dwell on these little details for she'd reached the top of the steps, and entered what seemed like another world.

There was nothing flashy about the interior of the plane, just opulent comfort, with wide, well-padded armchairs in off-white leather, colourful cushions stacked on them, and more, larger, flat cushions on the floor near the walls of the aircraft. A faint perfume hung in the air, something she couldn't place—too delicate to be musk, more roses with a hint of citrus.

'Sit here,' Saif said, then he waited until she sank obediently into one of the armchairs before showing her where the seat belt was and how a small table swung out from beside the chair and a monitor screen opened up on it.

'You will find a list of the movies and other programmes in the book in the pocket on the other side of the chair, and you can use your laptop once we're in the air. Press this button if there's anything you require and I will do my best to help you.'

Saif turned away, and Liz realised Khalifa had entered the plane. He came towards her, enquired politely about her comfort, handed back her passport then took the chair on the other side of the plane.

'All this space to carry two people?' she asked, unable to stop herself revealing her wonder in the experience.

'It can be transformed into many configurations,' Khalifa replied. 'The flight time is fifteen hours, and I thought you might be more comfortable in a bed, so the back of the cabin is set up for your convenience.'

'With a bed?'

It went beyond Scheherazade's fantastic stories, and now Liz forgot about hiding her wonder.

'I've read about executive jets, but never thought I'd experience anything like this. May I have a look?'

Was it the excitement in her voice that stirred the man? She had no idea, but at least he'd smiled, and as she felt a slight hitch in her breathing, she told herself it was better that he remained remote and unreachable— far better that he didn't smile.

'Wait until we're in the air. The aircraft door is closed and I assume the pilot is preparing for take-off. Because we have to compete with both the international and the domestic flights for take-off slots, we can't delay. But while we're on the ground, Saif could get you a drink.

Perhaps champagne to celebrate your first flight in an executive jet?'

'I can celebrate with orange juice,' Liz said, and although Khalifa was sure he saw her right hand move towards her stomach, she drew back before she touched it. The mystery of her pregnancy—or her attitude to it—deepened. He'd seen a lot of Liz Jones in the last ten days, and not by even the slightest sign had she acknowledged the baby she carried.

Neither had she ever mentioned the baby's father, and although he had a totally irrational desire to know about this unknown man, he couldn't bring himself to ask.

Oh, he'd thought of a dozen ways he could bring it up. *Does the baby's father not mind your leaving now? If you're still in my country, would the baby's father like to fly to Al Tinine for the birth?*

But every time he thought of a question, he told himself it was none of his business and quashed the desire to ask.

And it *was* none of his business, apart from the fact that the woman was coming to work for him and he'd have liked to know what made her tick. Having seen her in action in the Giles neonatal unit, he knew she was deeply involved with all her little charges, and genuinely caring, which made her apparent detachment from her own pregnancy all the more puzzling.

An enigma, that's what she was.

Saif had returned with freshly squeezed orange juice for them both and she smiled as she thanked him— smiled the kind of smile he'd seen her use around the unit, the smile she gave the other staff, the parents and the babies.

And just as irrationally as his desire to know about

her baby's father came the thought that he'd like her to smile like that at him...

She'd pulled some papers out of the bag she'd carried on board, and as she sipped her juice she was studying them.

In order to avoid conversation?

The thought aggravated him. Most women he'd had aboard his plane had been only too keen to talk to him.

But, then, most women he'd had aboard his plane had been diversions—pleasant playmates—not work colleagues, and pregnant work colleagues at that.

And, come to think of it, the days of pleasant playmates were long gone, too.

Though surely the woman had *some* conversation.

'The baby in the unit, Alexandra,' he began, deciding he'd start one himself. 'Was anything sorted out for her?'

As the delightful smile flashed across Liz Jones's face he regretted his impulse, because having had it directed at him once, he immediately wanted to see her smile again, to keep her smiling.

'Alexandra's grandmother turned up. It was like a miracle. The woman was from Melbourne and her daughter had taken off around Australia, backpacking with a group of friends. Her mother, Rose her name is, suspected there was something wrong with her daughter, who'd been moody and unhappy even while she was planning her trip. It was only when Rose saw something on the television about Alexandra that she began to put the pieces of the puzzle together.'

Khalifa tried to picture the scenario. In his family, many of the women still lived together, three generations, sometime more, and other women in the family visited every day for breakfast or coffee. His grand-mother would have picked up a pregnancy in an instant.

'Was this daughter living with her mother?' he asked, intrigued now. 'Or seeing her regularly? Would the mother not have noticed her pregnancy?'

He won another smile, only a small one but still it felt like a victory.

'Her daughter had always been big, and had put on more weight, but she hadn't been obviously pregnant before she'd left on the trip. She'd kept in contact with her mother, so Rose knew she'd been with her friends in Brisbane at the time Alexandra was found, but left almost immediately afterwards. By the time Rose saw the appeal for information, the daughter was in Central Australia somewhere, and, from photos sent on the mobile phone, considerably thinner.'

'And this Rose contacted you?'

'She phoned the hospital while the programme was still running on her television. She'd tried to phone her daughter but couldn't get through, but Rose turned out to be a determined woman and no grandchild of hers was going to be brought up in care. She offered to have a DNA test the next day and get the lab to send the re-sults straight to the hospital, but even before she knew for certain, she was on a plane to Brisbane.'

'And she *is* the grandmother?'

Was he really so interested in one tiny baby, Liz wondered, or was he talking to divert her as the plane was rising smoothly into the sky? She had no idea, but Rose and Alexandra's story was a good one, so she con-tinued to explain.

'She not only is, but she's a force to be reckoned with. She slashed her way through all the red tape, parried any objections and took her grandchild back to Melbourne yesterday. She says it's up to her daughter to decide what they tell Alexandra—she's keeping her name, too—but Rose is more than happy to bring the infant up as her own.'

'So, a happy ending all round,' Khalifa said with a broad smile, and Liz forgot about toes curling because this smile was enough to make her entire body spark and fizz in a most unseemly manner.

She'd heard about physical attraction but had obviously never experienced it, because this was something entirely new, and entirely ridiculous because she was going to be working with this man and couldn't go around all sparky and fizzy every time he smiled.

Although perhaps he wouldn't smile too often!

'It *was* a happy ending,' she said, 'and a great relief as far as I am concerned as I'd have hated to go away leaving Alexandra in limbo.' She hesitated, then the words she knew she shouldn't say came out anyway. 'It's not a very comfortable place, limbo!'

She turned her attention back to the papers in on lap, although she knew their contents by heart. She hadn't needed to check out neonatal units on the internet, as she'd always kept up with latest developments, but she didn't want to get anything wrong or miss out on something that might work in Al Tinine.

Al Tinine... If Najme meant star, did Tinine also have a meaning? She pulled out the little table Saif had shown her and set down her file on the new unit, digging into her bag for the brochures on the country, certain there'd be an explanation somewhere.

She could ask.

But asking meant starting another conversation and

having a conversation meant looking at him, and while she was looking at him he might smile and…

Klutz!

As far as she could remember, she'd never been a mental klutz, confining her clumsiness to the physical, but now her mind was running wild and bumping into things and losing the plot completely.

Could she put it down to a slight release from the grief and tension of the last few months?

She had no idea but hopefully it would sort itself out before too long and return to the focussed, professional brain she would need to do her job.

And to work out what was going to happen to the poor baby!

Surreptitiously, hiding her hand under the papers still resting on what was left of her lap, she gave it a pat, mentally reassuring it that things would sort themselves out, though what things, and quite how, she had no idea. Oliver was, after all, the father of the baby, and should he want it, and be fit enough to care for it, then all would be well, but there were too many uncertainties to even consider the poor thing's future at the moment so, to distract herself from the depression she was teetering towards, she forgot about not talking to Khalifa.

'The name, Tinine, does it, too, mean something?'

Of course he *had* to smile!

And now she was reasonably close to him, she could see a twinkle in the depths of his dark eyes.

A very beguiling twinkle.

Fizz, spark, spark, fizz—surely pregnant women shouldn't feel this level of physical attraction!

'You will have to wait and see,' he replied, and the promise in his voice made her physical reactions worse—far worse—though all the man was discussing was the name of his country, not some riotous sexual encounter in the back cabin of the plane.

Was it a double bed?

Queen size?

King?

Her wayward mind was throwing up the questions and it took all her determination and discipline to pull it back into line.

Forget about the destination, concentrate on the unit. She pulled out the figures, playing with what she already knew. Najme had a population of approximately fifty thousand people and a high birth rate of twenty per thousand. Khalifa had already explained that about a third of the population were expats, doctors, teachers, scientists and labourers, all brought in from other places to help in the modernisation of the country.

Fiddling with the figures, knowing full well that they told her only three basic beds would be required, she began to wonder just why her new boss was planning a larger facility.

'Are you expecting the population to grow fairly swiftly, or more people to move into the city? Or is there some other reason you want the larger unit?'

The question had come out before she realised Khalifa was speaking to Saif.

'I'm sorry, I shouldn't have interrupted. I was thinking out loud.'

No smile this time, which was just as well—and the little twinge of disappointment was stupidity.

'I'm discussing our menu for the flight and you're thinking work,' Khalifa said, enough amusement in his voice to start the fizzing. 'Do you never relax?'

'It's Tuesday, that's a workday for me. And, yes, I can relax, but I did want to check over these figures again.'

He almost smiled.

'The surrounding area supports probably as many people again, although the majority of them are living as they've always lived. Traditions dating back thousands of years are hard to change, and I am afraid if I rush things, we will lose too much.'

'Lose too much?' she queried.

'Traditional skills and values,' he said. 'I don't mean camel milking, or even spinning thread from the wool of goats, but what we call our intangible cultural heritage. The patterns the women wove into the rugs told the history of our tribe, told it in pictures they understood, and using these rugs, which they spread on the floor in summer and hung on the inside walls of their tents in winter, they taught the children. Now the children learn in school, learn skills and information they will need to equip them for the modern world. But how do we keep our tribal history alive?'

'You've spoken before about keeping tradition alive,' Liz remembered, 'and while I can't help you with any ideas about the cultural side, I do wonder, if these people live as they've always lived, will they use a hospital to have their babies, and would they be able to adapt to the situation if the baby needs special care?'

Her companion sighed deeply.

'I'm not really expecting them to use an obstetrician and have their babies in a hospital. Not immediately anyway, but once a baby is born, that life is precious and if it needs help, I am certain they will seek it.'

He paused and she wondered just how much pain this

discussion might be causing him—how much it might remind him of his wife.

'We have always had midwives, for want of a better word: women within the tribe who were taught by their elders to help other women through their pregnancy and childbirth. Now young local women are training not only as modern midwives but as obstetricians, and although they can't be everywhere, they can work with the older women, explaining new ideas and methods. Maybe through them we can introduce the idea of special care for fragile infants so, should the situation arise, the women will more readily accept the unit.'

'Or perhaps, with a translator—even with you if you had the time—I could visit some of these outlying areas, take a crib, show them what we can do, and how we can help the babies, explain that the family can be involved as well.'

To Liz's surprise, the man laughed, a real, wholehearted laugh that changed his face completely.

'Not families, I implore you,' he said at last, still smiling. 'You will get aunts, cousins, sisters, grandmothers—forty or fifty people all wanting to sit with the baby.'

'That many?' Liz teased, smiling back at him, and something in the air stilled, tension joining them together in an invisible bond, eyes holding eyes, a moment out of time, broken only when Saif said, in a long-suffering voice, 'If we could please get back to the menu!'

The menu proved delicious. Slices of melon and fresh, sweet strawberries with a slightly tart mint syrup poured over them. Delicate slivers of duck breast followed, the slices arranged on overlapping circles of potato, crispy on top and soft underneath, while fresh white asparagus with a simple butter sauce completed the main meal.

Offered a range of sweets, Liz declined, settling instead for a platter of fruit and hard cheese, finding, to her delight, that the dates accompanying it were so delicious she had to comment on them.

'They are from Najme,' Khalifa explained. 'We have the best dates in the world.'

Liz, replete and happy, forgot about the moment of tension earlier and had to tease again.

'You'd know that, of course, from the World Date Olympics, would you? Do they judge on colour and size as well as taste?'

Khalifa studied her for a moment. Where was the stressed, anxious, and obviously sad woman he'd first met at the hospital? Was this light-hearted, teasing Liz Jones the real Liz Jones?

He had no idea, although the thought that she might have relaxed because she'd escaped from the father of her child did sneak into his mind.

'We just know ours are the best,' he said firmly, 'and while we don't have a date Olympics you'll be arriving just in time for the judging of the falcons—a kind of falcon Olympics.'

Interest sparked in her eyes and she studied him in turn—checking to see if he was joking?

'Falcons?' she repeated.

'Our hunting birds,' he explained. 'It's one custom we are determined not to let die. The birds are part of our heritage and at Najme you will see them at their best, for everyone wants to have the best bird.'

'Falcons,' she whispered, smiling, not at him, he

thought, but to herself. 'Now I really know I'm heading for another world. Thank you,' she said, 'not just for giving me this opportunity but for so much else.'

She pushed aside the little table and undid her seat belt.

'And now,' she said, 'if it's all right with you, I might check out that bedroom.'

Saif must have been watching from behind the front curtain, for he appeared immediately, taking Liz's arm and leading her into the cabin.

And, no, he, Khalifa bin Saif Al Zahn, was not jealous of Saif walking so close to her.

Why should he be?

The woman was nothing more than another employee, if a somewhat intriguing one.

But as he remembered a moment earlier when they'd both smiled and something in the atmosphere around them had shifted, he knew that wasn't entirely true.

CHAPTER THREE

SHE was sleeping soundly when he knocked quietly and entered the cabin some hours later. Her lustrous hair was loose, spread across the pillow, a rich, red-brown—more red, he felt, but a deep, almost magenta red.

Beautiful against the white of the pillow and the rich cream of her skin, her hair was shiny, silky—his fingers tingled with a desire to feel the texture.

He moved into the cabin, slightly embarrassed at having to invade her privacy, and more than a little embarrassed by his thoughts. But the pilot had warned they were approaching turbulence, and Khalifa didn't want her thrown out of the bed. It was fitted with what in a chair would be called seat belts, simple bands that stretched across the bed to restrain a sleeping passenger.

Could he strap her in without disturbing her?

Was it even right to be doing this?

He wondered if he should wake her and let her do it herself, but she seemed so deeply asleep, and the little lines of worry he'd sometimes noticed on her face were smoothed away, the creamy skin mesmerising against the dark, rich swathe of hair.

No, he certainly shouldn't be looking at her as he strapped her in! He found the far side restraint and drew it across the bed and over her body, curled on its side, the bulge of her pregnancy resting on the mattress, one leg drawn up to balance her weight.

He picked up the other end of the strap, and clicked the belt shut, then tightened it, just slightly, so it would hold her firmly if the plane dropped suddenly, but not put pressure on her belly.

Even under the sheet he could make out the shape of her, but his eyes were drawn to her face, vulnerable somehow without the dark-framed glasses, an attractive face, full of strength and determination, though he'd seen it soften when she'd spoken of the baby, Alexandra.

But not when she mentioned her own pregnancy.

He had to leave.

Heaven forbid she woke and found him staring at her.

Yet his feet seemed rooted to the floor, his eyes feasting on the woman, not lasciviously at all, just puzzled that she remained such a mystery to him.

Puzzled that he *was* puzzled, for of course she was a mystery to him—he barely knew her.

And probably never would.

Looking at her isn't going to help you, he told himself, and after checking the cabin was free of loose objects that could fly about in turbulence, he did leave the room, but reluctantly.

Returning to his seat, he began to wonder if he'd made a big mistake, taking this woman to his homeland.

But why?

Having been educated in the West, he accepted equality in all things between men and women. A different equality existed in his own land, but never, in the history of the tribe, had women been seen as inferior for they were the carriers of history, the heart of the family, the heart of the tribe, so it wasn't the fact that she was a woman…

Except that it was!

Not only was she a woman but she was a woman who, for some totally perverse reason, he found attractive.

Extremely attractive.

Physically attractive.

Could he put it down to prolonged celibacy after Zara's death? Prolonged celibacy brought on by guilt that he'd not been there for her—not been closer to her—close enough to realise his own wife had been in trouble with her pregnancy…

Memories of the time made him wince and put the woman on the bed right out of his mind. Having failed one pregnant woman, he had no intention of getting involved with another one. She was an employee like any other, and he could treat her as such. Right now he had a mountain of work to get through, business matters that he'd set aside while he was in Australia.

Quickly absorbed in the details of a new university for Najme, in the number of departments the fledgling institution would have and the balance of staffing, he was surprised to find five hours had passed. The turbulence was also behind them, although when he shifted in his seat, wondering what movement had distracted him, a different turbulence made its presence felt.

Internal turbulence.

Liz Jones was standing in the doorway of the cabin, dark, red-brown hair tousled around her face, her eyes unfocussed as she cleaned her glasses with a tissue.

'I'm sorry to disturb you,' she said, stepping cautiously forward, 'but I need my bag to have a wash and fix my hair.'

'You might be more comfortable if you leave it down for the rest of the flight,' Khalifa heard himself say, although he knew he wasn't thinking of her comfort but of the glory of that shining tumble of hair.

I might be more comfortable if I'd never stepped onto this plane, never met this man, let alone agreed to travel to his country, Liz thought, but, contrarily enough, excitement was stirring in her. Refreshed by the sleep, all the doubts and questions left behind, she was now looking forward to whatever adventure this strange new country would offer her.

Once she was off the plane, that was.

Once she was away from the man who was having such a strange effect on her body.

Distracted by *that* thought, she grabbed only one of the handles of her bag, so as she lifted it the contents tumbled out, spilling files, and toiletries, her wallet and passport, her hairbrush and—

Her boss was out of his seat immediately, helping retrieve the scattered items, seeking out coins that had rolled away.

'Don't worry about the change, it will be useless in Al Tinine anyway,' Liz told him, totally mortified by the mess and sorry she'd ever mentioned being a klutz, as this was surely proving her point to him.

She scooped things into the bag, ramming them in any old how, until he held out the photo, grabbed at the last minute from her bedside table, still in its silver frame. Bill and Oliver, arms around each other, laughing as she'd snapped them...

Her companion was looking at it, perhaps a little

puzzled, and she could hardly snatch it from his hand no matter how much she'd have liked to.

In the end, he passed it to her and she ran her finger, as she'd done a thousand times before, over Bill's image. The three of them had been surfing at Coolangatta when the photo had been taken.

'He was my brother, Bill,' she found herself saying. 'More than a brother, really. Our parents died in the World Trade Center in 2001. They were on holiday in New York, a cousin worked in the building and they'd gone in to have a look. I was in my second year at university, and Bill and his partner Oliver became my lifeline—the only family I had left. Then three months ago Bill was in a fatal motor vehicle accident. That's what the policeman said when he told me, not a car crash—nothing that simple—but a fatal motor vehicle accident, as if Bill was already a statistic of some kind.'

She slumped into the chair, as memories of that moment—memories she'd never shared with anyone—came flooding back.

I will not cry, she promised the image of her beloved brother. I might have blurted all that out to a stranger but I *will not cry!*

She breathed deeply, recovering her equilibrium, willing the tears she knew had welled in her eyes to not betray her by brimming over and sliding down her cheeks. And then she felt better—not only for now, as in not so teary, but better all through, somehow.

'I'm sorry,' she said to her companion, aware he was watching her intently, although those dark eyes revealed nothing in the way of emotion. 'I haven't talked about it much. Now I'd better tidy up.'

She made sure she had both handles of her bag in

her hand and stood up, escaping as rapidly as she could without actually running to the cabin at the rear of the plane. She had a wash and tidied her hair, pulling it back into a low knot on the nape of her neck so she could relax back against the seat.

What she'd have liked to do next was hide away in this cabin, but she'd never been a coward.

She strode back in and took her seat, tucking her bag with its memories in a compartment to one side. Khalifa nodded acknowledgement of her return, and turned back to the papers on the table in front of him almost immediately, making it plain he didn't expect to be engaged in conversation.

Which was a good thing, as most of her conversations with him led down paths she didn't want to follow. She spread out her own papers, the ones about the size of units for different population figures. In all, they needed three spaces. One in the labour ward but surely they'd have that already—a care corner for the newborn.

Or would they?

Intent now on the project, she forgot about not engaging him in conversation.

'Do you already have a newborn care corner in the labour rooms and operating theatres?'

He looked across at her, frowning slightly.

'I beg your pardon?'

She *knew* she shouldn't have spoken!

'I'm sorry, I'm thinking through what you'll need, beginning with the infant's birth. I'm sure you do have an area where immediate care can be provided, and possibly a neonatal stabilisation unit close by where low birth weight or fragile newborns can be stabilised. These two centres are not really part of the unit because they have to be in or close by the labour rooms, but they come under the director of the neonatal unit at most hospitals, including Giles, so I wondered.'

Was she making sense?

She was talking work, at which she was more than competent, yet this man seemed to undermine her confidence in herself to the extent that she always sounded as if she was babbling at him.

Was it his stillness that threw her into turmoil? The air of other-worldliness he wore like an invisible cloak?

'I'm sorry,' he said, smiling—how she wished he wouldn't, and apparently the sleep hadn't help the fizzing or the sparking or her toes. 'I was involved in plans for a university and thinking of disciplines and staffing. I don't want to duplicate everything we already have at Al Jabaya, although some degree courses, like science, teaching and nursing, should be available at both. But to answer your question, we do have a newborn care corner in all the labour rooms, and we use that corner for stabilisation as well. Without a special care neonatal unit, up till now babies needing special care are airlifted to the hospital in the capital, which is very traumatic for the mother and the rest of the family.'

He really cares about things like that, Liz realised, hearing the depth of emotion in his voice. It made her want to like the man—but liking him, given the unexpected physical attraction, was probably not a good idea.

'So we'll need a stabilisation room and experienced staff for it. The equipment is much the same as we'll have in the unit, a crib with a radiant warmer, oxygen, a hand-operated neonate resuscitator, suction pump, examination light, laryngoscope set, and all the usual renewable equipment. I think two cribs in there would be enough, and with the provision for hand washing and infection control—bins, etc.—you'd need close to a hundred square feet. Is that doable?'

'It will be,' he said, and she heard it as a promise and wondered just how it must feel to be able to decide you wanted something then go right ahead and get it, or get it done. He'd wanted a neonatal paediatrician and here she was on a flight to a place she'd never heard of two weeks ago.

He'd lost her, Khalifa realised. She'd returned from the cabin and slid into her seat, and though he'd longed to talk to her—to ask more about the tragedies in her life, and things that weren't tragedies—he knew he had to respect her silence. In all truth, he knew silence was best, because he couldn't understand his desire to know more and that bothered him more than anything.

Then she'd asked a question and when he could have kept her talking because even if the talk was work related, hearing her voice gave him pleasure, but, no, he'd cut her off with one short sentence and now the opportunity was gone.

Telling himself this was for the best didn't work, and the words and numbers on the pages in front of him danced around so he could make no sense of them at all. Fortunately, Saif came in, offering light snacks, telling their guest about mint tea which, he felt, would refresh her.

'Or perhaps you would like to try mint lemonade,' he said.

'Mint tea sounds lovely,' Liz told him, smiling so naturally at him that once again Khalifa felt a twist of what he refused to consider was jealousy.

Saif returned with the tea and crescent-shaped almond biscuits dusted with icing sugar, a delicacy he knew was Khalifa's weakness. Liz relaxed back in her seat as she sipped the tea, and nibbled on a biscuit. It meant that, without being too obvious about it, he could watch her—see her in profile—a high forehead and long straight nose, full lips, a darkish pink against her creamy skin, slightly open at rest, and a chin that suggested she'd hold her own in any argument.

The shapeless garment she wore—so like the all-concealing gowns he knew from home—was made of fine enough material for it to lie softly on her body, showing him the shape of heavy breasts and the bulge of her pregnancy, her body, hidden though it was, so obviously lush and ripe.

It *had* to be the celibacy—not actually deliberate, although early on his guilt over not spending enough time with Zara before her death had certainly meant he'd not looked at another woman. After her death he'd thrown himself into work, continuing to learn exactly what it meant to be leader of his country, and an affair had been the last thing on his mind.

As it was now, he told himself firmly, but just as he forced himself to make sense of the words on the papers on front of him, the distraction in the plane with him spoke again.

'Leaving the stabilisation unit for the moment, the rule of thumb for a neonatal unit is three beds for every thousand deliveries, so realistically we'd only need three beds. If we add one or perhaps two critical-care beds to that, and another two for babies that might be brought in from elsewhere, we're up to six or seven, with two in the stabilisation unit. I know I should wait and see the space, but I'm thinking if it's close enough to the labour rooms for us to handle the stabilisation, perhaps in a divided-off corner of the neonate unit, it would ease any staff pressures and make the whole unit more financially viable.'

Was she as involved in this as she sounded, or was she attempting to sound detached because the brief glimpse of her life she'd revealed earlier had embarrassed her?

He guessed it would have. Even on such brief acquaintance he was reasonably certain she was not a woman who would confide in any but the closest of friends. So telling him about her brother had been a sign she was unsettled.

Because she was on her way to an unknown destination?

Or because of him?

He *had* to concentrate on work.

'Don't worry about financial considerations—stick to what you feel will work best.'

She flashed a smile in his direction.

'That's a dangerous statement to make, but I won't spend your money foolishly. We don't want staff hanging around doing nothing, because they'd become bored, and bored staff can let something slip. Better that we train a pool of staff for the unit, nurses who already work with babies in the nursery, then we can call on them when we need them. We can do the same with the hospital doctors. Interns on roster in the nursery can do some special-care training, spend two or three days with us so they see the routine.'

'You'll do the training?'

Another smile.

'Let's get the unit up and running first,' she said. She

was packing up her papers as she spoke, and added, 'And I really can't do any more until I see the space, so perhaps you'll tell me about the falcons.'

The smile slipped away, and she added quickly, 'Although I have a book to read if you're busy.'

But falcons were his passion, his one diversion from the world of work, so the invitation to talk about them was tempting.

'You know they're hunting birds?'

'Birds of prey, yes,' she said, warm interest in her voice and the sparkle back in her eyes.

'We train them to hunt for us. In days gone by, they provided food for the tribe, but now we hunt for pleasure. Although there are many, many breeds of falcon, we have three main ones we use, the gyr, the saker and the peregrine. We cross-breed them for strength and speed, and in all breeds the female is the bigger and the stronger.'

'I suppose she needs to be to ensure her babies have food,' Liz said, and for the first time he saw her hand rest on her swollen belly.

Perhaps she wasn't as detached as she had appeared...

'They're migratory birds but these days we don't catch and train wild birds visiting our land. They are protected and we have breeding programmes aimed at increasing their numbers. The birds we breed for hunting have passports, much like you and I do, with a photo of the bird and details of its genealogy.'

'To prevent inbreeding?'

It was a natural question, but Khalifa was warmed by her interest.

'Partly,' he admitted, 'but also to prevent theft, and

so a lost bird can be returned to her owner, but the main reason is so unscrupulous people can't pass off wild birds as bred ones.'

Now she was frowning.

'Is it such a big business that people would do that?' she asked, and he had to laugh.

'Wait until you see a falcon judging at one of our hunting expos. Every man there thinks he has the best bird. Envy, greed, pride—these qualities are universal, and in our country, no more so than at a falcon judging.'

The laughter made him human, Liz decided. That's why it affected her so much. One minute he was the complete businessman—an aloof, even kingly, businessman, and then he laughed and it wasn't just the fizzing and the sparking, but warmth spread through her, seeping into all the places that had been frozen solid since Bill's death.

Renewing her.

He talked on, about his birds, about watching them in flight and feeling a surge of freedom as they rose into the air, then the swoop as they sighted prey and plunged back to earth.

'They can travel at three hundred and fifty kilometres an hour,' he said.

'And if they mistime their swoop and hit the ground?'

He laughed again.

'It happens more often than you'd think and, yes, they can be killed or badly injured. In our falcon hospital we have a cabinet with drawers of feathers, so damaged feathers can be replaced, the replacement chosen from hundreds to most closely match the bird's plumage.'

'How do they attach a feather?'

'With a needle and thread, of course.'

Liz found herself laughing, not at the story but with delight that in this strange world to which she travelled was a land where people sewed carefully matched feathers back onto their birds.

Saif broke the merriment, coming in to ask what she would like for whatever meal they happened to be up to now, offering a choice of salads and open sandwiches, small meatballs or arancini. He handed her a menu, pointing out larger meals if she wanted something more substantial but in the end she left the choice to him.

'You are hungry?' Khalifa asked, after Saif had consulted him and departed.

'All the time, it seems,' she admitted, and for a moment Khalifa wondered if she'd say more—blame her pregnancy for her hunger maybe—but once again it seemed the subject was off limits.

Had the father of her baby hurt her in some way?

Could, heaven forbid, the pregnancy have been the result of a rape?

But no matter how it had been conceived, surely once she'd decided to carry the baby to term, she should have been bonding with it, talking to it, comforting it with touch as well as her voice. He remembered how he'd felt when he'd heard he was to be a father—proud and pleased, a little anxious that he'd prove up to the task, and even though he'd not been as involved as he should have been, a small kernel of excitement and anticipation had come to life within him.

Only to die with his wife and child.

Was this why her attitude towards her unborn child bothered him? Because to him it spoke of a lack of caring, yet in other ways he knew this woman to be extremely empathetic, and very caring.

He longed to know more, yet knew it wasn't his business, and as for the attraction he felt towards her—that was nothing more than a distraction. Saif had set a tray of diverse snacks in front of her, and she was smiling with delight, thanking him for his kindness, sampling things and praising him.

And undoubtedly it *was* jealousy he, Khalifa, was feeling.

What he needed was a parachute.

He pictured flinging himself off the plane and smiled at the stupidity of the thought, but deep inside he knew he'd have to do whatever he could to avoid this woman's company. Yes, they'd have to consult from time to time, but he would throw himself into work, both the work of government and his work as head of the surgical department at the hospital, so there'd be no time for him to be distracted by a flame-haired siren.

A pregnant, flame-haired siren!

CHAPTER FOUR

SAIF took the dishes before asking Liz to prepare for landing, and as the plane dropped lower in the sky and banked, she looked out of the window, seeing a land mass emerging from the clouds, then as the mass became clearer, she made out a long ridge of mountains like a spine running down the curving stretch of land—the land looking golden against the brilliant, blue-green sea that surrounded it.

'Oh,' she cried, as the island took shape. 'It's a dragon!'

Khalifa nodded, his smile one of approval and delight.

'Al Tinine—the dragon,' he said, and Liz felt a shiver of excitement. What might lie ahead in this magical place, this dragon land of myths and legends? A land of deserts and oases, of hunting birds with passports, and an enigmatic man who made her fizz and spark when he laughed?

She watched as the plane dropped lower, seeing now the red harshness of the mountain range, the softer red of desert sands spreading away from it, splotches of green here and there—oases, she imagined—and then a city that from the air looked pink.

Could it really be?

The wheels touched down and the engines roared as it slowed. They were here—in Al Tinine. In Najme, in fact, for Khalifa had told her they'd fly straight to the city where his new hospital awaited her.

Disembarking from the plane was a relief, Liz told herself, yet as she walked down the steps to where a big black four-wheel-drive vehicle waited, she felt a sense of regret.

She and Khalifa hadn't actually become friends, but they'd laughed together once or twice and she'd felt a connection to him—as if some indefinable bond was holding them together.

As wild a thought as the stories of Scheherazade, she told herself, looking around the flat expanse of the airfield and smiling as she noticed not high-rise buildings or even factories on its outer limits but hills of sand.

The Endless Desert—wasn't that what Khalifa had called it?

And suddenly she was excited, looking forward to every minute of this experience, looking forward to being positive and cheerful and, yes, successful in this new venture. She even gave the baby a pat, although getting too attached was still definitely not on—not when Oliver was likely to come out of his coma and want his child.

She'd be its aunt—Oliver couldn't take that away from her—but whether, with Bill gone from his life, Oliver would let her get close to the child, she had no idea.

Neither could she think about it right now for Khalifa, who had exited the plane before her, was talking to the driver of the big vehicle, talking anxiously, then taking out his mobile and pacing back and forth as he spoke to someone.

He glanced towards her, shook his head, then ended the conversation.

'I'm sorry,' he said, moving to stand in front of her, 'but there's an emergency at the hospital and I'm needed there. I would have liked to take you to the palace and see you settled in, but I will have to go directly to the hospital and then my driver will take you from there.'

Palace?

Maybe she'd misheard.

Setting that aside, she hurried to assure him she'd be all right.

'What kind of emergency?' she asked as she slid into the car.

Khalifa was in the front seat and turned to look at her.

'A pregnant woman with a meningioma in the occipital region of her brain. It must be a fast-growing one as the first sign she had was the loss of vision in one eye. Given her condition, we can't use drugs, or radiotherapy so—'

'How pregnant is she?' Liz's brain switched into work mode.

'Thirty-four weeks.'

'And the surgeon needs to get into the back of her skull.' Liz was thinking out loud. 'At thirty-four weeks you could take the baby—give the mother some beta-methasone to accelerate foetal lung maturation, then do a Caesar. We can provide care for a thirty-four-week neonate.'

'We?' Khalifa queried, a slight smile lurking on his lips.

'I'll be there. I'll come in with you. What's the point of bringing me all this way to loll around in some palace when a baby might need my help?'

'But you can't— You've just got off a plane.'

'And if you say it's because I'm pregnant I'll probably hit you.' Liz interrupted his faltering arguments. 'This is what I do, Khalifa. And if you're removing a tumour from this poor woman's brain, the last thing she'll need is to wake up and find you've sent her baby off to some hospital miles and miles away.'

Liz hoped she'd made her point, but when Khalifa did respond it was with a question of his own.

'You understand I'll be doing the operation? You know I'm a surgeon with special interest in tumours of the brain?'

Liz grinned at him.

'Do you really think any woman would go off with a man to a strange country without at least checking him out on the internet?'

He returned her smile.

'You'd be surprised,' he said, 'at how many women would do just that.'

'Not this one,' Liz assured him. 'You'd told me you'd studied medicine, but hadn't talked much about your surgery or said whether you were still practising. I must admit it was reassuring that as a doctor you'd at least understand what is needed in any hospital unit. The fights I've had with bureaucrats who think the setting-up and staffing within a hospital are all about getting the numbers right and meeting something they invariably call the bottom line.'

Khalifa nodded.

'These men exist in my life as well, but at least I have the power to cut off their heads if they annoy me.'

The lurking smile told her he was joking, and she smiled back as she said, 'I'd better remember that, hadn't I? I don't think my head would look too good raised on a pike outside this palace you talk of.'

She hesitated, then, aware she was showing her ignorance or possibly naivety, added, 'Is it really a palace? And, anyway, I don't need to stay with you. Surely there are staff quarters at the hospital.'

His smile broadened and warmth rushed from her curling toes to the top of her head, revealing itself, she was sure, in a rich blush.

'You will stay with me. The place is big enough for dozens of visitors—welcoming strangers and taking them in is part of our culture. And while not a palace in the style of a western fairy-tale, as the home of the ruler, it is called that.'

'But wouldn't the home of the ruler—the real palace—be in the capital?'

The smile turned to laughter.

'Does not the English queen have many palaces? Balmoral and Windsor and who knows what others, as well as the one in London. Now, we will stop talking nonsense about palaces, and you will see Najme as we drive into it.'

It *was* pink! All the buildings not pink stone but pink bricks or pink earth, made perhaps from the local sand—red desert sand. Liz was fascinated, and wanted to ask many questions, but Khlaifa was back into work mode, speaking crisply and confidently on his mobile to someone at the hospital, giving orders for the preparation of a theatre, for a crib, for specialist staff.

In English, Liz realised with a surge of relief. If most of the staff spoke English she wouldn't have to learn Arabic, although as she looked at the flowing script on signs in front of buildings she knew she'd like to learn it—to speak it and to write it.

Another challenge.

One she could forget, she told herself firmly. She probably wouldn't be here long enough to find her way around, let alone learn the language.

Best she should concentrate on work. What could she remember from her early studies about the tumour called a meningioma? Usually benign, she thought, but its growth within the outer covering of the brain—the meninges—could be causing compression on areas of vital function—in this case on the occipital region.

'Has she had any treatment for it?' Liz asked as Khalifa folded his phone and slipped it into his pocket.

'Normally the patient would have been given steroids in an attempt to shrink the tumour, but with her pregnancy it was thought an immediate operation was the best option. We have cribs with radiant heaters at the hospital because we use them to fly at-risk babies to the capital. I've asked one be prepared for you and for staff to be available.'

He paused, turning to look directly at her.

'Are you sure about this?' he asked. 'The journey—you must be tired...'

Liz had to smile.

'When I slept for most of it? Hardly,' she said. 'And isn't this the best way to tackle a new job? To leap right in and find out exactly what you do and don't have on hand? I'm very sorry for the poor woman, but I have to admit I'm excited at the same time.'

She really was, Khalifa realised as he took in the shine in her eyes and the slight flush of colour in her cheeks. He shook his head, unable to believe he'd, just by chance, found a colleague who obviously felt as he did about their profession, felt the physical thrill of a challenge.

Though it was probably best he not think of physical thrills and this woman in the same breath...

'Oh, it's pink as well.'

She whispered the words but he saw wonder in her face and felt a surge of pride because his hospital was truly a beautiful building. Stretched out in a swathe of parkland, the architect had somehow managed, with the design of the multi-level building, to still hint at the shape of the tents his family had used for thousands of years, while the dark pink colour of the walls spoke of desert dunes, the gold highlights desert sunsets.

But all he'd said was, 'We can leave our luggage in the vehicle.'

It was the most unusual hospital Liz had ever seen, arched openings leading into wide verandas that spread out from every floor, bright rugs and cushions thrown with apparent abandon across the marble tiling. Here and there black-robed women and turbaned men sat around low tables, drinking coffee from tall silver pots set over braziers that looked as if they held live coals.

In a hospital?

'Families like to be close to their loved ones, and this seemed to me a practical way to provide accommodation for them,' Khalifa said, making Liz realise her amazement must be showing.

'And presumably they don't take their cooking fires inside near the oxygen tanks,' she remarked, following him through a self-opening door into the foyer of what looked like a six-star hotel but was obviously the hospital's main entrance.

Voices called what she took to be greetings to Khalifa, some men bowing their heads in his direction, not, she felt, subserviently, but merely an acknowledgement that he was among them again.

He spoke briefly to a woman in loose trousers and a long tunic, a uniform not unlike the clothes Liz had brought with her. *So she'd got that right*, she was thinking when Khalifa took her arm and steered her towards another foyer with a bank of lifts.

This was the bit she still had to get right, she realised as her body reacted with volatile enthusiasm to his touch. She could have lit up an entire fireworks display had the fizz and sparks been visible. It had to be the hormonal shift of being pregnant. She'd put it down to that and, in the meantime, avoid opportunities that involved touch—or smiles, or laughter, or even, if possible, hearing his voice. Toes could only take so much!

'This is the theatre floor,' he said, preparing to lead her out of the lift, but she dodged his hand and strode ahead then realised she'd turned the wrong way. That was okay. Now she could follow him, trailing in his wake, taking in the ramrod-straight back, the sleek sheen of his hair, and the neat way his trousers hugged—

Totally not going there, Liz!

He led her into a theatre anteroom where a group of men and women were already pulling on hospital gowns over T-shirts and shorts, or were fully gowned and discussing what lay ahead of them.

'This is Dr Elizabeth Jones,' Khalifa announced

above the rush of greetings. 'I won't confuse her with all your names at this stage but she'll take care of the baby once it's delivered.'

He beckoned to a woman at one side of the room and she came forward, her dark eyes studying Liz.

'Laya is the head nurse in our nursery,' he explained, and Liz held out her hand.

'Call me Liz,' she said. 'And lead me somewhere I can have a shower and change. Who knows what foreign germs I could be carrying?'

Laya led her into a large bathroom with several shower stalls.

'Theatre gowns are in these cupboards,' she explained. 'I'll wait and get you kitted up.'

Liz grinned at her.

'Kitted up? Is that a local expression?'

'I trained in England,' Laya said. 'I could have chosen the USA but my family had been visiting London for years so I knew people there who were happy for me to live with them.'

She'd been stacking clean theatre gear on a bench so hadn't noticed Liz's baby bump until she turned back towards her.

'Oh!' she said.

'Exactly,' Liz told her, 'though it's not what it seems and, anyway, I'm perfectly well and quite capable of doing my job. Just get me a couple of sizes larger of everything.'

Laya looked as if she'd have liked to protest, or maybe ask more, but Liz hurried into a shower stall, stripping off her underwear then grimacing as she realised she'd have to put it back on again afterwards—or wear some of those enormous paper undies that were available throughout most hospitals. Pity they didn't do large size paper bras.

'Now we're organised,' she finally said to Laya, 'so lead on.'

Scrub up next, then into Theatre, gowned and gloved, where the patient was already on the table, one of the men from the anteroom in place at the patient's head, another man, obviously the obstetrician, preparing for an incision on the woman's swollen belly. Khalifa was on the far side of the room, examining the X-rays and scans on what looked like a flat-screen television fixed to the wall.

Liz checked the preparations Laya had made in the hastily set-up newborn care corner. A trolley of fixed height with radiant warmer, drawers that would hold equipment, an oxygen bottle, a hand-operated neonate resuscitator, scale, pump suction with foot operation, IV cannulas, mucus extractors, soft towels for drying and wrapping the baby, sterile equipment for tying and cutting the cord, feeding tube, sterile gloves—everything seemed to be in place.

As the obstetrician reached into the small incision and drew out the tiny infant, Laya wheeled the trolley close and Liz took the baby—a boy. She used a fine tube to clear his mouth and nose, squeezed his little chest so he began to breathe and then to cry. She held him against his mother's chest, only for a moment, but it felt the right thing to do for both of them, then, when the obstetrician had tied and cut the cord, she set the infant on the trolley and wheeled him to the corner of the room while the surgeons prepared the woman for the next stage of her operation.

'He's come through this well,' she said to Laya, as

the vital Apgar numbers added up to six at one minute. She'd used a bag and mask to give him a little extra oxygen, and by five minutes his score was up to nine.

Once dry and warm, they weighed and measured him.

'Fifteen hundred and fifty-eight grams—it's low for thirty-four weeks,' she said to Laya, then glanced over at where Khalifa was preparing to open the woman's skull. 'She possibly hasn't been feeling well for some time, maybe not eating properly. Would she have been seeing a doctor or midwife regularly?'

'I don't know her, but she's from the desert so I doubt it,' Laya said. 'It's all very well to build hospitals and clinics but getting our people, particularly the women, to use them will take a lot longer than His Highness realises.'

'His Highness?' Liz echoed, and Laya nodded towards Khalifa.

'He's our leader—a prince, a highness,' she explained.

Well, that settled all the fizz and sparking stuff, Liz thought, not that she'd ever had any indication that the man might be interested in her. As if he would be, pregnant as she was, and probably not even if she hadn't been pregnant.

A highness, for heaven's sake! And she'd been joking with him!

Though she should have twigged when he'd talked about the palace!

'Did he not tell you?' Laya asked as Liz wrote down the baby's crown-heel length of forty-four centimeters.

'Well, yes,' Liz admitted, 'but somehow you don't connect a bloke you meet in the corridor at work with royalty. I thought maybe like our prime minister—that kind of leader—an ordinary person with a tough job. Head circumference thirty-three.'

She made another note, her mind now totally on the baby, although the murmur of the surgical teams voices provided a background to all she did.

'I've got a special-care crib waiting. Should we take him to the nursery?' Laya asked when the little boy was safely swaddled and ready to be moved.

Liz glanced over at the woman on the table. The baby's mother was unconscious, of course, but would she have some awareness? Would she know her baby had been taken? Would she need him nearby?

'I think we'll stay here to do the stabilisation,' Liz responded. 'The crib has monitors on it so we can hook him up to them to watch him, and give him anything he needs as he needs it. At this weight he'll probably have some apnoea and will need oxygen support, caffeine to help his lungs…'

She knew she was thinking aloud, but the situation was so strange she wanted to make sure she was ready for every possible problem that could arise. CPAP, the continuous positive airway pressure, could be delivered through a nasal cannula, and if she put in a central venous catheter for drugs and measurements and a peripheral line as well, all the bases would be covered.

But without a special-care unit, where would they take the baby?

To the nursery?

No, from what Khalifa had told her, under normal circumstances they'd fly any premature baby to the capital.

Not a good idea, given what the mother was going

through. Liz glanced towards the tall surgeon bent intently over the operating table.

'Do new babies room in with their mothers here at the hospital?' she asked Laya.

'Some do,' Laya told her. 'It's a choice the mothers are offered.'

'And are there on-call staff rooms at the hospital—places where staff can stay over?'

Laya frowned at this question—not a big frown, more a worried grimace.

'Of course. Why are you asking?'

Liz grinned at her.

'I'm thinking maybe *this* baby can room in with his mother,' she said. 'Khalifa—' should she keep calling him that now she knew about the Highness thing? '—said there were few financial restraints and, anyway, it would only mean maybe a couple of shifts of nursery nurses, preferably ones who've worked with fragile newborns, helping stablise them before they're flown out, and we could keep him with the mother. I'd be happy to live in at the hospital to take a couple of shifts, and I'd still be able to do the preliminary work on the new unit at the same time. What do you think?'

It was Laya's turn to glance towards the surgical team.

'I don't know what to think,' she said. 'But once she's out of Recovery, the mother will go into Intensive Care…'

'A very sterile environment for a newborn,' Liz reminded her. 'Of course, we'll have to make sure there's room for the crib and a nurse to watch his monitor, but if there is, wouldn't it be best to have the baby near the mother? Wouldn't that be more of a help to her recovery than a hindrance?'

Laya shook her head.

'I don't know,' she said, glancing again at the table—or more particularly at the lead surgeon, who was still bent over the patient.

'You think he'll be a problem?' Liz teased, then she realised Laya was genuinely distracted.

'I know he lost his wife and child,' Liz said gently, 'but I would have thought that would make him all the more determined to achieve the best outcome for this mother and child.'

'Of course,' Laya told her, 'but...'

'But what?'

Laya hesitated, before saying, in a very quiet voice, 'Will *you* ask him?'

The way she spoke reminded Liz of the fear some surgeons managed to instil in their theatre staff, roaring at the slightest mistake, swearing and cursing when things went wrong. Now she, too, looked back at this particular surgeon. She didn't know him from Adam, but from the time she'd spent with him, she'd have put him down as the very opposite—quiet, reserved, not given to tantrums.

'Is it because of the highness thing you don't want to ask him?' she said to Laya, who looked even more uncertain.

'Not really. But I suppose it must be, because when he was just a doctor, if I did happen to run into him, it was just "Good morning, Doctor" like you do with all the staff you don't know really well. But since he became our leader—well, it changes things, doesn't it?'

Liz adjusted the cannula in the baby's nose.

'Did *he* change?' she asked, and Laya gave the question some thought then shook her head.

'He's not here as often, of course, but when he is he's just the same. And he always knows everyone's name, which most of the doctors and even nurses from other departments don't, but I don't think he's changed. It must be me who's changed.'

'I wouldn't if I were you,' Liz told her. 'Just carry on as you always did. But, anyway, it was my idea we room the baby with the mother so I'll ask him and make the arrangements, okay?'

Laya's smile told her the nurse had relaxed, and her words delighted Liz even more.

'Will you ask if he can arrange for me to be one of the nurses? I've travelled with preemie babies to the hospital in the capital so I know how to care for them, and I've already put my name down for training in the new unit.'

'Then I'll certainly ask for you,' Liz promised as Khalifa straightened up, stepped back from the patient and pulled off his gloves.

'Clean gown and gloves,' he said to one of the surgical staff, then he walked over to look at the baby, tilting his head to one side as if to take the little being in more clearly.

'You're still here?' He looked up at Liz as he asked the question and though she was about to make a joke about just being a mirage, the strain in his eyes told her this wasn't the time.

'No unit to take him to,' she said lightly. 'And I felt it was important to keep him close to his mother. In fact, Laya and I have just been talking about it, and we'd like him to room in with her if that can be managed. I'd be happy to live in here so I'm always on hand, and Laya and another nurse can share shifts with me. I realise the mother will be in the ICU for a while, but at least the atmosphere will be sterile and when the mother becomes conscious we'll have the baby on hand for her to see so she doesn't feel any anxiety or fear for him. I realise if you're not done there, you can't discuss it now, but we'll wait here until you finish and maybe talk about it then.'

He probably wouldn't understand the slang expression 'stunned mullet' but it described him to a T. Fortunately the scrub nurse called him for his fresh gown and gloves and one of his colleagues needed him back at the table, so any further discussion was suspended.

'He didn't look too happy about your idea,' Laya ventured, and Liz grinned at her.

'That's probably only because he's used to being the one with the big ideas,' she said. 'Once he's had time to think about it, he'll see it makes sense.'

And living in at the hospital would keep her safe from fizzing and sparks—but that was a side benefit. The baby definitely came first.

CHAPTER FIVE

Two hours later, as he stepped away from the operating table, leaving room for one of his assistants to close, Khalifa remembered the baby in the room—the baby and the woman caring for him!

She wanted the baby rooming in with his mother in the ICU?

The idea was bizarre, but even more confusing was her determination to stay at the hospital to care for the newborn. Was her own pregnancy making her ultra-sensitive?

Not that he'd noticed the slightest sensitivity on her part towards her pregnancy—the subject was not open for discussion. Yet it niggled at him, both the pregnancy and her seeming lack of interest in it.

He shoved his soiled gown and gloves into a bin, called for a fresh gown, although he'd finished at the operating table, and eventually, clean again, moved across the room to where the two women waited by the crib.

'The mother will be in Recovery for some time,' he said, addressing the air between Laya and the newcomer. 'I suggest the baby goes to the nursery where Laya can keep an eye on him.'

Now he had to face his new employee. With her

richly coloured hair hidden by a cap, the black-rimmed glasses dominated her face, making her skin seem creamier, her eyes a deeper blue.

'Not a good idea,' she said. 'Look at him. You say he's thirty-four weeks, but the mother may have miscalculated. Either that or he's not been well nourished. Put him in among healthy newborns and he'll look more like a skinned rabbit than he already does. Apart from anything else, it would be upsetting for the other mothers, with their chubby little pink-cheeked babies, to see him.'

Khalifa felt a twinge of annoyance. Dr Elizabeth Jones might have seemed the perfect person to set up the new unit at his hospital, but if she was going to argue with him every time he opened his mouth...

'Apart from anything else?' he queried, allowing his voice to reveal the twinge.

'He should be with his mother,' the annoyance replied. 'Not while she's in Recovery, of course, but surely you know where she'll be sent. I can accompany him there and keep an eye on him, and Laya can return to her own shift in the nursery.'

She looked Khalifa in the eye, daring him to argue.

'Minimum fuss, right?' she challenged.

'It is *not* right,' he muttered, glowering at her. 'You've barely arrived in the country, you could be jet-lagged—'

'And might make a mistake?'

Another challenge but before he could meet it she spoke again.

'That's what monitors are for,' she reminded him. 'I fall asleep beside the crib—which, I might add, is highly unlikely—and something goes wrong then bells will ring, whistles will blow and people will come running. I'm a neonatologist, remember, this is what I do. This hospital or Giles, this is my work.'

Again the blue eyes met his, the challenge still ripe in them.

'Any other objections?'

'Wait here!' he ordered, then realised that was a mistake for the baby's mother was already being wheeled into Recovery and the staff beginning to clean away the debris of the operation.

'No, wait outside in the corridor.' He spoke to Laya the second time, avoiding the challenging eyes *and* the disturbing feelings just being near the other woman was causing him. He headed for the changing rooms but once there he realised he should have showered and put on clean clothes on the flight but with Liz—would thinking of her as Dr Jones be better?—in the bedroom he'd not wanted to disturb her.

Now, showered again, changing back into his travel clothes was unappealing and the only apparel he had in his locker was a row of white kandoras and a pile of pristine red and white checked headscarves—kept there for any time he might have to leave the hospital for an official duty.

Not that he minded getting back into his country's clothing. Too long in suits always made him feel edgy, but walking hospital corridors as a sheikh rather than a doctor could be an offputting experience.

He wouldn't wear the headscarf—no, of course he would. Both it and the black cord that held it to his head. He was home!

He was beautiful! Liz could only stare at the apparition that had appeared before her in the corridor. Khalifa and yet not Khalifa, remote somehow in the clothes of his country, a disturbing enigma in a spotless white gown, the twist of black cord around his head covering giving the impression of a crown.

His Highness!

She ran her tongue over suddenly dry lips and tried for levity.

'Good thing it's you, not me, in that gear,' she said. 'White is not a colour for klutzes. I'd have tomato sauce stains down it in no time flat.'

Laya, she noticed, was suddenly busy watching the baby, her head bowed as if Khalifa in his traditional dress had overawed her.

To be honest, he'd overawed Liz as well, but it wouldn't do to show it.

'Follow me,' he said, ignoring her tomato-sauce remark and leading them along the corridor. Laya followed with the crib and Liz brought up the rear, telling herself that staying at the hospital was the best idea she'd ever had. Her body might have behaved badly to Khalifa in civvies, but that was nothing to the rioting going on within it now.

Stupidity, that's what it was.

Hormones.

Oh, how she hoped it was just hormones.

Although, given the impossibility of anything ever coming of her attraction to the man, providing she kept that attraction well hidden it wouldn't matter, would it? Just another unrequited love. She'd survived that once before when her fourteen-year-old self had fallen in love with Mr Smith, the school science teacher. Smith and Jones, she'd written in tiny writing all over the covers of her physics book.

And as she couldn't remember all the elements of

Khalifa's name, she couldn't write it anywhere, which was an extremely good thing.

'Here,' a soft voice called, and she turned to find her thoughts had distracted her enough for her to miss the lift foyer so Laya had to beckon her back.

'She's a klutz,' Khalifa was saying to Laya as Liz joined them. 'Do you know that word?'

Laya shook her head and Khalifa proceeded to repeat the explanation Liz had given him in what seemed like another lifetime. She stood there, feeling her cheeks growing hot, uncertain if he was teasing her deliberately or simply passing on something he found of interest to his compatriot. Not that it mattered. While he was talking to Laya he wasn't talking to her and the best thing she could do was avoid all conversations with him.

Fortunately, before she could become too mortified, the lift arrived and they were whisked up to the next level.

From the inside, the ICU looked like any other ICU, although this place was still sparklingly new. But beyond the glass outer walls Liz could see the big arches and the sheltered balconies that must run along the length of the building.

'For the families?' she asked Khalifa, so intrigued her decision to not talk to him was forgotten.

'Of course,' he said. 'Close family members can, as you'd know, come into the ICU for short visits, but the others have to make do with being outside. Most of the time the curtains are open so they can see in, and the patient has the comfort of knowing they are there.'

'So different,' Liz murmured, although the room they were now in could have been in any hospital in the world with its well-positioned monitors, external pacemaker, defibrillator, suction pumps, drains, catheters, feeding tubes and IV lines—a veritable web of tubes that would soon be connected to the baby's mother.

On the other hand, few hospitals would have ICU rooms this big.

'There! In that corner,' she said, pointing to a clear space by the outer window. 'A perfect position for the baby because the mother in the bed will only have to turn her head to see the crib. On the other side, there's just too much gear.'

Laya began to push the crib towards the space Liz had indicated but Khalifa stopped her with a touch of his hand—long, slim fingers—and turned to Liz.

'You're sure about this?' he asked, a slight frown marring the smooth skin on his forehead.

'About the baby rooming in?'

He shook his head, the frown deepening.

'About your own involvement? I could have another neonatal paediatrician here within a couple of hours. You do not have to do this.'

He spaced the words of the last sentence out very carefully, giving each one equal emphasis.

Was it an order in a polite form?

Liz had no idea, she just knew that when the woman woke up, her first thought would be for her baby.

'Quite sure!' Liz, too, spaced her words so he couldn't help but get the message that she was determined to go through with this. 'I'll just need someone to bring my luggage in from the car.'

He shrugged, the white robe lifting on his broad shoulders, the headscarf moving slightly so it showed his face in profile, a stern profile with that long straight nose and determined chin. The lips should have softened it, but they were set in a straight line—not thinned exactly, but straight enough to make Liz wonder if he was far too used to getting his own way.

She smiled at the thought and he caught the smile, raising his eyebrows but actually allowing the line of his lips to relax.

'Do you always get your own way?' he asked, echoing her thoughts so neatly she felt the blood rising to her cheeks once again.

What was wrong with her? This blushing business was totally out of character, and she doubted she could blame it on hormones. After all, she'd got through thirty-plus weeks of pregnancy without blushing when a man teased her...

Not that many men *had* teased her.

Fortunately Khalifa's pager went off with a soft beep and he departed, leaving Laya to wheel the crib into the corner and Liz to collect herself.

'Did you know him before? When you were studying perhaps?' Laya asked, as Liz checked the monitor leads were still attached and the baby seemed comfortable.

'The baby?' Liz joked, although she knew exactly what 'him' Laya had meant.

'No, His Highness,' Laya explained, while Liz wished the nurse would stop calling him that. The words made her, Liz, feel slightly squeamish. 'Did you meet him when he was overseas, training?'

The question was puzzling and although Liz would have liked to ask why, she contented herself with explaining about Khalifa buying the hospital where she worked with the idea of staff interchanges between the two facilities.

'It's a wonderful idea,' she continued, hoping to get

Laya's mind off whatever it was she really wanted to know. 'Think what the staff from both countries will learn and how the patients will benefit as a result.'

'But he seems at ease with you,' Laya protested, and it took a moment for Liz to realise she hadn't diverted the other woman at all.

'Oh,' she said, then she conquered the little flash of excitement the simple words had caused and squashed the whole conversation. 'I think he's the kind of man who would be at ease with any woman,' she told Laya. 'Now, we need to gather some supplies for this baby. Can I get you to do that? Do you have special packs on hand for when you airlift babies to the hospital up north? We'll need a couple of them to begin with and a trolley to hold supplies, and scales of course.'

Laya assured her such packs were available and departed, leaving Liz and one very small baby boy in the impressively equipped room. She looked down at the sleeping figure and felt movement from the child she carried.

Her hand moved to touch it—to feel the life within her—but she'd been so strong all through the pregnancy, she knew she shouldn't weaken now.

Although with Bill gone, could she not keep this baby?

Selfishness, she told herself. It wasn't hers—it was never going to be hers—that had been the biggest hurdle she'd had to leap when she'd decided to go ahead with the pregnancy. Everyone she knew had warned her of maternal bonds and attachment and she'd been determined it wouldn't happen to her, but now…

To Khalifa's astonishment, the situation with the baby rooming in the ICU seemed to be working. Admittedly, *his* patient had been very groggy when she'd come out of the anaesthetic, but of course Liz Jones had been right—the patient's first thought had been for her baby. In fact, her distress had been so evident that she'd been moved from Recovery to the ICU far more quickly than was usual.

Now, three days later, she lay, as she always did, with her heavily bandaged head turned towards the infant's crib. Only today the crib had been moved closer to his patient's bed and the woman's hand rested on her son's arm, her fingers moving very slowly and gently over his skin.

No need to see who was on duty with the baby. Khalifa doubted either of the nurses would have orchestrated this arrangement.

Liz nodded at him by way of greeting, as if all this was perfectly normal.

Yet wasn't it?

Mother and baby together—yes, that was normal. But—

'It bothers you?'

Was his confusion so obvious?

'Hospitals have systems and procedures and rules because in that way we can ensure the best outcomes for our patients,' he muttered, grumpy now as well as confused.

The woman had the hide to smile at him.

'And this isn't the best outcome for both our patients?' She nodded towards the pair. 'The two of them linked by the touch of love?'

The touch of love?

Her words struck deep into Khalifa's heart and a sense of loss that had nothing to do with Zara and the baby all but overwhelmed him. Had he ever known it? Certainly not from his mother, who had lived to please one man and one man only, his father. Her children, once born, were cast in among all the other children at the palace, anonymous in the crowd, although his grandmother, his mother's mother, had always sought him out, made him feel special.

Had that been love?

And did Liz know the touch of love, or were they just words? She'd certainly not given any indication that *her* baby had felt that touch.

He shouldn't judge, but her behaviour puzzled him, and now those words.

'You're probably right,' he admitted grudgingly, getting back to the conversation.

'Only probably?' she teased, then she turned the small computer screen so he could see it.

'I can't talk about your patient, but this little chap is doing well,' she said. 'His birth weight fell one hundred and seventy grams but we started feeding him through the orogastric tube on day two—was that only yesterday?—and I hope to have him on full feeds within a week. He's still on the CPAP but we took him off that for an hour this morning and he coped well so we'll gradually wean him off it.'

She was nattering on to him as if he was just another colleague in her life. Which, of course, he was, but...

His mind wanted to follow the 'but' but his instinct warned him not to go where it might lead. Instant attraction was dangerous enough—far too unstable to lead anywhere, in his opinion—but instant attraction to a pregnant woman—that was madness...

'Is she doing well, *your* patient?' the pregnant woman

was asking, and he brought his mind firmly back to work.

'Extraordinarily well,' he had to admit. 'Given that she's just had major brain surgery, I actually can't believe how much progress she's made.'

He'd thought his colleague might take advantage of that admission with a smug grin at the very least, but all she did was offer a whole-hearted smile, and a quiet 'I am so glad it's working out for her'.

Some undercurrent in the words made him look at her more closely and he was sure he detected shadows in her lovely eyes.

Shadows of sadness—though how could that be? And why would he think sadness?

Then, on the faintest of sighs, she explained.

'I have a friend in a coma,' she said quietly. 'It's a terrible place to be.'

He wanted to touch her, just a touch of comfort—on her shoulder, or perhaps her arm—but she moved away, clicking off the computer screen, tidying the trolley that held the baby's needs in the corner of the room, although it had looked perfectly tidy when he'd glanced at it earlier.

There'd been something deeply personal in her admission and he couldn't help but wonder if she'd been speaking of the father of her baby.

But in that case, surely she'd be giving the baby *more* reassuring touches, not fewer...

He *had* to get his head straight. He had to stop thinking about the woman, yet how could he when she was here every time he visited his patient?

Every time?

He thought back.

'Have you been getting any rest?' he asked her. 'Are you actually trusting other staff to take care of the baby?'

She looked up from the trolley in the corner and smiled at him.

'Of course I trust the staff and, yes, I'm getting plenty of rest. My body clock is still a bit wonky with the travel, so I come and go at odd hours, and if I'm here I give the nurse on duty a break.'

She made it sound so—*normal*, somehow, yet he knew it wasn't. For one thing, the nearest on-call room was way down the other end of the long corridor.

She must have read his thoughts because she smiled and said, 'And all the walking is the best possible exercise for me.'

He wanted to argue, to tell her she should be living in the palace, but he had no reasons to back up his argument, not one—none!

Yet he wanted her there—he wanted her to see his home, to walk through his gardens, to relax in a hammock beneath the shade of a peach tree...

Though perhaps a klutz in a hammock...and pregnant at that?

On a couch under a peach tree.

'I've seen the area for the new unit.' The shift in conversation startled him. 'And I've drawn up a list of equipment and passed it on to the manager of the children's section of the hospital. Laya tells me the nursery comes under his control so I assumed the new unit would as well. No doubt he'll run the purchases past whoever has to okay them. I'm sure you don't have to be bothered with minor details like that.'

He had to smile.

'I have a niece who uses that phrase—minor details like that—usually when she's spent an inordinate amount of money on some article of clothing.'

To his delight, Liz returned his smile.

'I can assure you I haven't overspent. In fact, I thought we'd start small. No point in having equipment we might never need cluttering up our space, but I have included things like comfortable, reclining armchairs for parents and a plan for the alterations we'll need to the internal space.'

Her smile slipped away, replaced by a slight frown.

'I couldn't cost things like the internal carpentry and plumbing and hadn't a clue who to ask but I'm sure Phil will sort it out. He seems to be on top of everything—fantastic bloke.'

Phil?

Who was Phil?

Of course, Philip Cutler, the young man Khalifa himself had headhunted from a children's hospital in the US to manage the department.

'I'm sure Mr Cutler will manage,' he agreed, aware he sounded stiff and stuffy, but inordinately put out by her seeming friendliness with 'Phil'! She'd only been here a couple of days!

He made a mental note to see the man and check the requirements.

Why? his head asked. Do you not trust one or the other—both—of these staff members?

He didn't answer his head's question because he knew full well his interest was in Dr Liz Jones, not in her lists, but if he kept abreast of her plans then he'd have more to discuss with her, more reasons to see and talk to her.

She is pregnant!

His head was yelling at him now.

She already has a man in her life, or did have within the last nine months!

Yet, for reasons beyond his comprehension, neither issue seemed to affect the attraction he felt towards her, or his—need?—to see her as often as he could, to hear her speak, to make her smile.

Madness!

Had she said something wrong? Liz wondered. Done the wrong thing, giving the list and plans to Phil—somehow made a mistake in this strange situation in which she found herself?

Unease coiled in Liz's stomach as she eyed the man—His Highness—though today he was more a doctor in his civvies, just standing there.

Lost in thought, or just plain lost?

She was lost, so she knew the feeling, but why would this man be feeling lost, here in *his* hospital, in *his* country?

Could it be that he was lost as she was, emotionally?

Of course he would be, she told herself. His wife and child had died. How long would it take to get over such a thing?

For ever?

His state of mind was enough to distract her—just a little—from the usual array of bodily reactions she was experiencing in his presence, although seeing him every day made it easier somehow to cope with—or simply hide—the fizzing and sparks.

'Are you worried about the unit, or is it your patient's condition bothering you?' she asked, to break a silence that had become uncomfortable.

It took a moment but her words must eventually have penetrated his distraction.

'Neither,' he said, then he turned and left the room, not having checked his patient at all, although the ICU doctors were in and out all the time.

It was two days before she saw him again, and this time he whisked into the room with enough purpose in his stride for her to guess this was a medical visit and nothing more. He was also in full highness uniform of white gown and headscarf, so imposing her breathing stilled, faltered, and hitched somewhere in her chest before she pulled herself together.

She concentrated on the baby, in the corner this morning while she changed his feeding tube, and forced herself to breathe normally—to ignore the man in the white gown and folded red and white checked headscarf.

Although hadn't she wanted to talk to him about something?

Something that had been worrying her?

Work, brain, work! she ordered.

What had it been?

Oh, well, if she couldn't remember, surely it hadn't been important enough to bother him with it.

Or had it?

Before she'd sorted out an answer to that question, he'd finished with his patient and was gone.

And, of course, she'd remembered her concern.

She pressed the little bell that would summon the nurse on duty from the tea room and when Laya appeared, left her in charge of the baby, hurrying down the corridor to catch Khalifa.

'There *was* something I wanted to talk to you about,'

she said, coming up behind him and touching him lightly on the shoulder.

He turned abruptly, as if her touch had stung him, and she wondered, briefly, if one shouldn't touch a highness. Then her concern for her patient's wellbeing swept that worry aside.

'The woman, the baby's mother, she's not had family visiting, or anyone outside on the veranda. Laya said she was from the south and you spoke of an Endless Desert. Do you think perhaps her family don't know they can visit—or maybe they don't know she and the baby are here? Has anyone tried to contact them? I don't know the protocol, of course, but I walk around the other wards and see the families by the windows and I love the idea of such support for the patients, but our little mother and her baby seem to have no one.'

Khalifa just stared at her, and again she wondered if she'd done the wrong thing—spoken out of turn, interfered where she shouldn't.

But when he spoke it was against himself, not her.

'Have you bewitched me in some way that not only do I allow you to rearrange the ICU to suit your ideas but I've let slide my concentration on my own patient? Of course her family should be somewhere near her, although...'

He looked concerned and she'd have liked to touch him again—a comforting pat on the arm, nothing more...

Instead, she prompted him.

'Although?'

'She *is* from the desert, from one of the tribes who are finding the new ways more difficult to accept. The fact that the family aren't here tells me we haven't made it clear enough that they are free to come and go, to visit when they wish, and remain within their family group on the veranda. We're not getting the message across that although the buildings are different, our customs can remain intact.'

'I'm sure you will,' Liz told him, and she meant it because the more she saw and heard of this man, the more she understood his deep, abiding love for his land and his people, and his concern for every one of them.

Khalifa knew it wasn't an empty assurance. She really meant it, as if she already knew him in ways even friends might not fathom.

The thought was so strange it took him a moment to process it, then he dismissed it as some fantasy that was part of whatever happened to his brain whenever he was around this woman.

Though his brain's reaction wasn't nearly as bad as his body's. Two days since he'd seen her, and one glimpse in that ICU room had had his body hardening, heating, burning…

Escape had been the only answer, although, now she'd caught up with him, hadn't he come to the hospital this morning to tell *her* something?

Of course, the paediatrician!

'On the subject of *your* patient,' he began, reverting to head of the hospital, even head of the country mode, 'I should have told you earlier. A trained neonatal paediatrician will be here…' he checked his watch '…within the next hour. She's flying down from Al Jabaya and will take over the care of the baby here at the hospital.'

Liz Jones turned towards him, her eyes narrowing slightly.

'You're sacking me?'

The question was asked lightly, but it was not quite a tease.

'Just freeing you up to do the work I brought you here to do,' he replied, equally lightly—he hoped! 'You will be welcome to visit the baby, of course, and I know you'll want to talk to Dr Hassan when she arrives, but this afternoon a driver will collect you and your luggage and drive you out to the palace. Four o'clock at the main entrance? That would suit you?'

She wanted to argue—he could see it in the stiffening of her body and the flash of some emotion in her eyes. Not anger, he thought, perhaps offence at his attitude. A dislike of taking orders? He had no idea, but once again, when he knew full well he should be distancing himself from her, the woman had intrigued him to the extent that he was making guesses at her reactions.

Enough!

Anyway, she'd relaxed again, her face now blandly composed.

'Four o'clock at the front entrance,' she repeated, and he sensed she'd have liked to snap a salute. 'I'll make sure I'm there.'

CHAPTER SIX

OF COURSE *he* was waiting for her. Yes, a driver would have been far more sensible, but where this woman was concerned he seemed to have lost touch with what was sensible. No matter how much he told himself there was other work to do, that there were things he shouldn't be putting off, he couldn't overcome his urge to see her reaction to his city, to the drive to his home, to his home itself.

'Is this chauffeuring a part-time job, something you do for extra cash when you're not being a highness?' she teased as he took her bag from her hand and tossed it in the back seat of the big, black, four-wheel drive vehicle.

'I was going home anyway,' he said, not quite a lie as he could work from the palace. But the 'highness' jab had struck home.

'Highness is nothing more than a title, like Mr or Dr,' he told her. 'It was never used in our country until recently when the paparazzi began to shove it in front of our names. Now suddenly every tribal leader in the region is His Royal Highness, as if we're European royalty. The problem is, our people are picking up on it as well.'

He glanced towards his passenger.

'Does it bother you?'

But apparently she didn't hear the question, for as he'd asked it she'd turned to look out the window. The moment coincided with his driving out of the hospital gates and they were passing a new souk that had sprung up at the entrance to the new building, market stalls appearing almost overnight, selling everything from herbs and spices to women's underwear.

'Oh, the colour! I didn't see this as we drove in,' his passenger murmured. 'Can we stop? May I get out and have a look?'

He pulled over on the other side of the road, tossing up in his mind whether to stay in the car, knowing there'd be deference if he walked through the market yet wanting to share the experience with her.

The latter won and he slipped out of the car, coming around to take her arm as she clambered awkwardly down from the high seat.

She breathed deeply, taking in the many different aromas of the market, smiling already, although they hadn't entered any of the narrow pathways between the stalls.

'What is the smell?' she asked, turning to him, the delight in her smile causing havoc in his chest.

'Spices, rosewater, incense, coffee, lemons—a mix of all those and probably a dozen other things,' he told her, keeping his hand on her elbow and guiding her across the road, nodding to people who greeted him but concentrating on keeping her steady on the rough, stony ground.

'Oh, look at that—pyramids of colour. How do they do that? What is it?'

She'd stopped only metres down the first alleyway

where tall cones of gold and russet and green and black
drew the eye.

'This is the spice seller,' he explained. 'Spices and
herbs.'

He pointed to the drying herbs hanging in bunches
from the supports that held the sheltering tent upright.

'So, tell me what the spices are,' she demanded, moving closer, her hands not quite touching the solidly built
cones of spices.

The fact that she assumed he knew which spice was
which amused him. Names of spices? He knew the
tastes but…

Asking the stallholder, he translated.

'The deep red is paprika, the yellow is tumeric, the
greenish-grey is cumin and the black, of course, is pep-
per. In the big glass jar, saffron threads—see.'

The stallholder had pulled some threads of saffron
from the jar and handed them to Khalifa.

He pressed them into Liz's hand, feeling the softness of her skin—

'But such huge stacks of it when all you use is a
pinch,' Liz said, sniffing at the saffron, half turning
towards him so the softness her breast was pressed
against his hand and the havoc in his body strength-
ened to chaos.

'I think they do it to attract attention to the stall,' he
said, hoping the prosaic reply had hidden his reaction
to her closeness.

'Well, that works!' she said, smiling at him in such
a natural way he wanted to stay right here, holding her
arm, surrounded by the noise and scents and bustle of
the souk, possibly for ever.

But she'd plunged on, finding a tall, silver coffee pot

and holding it up, turning it this way and that to catch the few rays of the sun penetrating the narrow passage between stalls.

'It's a design from the south,' he said, pointing to a triangular symbol etched on the side. 'That's one of the tattoos the desert women might have worn to ward off evil spirits.'

She put the pot down, serious now.

'I forgot to ask you. What happened with the relatives of your patient? Did you get in touch with them?'

'My grandmother has gone down to visit them. She will tell them what has happened and bring back as many of the relatives as wish to come.'

'Your grandmother? You still have a grandmother? You *are* lucky!'

He had no doubt that she meant it, and remembered now her telling him of her parents' deaths then her brother being killed.

'You have no living relatives?' he asked, and she shook her head, then she smiled and for the first time that he could remember, right there in the colour and clamour of the souk, she patted the bulge of her stomach.

'Well, I suppose you could say this one will be a relative—a niece or nephew. We'd thought later…'

Liz felt the tears sting her eyes and couldn't believe this was happening to her. Right here, in a marketplace, in a strange country, with a strange man, she was about to give in to the tears she'd held back for so long.

And that she *was* going to give in to them she had no doubt, for they were welling up inside her like a wave about to crash onto the shore.

'Let's get out of here,' she gabbled at her host, and

without waiting for his reply she plunged back the way they'd come, past the silver coffee pot and the pyramids of spices, heading blindly for the big black vehicle, thankful it had tinted windows so her feeble-minded collapse wouldn't be witnessed by the crowds of people entering and leaving the marketplace.

Khalifa put his arm around her, sheltering her from the crush, feeling the tension in her muscles as she drove forward, helping her into the car, closing the door, and quickly starting the car. Just down the road and off to the left was a small oasis, rarely visited as most people preferred the big parks in the centre of the city.

It was a beautiful place, where the red desert sands met the soft green of the tiny area, the sand hills slowly moving closer to the water but the vegetation fighting back.

He took her there, aware that some emotion was tearing her apart, helpless to help her as she held her hands to her face, unable to stop the tears that streamed between her fingers or the sobs she muffled with her fists.

But once he'd stopped in the shade of a squat date palm, he could put his arm around her and draw her close to his body, hoping human contact might be of comfort.

Holding her, was, of course, a huge mistake on his part, for this close he could smell the fragrance of her hair, the scent of her body, feel the softness of her flesh, the rise and fall of her breasts as she struggled to regain her composure. He stroked her arm—her skin silky smooth, lightly tanned, with fine, sun-kissed golden hairs that flirted with his fingertips.

And *his* flesh, weak as it was, delighted in all of this;

his skin heated—that thin line between attraction and lust dangerously close.

Thankfully, she moved, just slightly, in his arms, then pushed away, her glasses dropping onto the floor of the car, her hands rubbing furiously at her face, dashing away remaining tears, reddening her cheeks, tousling her hair, so when she turned to him she could only shake her head.

'I'm sorry, I truly am! I had no idea all that emotion was going to come pouring out! I didn't even know it was in there! And, believe me, I don't do tears—not like that. Blame the hormones.'

She was acutely embarrassed and angry with herself as well, that much was clear to see, but...

'I don't think there's anything to be ashamed of in emotion,' he said quietly. 'We all feel it, so can't we be allowed to show it?'

He won a smile—not the reaction he'd expected but one he enjoyed nonetheless.

'Do you?' she teased, and he must have looked bemused because she clarified the question for him. 'Show emotion?'

'Me?' he said, but he had to smile, teasing her back. 'But I'm a highness, remember. It wouldn't do for me to be weeping all over the place.'

He touched her lightly on the cheek.

'Seriously, though, those tears probably needed to come out, hormones or not. It's all very well to carry on working as if nothing has happened in your life, but losing your brother, your last living relative, that must have brought terrible pain.'

She turned away from him—from his touch?—and...

A memory stirred, a recent memory that had been lost in *his* emotional reaction to holding her in his arms.

'You said the child…'

How to put it?

'The child you're carrying—a relation—a niece or nephew? It's not your child?'

For a moment he thought she was going to ignore him, then she rested her hands on the bulge of her belly, smoothing the material of her tunic over it.

Hesitating…

Debating whether to tell him something.

'The baby is Bill and Oliver's,' she said quietly. 'I think I told you how they saved my sanity and kept me going when our parents died. They were my only family, and I loved them both. For years they'd talked of having a child, of getting a donor egg, finding a woman willing to be a surrogate, but every time they discussed it with me—Bill was a lawyer and Oliver's in finance so I was the best person to talk to about it—I felt this twinge deep inside me. It took me a while to figure it out, but in the end I knew it was something I could do for them—that I *wanted* to do for them.'

'To carry their child?'

She looked up at him, her eyes clear now, and smiled, a smile so full of loving memories he felt his heart tear.

'It made sense, you see. Using my egg would be as close to Bill's DNA as we could get, so Oliver donated sperm and that was it.'

'You make it sound so normal, but carrying someone else's child? Giving over nine months of your life to provide your brother and his partner with a baby? Was it legal? And personally did it not bother you in the slightest? Did it not bother the two men that you wanted to do it?'

She shook her head, the dark red hair, which had come out of its knot as she'd cried, now tumbling about her shoulders.

'The legal side was okay. Surrogacy is legal as long as it's not for profit. And of course it bothered Bill and Oliver, especially when the bloke I was going out with at the time was so horrified he dropped me like a hot potato. But once they knew I was serious, they were delighted, and just so excited. They made me see a counsellor first, and they discussed it with the same psychologist, but eventually it all fell into place.'

Liz smiled as she remembered the joyous delight of that time—a sad smile maybe, but the pair had been beside themselves.

'They went nuts,' she told Khalifa. 'They made recordings of their voices singing lullabies and talking— recordings I could play to the baby day or night, always changing them, telling the baby things about their lives and the lives all three would have together.'

'And you? Where we you in all of this?'

He sounded stern, almost angry.

She met his gaze, knowing other people had found the decision hard to accept but wanting this man to understand.

'I did it willingly. It was my idea to carry their child—you have to believe that. Oh, I knew the dangers. I knew I couldn't get too emotionally attached to the baby, but Bill and Oliver were so besotted that was easy.'

'Until the accident?'

Emotion closed her throat again but she was *not* going to cry! Not again!

Instead she nodded.

'Bill was killed, Oliver is in a coma, and the poor baby is in limbo.'

'But surely now you'll keep him or her,' Khalifa protested.

Liz sighed.

'You'd think it would be that easy, wouldn't you? But, in fact, if Oliver comes out of the coma, and if he still wants the baby, really it's his.' She tried for a smile but knew it hadn't worked too well when Khalifa reached out and drew her close again, holding her against his body, stirring *her* body so heat moved in places she hadn't known existed and tremors of excitement not only fizzed but bounded along her nerves.

She wanted to snuggle closer, to bury herself in him—not an easy task given the size she was—but to lose herself in sensation for just a short time would be so blissful, so soul-restoring. She snuggled just a little bit...

The kiss began as nothing. All he did was hold her close to comfort her, then press his lips against a bit of skin that was right there beside them. The pale bit near her temple where a pulse fluttered as his lips touched it.

How it became a lip kiss he later couldn't work out, but lips *had* certainly been involved and awkward as it had been in the front of a vehicle, with a very pregnant woman, it had galvanised his body in a way he'd never felt before.

She tasted of peach and honey and warmth and woman, her lips opening to him, her breath coming in little gasps that tightened his body even more. His hands found her breasts, and a tiny moan escaped her lips, catching on his tongue—igniting him.

A thousand reasons not to be here—not to be doing this—were thundering in his head, but nothing mattered except the kiss…and holding her and having her kiss him, feeling her hot, soft body up against his, tasting the honey and the peaches and the woman…

He supposed it had to end, yet he felt distinctly put out when she drew away, rubbing her hands across her face then turning to look at him.

'Oh, I'm sorry!' she cried. 'Oh for heaven's sake! I can't believe I did that!'

He was assuming she meant the kiss, but when she pulled a handkerchief from her handbag and reached out towards him, he realised the kiss, apparently, had meant nothing more than comfort and her distress was the result of something quite different.

As she rubbed ineffectually at a bright yellow streak of saffron across his kandora, he wasn't sure whether to be offended or amused.

'It doesn't matter,' he told her, taking her hand and closing it gently over the handkerchief.

She looked at him now, at his face—met his eyes, her own seeming naked, defenceless, without the terrible glasses.

'None of it?' she asked.

'Ah!' he said. 'As to that, I don't know! Can you deny the attraction between us?'

A shake of her head, a grimace, then she sighed.

'At least I can blame my hormones being out of kilter,' she said, attempting a smile so valiant it made his toes curl. 'What's your excuse?'

And when he didn't answer—how could he when he didn't know?—she spoke again.

'And what's even more bizarre is how you could possibly be attracted to so hugely pregnant a woman? Is it a kinky thing?'

He laughed and reached out to push the hair back off her face.

'I've no idea,' he told her, knowing she deserved honesty. 'Though I can tell you I've seen my fair share of pregnant women and it's never happened to me before.'

'Which is probably a good thing,' Liz replied, the sternness in her voice belied by the smile with which she said the words. 'So let's put it down to an aberration and ignore it,' she suggested. 'I've got a job to do and from all I hear you've got about a hundred different duties on top of your hospital work, so we've really no time for a dalliance.'

'Dalliance?' he echoed, not knowing the word.

'A little fling—a flirtation—that kind of thing,' she told him.

'Ah,' he said again, and wondered just what else there was to say.

Not that she gave him a chance.

'It was just a kiss,' she said, setting her glasses firmly back in place. 'Let's not make too much of it. Now you know where I am at the moment, you'll understand I don't need any further complications. I'm here to do a job and I'll do it. I'll get the unit going for you then return home to have this baby and sort out something for it. Honestly, Khalifa, that's about all I can cope with at the moment.'

He heard truth in her words—heart-rending truth—and marvelled that she'd coped as well as she had up to now. He wanted to tell her how much he admired her, and offer any help within his power, but she'd obviously decided the conversation was finished for she was clambering out of the car then steadying herself on the door as she slid off her sandals.

'Do you realise this is the first bit of desert I've seen since the plane landed and I saw sand hills in the distance? I want to feel the sand, to see if it's as soft as it looks.'

She stepped away from the car, squishing her feet in the sand, then bent to take a handful and let it fall like water from her fingers.

'It is!' she called to him, her delight so obvious he had to smile.

And had to join her as she climbed the hill. He took her hand as it grew steeper and hauled her up to the top.

They sat together, not too close but close enough that he knew she could feel his warmth as he felt hers. Not far away a random gust of wind stirred the sand into an eddy.

'There's a sand sprite,' he said, pointing to it.

'We'd call it a whirly-whirly,' she said, as the lifting twirl of sand danced across the surface of the dune.

'But are your whirly-whirlies real?' Khalifa asked her.

'Real?'

He nodded, smiling at her surprise.

'My people believe the sand sprites are good spirits—a little like djinns but less mischievous. There's a story of a sand sprite we tell the children.'

Liz lay back in the sand, so at ease with this man she barely knew, so delighted to be in this strange place, she wanted the moment to go on and on.

'Tell me?'

He smiled at her, then relaxed, easing back on to one elbow so he could watch her face as he talked.

'The legend tells us that once, long ago, there was a sand sprite who had magical powers. At night she turned into a beautiful woman, and she went about the land, fixing things that the djinns had interfered with, making things right for people, helping them.'

He paused then added, 'Not unlike a certain Australian doctor in that way.'

'I've been doing my job, nothing more. Just get on with the story.' She was embarrassed by his words but not as embarrassed as she felt every time she saw the smear of yellow across his white gown, or thought of how she'd reacted to his kiss.

'Well, one night she met a prince who was so handsome and dashing she couldn't help but fall in love with him, so now, every night, instead of doing good deeds she sought out the prince and spent her time as a human kissing him.'

'Which just shows the danger of kisses,' Liz put in, only half joking.

'It does,' Khalifa agreed very solemnly, 'for kisses led to other things and in the end they spent a night making love, but what the sand sprite didn't realise was that once she'd made love with a human, she couldn't go back to being a sand sprite ever again and had to stay as a human for ever.'

'They made love? This is a children's story?' Liz queried.

Khalifa grinned at her.

'In the children's version they get married.'

'But if it's told as a cautionary tale, what's the catch? Did they not live happily ever after? Did she prefer being a sand sprite to being human and pine away and die? Did the djinns take over the world, without her to undo their mischief?'

'I'm not entirely sure,' Khalifa admitted. 'My grand-mother told me the story and her stories usually carried a warning of some kind. "Be good or the djinns will get you" was the most common.'

'Perhaps the story was more for girls,' Liz offered. 'A warning about the dangers of kissing handsome princes.'

She sat up and dusted the sand off her hands, then gasped in wonder as she turned and caught the full beauty of a desert sunset. Above the sea of dunes, the sky was aglow with orange fire, streaks of red along the horizon and paler gold melting into the dark blue of the evening sky.

'I hope she came to life in time to see this every evening,' Liz whispered, reaching out to rest her hand on Khalifa's because she had to share the beauty and the wonder of it, for all she knew touching him was dangerous.

'I'm sure she did,' he told her.

They sat in silence, hand in hand, until the colours faded from the sky, then he helped her to her feet and steadied her as they clambered down the sand hill and back to the vehicle.

'Thank you,' she said, when she'd fastened her seat belt and he was about to shut the door. 'Thank you for giving me comfort when I needed it, for telling me the story, and most of all for sharing the beauty of that sunset with me.'

He touched her lightly on the cheek.

'It was my pleasure,' he said, and for some obscure

reason the words made her feel sad again, as if something wonderful had ended when, in fact, there was so much still ahead. The palace, and seeing more of this magical country, and then there was her job—setting up the new unit—a challenge she'd been looking forward to.

So maybe the sadness was hunger.

She was silent as he drove back to the main road, silent as they passed through the outskirts of the city, where streetlights were coming on and the dusk masked any difference she might have noticed in daylight. But as they approached the palace Khalifa watched her turning this way and that as if the rammed-earth walls of what had been an old fort needed to be viewed from many different angles.

'This is your palace?'

'Close,' he told her. 'The fort was built in ancient times. See the turrets there along the western wall? They were the lookouts for the enemies.'

'Did enemies only come from the west?'

'Foreign enemies,' he admitted. 'Though there were plenty of fights between the tribes themselves but that was more a sport—which team would win the competition this year, that kind of thing. When foreign enemies came, all the teams—the tribes—joined together.'

The vast wooden gate into the fort swung open as the car approached, the two men who had lived to open the doors now replaced by an automatic opening mechanism. Although the two men still sat, one of either side of the door, rising to their feet and saluting as he drove in.

'Oh!'

A small sound, but enough to delight him, for it told

him Liz had been startled by the beauty of the court-yard that lay behind the walls. Formally laid out with a sparkling fountain in the centre, it held fruit trees as well as ornamental plants, and gardens filled with roses, all now in full bloom.

'It's unbelievable,' she said. 'To see such beauty when all around is dry and barren. Of course the desert is beautiful, too, in its own way, but this is lovely.'

She shook her head and Khalifa was filled with absurd happiness at her appreciation.

'Has it always been this way?' she asked, as he pulled up at the bottom of a shallow flight of steps that led up to the veranda in front of the guest quarters.

'Always,' he said. 'I think I told you Najme was built on an oasis. Many centuries ago the caliph—that is our term for highness—ordered water to be channelled underground so the garden would always be green. And although the gates are kept closed at night, by day anyone can enter the courtyard and rest in the garden. Children can splash in the fountain and their mothers can pick fruit. The rule is you take only what you and your family will eat that day, so there is always plenty for everyone.'

'And that happens? People take only what they need?'

'Of course,' he said, but in his head he was putting the words into another context, remembering the kiss, certain from her reaction that she'd taken only what she'd needed—comfort—from it. Then she'd warned him off. Put it down as an aberration, she'd said.

Which was just as well, given his track record with pregnant women! An image of Zara popped obligingly into his head and he knew with total certainty that nothing must come of the attraction.

CHAPTER SEVEN

Liz was still gazing around at the lush colour of the courtyard, unable to believe such beauty had been hidden behind the dull red walls of the fort. Khalifa opened the door and helped her down from the car and his touch on her arm not only brought the usual reactions but with them a determination to ignore all physical manifestations of this attraction and to steer clear of this man whenever possible. She would treat him as her boss, nothing more—no chats or teasing or bleating out her problems...

He led the way up shallow steps and kicked off his sandals at the front door. She stared at the jumbled collection of sandals already there and forgot her good intentions, reaching out to hold his shoulder as she slid her own sandals off, asking, at the same time, 'This is a guest house? Do you have so many guests? There must be more than a dozen pairs of sandals lined up there.'

He steadied her then bent to add her sandals to the rather ragged line, then pointed out the small pairs.

'Four children, I would say, although my grandmother has tiny feet so if she's back from the Endless Desert one pair could be hers. Then the...'

He paused, frowning, and Liz wondered if he recognised one pair in particular, but when he continued, she realised he'd been working out how to explain.

'We have young women who look after the house and cook and mind the children. They are not exactly servants for they are usually related—members of our tribe—and their families live here with them so all the children grow up together. My child, if she had lived, would have grown up with the other children, and everyone who is in the house for a meal sits down together for it—all the women and children.'

It sounded very democratic, yet Liz had to ask.

'And the men?'

'In the past, when we were nomadic and our people roamed the desert, the men ate together by the fire outside the tent. This was to guard the women and the children inside. They could also discuss the days ahead, plan hunting trips or forays into foreign territories. Now the men talk politics, which is probably the same thing, but many men now eat with their wives and children— the evening meal at least. Many of the family now live in Al Jabaya, so you'll find mainly older family members here and the young women who look after them.'

He was leading the way into a wide vestibule as he spoke and Liz followed, although her mind had snagged on the image of the fire outside the big tent, the men around it, cleaning guns perhaps, guarding their women and children.

'Khalifa!'

The first child who appeared was a very small girl who raced towards Liz's boss and threw herself into his arms. Other children followed, then a couple of older women, three young women, heads demurely covered with bright scarves, but their faces alight with happiness at seeing the man she was with.

'This is Dr Jones,' he said to the gathering crowd. 'I would introduce you all, but learning too many names at once will confuse her. Who will be taking care of her?'

A young woman in a blue headscarf stepped forward.

'It will be my pleasure,' she said, in prettily accented English. 'I am Mori.'

'And I am Liz,' Liz told her, stepping forward and holding out her hand.

Mori took it shyly and gently squeezed Liz's fingers then said, 'If you would like to come this way, you can rest before dinner.'

Liz began to follow, then realised she hadn't thanked Khalifa for bringing her here. But when she turned he'd moved away and was deep in conversation with an older woman in black. The woman's hand was resting on his arm, and from the way he looked at her—with love, Liz thought—it had to be his grandmother.

She wanted to ask if the baby's mother's relations had been found, but Mori was moving further away and one glance down the seemingly endless corridor off the vestibule told Liz if she didn't follow she might be lost for ever.

The room Mori showed her into was bigger than her entire flat back home, the *en suite* bathroom the size of her living room. The floor was tiled in what looked like marble, the walls the dark pinkish red she'd seen on buildings in the city, but they were striped with horizontal bands of gold that matched the elaborate patterns woven in gold thread in the curtains around the bed, and the gold and red embroidery on the thick carpet beneath her feet.

'This is beautiful,' she breathed. 'All the colours of the sunset over the desert dunes.'

'Khalifa calls it the sunset room. When he rebuilt the palace so he'd have a home in Najme he named all the guest rooms.'

Did he, now? Liz thought, pleased with this tiny glimpse into a sentimental part of the man she was only beginning to know.

Beginning and ending, she told herself. He'd comforted her when she'd needed it, and comfort had led to a kiss, but her life was already swamped in confusion, and she had no intention of making it even more convoluted by giving in to her attraction to the man.

She opened her small bag and realised that just about everything in it was dirty. She'd gone through all but one of the outfits she'd brought with her. This last she'd shoved in on the off chance she might have to get dressed up some time—a long, floaty dress in different shades of blue. Holding it up, she wondered whether it was appropriate, but Mori, looking at it, assured her it was beautiful and that most of the women dressed up for dinner.

'I will take your other clothes and wash them, and if you need something else to wear, the cupboards in the dressing room have a selection of clothes in different sizes, all of them new.'

'Why is that?' Liz asked, intrigued by a guest room that came complete with clothing for the guest.

'In other times, people who had nothing would be taken in by the tribe. In the desert you cannot turn strangers away, for on their own they would surely die. If a person is hungry you must feed him or without clothes then you must cover him. That is our way.'

And when a person needs comfort, you comfort her, Liz added to herself just to make sure she understood that the attraction was going nowhere.

Once showered and dressed, she followed Mori to a huge room where women were already seated around a long piece of woven material stretched out on the floor. It would have been a tablecloth, Liz realised, had there been a table.

She joined Mori on a cushion on the floor.

'This is Rimmi, Khalifa's grandmother.' Mori introduced her to the small woman on the other side of Liz. 'She is the head of the house and likes to keep to the old ways, which is why we eat like this for breakfast and for dinner, everyone together.'

Mori rattled off a conversation Liz couldn't understand, but it must have been an introduction for the older woman, Rimmi, turned and took Liz's hand, squeezing her fingers gently and smiling with a warmth that had Liz immediately smiling back.

'Could you ask her if she has been down into the desert and found the relatives of the woman in hospital?' Liz asked Mori, who spoke again.

Rimmi's grasp tightened on Liz's fingers and she nodded then spoke, her voice a husky whisper.

'She says the family is already at the hospital and you are to be thanked and most blessed for all you have done.'

Liz smiled at the compliment and thanked Rimmi, then glanced up, startled, as an excited chatter spread among the women, while the children were positively yelping with glee.

As was Liz's stupid heart, for Khalifa had entered

the big room and apparently intended to share the meal with the women and children.

She watched the reactions around the table as he bent and kissed the women one by one, tousling the hair of the little ones he passed before settling down on the other side of his grandmother.

Liz told her racing heart to stop its nonsense, and nodded to the man. She longed to ask Mori about his presence, but obviously she couldn't with him sitting so close.

And so at ease! His long body settled comfortably on the cushion, his legs hidden beneath a clean white gown, the sides of his headscarf tucked up tonight in some complicated fashion so she could see more of his face than was usually revealed when he wore his traditional dress.

Such a strong face. Having heard his stories of the men around the campfire, she could picture him in olden times, a rifle slung across his lap, perhaps a child held against his shoulder, for this man, she guessed, could be both hard and soft.

Now food appeared, great bowls of it, the steam rising from the bowls carrying all the scents of the market they'd visited earlier, deliciously woven into mouthwatering dishes.

Rimmi served Liz, Khalifa explaining what each spoonful was as it was placed on her plate. He passed her bread to eat with it, then demonstrated on his own plate how to use it to scoop the food to his mouth.

'Although there is cutlery if you'd prefer. You'll find it wrapped in that napkin in front of your plate.'

Liz grinned at him and picked up the napkin.

'Better safe than sorry,' she said.

And was surprised when he murmured, 'Klutz,' very softly but with an undertone of affection that caught her off guard so for a moment she forgot about keeping her distance from him and smiled.

He'd known he shouldn't come—should have eaten at his own house—but all his brothers and their families were up in the capital, and he'd felt like company.

Felt like Liz Jones's company, the last functioning cell in his brain had whispered, and he'd been unable to deny it.

Fortunately, before he could become too entangled in his thoughts, Rimmi demanded his attention, talking to him but apparently meaning the conversation to include Liz Jones as well, for she had asked Mori to translate.

'The people of the desert—the people I spoke to—do not understand the hospital,' she was saying. 'To them it is a place where people die, so they do not wish to go there. Somehow you must explain better, to the women in particular, that going to the hospital, or to one of the clinics in the oasis villages, is the best thing to do for themselves and their children.'

'And the men?' Khalifa asked.

Rimmi shrugged her shoulders.

'Ah,' she said, 'the men! As good to talk to the camels or the date palms. But you must talk to the women. Take Dr Jones with you so they see it is a woman they will deal with, and let her explain about what can be done when pregnancy or births go wrong. A woman can tell other women.'

Khalifa glanced at Liz. Had she taken it all in? Had Mori translated it properly?

She smiled at him and nodded as if he'd asked the

questions aloud, and her eyes sparkled as she said, 'You and I talked about doing this earlier—was it on the plane or before that? I can't remember. Talked about taking a crib and explaining what happens in a special-care unit. I'd be happy to go. Just tell me when. After climbing one of your sand dunes, I'm dying to see more of the desert, and I think until the internal changes are made to the unit there's not much I can do there. So, when do we go?'

Now?

Tonight?

That was his libido talking, and he knew it could no longer be considered in this situation. She'd made if perfectly clear there'd be no more 'complications', as she'd put it, and it was only right that he should honour her request.

And she was right about the dalliance. Was that the word she'd used? Whatever might have happened between them, it could have been no more than that. How could he, who'd already failed one woman, and her child, take on responsibility for another?

Although to have a child...

He spoke before melancholy swamped him.

'I understand Phil has the alterations in hand for the space where the unit will be. The hospital tradespeople are beginning work in a couple of days,' he replied, when he realised his silence had stretched for far too long. 'Do you feel you need to be there to supervise that part?'

She bit her lip—something he hadn't seen her do, and rather wished she wasn't doing so now given the way his intention strayed to the pinkness.

'I can't see that I'd be needed,' she said eventually.

'Would we have mobile coverage or access to tele-
phones? Some way for Phil to reach me if he needed to
ask me something?'

Phil again!

'In most areas,' Khalifa assured her. 'It might be
called the Endless Desert but it's not the end of the
world.'

She smiled at his defence of his country and he
realised this trip might be a big mistake. Wasn't he
supposed to be spending less time in this woman's company, not more? Hadn't he decided that only hours earlier?

Then Rimmi was speaking, asking how he'd travel,
who he'd take with him, whether they would be staying overnight and what arrangements she should make
for the doctor's comfort.

Mori was explaining Rimmi's words to Liz, who was
looking more puzzled by the moment.

'When your grandmother wants to know how you'll
travel, she's not talking camels, is she, because right
now I'm not sure—'

He had to laugh.

'I think she meant helicopter or car,' he explained.
'Going by helicopter, we could cover a lot more villages
and tribal camps in one day.'

Now Liz was frowning at him.

'But dropping out of the sky and telling these people
stuff then whirling away again—isn't that what you're
wanting to avoid? From what Mori tells me, most of the
nomadic tribes now travel in four-wheel-drive vehicles
and trucks, although they still keep camels. Aren't we
better, if we're trying to introduce new ideas without

changing their lifestyles too much, approaching them in a vehicle they're used to?'

It made sense, but before he could agree she was speaking again.

'And on that subject, I think if you're coming with me, you should come as a bloke, not a highness. Oh, they'll know who you are, but if you're in casual clothes—do you do casual clothes?—they might be more receptive. It seems to me the white gown puts up a kind of barrier, which you probably need at times, but in this case—'

She stopped suddenly, her fingers covering her mouth as if to stop more words coming out, her cheeks slightly flushed with embarrassment.

'I *do* talk too much!' she muttered from behind those long, slim fingers with their pale, unpainted nails.

'No, you're right,' he assured her. 'I see your point, but if we're to cover all the tribespeople we will, as my grandmother says, have to stay overnight, and though we'd be welcome in the camps you might enjoy the experience of a night in the desert. With inflatable mattresses and sleeping bags it can be quite comfortable. What do you think?'

And what was *he* thinking, even to be considering spending a night in the desert with this woman? He, who knew the magic the desert skies could weave, the mischief the djinns could get up to? He'd forget the night in the desert and work it so they stayed in a village— all villages had buildings in which to put up guests.

'I can manage an inflatable bed, although getting into a sleeping bag might be a bit tight,' Liz responded, then she smiled, and her eyes shone with excitement as she said, 'But, oh, a night in the desert! I've never dreamt I'd experience such a thing! It would be fantastic!'

So there he was, stuck. But if he took Saif to set up camp and cook—wouldn't that be best? Although taking Saif when they were visiting the tribespeople would be a bit like wearing his kandora and headscarf—proclaiming his leadership by bringing a retinue, if only a retinue of one.

Saif in another vehicle—would that be best?

'What are you thinking, my boy?' Rimmi asked, and he turned to her, wondering just what she meant by the question.

'Are you doubting the wisdom of my taking the woman into the desert to speak to the tribespeople?' he asked, and she smiled and shook her head.

'Not at all, the idea is a good one for, if you remember, it was mine. I am wondering about the thoughts that make you frown?'

Khalifa was sure his frown had deepened, for he could hardly tell his grandmother he feared taking the woman into the desert because he lusted after her. She would remind him Liz was a visitor and order him to put such thoughts from his mind.

At least, he thought she would, and now she was waiting for his answer.

'I wouldn't like Dr Jones to be uncomfortable,' he said.

Rimmi smiled.

'I think Dr Jones is more than capable of looking after her own comfort,' she said. 'And I think it is you who will be uncomfortable, although you must be aware she will get tired. Make sure she rests in the afternoon and do not let her overstrain herself.'

Khalifa eyed his grandmother suspiciously. The older he got, the more he suspected the woman could read his mind, especially the bits of it he'd preferred remain unread.

Liz wondered what the pair was saying. Mori had stopped translating so obviously it was some private conversation, although Liz had heard Khalifa use her name.

The meal continued, more dishes appearing, more strange morsels of food to try, but finally Liz pushed aside her plate and turned to Mori.

'I realise it might be rude to leave the table, but I really need to stand up and walk around. Could you please explain that to Rimmi?'

Mori had barely nodded when Khalifa got to his feet, spoke to his grandmother, then reached out to support Liz as she struggled upright.

'Too much food,' she said, hoping to conceal the sizzling heat his touch was transferring to her hand.

She looked down, wishing there was some way she could offer Rimmi a direct apology, but when she tried, the old woman held up her hand and spoke through Mori.

'My grandson will take you for a walk in the garden. In your condition you must do this before you go to bed. It will help you sleep.'

Liz thanked her and followed Khalifa from the room, waving a general farewell to the women and children. A walk in the garden was just what she needed, but with Khalifa?

Perhaps if they talked about work…

She paused outside the door to push her feet into her

sandals, keeping her hand on the wall to balance herself so there was no need to touch Khalifa again.

'I know Dr Hassan had two special-care cribs flown down with her when she came. If we take one of them, would it leave the hospital short?' she asked, as they walked down the steps and onto the main path through the garden.

Khalifa didn't answer, although he paused and she stopped, just a little ahead of him, and looked back to where he stood, a dark figure lit by small lanterns burning at intervals along the path.

'Look around you. Do you really want to talk of work out here in the magic of the moonlight and the beauty of the garden?'

She smiled before she answered.

'Yes, I do,' she said firmly. 'Magic's all well and good, but it doesn't save babies, neither will it help the women of these desert tribes you talk of to visit a doctor or nurse if they need it during their pregnancy.'

'Then, yes, we can take a crib and whatever else you need,' he replied, sounding distinctly grumpy. 'Tomorrow I will take you to the hospital and you can organise whatever you want. There, are you satisfied? Can we now walk in the garden in silence, doing no more than enjoying the beauty of the evening? It is for your peace of mind, so you will sleep well, that my grandmother suggested the walk.'

Peace of mind! That's a joke. Peace of mind with him around?

Liz wanted to yell at him, to rail against the feelings he stirred in her without any apparent effort on his part. But it seemed he'd accepted her edict on the kiss, that it had just been a kiss and they shouldn't make too much of it, and had withdrawn behind the persona of the perfect host.

Perhaps that was all he'd ever been, his talk of attraction to her just that—talk!

So she walked with him in the garden and slowly the fizzing and sparks died down and the peace and beauty of the place entered her soul.

'It *is* beautiful,' she said, pausing by the fountain, trailing her hand in the shimmering water. 'I am glad we walked.'

Well, good for her!

Khalifa's mood was savage. Walking beside this woman in this place that was so special to him had been nothing less than torture. Walking beside her and not touching her, not feeling the softness of her skin or tasting the ripeness of her lips, captured in a kiss in the shadows of an olive tree. His body ached to feel her softness, his arms to hold her, but in his heart he knew he couldn't, and his head told him it was just as well she'd put a stop to further dalliance—because once he did touch her, he wasn't sure he'd ever be able to stop.

He held himself up to his full highness bearing, but the façade cracked and fell apart when she put out a hand, slightly damp from playing in the fountain, and grasped one of his, splashing water, klutz-style, all down his kandora.

'Thank you for the walk. There must be magic in this garden to have given me such ease,' she said, as cool as the hand that still held his. 'I hadn't realised just how badly my body needed to absorb some peace and beauty, to relax and let fate take its course. I've been pushing for things to fall into place, desperate for some certainty ahead, but now I realise I need to be patient and let whatever happens happen.'

He took her other hand and looked into her eyes, liking it that she was a tall woman, only a few inches shorter than his considerable height.

'You've had every reason to be lost in uncertainty,' he said, 'but I'm glad our garden brought you peace. Use it whenever you like, stay as long as you like. You will be looked after here and when, as you say, whatever happens happens, we will deal with that then.'

She smiled and he had to grip her hands more tightly because the urge to lean forward and take off her ghastly glasses and then press kisses all over her moonlit face was so strong that only by anchoring himself to her could he resist.

He walked her back to the guest house and saw her safely into Mori's care, then headed home, already on the phone making arrangements for their journey. Phil Cutler could make himself useful getting the things Liz would need ready for the trip, and Saif could pack the necessities for a night in the desert.

Yes, he was tempting fate by spending a night with her in the desert, whose magic was even stronger than the magic of the garden, but if the garden had given her peace, how much more at ease would she be after a night in the desert? And now he knew the torment she'd been suffering in recent months, how could he not offer her that one night?

CHAPTER EIGHT

It took a day to get organised but they left before dawn the following day, Liz assuring Khalifa that she loved early mornings, which wasn't entirely true but she had been sleeping so fitfully lately that getting out of bed had become a relief.

Now, driving through the desert, she was glad they'd left early. Already the dark shadows cast by the waves of dunes were lightening and the sands were changing colour, turning from black and grey to red and gold, so she felt she was in a world filling with colour.

'It's so beautiful,' she murmured, hardly daring to speak lest noise break the spell that beauty had bound around her.

'And treacherous, never forget that,' Khalifa told her. 'The beauty can lull the unwary into thinking nothing bad can ever happen here, but the desert is a cruel master and must always be treated with respect.'

She turned away from the magic beyond the window to look at him.

'You sound as if you know that from experience—but surely you grew up in the city.'

He nodded, and although he was in casual clothes—jeans, even, and a polo shirt—she could see the strength of his breeding in his face and in the hands that held the wheel of the big vehicle with the same ease as a good horseman might hold the bridle of a mettlesome stallion.

'I was, but my father felt all his boys should know their heritage, so for two years, from ten to twelve, we lived with relatives down here in the Endless Desert. We dressed like them, hunted with them, rode on mock attacks on other tribes. We mended our camel saddles and horse's bridles, and learned to shoot while mounted. And, most fun of all, we began to train our falcons, the ones our father gifted us.'

She thought of boys she knew, sons of friends and colleagues, who were ten, and wondered.

'Did you enjoy it?' she had to ask.

He didn't answer immediately, looking out across the waves of dunes—a dry red ocean.

'In the end, I enjoyed it so much that I stayed another year. I still return to that tribe for time out whenever I can manage it. Others hated it, and seeing their discomfort I believed my father had been wrong to make it a blanket rule. My oldest brother, for instance, had his spirit broken here. He became a man who needed others to help him make decisions. Oh, he chose well with his advisors, and has been a great ruler for our country, but his heart was never in it. He felt rejected by the desert, so he rejected it.'

'Which is why you're so determined to do more for the people of the south,' Liz said, and he glanced her way and smiled.

'I'd never put that into words before, but now I have, I realise the truth of it. Yes, it *is* why I am so anxious to help the desert people, but to help them without pushing them into a life they may not wish to live.'

Liz wanted to ask more about his childhood experiences but she sensed he'd said all he wanted to say about it—possibly more than he'd wanted to say. So she sat and thought about it—about a small boy sent to live with strangers.

'I guess it's not that much different to sending kids to boarding school,' she decided, then realised she'd spoken out loud right when she'd decided not to talk more about it.

But Khalifa turned to her and grinned.

'Very much so,' he said, 'although totally different from the boarding school I eventually attended. But the family sends the child away to learn the ways of the tribe—even in Western civilisation this is the case.'

'I hadn't thought of it that way,' Liz admitted. 'I was just lucky we lived in a city with schools all around so boarding school wasn't necessary. Where did you go? And did you enjoy it?'

'England, and no,' he said. 'It was cold and wet and always grey—can you imagine that after living with this colour? But the people were kind, and I learned things I couldn't have learned in the desert, things I needed to know to help my country move forward. I suppose you could say I learned the ways of other tribes.'

'And things you needed to know if you wanted to practise medicine,' Liz suggested, and again he grinned.

'Of course. Actually, I soon realised I wasn't very diplomatic, so decided my way to help my country would be through service of another kind. Medicine appealed to me.'

'Yet now you must be diplomatic,' Liz pointed out, wanting him to smile again.

But he shook his head.

'Not very. But, like my brother, I have people around me who can do the diplomatic niceties. The one good thing about the highness business is that people don't expect too much of you. A bow of my head, a touch of my hand, perhaps a smile from time to time, that's really all that's required of me in public.'

Not only was he not smiling but his voice had deepened, darkened at the edges by something like despair.

Why?

'Do you hate it so much?' Liz asked the question quietly, disturbed by the tension that seemed to have built up in the car.

He shook his head then glanced her way again.

'I do not hate the job,' he said, 'but what it did to me.'

Now he'd really stopped talking, Liz decided, and although she longed to know what he had meant, she stayed silent, looking out at the now fully lit landscape, marvelling at the colours all around her.

And there, ahead, in the gold and red and orange of the desert, she spied a darker shadow. As they drew nearer, the darkness turned to green, the huge fronds of the date palms shining in the sunlight.

'An oasis?'

'Our first stopping place,' Khalifa told her. 'This is a small village, too small to have a clinic, but the old midwife here has been handling minor accidents and illnesses for nearly fifty years. She is the power in the village, for all there is a chief who thinks he is.'

Liz smiled, thinking of the many women she knew who were the powers behind various thrones, from the personal assistants of big businessmen to the wives of politicians.

Although…

'If she's been running things her way for fifty years, will she be willing to listen to what I have to say?'

Khalifa turned towards her, and now he smiled, something she wished he wouldn't do, as her body was already excited about being in the car with him and her toes could only take so much curling.

'She has already visited the hospital to see what we have there and has probably set herself up with enough medicines to cure the entire population of the Endless Desert so, yes, she will listen. Not only will she listen but she will be happy to pass on what she learns to others.'

Looking around, Liz had to wonder if it was the desert that made the little oasis seem so isolated. They'd driven less than three hours from Najme, yet as the cluster of mud brick houses became obvious, it seemed to Liz that they were in the middle of nowhere.

'Ha! News of our visit has spread!' Khalifa said, pointing to a row of dust-covered vehicles drawn up at the edge of the village. 'Those belong to one of the remaining nomad tribes. They must be camped somewhere nearby at the moment.'

'And they've come to listen to me talk about preemie babies?' Liz queried, as Khalifa stopped the car and she saw that most of the visitors were men. 'It seems highly unlikely.'

Khalifa smiled again.

'It *is* highly unlikely. It's far more probable that they're here to ask a favour of me, or to tell me how badly a neighbouring tribe is behaving, or to offer me a daughter or sister as a new wife.'

His smile widened.

'Perhaps having a very pregnant companion will be a good thing after all.'

'I don't know about the "after all" part of that sentence,' Liz told him, 'but feel free to use my presence as a marriage deterrent, should you feel you need it.'

It had been a light-hearted moment, so she was surprised when he touched her fleetingly on the arm and said, 'Would that I could.'

His comment, as far as Liz was concerned, made no sense at all, but as a very elderly woman had emerged from one of the houses and was waving and smiling brightly at the new arrivals, Liz set the puzzle aside and concentrated on her job.

Khalifa greeted the woman with a kiss on both cheeks then, to Liz's surprise, he lifted the woman in the air and swung her around as he had with the children at the guest house.

She flapped and slapped at his arms but the smile on her face told Liz he was a welcome and much-loved visitor.

"This is Jazillah,' he said to Liz. 'Jazillah, this is Dr Elizabeth Jones.'

'Just call me Liz,' Liz responded, then turned to Khalifa as she realised they were both speaking English.

'I learned English from a friend,' Jazillah explained, taking Liz's hand in hers and turning it over as if to examine the lines on it.

The older woman held it, studying it, while Liz took in the dark colouring henna had left on Jazillah's hand.

'You are well, but troubled,' Jazillah finally declared, giving Liz back her hand. 'I know your machines can tell if there is cancer in someone's bones but are there machines yet that can probe the problems of the heart and mind?'

'Not yet, and probably not ever,' Liz told her, while Khalifa lifted the crib and other equipment they'd brought with them out of the back of the vehicle.

He carried it to the front porch of the house from which Jazillah had appeared, and set it down, and to Liz's surprise other women emerged from the tiny dwelling—surely too many to have been waiting inside.

Some, she saw, were pregnant, while others were probably grandmothers by now. A few were young, teenagers maybe, all cloaked in black, their hair covered, although their faces were visible.

'Serves me right for being suspicious,' Khalifa whispered from behind her. 'The men have not come begging favours but have brought their women in. That is good.'

Then, in a louder voice, he greeted the women in their own language, before telling Liz that Jazillah would translate and he would spend some time with the men.

As he departed, Liz watched the women folding themselves neatly and effortlessly down to sit on the ground. They were all attractive women, some of the young ones beautiful with huge doe-like eyes and clear olive skin.

Prospective brides for the ruler?

Liz smiled to herself and let the women settle, then introduced herself and explained what she did, thankful she had the excuse of showing the crib to avoid having to sit on the ground.

Though the sitting was relatively easy compared to the getting up.

'Sometimes babies are born too early, or are born with problems that mean they need special care in order to survive. I am the kind of doctor who can give them that care. I look after new babies, especially ones with problems.'

She paused while Jazillah translated and the women chattered among themselves, Jazillah explaining that they were talking of babies they knew who had died and remembering things that had gone wrong.

'Some of the things that can go wrong can be picked up during pregnancy through a scan,' Liz continued. 'Khalifa tells me that there are facilities for pregnant women to have a scan at the clinics in the larger villages. Sometimes it is possible to make things right for the baby even before it is born.'

She paused again, and again listened to the chatter.

As the group quietened, she showed them the crib and explained how everything attached to it worked, adding, 'For a baby born too early, we try to give it everything it would have received if it had still been in the womb.'

Now the questions began, and as she answered them, always with the lag for the translation, she began to wonder just how many villages they would manage to visit, and to wish someone had produced a chair, and to hope that soon they'd have a break so she could make a bathroom visit.

She was rescued by Jazillah, who apparently had the gift of reading minds as well as palms.

'We will break for coffee and you will drink mint tea,' the older woman decreed. 'But first you might like the bathroom. Come!'

She led Liz through the tiny house to the back, where a sparkling new bathroom had been added.

'It is good Khalifa spent time in the desert as a child, for he understands our needs,' Jazillah told Liz, then she slipped away.

By the time Liz returned, a chair had materialised beside the crib, and a small table beside it held a cup of mint tea and a selection of biscuits and fruit.

The women continued to talk while they sipped coffee from their tiny cups and ate dates and biscuits, so every now and then Jazillah turned to Liz to translate a question. Eventually they got on to the hospital, and all the services offered there, including the setting-up of the new unit.

'Will we be able to stay with our baby?' was the first question, and Liz assured the women they would be welcome there, then went on to explain about the verandas where family could also come and go so the woman had the support she needed.

'And men, they can visit?' Jazillah asked, and when she translated Liz's reply that the father could spend time in the unit with the baby, it raised a great deal of merriment among the women.

'They are telling me which of their husbands might do such a thing and which of them would be too scared of showing their emotion if their baby needed help,' Jazillah said.

Liz had to laugh.

'It's the same everywhere. It hurts fathers to see their baby in trouble, but often they don't want others to see their tears.'

More chatter and more questions, then finally Liz felt she'd covered as much as she could. She also had the sense that the women were accepting of the things she had told them and would be less reluctant to use the services Khalifa was providing.

But she was exhausted.

Had the language barrier made a fairly simple task more difficult, or were the effects of a busy first week in this strange land finally making themselves felt?

'You must rest now,' Jazillah decreed, perhaps not reading Liz's mind but seeing fatigue in her bearing.

'But we have other villages to visit, other people to see,' Liz protested.

'After you have rested.' Jazillah was firm. 'I have prepared a bed for you. Come!'

And suddenly Liz was happy to be led, to be bossed around and told to rest. In fact, she felt almost weepy that someone was taking care of her, as if her mother had returned from the dead and taken over just when she was needed.

Jazillah showed her a thick mattress on a floor just inside the door. It was covered by a bright, woven cloth and looked so inviting Liz forgot about the problems of getting up again from ground level, and sank down on it, turning on her side to get comfortable and falling asleep almost immediately.

Khalifa realised she was missing when he saw the empty chair, but the other women were still chatting on the porch so he assumed Liz had taken a short break. Jazillah soon put him right.

'You are not looking after that woman.' Her reprimand was sternly delivered, her face serious. 'You must make her rest and treat her well or her baby will be needing one of those special cribs you are carrying around.'

'Where is she?' he demanded, seriously disturbed by Jazillah's words.

'She is resting and she will stay resting until I say she can continue in the car,' Jazillah told her. 'And don't tell me you have to do a doctor check of her. I have checked and all is well, but she is very tired. And she is unhappy. Is that your doing?'

Here I am, leader of the country—and I'm being told off by an ancient medicine woman! Khalifa thought, but he was troubled by Jazillah's reading of the situation.

'She has reason to be unhappy,' he said quietly, 'and, no, not because of me.'

Unfortunately, his head added, although he knew full well he'd never willingly do anything to make Liz unhappy.

'Then you must take extra care of her,' Jazillah decreed. 'Unhappiness is bad for the baby, and is just as likely to cause problems as a medical condition.'

He frowned at that. Did she mean it? Had she proof?

Uncertain what to do next, he packed the crib and other paraphernalia back into the car. Though he longed to enter the house, if only to look at Liz, he remained outside, walking instead to the oasis, speaking to men who were there, fixing one of old pumps that fed water into the irrigation channels that ran between the date palms.

They talked of the prospects of the season's crop of dates, of the likelihood of sandstorms over summer, and of village politics. A new headman was making his mark, but not everyone liked him—would Khalifa keep an eye out for trouble?

The typical village talk soothed him, although the

little niggle of anxiety he felt over Liz's health refused to go away.

'Exhausted? What nonsense,' she told him only minutes later when he returned to the house to find her not only rested but ready to move on again. 'All I needed was a nap. I don't sleep well at night, but a nap now and then makes up for it. Where next?'

The blue eyes challenged him to argue and he glanced towards Jazillah and shrugged.

'Just make her rest,' the older woman said, then, to Khalifa's surprise, she took both of Liz's hands in hers and said, 'I will see you again soon. Soon and often.'

'I hope that doesn't mean I'm about to go into labour and you'll have to rush me back here for her to deliver the baby,' Liz joked as they drove away from the village.

'Don't joke about it,' Khalifa told her, more disturbed than Liz would realise by Jazillah's pronouncement. 'And, unlikely as it might seem to that woman, I *am* a doctor and I *can* deliver babies!'

'I'm sure you can,' Liz responded soothingly, 'but let's hope it doesn't come to that.'

He hoped it wouldn't as well, but there was no denying that his conversation with Jazillah had unsettled him and he was more than half-inclined to turn the vehicle around and head back to Najme.

'Don't even think about it.'

Liz's words made him realise he'd actually taken his foot off the accelerator as he considered this move.

'Are you reading my mind?' he demanded.

'Only the obvious bits,' Liz told him, then she reached out and touched his forearm. 'I'm not stupid, Khalifa. I know I have to look after myself. Yes, I was more tired than I realised this morning, but I'll take that as a warning and rest whenever I can. Let's do the next place then see how I feel, okay?'

Her touch had burned his skin—burned it as surely as a brand would have. How could that happen? How could it be that a foreign, pregnant woman could have sneaked beneath his emotional guard and be firing his body with need and his mind with any number of erotic fantasies?

And worse, he had yet to spend the promised night in the desert with her! In the desert where he was most alive, beneath the stars he knew like the skin on his own body, and with djinns around making mischief and no sand sprite to undo their spells…

Liz was glad the conversation about her health seemed to have finished, and was equally pleased to be travelling in silence. It meant she would think. And she needed to think. She needed to work out if her fatigue was simply physical or if the added complication of her attraction to Khalifa was contributing to it. Certainly, it took a lot of effort to pretend the attraction didn't exist.

'Oh!' she said, as they topped a dune and the wonder of the sight before her eyes drew the breathless exclamation.

Khalifa stopped the car so she could take in the great lake spreading from the bottom of the dunes.

'I can't believe it,' she finally said.

He smiled and said, 'Nor should you. It is a mirage.'

'No, it can't be, it's too real!'

'Unfortunately it is. It's often here and there are various explanations for it. Some say it's a reflection of the water in the oasis bounced back somehow from the sky but the oasis is surrounded by palms and very little of the water is visible so it seems unlikely. Science tells us it's caused by the deflection of light rays but to me it always has a kind of magic about it, and a lesson for us poor humans as well.'

'That things aren't always what they seem?' Liz guessed, and he nodded, then smiled and touched her baby bump.

'You'd be a prime example of that,' he said quietly, then he put the car into gear and drove down the dune, while Liz watched the water disappear and sand take its place once again.

They drove on in silence, Liz relaxed enough to find herself nodding off, so she let the back of the seat down and slept properly for a while, waking only when Khalifa stopped the car.

'This is the village closest to where I lived when I was in the desert,' he explained as she sat up and looked around. 'It has a clinic, and the clinic sister will have rounded up all the women from far and near to come and listen to you. She will also do the translating.'

Liz left her study of the village to turn towards him.

'If there is a woman in every village who can translate, why did you need to come?'

Khalifa looked at her and smiled.

'This may sound very pompous to you, but my presence means they will take you and what you tell them more seriously. And while you are talking to the women, I am not discussing camel prices with the men but explaining all the same things to them. It is important to them that they know what the women know, for how else can they make decisions together with their families?'

Liz nodded.

'Now, the clinic sister here is English. She came to teach first then trained as a nurse in Al Jabaya when she saw the need for nurses in the Endless Desert. She is married to the headman of the village and they have four children.'

'Then she probably knows far more about what I'm going to talk about than I do,' Liz told him.

'Possibly,' he conceded, 'but we add gravity to things she tells the women. The visit is not wasted for that reason.'

Liz found herself shaking her head again—there was so much to learn about this country and its culture, a lifetime wouldn't suffice.

Not that she'd have a lifetime here, a voice in her head reminded her, making her feel a little sad and sorry for herself. Although when a woman, all in black but with greying blonde hair peeking from beneath her head-covering came bounding out of a house to greet them, she forgot about everything but the job she'd come to do.

'Good heavens, you're pregnant. What on earth is Khalifa thinking to be dragging you around the desert in your condition?'

'I wanted to come,' Liz assured her. 'After all, what's the use of having a special-care unit at the new hospital if no one wants to use it? I'm Liz, by the way.'

'Jane,' the other woman said, holding out her hand and shaking Liz's before turning to Khalifa to berate him in person.

'Just make sure she rests after lunch,' was all he said, as he dumped the crib and the other gear at the front door, then he kissed Jane's cheek and departed, heading for wherever the men must have gathered.

Jane led Liz inside the house.

'The women are in here,' she said, and as Liz's eyes adjusted to the gloom she saw a couple of dozen women crammed into the room, all of them already settled on the floor, the coffee pot in the centre of the room burbling on a tiny, portable, gas ring.

The session went well, aided, no doubt, by Jane's understanding of everything Liz was saying. It ended with a lunch of salad and fruit. Then, as Jane showed Liz into a room where she could rest, she dropped the bombshell that put all thought of sleep from Liz's head.

'I'm surprised that Khalifa's letting you do this, given how he hid his first wife away throughout her pregnancy.'

By the time Liz had caught the subtext of the words, Jane was gone and she couldn't protest that she wasn't Khalifa's wife and neither was it his baby she carried.

How could Jane have got that idea?

And, worse, who else might think it?

It was only as she was drifting off to sleep that she remembered Khalifa's words in the car when they'd been setting off—something about her pregnancy protecting him from men offering their sisters or daughters as brides?

Had he guessed people might assume the baby was his?

Was he using her?

CHAPTER NINE

REFRESHED from her sleep, Liz was able to take more notice of the landscape as they drove deeper into the desert. She'd set aside her silly suspicions about this journey with Khalifa, putting them down to tiredness and the added problems the attraction caused her body.

Now, looking around, she realised the scenery was changing.

'It's still sand and dunes, but it's different somehow,' she said, when she'd tried and failed to pin down the difference.

His smile lit up his face.

'I call this the real desert,' he said. 'It's rare a stranger notices it because the differences are subtle. The dunes are slightly higher, the red of the sand is deeper in colour, and the wind carves shapes along the top of the hills so now you see a dog, and in a minute it might be a crocodile.'

'You're right. Look there—a prancing horse!' Liz didn't try to hide her delight, and she watched, bemused, as the shape of the horse turned into a big swirl of a wave.

'Is the sand shifting so that the shapes change?' she

asked, twisting in her seat to see what had happened to the wave.

'No, it's partly because we're moving, and partly because the sand is so pure down here—so uncontaminated by pollution of any kind—it reflects light in strange ways, giving the impression of shapes.'

'A different kind of mirage,' Liz whispered, looking all around her, trying to find other shifting shapes. 'No wonder the people believe in djinns and sand sprites when they see these transformations every day. How else would they explain them?'

Khalifa heard the wonder in her voice, and his heart hurt, for he'd never known a stranger even to see the shapes, let alone understand how his people felt about them. He wanted to stop the car and sit and hold her while they watched the dune shapes change in the shifting sunlight.

He wanted to stop the car and hold her.

He wanted to hold her.

That was the sum of it.

And this time it wasn't just his attraction to her prompting his thinking. It was something different, something deeper, something he didn't understand.

He didn't stop the car, driving on, driving just a little faster, hoping that once he was out of the car the feeling wouldn't be as strong.

'Damn it all, they must have moved on.'

Had she heard the frustration in his voice that she turned from her study of the landscape to look at him?

'Problems?'

None that he could tell her about!

'Not really,' he replied. 'I understood the next group

was camped down there.' He pointed to where he'd expected them to be. 'Can you see the well?'

To his surprise Liz laughed.

'I'd like to say yes, but what I'm looking at will probably turn into an animal of some kind, then back into a sand dune. You have wells? Out here in the middle of the desert, there's water?'

The laugh had made his heart hurt even more, but he covered his confusion with practicality.

'There's water everywhere under the desert. At the oases it has come to the top, but out here we dig wells. In fact, most of the wells are centuries old, dug by the nomadic tribes so long ago that no one remembers when. The nomads are happier camping near wells, because at most of the oases there are villages, and to the nomads villages represent civilisation.'

She was frowning now, and that hurt him too, although he knew it was just puzzlement on her part.

Or he hoped it was.

'But are there many nomadic people still living in the desert?' she asked.

'Not as many as when I was a boy, but still up to ten roaming tribes.'

She nodded and he knew she considered everything he said and that her interest wasn't superficial. It was empathy.

'Oh, now I see the well,' she cried, then turned back to him. 'But what do we do next, now we know they're not there?'

He drew up beside the well and *now* he stopped the car, but not to hold her. Instead he stepped out and dropped the bucket that stood on the rim, hearing it splash into the water. He wound up a pail full of the fresh, clean liquid, filled a beaker that was hung on the frame, filled it and carried it around to where she'd just alighted from the car.

'Try it,' he said, then watched with pleasure as she drank, tentatively at first then deeply, sighing with satisfaction at the end.

'Beautiful,' she said.

'But not as beautiful as you,' he murmured, taking the beaker and draining the last drops, then, with his lips still wet, he kissed her.

Liz was sure she didn't mean to kiss him back. She'd decided very firmly that kissing was off limits where this man was concerned. Probably, in her condition, where any man was concerned! But she was definitely kissing him back, leaning into him, tasting the water on his lips, tasting him, wanting more while her head rambled on about not kissing men.

Now her breasts were aching from the kiss, and she had to move so they could push against him, seeking relief, although his body heat made them ache even more, ache for his touch, for some release from the tension a simple kiss was causing in her body.

Except there was nothing simple about this kiss. If anything, it was the most complex kiss Liz had ever experienced, for it seemed to be saying things as well as asking things and she didn't understand any of it, except the need to keep on kissing Khalifa whoever, His Highness of Al Tinine...

The revving of an engine shattered the moment.

A vehicle approaching?

Out here in the desert?

She broke away from Khalifa, or maybe he broke away from her, although his hand stayed on her back, steadying her as yet another large, dusty vehicle approached them, driving not on the half-made road they'd been following, but rolling down a sand dune.

'Saif!' Khalifa muttered, dropping his hand from Liz's back and leaving a patch of skin that felt suddenly cold.

He walked away from her to meet the approaching vehicle, while Liz dipped the beaker into the bucket of water and sipped the clear, pure liquid once again, trying not to think of the kiss, and definitely not think of the reactions it had produced in her body. She focussed on the now—on what was happening—on why Saif had suddenly materialised, here in the middle of the desert.

She watched the two men talking, the low murmur of voices easily carrying across the silence of the desert, not that she could understand a word that was being said.

Khalifa's head was bent towards Saif, and Liz could study him, trying to make out why this man, of all the men she'd met at different times in her life, should affect her the way he did.

It wasn't that he had power—she'd barely been aware of that before they'd arrived in his country. And she knew plenty of men with money, so it wasn't the jet or the palace. It was just something about the man—something more than physical attraction, she was sure of it.

He was walking back towards her. Saif was already back in his vehicle, preparing to drive off.

'Is there a problem?' Liz asked Khalifa as he approached, while just looking at him walk towards her made her heart beat faster.

The smile he offered by way of answer sent her pulse into a further frenzy and she reached out to hold the top of the well in case her knees became too unreliable to hold her up.

'No problem, but Saif assumed we'd come here in search of the nomads. He tells me they're camped at the next well. It's some distance away, so we'll go to the camp he's set up for us and visit them in the morning.'

Liz studied him for a moment, trying hard to read his face but finding no clue about his feelings in it.

'Are you suggesting we stop now because you're worried I'll get overtired?' she asked, and the smile returned.

'I'd like to use that as an excuse, but I'm suggesting we stop for my own selfish reasons. Saif brought out my favourite bird and I'd like her to fly before dusk. She can catch her dinner, if she's not too out of practice.'

'Your bird? A falcon?'

Liz breathed the words, unable to believe she was going to see a hunting bird in flight—unable to believe an already amazing day could get even more extraordinary.

'Let's go,' Khalifa said, and he took her arm and led her to the car, opening the door for her then helping her in, something he'd done before, but this time it seemed...

More intimate?

No, she was imagining it—building on the kiss and the impact it had had on her body.

He was in the car himself now, starting the engine, his long, slim fingers relaxed on the steering-wheel.

Long slim fingers that had stroked her back—

Forget the kiss! Think of something else!

'You said Saif had set up our camp. You sent him out to do this?'

Khalifa glanced her way and smiled again.

'I didn't send him,' he said, a little stiff now. 'I am more than capable of setting up a camp but he insisted on doing it, or maybe Rimmi gave him his orders. All he'd say was that he wanted us to be comfortable, and to be sure there was food you could eat. He doesn't trust me as a cook. The bird was a surprise, something I hadn't expected.'

'But he knew it would please you? He knows you so well?'

He didn't turn this time, all his concentration on getting the vehicle up the sand dune, but he nodded, then said, 'Probably too well,' in such a rueful voice Liz had to wonder what he'd meant.

It seemed they must have driven up and over and down at least forty more dunes before once again she saw, in the distance, a dark shadow on the ground. As they drew nearer it materialised into a tent, but a tent unlike any Liz had ever seen. It was broad and low-set, slung a mere five feet above the ground, the sides sloping down onto the sand, poles and ropes holding and anchoring it.

'In the past, the tents were made from camel skins, the rugs woven from either camel or goat hair. These days the tents are made from factory-made fabric, but still keep the dark colouring of the originals, and the rug-weaving is still practised.'

He pulled the car up to one side of the tent and Liz saw, set out in front of it a brightly patterned rug and a stack of firewood, while a small fire was set beyond the rug. She could picture the scene from times gone by, with the men, backs to the tent, looking out past the fire into the darkness, looking out for trouble! Inside the tent she could make out two flat mattresses, not unlike the ones she'd been resting on earlier in the day. There was also a low table and, incongruously, a number of cool boxes, no doubt containing the dinner Saif didn't trust Khalifa to cook.

She slipped out of the car and stretched, then looked around for her companion, finding him bent over a box in the shade of the tent. Moving closer, she could tell it was the kind of cage used to carry small cats or dogs, and as Khalifa slipped a heavy gauntlet onto his arm, she realised the bird he'd spoken of, his falcon, was in the cage.

'May I come closer?' she asked, uncertain just how falcons might take to strangers.

'Of course,' Khalifa told her. 'She's wearing her hood so you won't frighten her.'

'More likely she'll frighten me,' Liz joked, but Khalifa was concentrating on the cage, undoing the latches then putting his gauntleted hand close to the ground, murmuring to his bird, words Liz couldn't understand.

The bird hopped out. She was far smaller than Liz had imagined, perhaps the size of an owl. She saw what Khalifa had meant by the hood, a little leather cap on the bird's head. It was sitting on the glove now, and she could see strings coming from around its legs, the strings now clasped between Khalifa's fingers.

'She's beautiful,' Liz whispered, taking in the snowy breast of the bird and the dark bands of colour on her back and wing feathers. Khalifa was petting her, stroking her, talking soothingly, and it seemed to Liz the bird understood exactly what he was saying. He took the hood off her head and she turned to look at him, her eyes bright and inquisitive.

'She looks like you,' Liz told him, as she saw the two heads in profile, both imperious, haughty, aware of their power and the attraction of it.

Khalifa raised his eyebrows then spoke again to the bird, carrying her away from the tent, holding his arm up, then releasing the strings he'd held between his fingers.

Wide wings raised high, the bird seemed to stretch, then she lifted into the air, circling as she rose with what seemed like effortless ease until she grew so small it was hard to see her. Just a speck, circling and circling.

'She must have fantastic eyesight if she can spot her prey from that height,' Liz said.

Just as she spoke the bird dived, arrowing towards the ground before rising again, a smaller bird in its talons.

'Oh!'

'Do you find it cruel?' Khalifa asked, correctly interpreting Liz's exclamation.

'Not cruel, because she has to eat—we all do. But it was unexpected, I suppose. I had no idea what she'd eat.'

'Quail tonight—but in the past the birds hunted to feed the families who bred and kept them. There's very little food in the desert and often whatever the birds caught was the only protein the families ate. Now it is sport, but back at Najme for sport we use small stuffed bunnies and birds that are flung from a bow to give the bird the impression of movement.'

The bird had returned, dropping the quail at Khalifa's feet and returning to perch on his gauntlet.

'I'll feed her now and then she will fly without hunting, fly just for the delight of it, to feel the air beneath her wings and the air currents carrying her upwards.'

He took the two birds back towards the shade, and Liz sensed he regretted letting her see the kill, as if it—or her reaction to it—had changed something between them.

She followed him and watched, understanding that she couldn't judge either bird or man. The bird had followed its nature, it had been born knowing it had to hunt to eat.

'I do understand,' she said, squatting awkwardly beside him, wanting more than anything to recapture the closeness they'd shared at the well.

Wanting him to kiss her again? her head asked.

Probably, was the honest answer.

Her meal finished, the falcon hopped back on Khalifa's arm and he held it high until the bird took off again.

'Do you want to catch her?' he asked, pulling off the gauntlet and offering it to Liz.

'Would she come to me?'

He dug in his pocket and produced a whistle.

'Put on the glove then blow this and hold your hand up high.'

Excitement rose as Liz pulled on the heavy leather covering, then put the tiny whistle to her lips. It made a sharp, high-pitched sound, barely heard, yet the bird turned in the air and as Liz raised her arm, it dived straight down, alighting, not at three hundred and fifty kilometres an hour but as lightly as a feather on the glove.

'Oh!' she whispered, this time in utter wonder, for the bird, close up now, was even more beautiful than she'd first thought, the soft feathers gleaming in the last rays of the sun, the proud head turning this way and that.

Khalifa guided Liz's hand down towards a stand. The bird stepped onto it and looked around, her bright eyes taking in her surroundings.

'Will she stay there?' Liz asked.

'I'll attach a leash to her jesses, the little strings that hang down from her anklets, and fix her there so she's safe. But I don't think she'd fly away unless she was startled by something.'

'She's amazing,' Liz said, spellbound by the beauty of the bird.

'She is,' Khalifa said, and he put his arm around Liz as she stood looking, and the arm made her wonder if he was still talking about the bird.

He guided her towards the tent.

'Will you relax inside, or should I bring some pillows out to the rug beside the fire?'

It was such an ordinary question Liz forgot about there being subtext in his conversations. He was nothing more than a kind man, and his touch was simply supportive, while the kiss...

Well, the kiss could have been nothing more than happiness at being back in his special place in the desert and wanting to share his delight.

'Outside, please,' she replied. 'I could sit and watch the desert change for ever.'

He turned towards her as if to say something, then shook his head and ducked into the low tent, returning with one of the padded mattresses and a couple of big cushions in his arms.

'Sit!' he ordered when he'd arranged them to his satisfaction on the rug.

He held her arm, supporting her weight, while she sank down onto the ground, then he insisted she make herself comfortable, helping adjust the cushions behind her back.

'A drink? I'll check what Saif has left us, but there is sure to be some iced tea, and I would think pomegranate juice if you'd like something more exciting.'

Liz smiled up at him.

'I think pomegranate juice is appropriate for the desert,' she said, stretching back against the cushions and smiling to herself as he disappeared into the tent.

'You are happy?' he asked when he returned.

She had to pause and think about it, then answered honestly.

'I am,' she said. 'Right now, this very minute, all my problems seem so far away, and being pampered, offered drinks, being waited on—that's special.'

He squatted beside her to hand her the drink, his dark gaze scanning her face.

'I imagine you are far too independent to accept much pampering,' he said, easing into a sitting position beside her—close but not too close.

She was about to agree, then remembered.

'Actually,' she admitted, 'I was showered with pampering when I first became pregnant. Bill and Oliver couldn't do enough for me. It was all I could do to take off my own shoes when I stayed overnight for a visit.'

Khalifa took her free hand and squeezed her fingers, although this was the first time he'd heard her speak of her brother and his partner with sadness but not deep pain in her voice.

'Everything will be all right,' he told her, and although it was an empty promise when so much in her life was in limbo, she accepted it with a smile and lifted her glass towards him.

'Cheers!' she said.

'*Shucram*!' he replied, lifting an imaginary glass and touching it to hers.

'*Shucram*? Is it Arabic?'

'It is what we say as a toast. You like the word?'

'I do,' Liz agreed and raised her glass again. '*Shucram*!'

It was a nothing conversation, words passing back and forth, but something else was passing back and forth as well—awareness.

Or was it only one-way traffic, he wondered, this tingling in his skin, the rush along his nerves, the tightening of his body?

She was pregnant!

Yes, but try as he might to reject the thought, he was beginning to believe that he found her pregnancy just as sexy as the rest of her. At first he'd thought it was just the hair, and then the way she laughed, and her creamy skin, and her eyes behind the glasses. But the pregnancy definitely wasn't offputting, and the more he got to know the woman inside the outer shell, the more the attraction grew.

'Are you not having a drink?' she asked, and he heaved himself off the rug and headed for the tent, not for a drink but to collect his thoughts.

He fished around in the cool boxes and found that the ever-reliable Saif had packed snacks, even labelling the flat platters with a sticker—'Use these for snacks'. Saif really did think his boss was an idiot.

Idiotic right now.

He wasn't even sure if he was reading the signs of a mutual attraction—kissing him back, pressing her body into his—correctly.

He put the snacks onto the platter, removing the sticker first, then poured himself a glass of juice and returned outside.

Liz was lying back, looking all around her, wide eyes taking in the beauty of the desert as the shadows grew longer and the sinking sun left the dunes black-shadowed and mysterious. But the sky was brightening in the west and soon the colours of the sunset would be reflected in the crystalline sand, so they'd be afloat in a sea of red and gold and orange, even vermillion and saffron, these last two better words because they held some of the beauty of the colours.

It held them silent, the nightly transformation of the desert sands, and only when the colours faded and dusk fell about them did Liz move, putting down her glass on the platter and turning to lie on her side, looking at Khalifa.

'I can see why you stayed an extra year,' she said quietly. 'As well as its spectacular beauty, this place brings a sense of peace, doesn't it?'

'It's because you can't fight it and win,' he told her. 'You can only survive in the desert if you learn to live with it, learning all its many moods, bending to its will rather than trying to bend it to yours. The road we followed to the oasis and the well is a great example. It was built by my brother to open up the desert, but slowly and surely the desert is reclaiming it. Not that it matters when we have vehicles that can traverse the sand, but no man can tame the desert.'

'Neither should they want to,' Liz said. 'We've already tamed too much of the world's land, and we need these wild places to—would it sound silly if I said to replenish our souls?'

He moved the tray so he could touch her face.

'Definitely not silly,' he said.

He wanted to touch more of her, to feel his hands slide over her skin, to lift her hair and kiss the nape of her neck beneath it, to lie with her so their bodies learned the shape and texture of each other.

'I'll get our dinner. Knowing Saif, he'll have stuck to cold meats and salads so I don't have to show my lack of cooking prowess, but as it's getting cool, I'll light the fire anyway.'

He edged away from the distraction of Liz and lit the fire, then went into the tent and lit the lantern and the candles Saif had left for them.

The light was soft, but it was enough for him to discover his guess had been right. Inside the largest of the cool boxes were platters of meat, already laid out, and salads in bowls. The last of the cool boxes held an array of fruit. That, he'd leave until later.

He brought out food, setting it beside his guest so she could reach everything with ease. Plates followed, and damp napkins in a thermos flask so they were still warm and faintly scented.

'A feast in the desert,' Liz murmured as she filled her plate with bits and pieces of salad and meat, trying everything as he'd been sure she would because this was a woman who lived for new experiences.

Yet she'd given up nine months of her life to produce a child for her brother? How much she must have loved him!

How great her capacity for love!

'You're not eating,' she told him, pointing at him with her fork.

'Thinking,' he said, and she smiled.

'Thinking makes me hungry,' she said, then laughed at herself. 'Actually, everything makes me hungry these days. But I'd feel a lot better about stuffing myself with food if you were at least nibbling on a lettuce leaf.'

He filled his plate and ate, enjoying the food, enjoying the company, enjoying most of all the desert, his spiritual home.

Liz wondered what he was thinking. Probably not how sexy she was, although his sexiness was one of the main topics of thought running through *her* mind. Something about the man stirred bits of her that had never been stirred before and she wasn't entirely certain it was all physical attraction. The more she saw and learned of him as a man—the way the people obviously loved him, the way he never spoke down to anyone, his tenderness with his grandmother—the more attractive he became.

While she was the very opposite—fat and even clumsier than usual, her life in chaos—no redeeming features at all, so why he kept on kissing her she had no idea.

Kept on kissing her? It had happened, what, twice?

But even thinking of the kisses had her body stirring, her breasts growing heavy, her skin going coming out in goose-bumps.

She set down her plate, afraid she'd start trembling, and looked at the dancing flames of the fire in front of them.

Fire, heat, burning…her attraction to this man could lead nowhere, so why get burnt?

Because I want to?

She hadn't really expected an answer to her silent question, so when it came it shocked her. What was she saying? That she'd like to make love to this man for the sheer physical pleasure of it?

Knowing nothing would come of it?

Knowing it would probably be a one-off experience?

Knowing she'd have something to remember him by—that was the real answer—a memory of a special night in a very special place with a very, very special man!

'*Are* you attracted to me?'

The question popped out without much forethought. Klutz!

She could feel the heat rising in her cheeks, burning there, but at least he was smiling.

'You have no idea how much,' he said softly, then he moved the platters and plates and shifted so he sat beside her, his body close but once again not touching her. 'But you are in a strange place, both physically and mentally. If we do something about this attraction, are you sure you won't regret it?'

She turned towards him and this time *she* touched *his* face.

'I won't regret it,' she said quietly, then she leaned forward and kissed him on the lips, tasting remnants of the pomegranate drink, tasting him.

The kiss was slow and easy, not tentative but definitely the beginning of a voyage of discovery. His tongue delved, invaded, starting the fires within, nothing more than glowing embers at the moment, but Liz knew they'd flare soon.

She slid her hand beneath his shirt to feel his skin, and heard his murmur—of pleasure? Of approval?— then felt his hand against her breast, felt her nipples growing hard, and raised her hand to touch his, to brush against them, gently, teasing the tight buds.

His murmur became a growl and now his lips had moved from hers, searching along her chin, finding skin to tease beneath her hair, shivers running down her spine. His tongue flicked against the hollow of her neck and this time it was she who murmured—cried out really—wanting more, so much more.

'I will take care of you.' He breathed the words against her skin and before she could protest that their satisfaction should be mutual, his hand had sought the very centre of her being and with one hand on her breast and the other brushing gently but insistently against her panties, she found herself squirming with delight and need, squirming and breathing hard, wanting more yet wanting him to stop what was becoming torture.

But she, too, could tease, so she felt for him and found the hardness pressed against his jeans, finding the tip of it and running her fingers lightly over it.

'Clothes,' he gasped, and they separated, but though she longed to see him naked, she was less inclined to reveal her own body in all its swollen glory.

'I *have* seen pregnant women before,' he said gently, obviously reading her reluctance to disrobe.

And with that he lifted the loose top she wore up and over her head, then with seemingly practised ease he dispensed with her bra before reaching down and sliding off her long trousers and panties.

'You are beautiful,' he said, pushing away the arms she had wrapped around herself. 'Radiantly beautiful.'

'Fat,' she retorted, 'while you…'

He'd shucked off his own clothes and knelt beside her, the light from the flickering fire dancing on his naked skin.

She touched him, more in awe than anything, but he took her hand and kissed her palm, then drew her thumb into his mouth and suckled it, taunting her to distraction before turning his attention to her breasts, teasing at one with his tongue, at the other with what seemed to her like magic fingers.

The slow dance of foreplay began again. Liz finally relaxed, telling herself it was for the memory, and that she had to grab as much enjoyment as she could from it. But conscious thought soon disappeared, her body revelling in sensation, her brain numbed by delight. Unhurried by some unspoken but mutual consent, they explored each other's bodies, learning the shape of them, the taste and texture of the skin, the places where the slightest touch stirred the embers of desire, making them flicker until suddenly they became flames.

He lay behind her now, pleasuring her with his hands, building the tension in her body to gasping point then easing back until he was certain she was ready. Only then did he slide into her, gently and carefully, but still touching and teasing so she was lifted to another plane then burst apart, coming with a shuddering sob, then coming again as he, too, climaxed and held her tightly to him.

They lay together, the crackling of the dying fire the only noise in the empty desert, the stars above so bright Liz felt she could reach out and touch them, pull them down and hold them in her lap in the same way she held the happiness their lovemaking had given her.

'No regrets?' Khalifa whispered in her ear, and she snuggled closer to him.

'How could there be?' she queried softly. 'This is an experience that I'll treasure for a lifetime.'

His arms tightened around her, then one hand slid down to rest on her belly where the baby kicked obligingly.

Had it been mine, I would never have to let her go, her or her baby, Khalifa thought, then he wondered where the thought had come from. This woman could never be his, for all he was fairly certain he might love her.

Love her?

An even more bizarre thought to be having. What did he know of love?

Yet melancholy enfolded him as he held the woman in his arms, and melancholy was something he never felt out here in the desert.

Did love always lead to sadness?

'Thank you,' the woman in his arms whispered softly, the words like a benediction.

He wanted to thank her, too, to talk about his feelings, but he didn't know how to start because men of his tribe didn't do that kind of thing.

'Talk to me,' she said—reading his mind.

She had turned so she faced him, resting her hand on his chest as if she needed to maintain physical contact with him.

'About what?' he countered, not certain enough of love to talk of it.

'About you,' she responded. 'About your wife—your feelings about the baby?'

She patted her naked belly and added, 'I've been so determined not to feel anything about this poor wee soul's arrival, I've no idea how a pregnant woman might feel, let alone a man. Were you pleased? Excited? Would you marry again? Have another child?'

Was there a shadow of pain behind her questions? Or was he imagining he heard it?

He didn't know, but she'd asked and now he wanted to answer her, to talk about Zara and his child as he had to no one else.

'My wife was over the moon, totally absorbed in her pregnancy, but me…?'

He hesitated.

'You will think this very silly, but to have a pregnant wife, somehow it is a confirmation of a man's virility. I was proud.'

Again he stopped, partly distracted by a finger drawing whorls around his nipple but also uncertain how to proceed.

'Keep talking,' the owner of the finger said, and now he found it easier.

'I was excited by the thought of a child, more than a baby. Seeing a child grow, explaining things as he or she explored and learned about the world.'

The finger stopped moving and in the moonlight he saw her turn her head so she could study him as she asked her next question—study him as he answered.

'And now?'

He touched the upturned face.

'Now I am a coward. Although I know if I had a pregnant wife I would be far more involved with her pregnancy, the guilt I felt—still feel—at not realising all was not going well for Zara would probably haunt me.'

She brushed her finger across his lips and asked, oh, so gently, 'Was there anything you could have done? Would being with her more have made a difference?'

He didn't want to answer, knowing answering would release him from his guilt, but his guilt was all he'd had of Zara after her death...

'Tell me.'

'No.'

The word came out far too bluntly. Could he really have *not* wanted to lose the guilt?

'I don't mean, no, I won't tell you but, no, there was nothing I could have done,' he said, more gently now, and going on to explain the genetic heart problem that had killed his wife and child, a problem that had never been known or even suspected.

The woman who'd prised this confession from him snuggled closer and reached out to clasp his head against her breast, running her fingers across his short hair, offering solace with touch.

He reached for her hands and held them, squeezing them gently, silently thanking her for the blessing of her understanding. Thanking her for pointing out how pointless his guilt had always been.

She eased her hands away and he touched the bulge of her pregnancy, running his hand over the taut skin, wishing...

Her hand closed over his.

'Thank you again,' she said, as if in telling her he'd given her some kind of gift, then she moved so she could lie in comfort, and whispered a quiet 'Goodnight'.

He lay, still propped on his elbow, watching how

quickly she slid into sleep, feeling guilt—was he ob-
sessed by it?—about their lovemaking, thinking she'd
already been tired...

Once certain she was sleeping, he eased away from
her and went into the tent to find a rug to cover her,
but when he returned he simply stood and looked at
her, bathed in starlight. He looked at the pale creamy
skin, the spread of hair, the swollen belly that stirred
him more than anything. To him, at this moment, she
was the epitome of womanhood and he was pretty sure
he loved her.

CHAPTER TEN

HE WAS asleep when Liz awoke to find herself covered by a soft, warm blanket. For a moment she lay there, remembering—first her body remembering, warming, delighting in reliving the sensations—then her mind remembered Khalifa's conversation and her heart ached for the pain he'd carried. Meanwhile, a tiny spark of delight glimmered in the darkness—delight that he'd talked to her about something so personal.

But remembering was wasting time, because right now she had pressing physical needs of a different kind. She eased herself away from him, trying not to wake him, then pulled on her clothes rather randomly, although it was stupid to think she had to get dressed when there was no one but the bird to see her as she crept around to the back of the tent for a bathroom break.

She squatted behind the tent, feeling the unfamiliar tenderness Khalifa's lovemaking had left behind, revelling in it and the sense of well-being in her body.

Satisfaction, that's what it was—satisfaction that had produced enormous pleasure and great release.

Straightening up, she looked up at the heavens, searching for the Southern Cross, although she knew she wouldn't see it in a northern sky. But all the stars looked friendly, and she thought about what people said—about stars aligning.

Her stars and Khalifa's had aligned, for just a short time, and now she had the memory of this very special night.

She sank her toes into the sand and wondered about the sand sprite. Had *her* lovemaking been as satisfying? Had it been so special that she'd had no regrets about having to remain a mortal?

'Sand sprites indeed!' Liz muttered, and she shook herself out of her fantasies and focussed on the purely practical.

Her teeth itched!

Could she risk opening the car to get out her small overnight bag?

She was walking towards it when she saw the bag sitting on the front of vehicle. She reached for it. She'd need to find water, maybe in the tent, so she could have a wash and clean her teeth.

And put on clean clothes.

She had opened the bag and was delving in it to find her toiletries when she felt the pain—a sharp jab, so agonising she forgot about the sleeping man and screamed, hopping around on one leg while she tried to find the source of the pain on her other ankle, hopping so she tripped and fell against the car, unable to stop her cry of dismay.

The scream came to Khalifa in a dream, but he was soon awake, aware Liz was no longer in his arms, aware it hadn't been a dream. He sat up, searching for her, angry he'd been so deeply asleep he couldn't place the direction the noise had come from.

'Liz?'

He heard his own panic in his cry, but her answer—'I'm okay, something bit me and I fell'—did little to reassure him.

He rushed towards her voice, to find her struggling to her feet beside the car.

'Stay still,' he ordered, and, with hands he knew were shaking he bent to lift her, carrying her to the tent where a lantern still glowed softly and placing her gently on the couch.

'The bite, where is it?' he demanded, his voice so rough she flinched, but she pointed to her leg and without hesitation he stripped off her trousers, shaking them, seeing the scorpion that fell from them, his heart stopping with fear even as his foot lifted to squash the life out of it.

But squashed, would he be able to tell?

He brushed it further from her then lifted the lantern, relief swamping him as he saw the square-shaped sternum rather than the triangular shape of the deadly Leiurus.

Now he squashed it, then returned to Liz, kneeling beside her, examining the reddened mark on her calf.

'I'm sorry, I should have warned you about the little beasts. It will be painful for a while, but it wasn't poisonous. Did you hurt yourself in the fall?

Even as he asked the question his hands were moving over her, calmer now, although not as calm as a professional's hands should be, for his heart was still racing, his mind now caught up in the inevitable 'what ifs', his chest tight with the knowledge that she could have died.

Had she felt his fear that she took his hands and looked into his face?

'Khalifa, I'm fine. Yes, my leg hurts—it's like a bad ant bite but that's all. Stop panicking.'

She smiled as she spoke, her beautiful, warm, open smile, and although he'd have liked to tell her he never panicked, the words wouldn't come because now he couldn't breathe properly, he was so overwhelmed by the thought of losing her.

He wanted to tell her, to explain how he felt—how the revelation that had come to him when he'd looked at her body in the moonlight, and how hearing her cry had nearly killed him—but he'd lost her. Her eyes were no longer on him but looking inward. There was a small frown of concentration on her face.

'What is it?' he demanded, but she didn't reply, her hands moving to her belly, holding it.

Now new alarm spread through him, especially when he saw the movement—the bulge of her stomach tightening into a ball, obvious because she was so slim.

She was in labour?

Out here?

Now?

Great!

'Is it a contraction?' he demanded. 'Was that the first? Are you timing them? Are you in pain? Did you fall heavily?'

Or had their lovemaking brought it on?

Whatever the cause, it was he who had, selfishly, wilfully, wished to spend the night in the desert with her—he who had made love to her.

Now another woman and her baby's lives were in jeopardy.

'Khalifa.'

One word, just his name spoken softly, brought him

out of his panic. He took her hands in his and looked into the blue eyes.

'I think this time it's for real,' she whispered, then stopped as another contraction ripped through her body, her hands clutching his, clamping on them, squeezing tightly.

'I'm sorry—such a nuisance,' she gasped as her grip loosened, telling him the pain was gone.

'Never!' he said. 'I might have put you in this position, Liz, with my own stupidity, bringing you out here, but I'll take care of you and the baby, believe me.'

She half smiled, although her abdomen was contracting again and the smile turned into a grimace, though she pushed out the words she wanted to say.

'Not your fault—no more guilt!' she told him, then grabbed his hands again as if they were her only lifeline, her main connection to reality.

And *he* should have been timing the contractions! They seemed to be coming far too close together, but she was right, no more guilt. This woman was *not* going to die! He was a doctor, he could deliver a baby, and even though it would be preemie, he could handle that until help arrived. Help would come. He had no radio contact here, but back at the well he could use his mobile and call in a helicopter to airlift Liz safely to the hospital.

She was resting, now, her face damp with sweat. He should wipe it, make her more comfortable, but getting her to the well where he could summon help was more important.

'I'm going to check the dilatation of your cervix,' he told her, brushing his hand across her cheek because he couldn't say all the things he wanted to say to her, not now when he had to concentrate on her welfare, not his feelings. 'If it's not too dilated, I'll drive you to the well. I can contact the hospital from there and get a helicopter to collect you.'

She pressed her hand over his and nodded her thanks, biting her lip, so he knew another contraction was on the way.

He also knew that they wouldn't get to the well.

What did he have with him? An emergency kit in the car—it would have scissors that would be useful to cut the cord but little else as far as he could remember.

Water—he'd have plenty of water.

Think!

The mental order slowed his panic, and he found more damp napkins in a sealed container and used one to wipe Liz's face. She smiled at him and he thought his heart might break, then she whispered, 'You *do* remember how to deliver a baby!'

The gentle tease was worse than the smile, as far as affecting him went, but just in case she wasn't teasing he was quick to reassure her.

'Of course!' he said, then teased her back. 'I'm already boiling water on the fire, although I've never been quite sure what the boiling water you read about it stories was for. Maybe to sterilise the scissors.'

He kissed her lightly on the cheek and added more seriously, 'I'm going to the car. I'll be right back.'

He left the damp napkin with her and made sure she was comfortable on the couch, then headed for the car, finding the first-aid kit easily, and the drum of water, which he took with him, although Saif had left plenty in the tent.

He returned to find she'd moved, and was standing, gripping the tent pole.

'Better this way,' she gasped through pain, and he remembered his grandmother telling him how she had given birth, squatting while she gripped a solid pole set in the ground.

He held Liz while the contraction racked her body, so much stronger now that he wondered she could stand it, but as it passed she leant back into him and, holding her in his arms, a weird kind of happiness, something he'd never felt before, pulsed through his veins and calmed his panicked mind.

Though not for long! As Liz's labour continued, at what seemed to him an alarmingly rapid rate, he wished he could remember more about childbirth. His obstetric days, back when he had been a student and an intern, were long behind him, and any knowledge he'd ever had about a situation like this had to be retrieved from a long-unused part of his brain.

What he did know was that he had to be ready— ready to handle a fragile, newborn baby. He searched the tent, found clean headscarves and a clean kandora, thanks to Saif, who believed his master should never appear with a spot on his clothing or the wrong crease in his headdress.

Leaving the kandora—he could put that on Liz later—he piled the other things he might need on a towel beside where Liz now squatted, her hands still gripping the pole, so involved with the process going on within her body he might as well not have been there.

A baby catcher, that's all he was—yet even as he had the thought, new excitement shafted through him. He was going to deliver Liz's baby!

Well, she'd do all the work, he'd just be on hand—
but now the tension in his body was different, more like
elation than panic. He held her again, squatting behind
her so his arms could support her, talking to her, encouraging her, whispering things he doubted she'd remember later but words he wanted to say.

He felt the moment she began to push and sat behind
her, his hands, washed and rewashed, ready for the arrival. He felt the head as it crowned, disappeared, then
crowned again, emerging fully, the little body twisting
so the shoulders would come through the narrow passage, then with a final push the baby was in his hands
and Liz had collapsed onto the blanket he'd spread beside the pole.

He stared at the baby, transfixed by her beauty and
perfection, and smiled when she gave a cry that sounded
full of resentment at being ejected from her sanctuary.
She even blew a little bubble when he used a straw to
clear her mouth and nose of mucus.

When he felt her chest moving as she breathed, he
held the little bundle towards Liz.

'A little girl,' he whispered, his voice so husky with
emotion the words croaked out.

But even in the dim light of the lantern he could read
the despair in Liz's eyes and see the way her hands
moved towards the tiny infant then were pulled back
with what seemed an almost superhuman effort.

'Will *you* cuddle her for me?' Liz whispered, tears
streaming down her face. 'Hold her against your skin
for a few minutes and talk to her. She's used to men's
voices.'

Liz's voice broke on the last few words and she

turned away, her hand pressed against her mouth to stem the emotion she was obviously feeling.

He held the baby as she asked, glad he hadn't had time to dress so she could feel his skin, but his mind was on the woman, not the baby, for all she, premature as she was, should have all his concentration.

'Just keep breathing, *farida*, my precious pearl.' he whispered to the little girl, wrapping her carefully before setting her down to turn his attention to her mother.

How could this be so hard? How could she possibly be hurting more than she had during the brief labour?

The questions jostled with more practical matters in Liz's head and although she knew she should be gathering her wits and making sure Khalifa was doing all the right things for the baby, the ache of loss, so unexpected, was too overwhelming for her to think straight.

Perhaps if she held the little girl?

Then gave her up when Oliver recovered and wanted her?

She doubted she'd be strong enough to do that, knowing how much she already loved this infant, for all her determination to remain detached.

The bulge on her abdomen told her she was ready for the third stage of labour but it seemed Khalifa had remembered enough of his obstetrics training to have also recognised this fact. He'd set the baby, wrapped, it appeared, in one of his red-checked headscarves, quite close but not right beside her, and was preparing to deliver the placenta.

What must he be thinking of her? All he'd wanted was to share his delight in the desert with her, and here she was, causing all this trouble. And she had no doubt, knowing him as she now did, that he'd blame himself for the baby's premature arrival.

She wanted to say something, to thank him, but the words wouldn't come, because now something else had bobbed into her erratic brain and she was crying again.

'Liz?' His voice was gentle. 'Is it the baby? Do you want to hold her?'

Liz shook her head, swallowed hard, then poured out more grief on the poor man, knowing she shouldn't but unable to stop herself.

'It wasn't meant to be like this! They should have been here, and we were going to keep the cord and donate it for research. It was all planned.'

She knew her voice had risen to a pathetic wail, but Khalifa, who probably should have found an excuse to be busy elsewhere, was lifting her so he could take her in his arms, lifting her and carrying her outside, setting her down on the mattress where they'd made love—had it only been hours earlier?

'You've had so much pain—too much really for anyone to bear—but you are strong, Liz Jones, the strongest woman I have ever known. Yes, it hurts, but you've brought life to a new soul and now, if you look over there, you will see the sun coming up on a bright new day. You've seen desert sunsets, now watch the sun rise over a new day and know that we are given new days so we can start again and make each day better than the last one.'

He kissed her lips then left her, leaning back against the cushions, thinking of his words as she watched the slowly rising sun bring the desert to life.

Khalifa lifted the baby and, holding her cradled in one arm, walked out to the car, checking the crib they were carrying around. But there was no way he could see to secure it in the vehicle so back at the tent he packed one of the picnic baskets with towels, making a nest for her for before settling her into it. Once sure she was secure, he carried the basket out to the car where he strapped it in as tightly as he could, using a seat belt.

He'd already mentally debated asking Liz to hold her, but had decided that was probably less safe than his makeshift baby capsule. One abrupt stop and she could fly out of Liz's arms.

He returned to Liz, sitting where he'd left her, watching the magic of the sunrise, her skin touched to gold by the reflection from the dunes, the slight smile on her lips enough to break his heart all over again, but this was not the time for emotion. He had a fragile premature infant to take care of, not to mention possible complications for Liz.

Heaven forbid…

'We must drive to the well,' he said, stifling any hint of emotion. 'I can radio for help from there.'

She nodded but didn't move until he bent to lift her.

'No,' she said, 'I'm quite capable of walking. I've been enough of a burden to you already. Besides, I need to go into the tent—to dress in something.'

He helped her to her feet, her hand in his, his arm supporting her, yet close as he was he knew he wasn't really there—not for her—some distance having grown between them, something having shifted in their admittedly brief and unlikely relationship.

Which was good, wasn't it?

'Then I must check the baby,' she said, confirming his impression, for she was back in Dr Jones the neonatologist mode, which left him where?

The chauffeur?

'You'll find a clean kandora in the tent, you can put that on,' he said. 'And plenty of water and towels.'

She walked away and as he watched the long slim legs beneath the slightly bloodstained tunic she still wore moving her away from him, a sense of loss invaded his soul.

What had she said?

She needed to check the baby?

He went to the car and released the seat belt, carrying the picnic basket into the tent where he could unwrap the little girl on a table.

Liz was standing there, his kandora looking far better on her than it did on him, but the pain he could see in her eyes and the lines of strain on her face told him this was going to be one of the hardest things she had ever done.

To examine her own child, yet not touch her with love.

'You are still her aunt—you can love her,' he said to Liz, wanting so much to ease her pain. 'And surely you love all the babies you examine—at least a little bit.'

Liz heard the words but for a moment they didn't sink in, and then, as her body relaxed and the hurt she was feeling grew less, she turned and smiled at the man who'd uttered them.

'It seems I keep having to thank you,' she said, still smiling as she looked down at the tiny baby.

Carefully she checked that all was well, guessing at the baby's weight, checking breathing and heart rate, stupidly counting toes and fingers—mother stuff—silly, really...

'She's all good but must stay warm.'

She wanted to suggest holding her, for warmth, not because her arms ached to do just that, but there were dangers in holding a baby in a moving vehicle.

'Here,' Khalifa said, handing Liz lots more towels. 'We can use these to wrap her in tightly'.

Together they settled the baby once again.

Together, Liz thought sadly. She had so enjoyed the togetherness they'd shared, every moment of it, but now—well, she could hardly expect the man to fall in love with a woman when he'd had to deliver her baby...

She watched Khalifa as he carried the picnic basket to the car, watching the care and concentration he gave to the task of securing it, surprised when he paused. Was he examining his handiwork? Checking everything?

But, no, he was studying the baby, for he smiled and reached into the basket, apparently to touch the tiny girl, his lips moving as if he was speaking to her.

Liz blinked away the tears, telling herself the cause was postnatal hormonal imbalance, not a longing to touch the child in just that way, to whisper to her— damn it all, *to hold her*!

She's Oliver's, she told herself, over and over again, but no amount of telling eased the pain.

'Ready?' Khalifa called to her, apparently surprised she wasn't in the car.

'Coming now,' she said, sniffing back the unshed tears and gathering the remnants of her courage around her like a tattered cloak.

'Exactly how early is she?' Khalifa asked as he took his seat behind the wheel and started the engine.

'Four weeks, give or take a day or so,' Liz told him, then had to ask, 'Why?'

'I wondered if we should head for the well where I can call for a helicopter, or if it would be safe to drive back to Najme. It will take an hour to the well, then the helicopter will probably be there in three-quarters of an hour, and have you both back to the hospital half an hour after that.'

Liz added up the times, then realised he was telling her this for a reason.

'There's an alternative?'

He turned to her and smiled.

'We could drive. It would mean cutting across the desert but I've done it dozens of times and have a GPS. Driving, we could be in Najme in three to four hours. What do you think? Should she be airlifted because that's quicker?'

This is just another patient, Liz told herself. What would you decide?

The little girl's responses had been good, her breathing and heart rate fine, there was no reason she'd even need a special crib in hospital, so...

But was she, Liz, leaning towards the drive because she wanted more time with the baby, even if she wasn't holding her? Somehow, just knowing she was so close was enough at the moment, but at the hospital, someone else would care for her and she herself...

Well, what would *she* do?

What *could* she do?

Keep pretending it was just another baby, a patient like any other?

Her heart cried out in denial, but she'd been so good, so strong in keeping faith with the fact that it wasn't her baby, she really, really didn't want to weaken now.

'I'll drive unless you tell me she really needs a helicopter.' Khlaifa's voice, gentle and understanding, broke into her silent debate. 'I can understand you wanting to have more time with her,' he added. 'For all you've denied any maternal instinct, it's only natural you wouldn't want to be separated from her.'

He turned his head towards her and she saw the smile that still started so much reaction in her body.

'*You* taught me that,' he said, then he reached out and touched her cheek, although his eyes were back on the sand across which they travelled. 'Taught me so many things.'

Like what? she wanted to ask, but perhaps it was better just to accept the compliment—to hold it to herself like a precious gift.

'What will you do?' he asked, his attention back on the trackless desert that stretched like an endless red ocean before them.

'Do?'

'In Namje,' he added. 'You'll need to be checked by an obstetrician, and you'd be welcome to stay on either in a hospital bed or in an on-call room, close to the baby.'

Close to the baby?

'Oh, Khalifa!'

His name came out on a sigh and she caught back the maudlin thoughts that once again threatened to over-whelm her.

'You're right, I'll see a doctor...' she had to smile for she was sitting right beside one, and was a pretty good professional herself '...then maybe an on-call room, not to be close to the baby but so I can get on with the work you brought me here to do.'

'Then stay at the palace. I'll make sure you have a

car and driver available at all times so you can come and go as you wish.'

She could hear the things he hadn't said—about the baby, and questions about why she was so adamant to stay detached.

'It's not just Oliver,' she whispered. 'If it was, I'd be okay because he'd want me to love the baby as much as he would. It's his parents. When Oliver regains consciousness he'll still be far from well, so his mother will be the baby's primary carer, and if she won't let me near Oliver, there's definitely no way she'll want me involved in the baby's life.'

She paused, trying to get all the permutations and combinations of the future that had jostled in her head since Bill's death into some kind of order. Khalifa, after all he'd done for her, deserved an explanation.

'I could push to keep her, or at least be allowed access, because legally, right now, she's mine. But I couldn't let her become a pawn in a tug of war between myself and Oliver's parents, particularly if Oliver never recovers completely.'

She turned to Khalifa and touched his arm.

'That's likely, as you know, after a head injury. And just think of the joy she'd bring him. A man, broken-hearted over his partner's death, broken in health as well, then suddenly there's this little girl, someone to live for, someone to love and cherish...'

She shook her head, sniffed back more tears and added, 'I couldn't take that away from him.'

Khalifa's heart was scrunched with pain for this woman who sat beside him, her own heart breaking so she could bring happiness to someone else. Someone she'd obviously loved, but still...

'Anyway,' she said, with false bravado, 'we'd settled all that long ago. I'm just a bit emotional about it all right now, but I'll survive. And although the palace is a beautiful serene place, I'd be better off at the hospital. I found out from Laya there's a breast-milk bank already established at the hospital so I'll give milk to that. It doesn't matter if she gets my milk or someone else's as long as it's the good stuff. And she's big enough to go into the ordinary nursery, but if you could wangle Laya to look after her, I'd be very grateful.'

He'd been lost in wonder that she'd shifted so swiftly from the emotional to the practical when he heard her voice waver on the last few words. He stopped the car, unclipped his seat belt and turned towards her, putting his arms around her as best he could and holding her close against him.

'We'll work it out,' he promised, '*we*, not you. You tell me what you want and you shall have it. I know you've had to rely on your own strength for a long time now, but do you think could you learn to lean on me, to let me help you in any way I can?'

He kissed her hair, mussed and sweaty, and rubbed his hands across her shoulders, rubbing at her back, offering comfort in the only way he could, with the physical caresses of a friend.

He felt her head nod against his shoulder and knew he'd have to make do with that for the moment. Right now he had to get them both to the hospital.

Easing her back into her seat, he started the car and they continued on their way. Fortunately the baby slept, for he'd have hated to imagine the emotional battle Liz would have had to fight if the infant had needed comforting or feeding.

Eventually the pink towers and minarets of Namje appeared in the distance.

'Another mirage?' Liz queried.

'No, that's the real thing,' he assured her, smiling because he knew from her voice she was feeling stronger now.

Could he really know her so well in such a short time, to be picking up intonations in her voice?

He knew he could, because it seemed he knew her in his bones, as if she was a part of him. How she felt about him was a total mystery, the arrival of the baby hardly a normal scenario for the morning after their first lovemaking.

And now his guilt returned. He'd let his passion for this woman put her and her baby into danger and although everything appeared to be working out all right, the guilt was still there.

The baby gave a cry as he turned into the hospital gates.

'She must know we've arrived,' Liz said, and although he'd seen her turn and her hand move as if to pat the child, she pulled back, biting at her lip, determined, he knew, not to give in to the welter of emotion that must be wrenching her to pieces beneath her composed demeanour.

He used his mobile to phone the hospital, although they were already in the drive, asking for Dr Hassan and explaining what had happened, requesting she be on hand to examine and admit the infant, asking her to get Laya to meet them. Then he contacted the hospital's head obstetrician, thankfully in the hospital at the moment, and explained about the desert birth.

'We'll go in the staff entrance, and Laya will meet

us there to take the baby while I take you to a private room where you can be examined. I'm sure the doctor will want to keep you in as a patient at least overnight, and…' he turned and touched her cheek '…it would make me feel happier if you stayed at least that long.'

'I can hardly say no when you've been so good to me,' Liz responded, but he knew the distance he'd felt between them at the campsite in the desert was growing stronger—a distance he had no idea how to breach.

Once examined and pronounced fit, Liz showered and changed into her own clothes, which had miraculously appeared while the obstetrician was with her. Pleased she knew her way around the hospital, she went down to the nursery where Dr Hassan assured her the baby was fine.

The doctor indicated the crib, although Liz hadn't needed to be told, for Laya was sitting beside it and Khalifa hovering over it.

She didn't want to see Khalifa—well, she could see him already—but she didn't want more conversation with him. This was partly because she already felt so beholden to him for handling her typical klutz-like emergency delivery, but also because something seemed to have shifted between them. The closeness she'd felt in the desert had whisked away like a sand sprite, lost for ever in another world.

Not that she could turn around and walk out…

'I've been passed all clear by your doctor,' she told him as she approached the pair beside the crib. 'In fact, he tells me you did a splendid job, so there you are. Perhaps a second speciality lies ahead for you.'

She sounded like a robot, rattling on about nothing,

but standing here, seeing the little pink face of the child she couldn't call her own, was tearing her apart, and while she longed to lean into the strength Khalifa had offered, the something that had shifted between them held her back.

She mumbled some excuse and left the room, although she'd intended asking about the procedures in place for donating breast milk. She couldn't return to her hospital room and brood—madness lay that way—so she walked further down the corridor to where the alterations to the new neonatal unit were well under way.

Khalifa found her there and, thankful the workmen had all departed, he took her in his arms.

'Talk to me,' he said, as she had said to him after they'd made love.

'I don't know what to say, or what to think, or what to do,' she whispered. 'It's as if I'm waiting for a sign, waiting for something to happen that will tell me which way to turn.'

He didn't have an answer so he kissed her, because it seemed the next best thing, and holding her like this it was difficult not to kiss her. Her response suggested the coolness between them might have been in his imagination, but common sense warned him that he was holding a very emotionally fragile woman in his arms, and her response might have been nothing more than a desperate need for comfort.

He would keep on kissing her, just for a while, and if that was selfish, because his body had been craving to hold her, then so be it, and hopefully she'd get some solace from it as well.

Eventually she broke away, an experimental smile on her face, so pathetic he wanted to kiss it off.

'I made a mess of things as usual,' she muttered. 'Going into labour like that, ruining what should have been a perfect night.'

'Nonsense,' he said. 'What could be more perfect way to finish a night than the arrival of a new child?'

He kissed her again but this time there was no response, and she eased herself away from his body and didn't even try to smile as she whispered, 'Oh, Khalifa, I am just so confused at the moment, I don't know where to turn.'

Turn to me, he longed to say, but though he might not have known her long, he knew she would have to work her own way out of her confusion. All he could do was be there for her.

For her and the baby…

CHAPTER ELEVEN

Liz returned to her room and, working out the time difference between Al Tinine and home, phoned Gillian to ask how Oliver was.

There had been no change. This information didn't help. Although she chatted to her friend for a few minutes, asking after the cat and the hospital, she didn't mention she'd given birth to Oliver's baby. If thinking about the baby made her teary, talking about her to Gill would have brought on an emotional tsunami!

'So, now what?' she said aloud in the empty room, but when she tried to think she realised her brain had turned to jelly and refused to cooperate.

Maybe if she slept…

She was a sand sprite, coming to life only at night. The darkness all around her told her it was night, so she moved, tentatively at first, feeling for limbs instead of whirling grains of sand, finding legs and arms and toes and fingers, realising she was alive.

Because it was night? Or because she'd made love to a human and been forced to stay alive for ever?

Wasn't that a good thing?

Yes, most definitely, when her body remembered the shivery excitement of their kisses, the languorous plea-

*sure of the human's touch, the smoothness of the couch
beneath them, the heat of his body curled into hers, his
tenderness, the gasping pleasure as they climaxed, lying
with him afterwards, held safely in his arms.*

*A prince. He was a prince, and beautiful, and staying
alive meant she could love him for ever and he would
love her, and so she'd have no regrets, would she...?*

She woke with a start, the dream so vivid her body
could feel the physical pleasure she and Khalifa had
shared.

But he *was* a prince, and him loving her for ever was
no more than a dream.

Restless now, she glanced at her watch. Past midnight—her body clock was all out of kilter again. But
past midnight meant there'd be few people in the nursery. She could safely go and look—just look—at the
baby. Oliver's baby.

She pulled on a gown and started down the corridors,
past the windows to the outside verandas where the
families of patients slept, and quietly into the nursery,
moving unerringly towards the baby's crib, stopping
when she realised the man asleep in the chair beside it
was Khalifa.

Khalifa?

She backed away into a shadowy corner because the
baby was stirring, and although the little one hadn't
made a sound Khalifa must have sensed she was awake,
for he straightened up and peered into the crib, then,
smiling, lifted the little bundle into his arms, talking to
her, rocking her, smiling all the time. The baby lay still,
yet Khalifa didn't return her to the crib but held her in
his arms, sitting down again, speaking so quietly Liz
couldn't tell if it was in Arabic or English.

Liz crept away, more confused than ever.

Was the baby a replacement to him—for the daughter he had lost? If not, why was he doing this, sitting with her, holding her, talking to her?

Bonding!

She should go and ask him, but in truth she was glad the baby had someone holding her and talking to her, especially a male so she'd know the man smell of him.

But thinking of the man smell of Khalifa was dangerous when she was in this muddled state of mind, so she returned to bed and forced herself to count camels until she fell asleep. Although, she thought muzzily as she drifted off, she couldn't recall actually seeing a camel since she'd been here.

She spent the next day avoiding Khalifa, avoiding the nursery when she saw him there, spending time with Phil as they worked out costings for the new unit, and checking equipment that was already coming in. But it was hard to avoid him when she returned to her room to find not only Khalifa in it, but a crib, complete with baby, presumably the one she'd carried, though not hers, never hers.

Her eyes filled with tears and she cursed her own weakness, but Khalifa's attention was on the baby, so maybe be hadn't noticed.

She dashed them away with her hand and hardened her voice.

'What's this?'

He turned abruptly, as if caught out in wrongdoing, then smiled the smile that touched her heart every time she saw it.

Coming towards her, he took both her hands in his,

guiding her to the bed and settling her on it, sitting beside her and curling his arm around her shoulders.

'Liz, there's been news and I had to tell you personally. But I didn't want to leave the baby so I brought her along as well.'

The words made so little sense Liz shook her head, but her eyes were darting towards the crib, towards the little pink and white bundle with a shock of dark hair lying, swaddled, in it.

Khalifa's arm tightened and his voice was deep and grave.

'Oliver is dead,' he said.

Shock held her silent but only for a moment.

'He can't be. I spoke to Gill last night.'

'I'm sorry, my love, but he is,' Khalifa responded. 'His parents decided to turn off the life support this morning.'

Although a little bit of her had grabbed those two words—*my love*—and clung to them, Liz knew she had to understand the real message, *and* the implications of it.

Implications that had started panic in her chest.

'But the baby? What about the baby?'

'We don't have to decide that right now,' Khalifa told her gently, 'but I rather hoped she might be ours.'

Confusion joined the panic.

'Ours?'

'Yours and mine, but we'll work that out later. Right now, do you want to hold her, nurse her, talk to her, think about a name?'

'But…'

Had he sensed her total confusion? For he left her sitting on the bed and went to the crib, lifting the baby, murmuring to it in a foreign language, the voice deep and soothing, switching to English as he took a step towards Liz.

'See, *farida*, precious pearl, this is your mother. I was telling you about her, and now she really can be your mother and hold you, just as I told you.'

Liz could only stare at him, but she held out shaking arms and took the infant, no longer concerned about the tears that flooded from her eyes and fell to dampen the tiny bundle's wrappings.

Khalifa stood and watched her, seeing the happiness behind the tears, understanding the welter of emotion Liz must be going through. The loss of her friend, but the confirmation that the baby she'd carried so generously for her brother and his partner would now be hers.

If only he could take the pain away from her, carry it for her, help her through it.

If only he had the right.

He sat and held them both, a million thoughts flashing through his head, but paramount among them was the need to make this woman his—so that he and she and the baby would make a family and he *could* help her through her grief.

'She's eating well and sleeping well and needs no special care,' he told her. 'If we take Laya to help you look after her while you regain your strength, can we take her home?'

'Home?' Liz queried, turning to look at him, dampness from her tears still lingering on her cheeks so he had to touch her to brush it away.

He took a deep breath and plunged into what he later realised was a *most* prosaic and loveless proposal. But he had to get it said before his courage failed completely.

The thought of losing this woman was so overwhelming he had to know where he stood.

'This is not the most romantic spot for what I want to say, but I don't know when there'll be another time for us to be together—just the three of us.'

He was frowning and Liz realised that his voice, for the first time since she'd met him, was slightly hesitant. Then he smiled, and while her body went into its usual reaction of delight, her brain told her that something important was coming up.

Tension built to snapping point as Liz waited.

And waited.

Now he tried for a smile, tightened his grip on her shoulders, and said, with a pathetic smile, 'How would you feel about marrying a bloke with more money than sense?'

Khalifa knew he was making a complete hash of this. The moment the words had come out he'd known they were wrong, but apart from yelling 'Marry me', which was what he'd most wanted to do, he'd not had a clue of how to propose.

No wonder Liz looked confused.

'M-m-marry you?' she stuttered. 'Why?'

'Because we like each other and we've got the baby. I've been bonding with her, like you said, and I can give you both a comfortable life, and you can still work if you want to, and you seem to like the country and the people you've met, and there's no one left for you at home—you told me that—and, besides, I'd like it.'

He had a vague feeling he'd made things worse but was still surprised by her reaction.

'Is this to do with guilt?' she demanded. 'Guilt about your wife and child dying, guilt about taking me out into the desert? I might not have known you long, Khlaifa, but I know how you treasure your guilt, piling it up inside you like the nomads pile their belongings on their camels.'

His turn to be stunned!

He tried to protest but she was speaking again.

'And would a replacement wife and child, no matter how well you've bonded with the child, ease that guilt?'

'Liz, no, believe me, that's not true.'

She eyed him with suspicion written clearly on her face, but when she spoke it was to comfort him. She took his hand and used both of hers to hold it.

'It wasn't your fault your first wife died,' she said gently. 'You know that. As for me, the scorpion stung me because I was there and I was careless. I knew about scorpions and should have shaken out my clothes before putting them on, so you don't have to marry me out of guilt, okay?'

'I didn't offer out of guilt,' he muttered at her, annoyed now that something he'd thought would be so easy was turning into a nightmare.

'Then why did you offer?' she demanded, her blue eyes behind the horror glasses so huge he could have drowned in them.

'I told you,' he said desperately. 'We're good together, I already love the baby, you like my country, there are plenty of reasons for us to marry.'

For a moment he thought those eyes had filled with tears but she turned away from him before he could be sure, looking out the window, her shoulders lifting with a sigh that seemed to echo around the desert beyond the car.

'No!' she said, just *no*, nothing more, sitting there, not even looking at him.

He stood up and began to pace the room, trying to work out how things had gone so disastrously wrong.

Would asking why help?

Not if her answer was she didn't love him.

In fact, that would make things worse.

Then he asked anyway, because he had to know.

Just one word—why?

Liz beckoned him back to sit beside her before she began to speak.

'You gave a lot of reasons for wanting to marry me,' she said, thinking through each word because she knew she had to get it right. 'But not the one I wanted to hear—the one I needed to hear.'

She moved and touched her hands to his face, cupping it and looking into his eyes.

'I know it will probably sound stupid to you, Khalifa, but all my adult life I've known the one thing I wanted out of marriage, and that wasn't money, or a job, or even a palace. Just love. I wanted love like my parents had, like Oliver and Bill's. Mutual love that transcends all else, that distracts you at the most inconvenient time, that maddens and annoys and makes you ache when your loved one isn't near. You told me of the sand sprite and somehow made it sound as if she regretted making love to her human lover. But if she loved him there'd have been no regrets. There *are* no regrets with love.'

He put his hands on hers where they still rested on his face, his heart so full he doubted he could speak.

But speak he must.

'You don't love me?' he asked, and to his surprise she laughed.

'Oh, Khalifa,' she whispered. 'If you only knew how much! I love you to distraction and probably have since soon after we first met. But that's not enough. It has to be returned, or our life would be like a see-saw with one of us always up and the other always down, never balanced.'

'And you think it's not returned?' he murmured, and now he took her face in hers and kissed her lips, claimed them, consuming her with kisses.

'You say I've driven you to distraction since we first met, but you…!' he murmured against the soft skin of her neck. 'You've blown my mind, you've turned my life upside down, you've got me in such a state the whole country could have fallen apart, so absorbed I've been in you. Then when you went into labour, I panicked that something would go wrong and I would lose you. Yes, I did feel guilt—but most of all I felt pain. Then I delivered your baby and it was as if heaven had given me a gift. I thought if I offered you a wonderful life for you and the baby you might stay here, but I should have known you better. Love? Of course I love you. More than I can ever say, more than you could ever know, always and for ever.'

'But you didn't think to mention it in your proposal?' she teased.

He rested his hands on hers and tried to explain.

'I was—I suppose scared sounds stupid, but that's what I was. Terrified more like—because after all it's just a word but…'

He couldn't do it, not sitting here so close, so he stood again and paced.

'I'd never realised quite how powerful a word it was, but even thinking about saying it made me feel vulnerable, and I doubt I'd ever felt that way before. Even when I was a child in the desert, or at boarding school. I'm a sheikh, with a long line of tough warriors behind me. We cannot be vulnerable. What if you hadn't loved me back—how much more vulnerable would that have made me? I know this must sound strange to you, but when I told you I loved you just now, that's the first time I've ever used the word—in English or in Arabic.'

She held out her hand to him and he drew her up and wordlessly they held each other, together protecting the vulnerability of love.

CHAPTER TWELVE

THE toddler went straight to the fountain, standing on tiptoe to splash her chubby little hands in the cool water, splashing Khalifa, who hovered over her, ready to catch her when her excitement brought her crashing down, as it inevitably would.

'A klutz, like her mother,' he said fondly, still waiting for the fall but turning part of his attention to the woman who lay back in a lounger beneath a nearby peach tree, the bulge of her pregnancy obvious beneath the fine cotton gown she wore.

'Demanding, like her father,' Liz countered, when her daughter grabbed Khalifa's snow-white kandora in her wet hands and scrunched a patch of it while yelling his name—or the Da, Da, Da she called him.

Farida Olive Wilhemina bin Khalifa al Zahn was prattling up at her father, and both Liz and Khalifa knew exactly what she wanted, which was to be stripped off and lifted into the water, where she would immediately fall over and emerge yelling her indignation.

'No,' Khalifa said, very firmly, but Liz could see he was already shuffling out of his sandals and hitching up his kandora, and in a minute would climb into the fountain himself so he could hold his daughter—the precious pearl he'd named her—while she splashed.

The year had passed so quickly. Settling into life at the palace, life as a mother, life as Khalifa's wife—this last made her body burn, pregnant though she was—had made the time pass quickly, but at last Liz felt at peace. Thinking of the loss of Bill and Oliver would always cause a little ache inside her, but the gift they'd given her, this beautiful little girl, eased it immensely, while the gift of Khalifa's love had made her complete in some way she could never explain, even to herself.

He turned towards her now, as if drawn by her thoughts, and smiled. Her toes curled and inside the sparks and fizzing was just as bad as ever.

Or as good as ever...

'The sand sprite would have had no regrets,' she said to him, and knew he understood.

* * * * *

TAMED BY HER
BROODING BOSS

BY
JOANNA NEIL

First published in Great Britain 2012
by Mills & Boon, an imprint of Harlequin (UK) Limited.
Harlequin (UK) Limited, Eton House, 18-24 Paradise Road,
Richmond, Surrey TW9 1SR

© Joanna Neil 2012

ISBN: 978 0 263 89792 0

Harlequin (UK) policy is to use papers that are natural, renewable
and recyclable products and made from wood grown in sustainable
forests. The logging and manufacturing process conform to the
legal environmental regulations of the country of origin.

Printed and bound in Spain
by Blackprint CPI, Barcelona

Dear Reader

Once bitten, twice shy... So the old saying goes. It's one that intrigues me... How, I wondered, would a young girl respond if the man she yearned for turned her away? Wouldn't she do her utmost to steer clear of him in the future?

That's exactly how it was for Sarah, after James Benson rejected her as a vulnerable teenager. Meeting him again, years later, she's alarmed to discover that she still has feelings for him—but she can't possibly act on them.

Besides, she has way too much going on in her life, with her young half-brother and half-sister to look after, as well as the responsibility of working as a doctor in a busy emergency department.

Add to the mix the tranquil setting of a picturesque Cornish fishing village—a favourite with me—and I think you'll agree we have the perfect prescription for romance!

Love

Joanna

CHAPTER ONE

'So, ARE you both okay…? Do you have everything you need?' Sarah's glance trailed over her young half-brother and half-sister, while she tried to work out if there was anything she had forgotten. It was a cool spring morning, with the wind blowing in off the sea, but the children were well wrapped up in warm jackets and trousers.

'Do you still have your money for the lunch break, Sam?' she asked, pausing to tuck a flyaway strand of chestnut-coloured hair behind her ear. He was such a whirlwind, she wouldn't have been surprised to learn that he'd lost it somewhere between the front door of the house and the school gates.

Ten-year-old Sam was clearly feeling awkward in his brand-new school uniform, but he stopped wriggling long enough to dig his hand deep into his trouser pocket.

'Yeah, it's still there.'

'Good. I'll organise some sort of account for you both with the school as soon as I can, but for now make sure you get a decent meal with what you have.' She gave Sam a wry smile. 'I don't want you to go spending it on crisps and junk food.'

His shoulders moved in brief acknowledgement and

she turned her attention to Rosie. The little girl wasn't saying very much—in fact, both children had been un-usually quiet this morning. Perhaps she should have ex-pected that, since it was their first day at a new school. They didn't know this neighbourhood very well as yet, and they'd had to adjust to so many changes of late that it was understandable if they were struggling to take everything on board.

'How about you, Rosie? Are you all right?'

Rosie nodded, her expression solemn, her grey eyes downcast. 'I'm okay.' She was two years younger than her brother, but in some ways she seemed a little more mature than him. It looked as though she was coping, but you could never tell.

'I'm sure you'll be fine, both of you.' Sarah tried to sound encouraging. 'I know it's not easy, starting at a new school mid-term, but I expect your teachers will introduce you to everybody and you'll soon make friends.' She hesitated for a moment, but when neither child said anything in response she put an arm around each of them and started down the path towards the classrooms. 'Let's get you settled in—remember, if I'm still at work by the time school finishes, Murray from next door will come and pick you up.'

A few minutes later, she kissed them goodbye and left them in their cloakrooms, anxiety weighing heavily on her, but there was relief, too, when she saw that the other children were curious about the newcomers and had begun to talk to them.

Sarah pulled in a deep breath as she walked back to her car, trying to gather sustenance from an inner well of strength. It was difficult to know who felt worse, she or the children, but somehow she had to push those concerns to one side for the moment and get on with the rest of what looked to be a difficult day ahead.

It wasn't just the children who were suffering from first-day nerves—she would be starting out on a new job, riding along in the air ambulance with the immediate care doctor for the area. That would carry with it its own difficulties…but that wasn't what was troubling her. As a doctor herself, she hoped she was well prepared to cope with any medical emergency.

She set the car in motion, driving away from the small Cornish fishing village and heading along the coast road towards the air ambulance base where she was to meet up with James Benson.

Her hands tightened on the steering-wheel. Now, there was the crux of the problem. Even recalling his name caused a flurry of sensation to well up inside her abdomen and every now and again her stomach was doing strange, uncomfortable kinds of flip-overs.

How long had it been since she'd last seen him? A good many years, for sure… She'd been a teenager back then, naïve, innocent and desperate to have his attention. Her whole body flushed with heat at the memory, and she shook her head, as though that would push it away.

She'd do anything rather than have to meet up with him once again, but the chances of avoiding him had been scuppered from the outset. Maybe if she'd known from the start that he was a consultant in the emergency department where she'd wanted to work, she would never have applied for the post as a member of the team.

And how could she have known that he was also on call with the air ambulance? It was a job she'd trained for, coveted, and once she'd been drawn in, hook, line and sinker, there was no way she could have backed out of the deal.

She drove swiftly, carefully, barely noticing that she had left the coast behind, with its spectacular cliffs and rugged inlets, and now she was passing through deeply wooded valleys with clusters of whitewashed stone cottages clinging to the hillsides here and there. The bluebells were in flower, presenting her with occasional glimpses of a soft carpet of blue amidst the undergrowth. Small, white pockets of wood sorrel peeped out from the hedges, vying for space with yellow vetch. It was beautiful, but she couldn't appreciate any of it while her heart ached from leaving the children behind and her nerves were stretched to breaking point from anticipating the meeting ahead.

At the base, she drove into a slot in the staff car park and then made her way into the building, to where the air ambulance personnel had their office. Bracing herself, she knocked briskly on the door and then went inside.

The room was empty and she frowned. She couldn't have missed a callout because the helicopter was standing outside on the helipad.

She took a moment to look around. There were various types of medical equipment on charge in here, a computer monitor displaying a log of the air ambulance's last few missions, and a red phone rested in a prominent position on the polished wooden desk. To one side of the room there was a worktop, where a kettle was making a gentle hissing sound as the water inside heated up.

'Ah, there you are.' She turned as James Benson's voice alerted her to his presence. Her heart began to race, pounding as those familiar, deep tones smoothed over her like melting, dark chocolate. 'I'm sorry I wasn't here to greet you,' he added. 'We've all been changing into our flight suits and generally getting ready for the off.'

She nodded, not trusting herself to speak just then. He was every bit as striking as she remembered, with that compelling presence that made you feel as though he dominated the room. Or perhaps it was just that she was unusually on edge today. He was tall, with a strong, muscular build, and he still had those dark good looks which, to her everlasting shame, had been her undoing all those years ago, the chiselled, angular bone structure and jet-black hair, and those penetrating grey eyes that homed in on you and missed nothing.

He was looking at her now, his thoughtful gaze moving over her, lighting on the long, burnished chestnut of her hair and coming to rest on the pale oval of her face.

'I wasn't sure if it really would be you,' he said. 'When I saw your name on the acceptance letter I wondered for a minute or two whether it might be some other Sarah Franklyn, but the chances of there being two doctors in the neighbourhood with the same name was pretty remote. I know you went to medical school and worked in Devon.' His glance meshed with hers, and she steeled herself not to look away. He'd obviously heard, from time to time, about what she was doing. She straightened her shoulders. She would get through this. Of course she would. How bad could it be?

'I expect my taking up a medical career seems a strange choice to you, knowing me from back then.' Her voice was husky, and she cleared her throat and tried again, aiming to sound more confident this time.

'You weren't in on the interviews, so it didn't occur to me that we would be working together.'

He inclined his head briefly. 'I was away, attending a conference—it was important and couldn't be avoided or delegated, so the head of Emergency made the final decision.' His mouth twisted in a way that suggested he wasn't too pleased about that, and Sarah felt a sudden surge of panic rise up to constrict her throat. So he didn't want her here. That was something she hadn't reckoned on.

His glance shifted slowly over her taut features and she lifted her chin in a brash attempt at keeping her poise.

His grey eyes darkened, but his voice remained steady and even toned. 'Perhaps you'd like to go and change into your flight suit, and then I'll show you around and introduce you to the rest of the crew. We'll have coffee. The kettle should have boiled by the time you're ready.'

'Yes. That sounds good.'

At least he was accepting her presence here as a done thing. That was a small mercy. And it looked as though he wasn't going to comment on what had happened all those years ago. Just the thought of him doing that was enough to twist her stomach into knots, but for now perhaps she was safe. After all, she'd been a vulnerable seventeen-year-old back then, and now, some nine years later, she was a grown woman who ought to be in full control of herself. Why, then, did she feel so ill at ease, so uncertain about everything?

But she knew the answer, didn't she? It was because, sooner or later, the past was bound to come up and haunt her.

He showed her to a room where she could change into her high-visibility, orange flight suit, and she took those few minutes of privacy to try and get herself together. She'd keep things on a professional level between them, nothing more, no private stuff to mess things up. That way, she could keep a tight grip on her emotions and show him that she was a totally different person now, calm and up to the mark, and nothing like she'd been as a teenager.

She cringed as she thought back to some of the things she had done in her early teen years. Had she really driven Ben Huxley's tractor around the village on that late summer evening? He'd forever regretted leaving the keys in the ignition, and his shock at discovering his beloved tractor stranded at a precarious angle in a ditch an hour later had been nothing to the concern he'd felt at finding a thirteen-year-old girl slumped over the wheel.

And what had been James's reaction when she'd broken into the stables on his father's estate one evening and saddled up one of the horses? It had been her fourteenth birthday and she hadn't cared a jot about what might happen or considered that what she had been doing was wrong. She had loved the horses, had been used to being around them, and on that day she'd felt an overwhelming need to ride through the meadows and somehow leave her troubles behind. She had been wild, reckless, completely out of control, and James had recognised that.

'None of this will bring your mother back,' he'd said to her, and she'd stared at him, her green eyes wide with defiance, her jaw lifted in challenge.

'What would you know about it?' she'd responded in a dismissive, careless tone.

She'd been extremely lucky. No one had reported her to the police. She'd got away with things, and yet the more she'd avoided paying for her misdemeanours, the more she'd played up. 'Mayhem in such a small package,' was the way James had put it. No wonder he didn't want her around now.

He made coffee for her when she went back into the main room a short time later. 'Is it still cream with one sugar?' he asked, and she gave him a bemused look, her mouth dropping open a little in surprise. He remembered that?

'Yes…please,' she said, and he waved her to a seat by the table.

'Tom is our pilot,' he said, nodding towards the man who sat beside her. Tom was in his forties, she guessed, black haired, with a smattering of grey streaks starting at his temples.

'Pleased to meet you, Sarah,' Tom said, smiling and pushing forward a platter filled with a selection of toasted sandwiches, which she guessed had been heated up in the mini-grill that stood on the worktop next to the coffee-maker. 'Help yourself. You never know if you're going to get a lunch break in this line of work, so you may as well eat while you get the chance.'

'Thanks.' She chose a bacon and cheese baguette and thought back to breakfast-time when she'd grabbed a slice of toast for herself while the children had tucked into their morning cereal. It seemed a long while ago now.

'And this is Alex, the co-pilot,' James said, turning to introduce the man opposite. He was somewhere in his mid-thirties, with wavy brown hair and friendly hazel eyes.

'Have you been up in a helicopter before?' Alex asked, and Sarah nodded.

'I worked with the air ambulance in Devon for a short time,' she answered. 'This is something I've wanted to do for quite a while, so when this job came up it looked like the ideal thing for me.'

He nodded. 'James told us you'll be working part time—is that by choice? It suits us, because our paramedic is employed on a part-time basis, too.'

'Yes. I'll just be doing one day a week here, and the rest of the time I'll be working at the hospital in the A and E department.'

'Sounds good. You'll get the best of both worlds, so to speak. It's unusual to do that, though, in A and E, I imagine?'

'Not so much these days,' Sarah murmured. 'And it suits me to do things this way.' She bit into her baguette and savoured the taste of melted cheese.

'Sarah supplements her income by doing internet work,' James put in. 'She writes a medical advice column for a website, and one for a newspaper, too.'

How had he known that? She looked up at him in surprise, and his mouth made a wry shape. 'I came across your advice column when I was browsing one day, and there was mention there of your work for the newspaper.' He frowned. 'I'm not sure it's wise to make diagnoses without seeing the patient.'

'That isn't what I do, as I'm sure you're aware if you've read my columns.' Perhaps he was testing her, playing devil's advocate, to see what kind of a doctor she really was, but she wasn't going to let him get away with implying she might not be up to the job. Neither was she going to tell him about her personal circumstances and give him further reason for doubting her suitability for the post. She needed to work part time so that she could be there for Sam and Rosie whenever possible, and the writing had provided an excellent solution in that respect. Working from home was a good compromise.

'I mostly work with a team of doctors,' she said, 'and we pick out letters from people who have conditions that would be of interest to a lot of others. We give the best advice we can in the circumstances, and point out other possible diagnoses and remedies.'

'Hmm. You don't think the best advice would be for your correspondents to go and see their own GP, or ask to see a specialist?'

'I think a good many people have already done that and are still confused. Besides, patients are much better informed these days. They like to visit the doctor with some inkling of what his responses might be, or what treatment options might be available to them,' she responded calmly.

He nodded. 'I guess you could be right.' He might have said more, but the red phone started to ring and he lifted the receiver without hesitation. He listened for a while and then said, 'What's the location? And his condition? Okay. We're on our way.'

Food and coffee were abandoned as they hurried out to the helicopter. 'A young man has been injured in a multiple-collision road-traffic accident,' James told them. 'He has a broken leg, but he's some thirty miles away from here, and the paramedics on scene feel they need a doctor present. He needs to go to hospital as soon as possible.'

They were airborne within a minute or two, and soon

Sarah was gazing down at lush green fields bordering a sparse network of ribbon-like roads. James sat next to her, commenting briefly on the landmarks they flew over.

'There's the hospital,' he said, pointing out the heli-pad on top of the building. 'We'll be landing there when we have our patient secured.'

A little further on, they passed over a sprawling country estate, which had at its centre a large house built from grey, Cornish stone. It was an imposing, rectangular building, with lots of narrow, Georgian windows.

'Your family's place,' Sarah mused. 'Do you still live there?' It was large enough for him to have the whole of the north wing to himself. That's how things had been when she'd lived in the area, though he'd been away at medical school a good deal of the time, or working away at the hospital in Penzance. His younger brother had taken over the east wing, leaving the rest of the house to their parents.

He shook his head. 'I have my own place now. It seemed for the best once I settled for working perma-nently in Truro. It's closer to the hospital. Jonathan still lives on the estate, though he has a family of his own now. He has a boy and a girl.'

'I wondered if he might stay on. He was always happy to live and work on the family farm, wasn't he?'

James nodded. 'So you decided to come back to your roots. What persuaded you to leave Devon? I have friends who worked there from time to time and, from what I heard on the grapevine, you were pretty much settled there. Rumour had it your mind was set on stay-ing with the trauma unit.'

'That's pretty much the way it was to begin with…
I was hoping I might get a permanent staff job but then
I was passed over for promotion—a young male doctor
pipped me at the post, and after that I started to look
around for something else.'

He winced. 'That must have hurt.' He studied her
briefly. 'Knowing you, I guess his appointment must
have made you restless. You wouldn't have let the grass
grow under your feet after that.'

'No, I wouldn't, that's true.' She wasn't going to tell
him about her situation—although it hadn't been voiced
at the time, she was fairly certain that she'd lost the
promotion because of her family ties, and now she had
to do everything she could to find secure, permanent
work. This job promised all of that, but she was on three
months' probation to see how things worked out on both
sides, and she didn't need him to go looking for excuses
to be rid of her before she signed a final contract.

By now they had reached their destination, and as
the pilot came in to land, she could see the wreckage
below. It looked as though a couple of motorcyclists
had been involved in a collision with a saloon and a
four-wheel-drive vehicle, and there were a number of
casualties. A fire crew was in attendance, and from the
blackened appearance of the saloon, it seemed that a
blaze had erupted at some point. She could only hope
the occupants of the car had escaped before the fire
had taken hold.

'You'll be shadowing me,' James said, unclipping his
seat belt as the helicopter came to a standstill, 'so don't
worry about getting involved with the other patients.
We'll take them in strict order of triage.'

Sarah bit her lip. She had no objection to following

his lead and learning the ins and outs of this particular job, but surely she'd be of more use helping with the other victims of the crash?

'Okay, whatever you say. Though I do feel I could be of help with the rest of the injured.'

He was already on his way to the door of the helicopter, his medical kit strapped to his back in readiness. 'Let's see how it goes, shall we? According to the paramedics, our primary patient is in a bad way. He needs to be our main concern right now.'

Sarah followed him to the side of the road where a paramedic was tending an injured youth. There were police vehicles nearby and a young officer was directing traffic while another was setting up a road block.

She knelt down beside the casualty. He couldn't be much more than eighteen years old. He lay on the grass verge, well away from the traffic, and his face was white, blanched by shock and loss of blood. The paramedic was giving him oxygen through a mask.

'There are two people suffering from whiplash and sprains,' the paramedic told them. 'They're being looked after by my colleague, along with another man who has chest injuries—broken ribs and collarbone, from what we can tell so far. This lad is Daniel Henderson, motorcyclist. He and his friend were on their way to the coast when they ran into trouble. The two motor vehicles crashed at a road junction and the lads had no way of avoiding them.'

James was already assessing the extent of the boy's injuries. 'His lower leg's grossly deformed,' he said in a quiet voice. 'It looks like a fracture of both the tibia and fibula. That degree of distortion has to be affecting the blood supply.'

The paramedic nodded. 'He's in severe pain, he's very cold and his circulation is shutting down. We can't give him pain relief because we can't find a vein.'

It was a bad situation, because if there was an inadequate supply of blood to Daniel's foot there was the possibility that gangrene would set in and he might lose his leg.

'Thanks, Colin. I'll do an intraosseous injection,' James said, reaching into his medical bag for a bone injection gun. He spoke directly to the boy. 'I'm going to give you something to take away the pain, Daniel. It's a strong anaesthetic, so after a minute or two you'll be feeling much better. There'll be a sharp sting and soon after that you'll start to feel drowsy. Are you okay with that?'

Daniel nodded and closed his eyes. It was a case of the sooner the better, as far as he was concerned.

'Shall I clean the injection site and prepare the ketamine for you?' Sarah asked, and James nodded.

'Yes, thanks.'

As soon as she had cleaned and draped an area on Daniel's upper arm, James located the injection site and pressed the device on the gun that would insert a trocar through the bone and into the soft marrow that was filled with blood vessels. Once he'd done that, he removed the trocar and taped the cannula, the small-bore tube, in place.

Sarah connected an intravenous tube to the cannula and then James was able to give the boy the medication he needed. 'How are you doing, Daniel?' he asked softly after a while. 'Are you okay?'

'I'm all right.' Daniel's voice became slurred as the drug began to take effect.

'Can you feel this?' James pressed a wooden tongue depressor against his leg.

Daniel shook his head.

'That's good, it means the anaesthetic's working,' James said. He glanced at Sarah. 'I think we can safely try to realign the bones enough to restore his circulation. If you and Colin hold him still—Colin at his chest, and you, Sarah, take hold of his upper leg—I'll manoeuvre his ankle and start to pull. We'll need to take great care—we don't know how much damage has already been done to the blood vessels. Let's hope we can do this without too much of a struggle.'

He spoke softly so as not to alarm his patient, but Daniel was by now well anaesthetised and wasn't much concerned about what was happening. Sarah guessed he was simply glad to be free of pain at last.

James worked carefully to straighten out the broken bones as best he could, and as soon as he had achieved that to his satisfaction, he began to splint the leg to prevent any further movement.

'That should do the trick,' he said. 'His circulation should be restored now.'

Sarah kept an eye on Daniel the whole time. She was worried about him. He wasn't saying anything, and had appeared to be drifting in and out of consciousness throughout the procedure.

'We should put in a fluid line,' she said in an undertone. 'He's lost a lot of blood.'

'Yes,' James answered. 'Do you want to see to that, and then we'll transfer him to a spinal board?'

She didn't waste any time, and as soon as she had set up the line they worked together to make sure the young lad was comfortable and covered with a space blanket.

Then they secured him with straps to the board so that he could be transferred to the helicopter.

James left them briefly while he went to check on the other patients, but he returned quickly and took his place beside Sarah in the helicopter.

'The others will be okay to travel by road,' he said. 'It'll take around an hour for them to get to the hospital, but they're in no immediate danger.'

He glanced at his patient. 'I've asked Tom to radio ahead and alert A and E to have an orthopaedic surgeon standing by,' he told Sarah. 'How's the lad doing?'

'His blood pressure's low and his heart rate is rapid, with a weak pulse,' she answered. The signs of shock were all there, but they'd done everything they could for now, and all they could do was wait.

Tom was already setting the helicopter in motion, lifting them up off the ground. Within minutes he had turned them around and they were heading out across the Cornish peninsula towards the hospital, some thirty miles away.

James checked on the injured youth, lifting the blanket to look at his feet. 'His toes are beginning to pink up,' he pointed out, glancing at Sarah.

'Oh, thank heaven,' she said. She smiled at him, her mouth curving, her green eyes bright with relief. With his circulation restored, the imminent danger of Daniel losing his leg had been averted. 'I'm so glad for him.'

James nodded. He gently tucked the blanket in place, but he didn't once take his gaze from Sarah. He was watching her closely, as though he was mesmerised, taking in the warmth of her response, the soft flush of heat that flared in her cheeks.

The breath caught in her throat, and a familiar hunger surged inside her as she returned his gaze. There was a sudden, dull ache in her chest, an ache that came from knowing her unbidden yearning could never be assuaged. He still had the power to melt her bones and fill her with that humiliating need that would forever be her downfall.

She closed her eyes briefly. How on earth would she be able to work with him over the weeks, months that lay ahead?

'We'll be coming in to land in about two minutes.' The pilot's voice came over the speaker.

'Okay, Tom. We'll be ready.' James turned his attention back to the boy on the stretcher. He was self-contained, in control, as always.

Sarah looked out of the window. She had to keep things between them on a professional footing. That was the only way she could survive. From now on it would become her mantra.

CHAPTER TWO

'You look as though you could do with a break. Has it been a tough week?' Murray laid a manila folder down on a corner of the pine kitchen table, avoiding the clutter of pastry boards and rolling pins. 'I brought the colour charts I promised you,' he added, tapping the folder. He stared at her, looking her up and down. 'You're not your usual jaunty self today. What's up?'

'Nothing's up.' Sarah smiled at her spiky-haired neighbour and waved him towards a chair. Perhaps she was a bit pale from being cooped up in the house, and since she was cooking with the children today there were probably traces of flour in her hair where she'd pushed it off her face with the back of her hand. 'If I look less than on top of the world, I guess it's because I was up till all hours last night, painting the walls in the living room. Sit down and I'll pour you some tea. We were just about to have a cup.'

'Sarah's going to paint our bedrooms next,' Sam put in eagerly. He was using a cutter to make gingerbread shapes, and he paused now to assess his handiwork. 'She said we can choose the colours—'cept for black. She won't let me have that.' His bottom lip jutted and he frowned as he thought about that for a second or two.

Then his eyes lit up. 'Purple would be good, though—
or bright red.'

'We helped Sarah with the living room,' Rosie put
in. 'Well, I did. Sam kept going off and playing on his
game machine.' She looked at her older brother and
shook her head.

'You were both a great help, all the same,' Sarah
said, her eyes crinkling at the corners. 'It's going to be
a long job, though,' she admitted, glancing at Murray
as she went over to the worktop at the side of the room.
She lifted up the sunshine-yellow teapot. 'I knew there
would be a lot of work when we moved in here a fort-
night ago. This place was in a pretty wretched state
when I bought it.'

Murray pulled a face. 'I guessed it was bad—the old
man who used to live here wasn't able to do much in the
way of maintenance—but I knew he was looking for
a quick sale once he'd decided to go and live with his
son and his family in Somerset. I did what I could to
help him out with things, but there was a limit to what
I could do, with company business getting in the way.
There were orders for goods coming in thick and fast
and supplies from the warehouses were delayed and
so on. There's been a lot to sort out over the last few
months.' He frowned. 'Perhaps I shouldn't have pointed
the house out to you,' he finished on a thoughtful note.

She poured his tea and came towards him once more,
placing the mug in front of him. 'You did the right
thing,' she told him, laying a hand on his shoulder and
squeezing gently. 'I'm really glad you told me about
this place. I don't know what I'd have done otherwise.
It was exactly what I needed.'

'Hmm… Well, I suppose a lick of paint here and

there will work wonders.' He glanced at the children, busy laying out gingerbread men on a baking tray. Rosie's were perfectly symmetrical, with raisins placed in exactly the right place to represent eyes. Sam, on the other hand, was far more slapdash in his approach, and his men looked like cross-eyed vagabonds, with bits missing here and there. Sarah suspected he'd been surreptitiously tasting the uncooked mixture every now and again—the greasy smears around his mouth were a dead give-away.

Murray looked at Sarah once more as she placed the first batch of gingerbread men in the hot oven. 'How's the job going? Is it working out for you?'

She sat in a chair opposite him, leaving it to the children to finish rolling out the remains of the gingerbread mix on a pastry board.

'I think so. It's early days yet. My boss is watching my every move.' She gave a wry smile. 'I think he's worried I might slip up and inadvertently kill off one of our patients.'

James had not made it obvious that he was concerned about her ability to make the grade, but for the last week he'd checked everything she did, going over her charts and medication logs with a keen eye. Every now and again she would be aware of him assessing her actions, scrutinising the way she handled various procedures. She'd no idea why he was concerned about her abilities as a doctor, but in the past she'd always been headstrong and haphazard in her actions, and maybe he thought she'd breezed her way through medical school on a wing and a prayer.

Murray laughed. 'As if!' Then he sobered, glancing at the children, and added in an undertone, 'Seriously, though, are you finding it all a bit much? You have a whole lot on your plate these days.'

'It's okay. I'm beginning to get used to the new routine. It's just that...' She broke off, her expression rueful. 'I don't know,' she said, after a moment or two. 'I don't seem to have time to sit and think at the moment. Everything seems to be going at a breakneck pace—moving in here, the new job, finding a school for the children, taking on the internet work. It's all come about in a short space of time.' She straightened up and sipped at her tea. 'I'm sure things will sort themselves out, though. Like I said, these are early days.'

'Maybe it would help if I took the kids out for a while. That would give you some time to yourself—unless you'd like to come with us?' He gave her a thoughtful look. 'I need to head into town to pick up some hardware for my computer and I thought about dropping into the pizza place while I'm in the area.'

Sam's ears pricked up at the mention of pizza. 'When are you going? Can I go with you?'

'Sure.' Murray laughed. 'If Sarah thinks it's okay, that is.' He glanced at her and she nodded. She'd known Murray for years, ever since they'd both taken part in a rock-climbing course at an outdoor pursuits centre. He ran his own internet company, working from home most of the time, selling sports equipment and accessories, advising people on how to keep fit, and setting up weekend sporting activities. She'd always found him to be reliable and trustworthy. The children would be safe with him, that was for sure.

'That's fine with me. I think I'll give it a miss, though, if you don't mind. I think I need some time to get myself together.' It had been a stressful week, one way and another, and being with James every day had been harder to handle than she'd expected. She'd always known she should keep her distance from him, but now that she'd taken the job that was never going to happen. Every instinct warned her that whatever way she became involved with him, she might end up being hurt. He alone had the power to affect her that way. Emotionally he could leave her bereft.

She dragged her mind back to Murray's offer. 'I have to go and buy some groceries from the village store, and I could do with a walk along the clifftop and maybe even along the beach.' She smiled. 'Rosie and Sam never seem quite as keen on doing that as I am.'

Murray nodded and turned to look at Rosie. 'How does pizza sound to you, Rosie? Are you in?'

'Yes, please.' She looked at Sarah and said hesitantly, 'I don't mind going for walks…not really… It's just that…' She broke off, her shoulders wriggling. 'Mum used to take us along the seafront in Devon. Now… I get… I get all sad now when we go to the beach.' Her eyes were downcast, and her lower lip was beginning to tremble.

'Oh, Rosie…' Sarah's heart swelled with compassion, and she quickly stood up and went over to her. 'I know how you must be feeling, pumpkin.' She put her arms around the little girl and held her close. 'I do under-stand. It's hard…but you'll see, it'll get easier with time.'

'We used to play football on the beach with Dad sometimes,' Sam said, a wistful, far-away look in his blue-grey eyes. 'He used to dive for the ball and then he'd fall over and we'd wrestle him for it.'

Sarah reached out and gently stroked his hair. She didn't remember her father ever playing rough-and-tumble games like that with her when she'd been younger, but obviously he had changed, grasping a second chance of happiness after he had found her stepmother and started his new family. She felt for Rosie and Sam. They were going through something that no child should ever have to bear, but she was doing whatever she could to make life easier for them. It was difficult, though, because memories would come flooding in at unexpected moments, like this, putting her on the spot.

'Sounds as though you could all do with a bit of cheering up,' Murray said, coming to her rescue. 'I think pizza with all the toppings will probably do the trick—and we could take some of your game DVDs into the store and swap them for those you were telling me about, Sam, if you like?'

'Oh, yeah…that'd be great.' Sam's mood changed in mercurial fashion.

'Rosie, you might like to check out some of the dance games,' Sarah suggested, following Murray's lead. 'You have some pocket money saved up, don't you?'

Rosie brightened and nodded, causing her soft brown curls to flutter and gleam in the sunlight that poured in through the kitchen window.

'That's settled, then,' Murray said. 'As soon as you're ready, we'll be off.'

After they had gone, Sarah cleared away and set out the cooked gingerbread men on racks to cool. A few were missing already, since Murray and the children had decided they smelled too good to leave until later. Sam's pockets had been bulging as he'd left the house.

She looked around, suddenly feeling the need to go out and get away from all the jobs that were crying out for attention. Sam and Rosie would be gone for much of the afternoon, according to Murray, so maybe she would make the most of things and go and get some fresh air. The walk into the centre of the village would do her good and she could pick up some fresh supplies from the grocery store while she was there.

It was a beautiful spring day, with a blue sky overhead and patchy white clouds moving in from the coast. As she walked down the hill towards the seafront, past colour-washed cottages and narrow, cobbled side streets, she could feel the light breeze lifting her hair and billowing gently round the hem of her skirt. In the distance, boats were moored in the harbour, and closer to home fishermen tended their nets, laying them out on the smooth sand as they looked them over and prepared for the next trip out to sea.

Instead of going directly down to the beach, she took a path that led to a raised terrace overlooking the cove, and from there she gazed out across the bay towards the craggy promontory she had once explored as a teenager. It was some distance away, but she could see the waves dashing against the rocks, sending up fountains of spray to splash into the crevices. She'd gone there once with friends, and James had joined them. He had been on one of his brief visits home from medical school. He'd walked with her along the shore as she'd looked for shells buried in the warm sand. It had been a magical day, with the sun high in the sky and James by her side, a day that had almost made her dreams come true.

There was a movement beside her and it was almost as though by thinking of him she'd conjured him up. 'It must seem a long time ago since you spent your days searching for crabs in those rock pools,' James said, coming out of the blue to stand alongside her. He followed her gaze to the boulder-strewn beach some half a mile away.

She gave a startled jump, taking a step backwards as he went to place a hand on the metal railing in front of them. He quickly put his arm out to steady her, and then when she'd recovered her balance he let his hand rest on the curve of her hip.

'Are you all right? I'm sorry if I surprised you.' He sounded concerned and his glance moved over her to gauge her reaction. 'I didn't mean to creep up on you like that. I thought you'd be aware of me, but you must have been miles away in your head.'

'Yes… I'm okay.' She rested her fingers against her chest, on the soft cotton of her top, as though that might somehow calm the staccato beat of her heart. Where had he come from? She couldn't think straight while he was so close, with his hand spreading fire along her skin, sending heated ripples of sensation to spread through her hips and along the length of her spine. 'What… what are you doing here? Where did you come from?'

'I was on my way home from the hospital and I decided to stop and pick up something to snack on from the village shop. Then I saw you standing here.'

'Oh, I see.' She frowned. 'I thought this was your weekend off.'

He removed his hand and stepped closer to the rail, turning so that he could look at her properly. That ought to have made things easier for her, but instead her mind went blank for a moment or two as she unexpectedly felt the loss of his warm, intimate touch. Perversely, she wanted him to go on holding her.

'Yes, it is, but one of the junior doctors was anxious about a patient and phoned me to ask what he should do. Apparently the consultant in charge was busy dealing with another emergency.'

'Were you all right with that?' She'd watched him work hard all week, putting in long hours, staying on to make sure his patients pulled through and were definitely stabilised or on the road to recovery before he would leave. He seemed reluctant to hand over responsibility until he had done everything humanly possible to make sure they were safe. It must have taken a toll on him, but it didn't show. Despite all that supreme effort, he still managed to look fit and energetic, on top form.

Weekends were precious for everyone, but some senior medical staff guarded them as sacrosanct, a time to recuperate and recharge their batteries, something they'd earned after years of study and acquiring specialist qualifications. From what she'd heard, one or two consultants took a very dim view of things if juniors called them in to work out of hours. Of course, things tended to operate differently in the emergency department.

'I was fine with it,' James said. 'I'd sooner I was there to see a patient if there are any worries about his or her condition. Junior doctors do their best, but they need support, and I try to give it as much as possible. Sometimes you can do it over the phone, but other times there's nothing for it but to go in.'

'Yes, of course.' She had finished her foundation years, but she wasn't much more than a junior doctor herself—James was far more experienced than she was. He'd started his training while she'd been about to begin her worrisome teens, and he'd always put his heart and soul into medicine. 'What was the problem with the patient?' She might be in the same boat herself

one day, in a quandary as to whether she should call
him out, and it would be helpful to know what kind of
things she ought to bring to his attention.

'A woman collapsed while she was being treated for
an abdominal injury. The doctor followed all the proto-
cols but she wasn't responding, so in the end he called
me to ask for advice. The senior staff were all too busy
with other emergencies. There was obviously something
more going on than the problems with her injury, but
her medical records weren't available. Her liver was
damaged, nothing too major—at least, not enough to
cause her total collapse. I've ordered a batch of tests,
so we'll know better what's going on as soon as they
come back from the lab. She's being given supportive
treatment in the meantime.'

His glance wandered over her, taking in the pale-
coloured cotton top that faithfully followed her curves,
and the gently flowing skirt that skimmed her hips,
drifting and settling around her calves as she moved.
His grey eyes seemed to glimmer as he studied her,
though of course it might simply have been a trick of
the light. 'You're looking very summery…just right for
this warm sunshine,' he said.

A wave of heat surged through her. She hadn't expected him to comment or even notice how she looked,
but perhaps it was the contrast between how she looked
now and the way she dressed at work that had sparked
his interest. One day a week when she went out with
the air ambulance, when she wore a flight suit, and the
rest of the time at work she dressed in scrubs, the basic
A and E outfit.

She gave a wry smile. 'It beats wearing scrubs, anyway, or even jeans. Just lately, when I'm at home I've

been trying to get on with some decorating any chance I get, so it makes a change to be out of jeans for a while.'

'Ah…of course, you only moved back here a couple of weeks ago, didn't you? I imagine there's a lot to do, settling into a new place.'

'Yes, you're right there. My back certainly knows all about it.' She laughed, rubbing a hand over muscles that had only recently made themselves known to her.

'Perhaps it's just as well you're having the afternoon off, then. Are you taking some time off from the decorating to explore the village? I expect you want to get to know the place all over again.' He leaned back against the rail, at ease, his long body thoroughly relaxed as he watched her.

'Yes, I thought I'd wander around for a while. Though, like you, I need to get some supplies from the store. I did a big shop when we arrived but now I'm running out of a few things.'

She glanced at him. He was smartly dressed, in dark, clean-cut trousers and a deep blue shirt, the kind of thing he usually wore for work in the emergency unit when he wasn't in scrubs. Perhaps he'd left his jacket in his car, along with his tie. His shirt was open at the neck, exposing an area of smooth, suntanned throat. She looked away. 'Did you park up somewhere around here?' she asked.

He nodded. 'By the quayside. I don't live too far away from here, but it's more than a short walk and it's uphill all the way.' He pointed to the steps that were built into the hillside, with a protective rail to help along the way.

Sarah glanced at the steep, green slopes, covered with a rich array of grasses and shrubs. At intervals there were houses dotted about, overlooking the sea. 'Do you live in one of those?' she asked.

'No. You can't see my house from here. It's further back, about a mile inland. I walk to the village sometimes to stretch my legs and take in the scenery.'

'It must be a big change for you after all those years of living on your parents' country estate.'

'Yes, it is. But I like having my own space.' He looked out to sea for a while, and they both watched a sailing vessel move across the horizon. 'I wondered if you'd ever come back to Cornwall,' he said. 'You were in Devon for several years, weren't you? Did you stay with your father there? He'd remarried before you left here, hadn't he?'

'Yes, he had...and Sam was already a year old by then. I did stay with my father in Devon for a short time.' She moved restlessly, uncomfortable with memories that crowded her brain, and he followed as she began to walk along the cliff path.

'But then...?'

'I began to wonder if I might be in the way. What newly married couple wants a teenager around?' She pulled a face. 'Anyway, it wasn't long before I went away to medical school, and I was glad to be independent. And it was easier to rent my own place, once I found friends to share with me.'

'How did your father feel about that? After all, you and he had quite a few years here in Cornwall when it was just the two of you together.'

She shrugged awkwardly. 'It was never all that comfortable for either of us once we were left on our own. He was withdrawn a lot of the time, and he preferred to be by himself. He'd have cut himself off from everyone and everything if it had been possible, but instead he had to go out to work to keep a roof over our heads. Then he met Tracy and everything changed.'

He frowned, looking at her with an intent expression. 'That must have been hard on you after all that time of being out in the cold, so to speak.'

She pressed her lips together briefly. 'She obviously sparked something in him that gave him a renewed zest for life. I guess I was glad he'd found some reason to join the human race once more.' The path led down from where they were to the centre of the village, where the grocery store and the post office stood side by side. 'I need to buy some fresh vegetables and a loaf of bread,' she announced. 'Are you heading in the same direction as me?'

'I am. I thought I might get some sticky buns and one of Martha's hot coffees to take away.' He sent her a quick glance. 'Perhaps you'd like to help me eat them— I didn't have breakfast and I missed out on lunch with being called out so early this morning. It's lazy of me, I know, but I can't be bothered to go back home and cook.'

Her green eyes widened a fraction. 'It's the middle of the afternoon,' she said in astonishment. 'You ought to know better than to go without food in our line of work.'

He nodded, his mouth making a crooked line. His whole countenance changed when he smiled, and her heart gave a small lurch. 'Consider me told off,' he said. 'How about the buns? Do you want to share?'

'Okay.' She pushed open the door of the shop and a bell jangled to alert Martha, the proprietor, to her customers. 'But I'll go one better than that. Why don't you come over to my place and I'll heat up some soup and warm some bread rolls in the oven? Then you can have the buns for afters. I only live about five minutes' walk from here.' The suggestion was out before she had time to consider whether she was wise to get in closer contact with this man who had haunted her, metaphorically speaking, ever since her change from teenage brat to emerging womanhood.

'Well, that's too good an offer to miss…if you're sure?' His brow creased. 'I don't want to put you to any trouble.'

'It's no bother. But if you were to collapse through malnutrition, I wouldn't want to have it on my conscience.' She gave him an admonishing glance and he laughed.

'Thanks, Sarah. Besides, I'm curious to see where you're living now. I heard you'd bought a place, rather than renting. That sounds enterprising, coming from a girl who wanted to be free as a bird and explore new pastures.'

'Hmm.' Her cheeks flushed with warm colour. 'I was very young and naïve when I came out with that statement.' She'd been brash, full of youthful defiance, keen to let him know that she wouldn't be staying around for much longer. In truth, in her mind, she'd been running away. Her mouth made an odd twist. 'It's actually not up to much, and I think you might be quite disappointed when you see it. I know I was, but I was already contracted to buy it.'

He gave her a perplexed glance. 'You mean you bought it without seeing it?'

'That's right. It came up for auction and I didn't have time to suss it out before putting in an offer. It was just about as much as I could afford.' She lifted her arms in a futile gesture. 'And I was in a bit of a hurry.'

'It sounds like it.'

'Can I help you?' Martha bustled forward, ready to serve them, her face creasing in a smile. 'Have you managed to sort yourself out, my dear?' she queried gently, looking at Sarah. 'You did quite a bit of stocking up last time you were in here, didn't you? I must say, you don't look quite as harassed as you did then.'

'I think it's all beginning to work out,' Sarah answered cheerfully. 'You had pretty well everything I needed to get me started with the cleaning and so on… but I just want a few bits this time around.'

Martha collected together everything off Sarah's list, and she and James left the shop a few minutes later, loaded with packages. James was munching on one of the buns he'd bought.

'Here, let me carry those for you,' he said, relieving her of a couple of bags. He peered inside them. 'There are a lot of vegetables in here for just one young woman.'

'Ah…perhaps you didn't know…' She sent him a quick, sideways look. 'I'm not on my own these days.'

'You're not?' His step halted momentarily and he frowned, glancing at her ring finger and then, seeing that it was bare, said, 'Have I missed something? Are you involved with someone?'

'No, it's nothing like that.' She walked determinedly up the hill towards her cottage.

He sent her a puzzled look, but they'd reached her house by now and she stood still, looking up at the blotchy, white-painted building with its peeling woodwork. 'This is it. This is where I'm living now.'

He stared, his gaze moving up to the roof where a few slates were cracked or missing altogether. To his credit, he managed to keep a straight face as he said slowly, 'I think you might have your work cut out here.'

She laughed. 'You said it...but that's nothing. Wait till you see the inside.' She'd already reinforced his view that she was as reckless as ever, buying on impulse, so what did it matter if he looked around and saw the pitiful state it was in?

They walked along the drab hallway to the kitchen, where he set the bags and packages down on the pine table. He glanced thoughtfully around the room for a moment or two, taking in the flaking ceiling and the windows that hadn't seen a lick of paint for quite some time.

'The cupboards and worktops look as though they're made of solid wood,' he commented after a while. 'I suppose they could be stripped back and restored to their original condition—or painted, depending on how you feel about it.'

'Hmm. Yes, you're right. I haven't quite decided what I'm going to do yet.' She smiled at him. He was being positive, and that made her feel much better. 'I'll put the soup on a low heat, and the rolls in the oven, and I could show you around the place while they're warming up, if you like?'

He nodded. 'Sounds good to me. Can I do anything to help? Shall I put the kettle on?'

'Okay, thanks. Mugs are over there, cutlery in the drawer.'

They worked together for a while, and then she took him on a whistle-stop tour of the three-bedroomed cottage, pointing out the best features, where she was able to find any.

'I knew the structure of the house was reasonably sound when I bid for it,' she told him, 'because Murray, my neighbour, is a good friend, and he knew about the property—from a layman's point of view, of course.'

'Ah…I see… I think.' He hesitated. 'Have you known him long?'

She nodded. 'For years, though of course we've been out of touch until recently. He's been a great help to me.' They were in one of the bedrooms, and she waved a hand towards the small fireplace. 'I'm not sure quite what to do about that. As you've seen, there's a fireplace in each of the three bedrooms.' She frowned. 'They say you should keep any character features like that if at all possible when you're renovating, but they don't look too good at the moment, and anyway I'm wondering if the rooms might be a bit chilly with the open chimney.'

He shook his head. 'The chimney shouldn't make any difference, and from the looks of things you have central heating, which should keep everything cosy. I think it would be a good idea to keep them. The house is Victorian and pretty solid in most respects, and it would be a pity to lose its character. It should be a fairly straightforward job to renovate them—you have to get rid of any rust, of course, apply a coat of red oxide and then when that's dry rub in some black grate polish. It doesn't come off once it's done, and the fireplace will look as good as new.'

'You're probably right.' She was thoughtful. 'I'll put it on my list of things to do—it's getting to be quite a long list.'

'I could do it for you, if you like.'

She blinked in astonishment. 'You'd do that?' She was completely bowled over by his unexpected offer. Why would he want to spend time doing anything at all in this old, neglected house? And why would he do it for her?

'I think it's something I would enjoy.' He went over to the fireplace and ran his fingers lightly over the partially engraved cast iron. 'I often did restoration work in the family home, don't you remember? There was that time I was up a stepladder, trying to decide what colours to use on the ornate ceiling in the dining room, when you walked in.' He sent her an oblique glance, a glimmer sparking in his dark eyes.

'Oh.' The breath left her lungs in a small gasp. How could he have brought that up? Did he recall everything, every tiny instance of when she'd brought havoc into his life? 'How was I to know you were balanced on a ladder?' she said. 'I didn't mean to take you by surprise. All I knew was I was supposed to go to the house and find someone who would get me started on the apple picking. I should have gone to the study, but I went into the dining room by mistake.'

'And I narrowly avoided taking a nose dive.'

'Because I managed to steady the ladder just in time—'

'Only after I grabbed hold of the mahogany cabinet and regained my balance.'

'Yes, well...' Sarah clamped her mouth shut. Perhaps it was for the best if she didn't say any more. It was an experience that had alarmed her greatly at the time. For a number of years she had worked on the estate in the summer holidays and this particular season she had been scheduled to spend time in the orchards. She hadn't meant to catch her employer's son off guard, and the consequences could have been disastrous. 'You made a good job of the ceiling anyway,' she said, breaking her vow of silence.

He grinned. 'I guess I did, in the end. It took a while, though. A couple of weeks at least.' He moved away from the fireplace. 'I'll make a start with the fires as soon as I get hold of the red oxide and the polish...that'll be sometime next week, I expect.'

'Um, okay. Thanks. That would be really good. I'm really stunned that you should offer.' She looked around for a moment at the fading wallpaper and gave a soft sigh. It would all get done eventually.

'As you say, the house is sound in most respects,' James commented, interpreting her rueful expression. 'It doesn't look much now, but with care and attention it could be something quite special.'

She smiled at him. 'Yes, you're right, of course.' She turned towards the door and said, 'I think you've seen everything now—shall we go and see if the soup's ready?'

The kitchen was warm from the old AGA, and Sarah soon had the table set for the meal. She put out butter, ham and cheese, along with a bowl of fresh salad, and invited James to sit and eat. Then she remembered the gingerbread men and laid some out on a plate, sliding it alongside the sticky buns James had bought.

'Help yourself,' she said, taking a seat across the table from him.

He smiled as he looked at the food, and sniffed the air appreciatively. 'Mmm,' he murmured, ladling soup from the tureen into his bowl. 'This smells appetising— like home-cooked vegetables in a rich, meaty broth.' He dipped his spoon in the soup and tasted the mixture, his eyes widening in surprise. 'Ah…this is wonderful. I don't think I've ever tasted anything quite like it.'

'Well, I'm glad to hear it—though if you're that hungry, I expect anything would taste good right now.' She grinned. 'Although I did spend a good deal of yesterday evening getting it ready.'

His dark brows rose, and he looked at her dubiously, as though he expected to see her nose grow like Pinocchio's had whenever he'd told a lie. 'You're kidding me,' he said in astonishment. 'You, spending time in a kitchen? I can scarcely believe it. As I recall, you'd sooner grab a burger or a baguette or stick something in the microwave so that you could be on your way. Wherever did you learn to cook?'

'Oh, here and there. It turned out to be a bit of a necessity once I was on my own.' She laughed. 'To be honest, I soon got very tired of convenience food and decided I needed to buy a cook book.' She helped herself to salad, adding grated cheese to her plate alongside the ham.

'You certainly look good on whatever it is you've been eating these last few years.' His glance trailed over her. 'You've filled out—as I recall, you were a skinny little thing with flyaway hair that was forever coming loose from the pins, or whatever it was you used to keep it in place.'

Her mouth made a brief, crooked slant. 'Not much change with the hair, then.' She'd brushed it before leaving the house, securing it in a topknot as best she could, and even now she could feel silky strands parting company with the clips.

She bent her head and pretended to be absorbed

with her meal. He'd called her skinny. No wonder he'd not even looked at her the way she'd hoped for back then when she'd been seventeen. Warm colour filled her cheeks. Skinny. He'd made a twosome with Chloe, the daughter of the local innkeeper—she'd had curves aplenty, along with golden hair and dreamy blue eyes. She'd seen them having lunch together at a pub, and his defection had been the final straw to a love-starved teenager. She'd vowed then she would get away from the village and leave James far behind.

And yet now she was sharing a meal with him in her fading, love-starved cottage. She must be mad.

She gathered her composure and forced herself to look at him once more. 'I made another pot of tea—would you like a cup?' She was already reaching for the teapot.

He nodded. 'Thanks. That would be great.' He was staring absentmindedly at the plate of gingerbread men. Some had bits of leg missing, or half an arm, and that made him smile. 'They smell good—more wounded soldier than fighting men, I'd guess,' he said.

'Oh, yes. They're Sam's addition to the feast. He's always in too much of a hurry to bother with perfection.'

He frowned. 'Sam—so there's someone else, as well as Murray? Your life must be getting quite complicated.'

'Yes.' She glanced at him and said quietly, 'Perhaps you haven't heard what happened to my father and Tracy?' It had been a terrible shock, and she had never felt more alone in her life when she'd heard the news of their accident.

'Something happened to them?' His expression was suddenly serious, and Sarah nodded unhappily.

'They were caught up in a road-traffic accident.' She

pressed her lips together briefly. 'Unfortunately their injuries were serious and they died almost instantly.'

He drew in a sharp breath, his features taut. 'I didn't know. I'm so sorry, Sarah. That must have been awful for you.'

'It was. It was a difficult time.' She closed her eyes fleetingly, resting a hand on the table, unable to concentrate on anything for that moment, while her mind was lost in the memory of those dreadful weeks when the world as she'd known it had come to a standstill.

His fingers closed over hers, in a comforting gesture that brought her back to the present and made her look up into his dark eyes.

'Did you have friends to support you?'

'Thankfully, yes.'

'I'm glad. I wish I could have been there for you.'

'Thank you.' She sent him a gentle smile. 'But I coped. The biggest problem for me back then was what to do about Sam and Rosie, of course…my half-brother and half-sister. Sam's ten years old, and Rosie's eight.' She frowned. 'I think you might have seen Sam when he was a baby…at the wedding reception of a mutual friend. Anyway, they both live with me now.'

'But…surely there was some other relative who could have taken them in? An uncle and aunt, perhaps?' He looked shocked. 'How can it be that you're looking after them?'

Her shoulders lifted. 'There's no one else, so they're my responsibility now. That's why we moved back here, so that I could take up this new job and hopefully keep a roof over our heads.'

He shook his head, a perplexed expression on his face. 'I'd no idea, none at all.'

'Why would you?' she said quietly.

They finished their meal and James helped her to clear away. It was plain to see he was stunned by what she had told him, and later, when he was getting ready to leave, he said, 'You've taken on something that others would baulk at, you know.' His features relaxed. 'But somehow I might have expected it of you. You were always up for a challenge, weren't you?' His mouth twisted. 'Let's hope this one doesn't turn and bite back.'

CHAPTER THREE

'How are you feeling today, Nicola?' James picked up his patient's chart and then moved to the bedside where he gave the woman an engaging smile.

'So-so.' She tried to smile in return, but Sarah could see that she was extremely fatigued and clearly very unwell. Nicola Carter was in her mid-forties, with anxious grey eyes and brown hair that formed soft waves around her pale face. There was an intravenous drip connected to a cannula in her arm giving her lifesaving fluids. 'I feel a bit dizzy, and I keep being sick.'

'Mmm.' James nodded, showing his understanding and concern. 'It probably doesn't help that your blood pressure is very low. Your liver was bruised in the car crash and there was some bleeding inside your abdomen, which is why it is so important that you have complete bed-rest for a few days. You were in a bad way when you came into A and E on Saturday, and we still need to find out exactly what happened. It wasn't just the accident that caused you to collapse.' He glanced briefly at her notes. 'You haven't been eating much these last few months, have you? You've lost quite a bit of weight recently.'

'I just don't seem to have much of an appetite.'

'Well, we'll have to do something about that, and make sure we get you feeling better as soon as possible.' He laid a hand on hers. 'With any luck we should have the results of the latest tests by tomorrow. In the meantime, get as much rest as you can.'

'Okay.'

James moved away from the bedside, and Sarah followed. She'd gone with him each day on these rounds of the observation ward, and she was used by now to his gentle manner and matter-of-fact way of dealing with his patients. Somehow he managed to put them at ease so that they could feel reassured they were in good hands.

'I want you to follow up on Nicola's case,' he said now, replacing the chart in the slot at the end of the bed. 'With any luck, the internal bleeding will stop completely and she'll start to heal.'

'I'll see to it.'

'Good.' They walked together towards the A and E department, and he sent her an oblique glance, his grey eyes thoughtful. 'Thanks for giving me lunch the other day. I appreciated you taking the time and trouble to do that.' His mouth curved. 'And it was great to have the chance to look around your house.'

'Do you know—I enjoyed showing you? You actually helped me to see the place through fresh eyes.' She smiled. 'I wasn't sure what I was going to do about the children's bedrooms, how I was going to make them cosy and child-friendly, but you had some great ideas about using the old furniture in there. I'm going to spruce up the Victorian dressing screen and put it in Rosie's room—she'll find all sorts of ways to use it for imaginative games, I expect. And Sam will love to have the desk from the front room. He's really into drawing and writing these days.'

They left the observation ward and headed along the corridor, and James held open the fire door to let her pass through into the A and E department. 'I hadn't realised you'd taken on quite so much, with the children, especially. It must be difficult for you. I mean, you're so young, and you have your whole life ahead of you. Were there really no other options?'

Sarah shook her head. He wouldn't understand her reasoning because he was a bachelor, used to the freedom of his bachelor lifestyle. 'Even if there were, I wouldn't have taken them. I know what it's like to be left, to lose a parent, and they lost both of theirs. I wanted to smooth things for them, to show them that they still had family, someone who cared about them and who would be there for them.'

His mouth made a crooked slant. 'Given your background, I suppose I shouldn't have expected you to do anything else.'

'I guess so. Their situation is different from mine, of course, but they've had to put up with a lot, leaving their home behind, moving from Devon to Cornwall, settling into a new house and a new school. It's all happened quite fast, but I think they're beginning to make friends, so it should be a little easier for them from now on. I'm trying to involve them in the renovations as well, asking them for ideas and so on and giving them small jobs to do so that they feel they're part of it.' At least she could give them love and tenderness, things that had been sadly missing in her own early years.

'With your help, I'm sure they'll do all right. And doing up the house is a project that's going to keep all of you busy for the next few months.' He sent her a questioning glance. 'Speaking of which, I could come round this evening to make a start on the fireplaces, if you like...if that suits you?'

'That would be great, thanks.' It was good to know that he'd meant what he'd said about helping.

'I'm sure Sam will be happy with his new bedroom.' James chuckled. 'Didn't you say you're going to paint one of the walls red? Better that than the all-round black he was talking about.'

'I think he must be going through a Goth phase.' She laughed with him. 'I thought of compromising and doing a midnight blue ceiling with stars. I haven't made up my mind yet, though.'

'Who knows,' he said in an amused tone, 'if you encourage an interest in the stars and planets, he might grow up to be an astronomer.'

'Yeah, maybe. I wonder if they do astronaut suits in black?'

'Ah...there you are, James.' The triage nurse looked pleased to see him, and hurried towards them as they made their way to the central desk. 'I was just about to page you.' She paused to catch her breath. 'We've a young girl, Rachel, about seventeen years old, coming in by ambulance. She's been partying all weekend from the sound of things. It's a regular thing with her, apparently. She collapsed at a friend's house—they say she'd been drinking and experimenting with Ecstasy.'

James winced. 'We've been getting far too many of these cases lately. And they seem to be getting younger.' He glanced briefly at the white board that detailed patients being treated in the emergency unit. 'Thanks, Gemma. We'll take her into the resuscitation room.'

'Okay. Do you want me to stand by?'

He shook his head. 'Sarah is shadowing me for these first few weeks, so she'll assist me on this one. I can see from the board that you have enough on your hands already.'

'Too right. It's been frantic here this morning from the outset.' Gemma walked swiftly away, leaving them to go and meet their young patient at the ambulance bay.

A paramedic was giving Rachel oxygen through a mask. 'She was talking at one stage—very upset and not making any sense, something about her family— but now she's unresponsive,' he told them. 'Her temperature's raised and her heart rhythm is chaotic. Blood pressure's high, too.'

By the time they had wheeled her into Resus, the girl had begun to have seizures, her whole body jerking in an uncoordinated fashion. James gave the teenager an injection of a benzodiazepine to control the convulsions while Sarah did a swift blood glucose test.

'She's hypoglycaemic,' she said, and James nodded.

'Give her dextrose, and thiamine to help with the alcohol problem. As soon as the seizure stops, we need to get in a fluid line.'

'Will do.' Sarah worked quickly to gain intravenous access. They both knew that the biggest danger to their patient right now was dehydration. Alcohol consumption caused loss of fluid volume due to increased urine output, and that could bring about problems with the heart and blood pressure and lead to collapse.

'I think it will be safer if we intubate her,' James said, gently introducing a short, flexible tube into the girl's windpipe and connecting it to a respirator. 'This way we can be sure she won't choke on her own vomit. And we need to get her temperature down.'

'I'll get the cool-air fan.' Sarah set that up and then paused for a moment to look down at the girl lying on the hospital bed. Her waif-like face was damp with perspiration so that her long brown hair clung to her cheeks and temples. She was dressed in party clothes, a skinny rib top and short skirt, with dark-coloured leggings that only emphasised her painfully thin frame.

'Apparently she talked about family,' she said quietly. 'From the notes, it looks as though Gemma hasn't been able to contact the parents yet. Perhaps I should talk to her friends and see what I can find out.'

'That's a good idea.' By now, James had set up the ECG machine to monitor the teenager's heart rhythm, and he had begun to write out the medication chart. 'I'm worried about the effect the alcohol and the Ecstasy are having on her heart,' he said, his mouth making a flat line. 'She's so young, and all this is such a waste.'

'They call it the love drug, don't they? It's supposed to make you feel warm and fuzzy and you want to hug everyone around you. Perhaps that was what she was looking for.'

'Maybe so, but she's ended up with a whole lot more that she didn't bargain for. If she comes out of this all right, she'll be a very lucky young woman.'

'I guess you're right. But perhaps we all do things we regret sometimes.'

He frowned, looking intently at her, his dark gaze searching her face.

She looked away, a rush of heat filling her cheeks. She didn't want to recall the things she'd done…especially that one time she'd had too much to drink…and she fervently hoped he'd forgotten it, that it hadn't made an impression on him. It had been as though she'd been determined to throw herself headlong into disaster. She shuddered, trying not to think about it. She wasn't the same person now.

She ran a hand through her long, silky, chestnut hair. 'I went a little crazy after my mother left. But I've had a lot of time to go over it in my mind.' She frowned. 'I think, all the time I was acting up, I was looking for something—something that would help me to make sense of my life and give me a reason to go on. After my mother walked out, I was hurt, desperately hurt, and bewildered more than anything else. I was sure I'd done something wrong, that I'd made her hate me so that she left me behind. I kept asking myself why else would she have done that. Didn't she know that I needed her? For a long, long time I went through a kind of grieving process.'

Her eyes clouded as she thought about those months, years of despair, and for a while she was silent, turning over the events of the past in her mind. Even now, she felt the bitter sting of that moment, watching her mother walk away, not knowing that was the last time she would ever see her—the revelation that she had gone from her life came later on, and it hit her as keenly now as if it had happened only yesterday.

'I'm sorry.' James placed the medicine chart on the bed and reached for her, his hand lightly circling her arm. 'You were only twelve years old when she left. It's no wonder that you were devastated after she'd gone.'

He drew her away from the bedside. 'Let's go and get a cup of coffee, take a break for a while. We can go outside in the fresh air if you like.'

'I…I don't know. Are you okay with leaving Rachel?' They'd been on the go for the last two or three hours and she could do with a short break, but even so she glanced doubtfully at the monitors. They were flashing up numbers and bleeping occasionally, signalling trouble, and for an instant she was uncertain what to do.

'The duty nurse will keep an eye on her. We've done all we can for her for the moment.' He signalled to a nurse who was writing up names and treatments on the white board and she nodded and came over to them.

She was young, conscientious and good at her job, but she coloured prettily as James handed her the medication chart. 'I've given her the first dose of cardiac medication,' he said, 'so her heart rhythm should begin to settle before too long. Let me know if there are any adverse changes, will you?'

'I will.' The nurse smiled at him, and Sarah wondered at the softening of her features, the molten glow of her eyes and the pink curve of her mouth. It was odd how he had that kind of effect on the women all around him. She'd seen it before, with the female foundation-year doctors, as well as with the ancillary staff. They all fell for him.

Perhaps it was understandable. She was far from immune herself, but of necessity she'd learned to steel herself against his inherent charm. Like she'd said, self-preservation was a powerful instinct. She'd heard on the grapevine that he'd dated a couple of young women doctors, but rumour had it he didn't want to commit and he'd let the relationships slide when it looked as though they were getting too heavily involved.

They bought coffees from the cafeteria and took them outside to the landscaped grounds beyond the building. Here the earth was gently undulating, grassed over, with trees and shrubs providing a pleasing back-drop, and here and there were bench tables and seats where the hospital staff could sit and eat while enjoying the sunshine.

James led the way to a table that sat in the shade of a rowan tree. The tree's pinnate leaves were dark green, rustling softly in the light breeze, a pleasing contrast to the clusters of creamy white flowers that adorned its branches.

'I'm sorry you were upset just now,' he said. His eyes darkened. 'I could see that it was difficult for you, going back over what happened.'

She gave a brief, awkward smile. 'It's all right,' she said, in a voice that was suddenly husky with emotion. 'I was young and troubled, but I found a way of getting through it eventually…with Murray's help. He helped me to see things in a different light.'

'Murray. Your neighbour.' He said it in a measured tone, a muscle flicking in his jaw. 'He seems to have been a strong influence on your life…both then and now.'

'Yes. He persuaded me to take up medicine.' Truth to tell, James had actually been the biggest influence in her life, but she wasn't about to admit that to him. He'd been patient, talking to her, making an effort to understand her, and she'd thrown it all back at him, too impulsive and reckless to care that he'd been trying to help her.

Her shoulders lifted in a negligent shrug. 'We kept in touch. Murray was always a good friend. He never judged me. Somehow he was just always there for me.'

'I suppose your father wasn't much help.'

'No, not much.' She pulled a face. 'I didn't get it at the time, why he didn't talk to me about my mother. He just clammed up, withdrew into himself. So, after I'd finished blaming myself for her leaving, I started to think it must have been his fault. He was the reason she'd walked away from us. He didn't talk about it. He kept his emotions locked up inside himself and I couldn't reach him so I started to kick out at anything and everything. I didn't care much about anything. And after the hurt there was just anger, a blinding, seething anger that seemed to grow and grow. The adults in my life had let me down and why should I worry any more about what anyone thought?'

'Do you ever hear from her or find out where she went?'

She shook her head and then sipped slowly at her coffee. 'Occasionally there would be cards. I think my dad tried to find her once, but by the time he tracked her down, she'd moved on. I know he wrote to her at the address he'd found, and a couple of months later there was a birthday card for me in the post. I was sixteen. It broke my heart.'

She rested her palm on the table, and he gently stroked the back of her hand as though he would comfort her in some small way. 'Did you ever try to get in touch with her?'

'Yes, I did, from time to time…when I got over my anger and frustration. I just wanted to know why she did it, why she went away without a word of warning. I wanted to understand how she could have been so heartless. So I wrote to the address my father had found and hoped that my letter would be forwarded on to her. I thought, if she could send cards, there must be a tiny bit of remorse for what she did, somewhere deep down. But she never replied.'

She pressed her lips together, making her mouth into a flat line. 'I still want answers, even now, but I haven't been able to find her. The Salvation Army made some enquiries for me, but nothing came of it. It's very frustrating.'

'Perhaps it would be better if you gave up on searching for her. It isn't getting you anywhere, is it?'

'I don't think I can do that. It eats away at me, the not knowing. I need answers, and somehow, without them, I don't feel as though I can move on.'

He shook his head. 'After all this time you have to find a way of putting it behind you. Going on the way you are, you might simply be raking up more heartache for yourself.'

Her chin lifted. 'Then that's the way it will have to be. I can't give up.'

They finished their coffee and went back to A and E. Sarah sought out the friends who had come along with Rachel to the emergency department and spent some time with them, trying to find out more about the demons that had driven this troubled young girl to drink herself into a coma. It seemed to her that it was a very thin thread that separated her from this teenager. By all accounts, both of them had to face up to insurmountable problems…or maybe the difficulty was that they weren't facing up to them.

At the end of her shift she was glad to go home and leave the worries of A and E behind her for a while. More patients had been admitted to the observation ward, and when she left the hospital Rachel was still unresponsive for the most part. It would be several hours before her blood alcohol level reached a safe point, and likewise the problems that the Ecstasy had caused with high blood pressure and overheating would take some time to resolve.

Murray had collected the children from school for her, and she spent half an hour chatting to him before going back to her own house with Sam and Rosie.

'My boss is coming to help out with getting the house shipshape,' she told the children as they had dinner together later in the warm kitchen. 'I'll be painting the walls in your room, Sam, so maybe you can play in the living room this evening. I don't want you and Rosie arguing while we're busy.'

Sam didn't answer, but his upper lip jutted out in a scowl, and it seemed to Sarah that might be a bad sign. He was obviously keeping his options open as far as keeping the peace was concerned.

'He had a fight with a boy called Ricky at school,' Rosie confided. 'Ricky ended up with a bruise on his leg and he told the teacher Sam did it.'

'You didn't have to tell,' Sam complained, his expression dark and his eyes giving out flint-like sparks.

'Yes, but Murray has the letter from the teacher,' Rosie said with a holier-than-thou attitude. She looked at Sarah. 'He must have forgotten to give it to you.'

There was a tap on the kitchen door at that moment, and Murray poked his head into the room. 'Is it all right if I come in?' he asked, and Sarah nodded.

'We were just talking about you,' she told him. 'Apparently you have a letter for me?'

He nodded, and held out an envelope. 'Sorry, it went out of my head when we were talking about your internet article. I came to give it to you as soon as I remembered.' He saw Sam's belligerent expression and added, 'Cheer up, old son. It could have been worse, and neither of you came out of it unscathed. Have you shown Sarah your war wounds?'

Sarah's jaw dropped. 'War wounds? What on earth happened?'

Sam began to fidget, hunching his shoulders as if he'd rather be elsewhere.

'Show me,' Sarah demanded, and he reluctantly held out his arm and rolled back the sleeve of his shirt. There were several red scratches along his forearm.

'I think you'd better explain,' she said, keeping a level tone.

'It wasn't nothin',' he muttered. 'Ricky said I couldn't play football 'cos I didn't have no football boots and I said I didn't need any, and I could play better football than him any day. Then we got into a fight.'

His grammar had gone to pieces, a sure sign that he was uptight. Sarah scanned the letter from the teacher. 'They're not taking any action because it happened outside the school grounds,' she said, and then added, 'Heavens, this all took place yesterday morning, after I dropped you off at school.' She looked at Murray, her eyes widening.

'The other parent complained to the head,' he explained. 'I didn't hear anything about it until the teacher handed me the letter today. Both boys have been reprimanded.'

'Hmm.' She glanced at Sam. 'Next time anything like this happens, you tell me straight away so that I know what I'm dealing with.' She sighed. 'And I suppose we'll have to get you some football boots. They weren't on the list, so how was I to know? We'd better go into town after I finish work tomorrow.'

Sam allowed himself an exultant grin. 'Yay!'

'Never mind "Yay",' she said. 'No more fighting.' The doorbell rang, and she stood up. 'That'll be James,' she murmured. 'Excuse me. I'll go and let him in.'

James was waiting patiently outside the front door. He looked incredibly sexy. He was dressed in casual clothes, black chinos teamed with a dark shirt that skimmed his flat stomach and draped smoothly over broad shoulders. He was long and lean and as she looked at him her heart missed a beat. Heat began to pool in her abdomen and an unbidden yearning clutched at her, causing the breath to catch in her lungs.

He studied her, those grey eyes all-seeing, assessing her in return, and a faint smile hovered on his lips. 'Aren't you going to invite me in?'

'Oh. Yes, of course. Come in.' She opened the door wider, stepping back a pace and waving him into the hallway. 'We're in the kitchen. We were just having a bit of a discussion about problems at school.'

He looked at her curiously. 'What sort of problems?'

'Boys. Fighting,' she muttered, as though that said it all.

'Uh-huh.'

They went into the kitchen, and she introduced him to Murray first of all. 'We met years ago at the rock-climbing club at the coast,' she said. 'Murray showed me all the things I needed to know, like how to use a belay device and hammer pitons into rock crevices for anchor points.' She frowned, seeing that the men were looking at one another with oddly quizzical expressions. 'Do you two actually know each other?'

'I think we may have met before,' James said, eyeing up Murray's lanky, relaxed figure. 'Didn't your company supply the equipment for one of the activity weekends on my father's estate? We held a gymkhana and a dog trial course, if I remember correctly. You came to help set everything up for the event.'

'That's right.' Murray was impressed. 'You've a good memory—that was some years ago.'

'Mmm.' James studied Murray, his grey eyes taking in everything about him, from his jeans and supple leather jacket to the square cut of his jaw and the protective, intent expression that came into his blue eyes when he glanced at Sarah.

Sarah thought back to those summer days she'd spent on the Benson estate. She remembered being invited to the events that were held there from time to time, and the gymkhana stood out particularly in her mind. She'd ridden one of the horses that day. Over the previous months James's father had had his stable manager teach her how to ride—maybe he'd taken pity on the girl whose mother had abandoned her. Whatever, she had been performing that day, and when she'd come to the end of a faultless round, she'd slid down from her horse into James's waiting arms. He'd laughed as he'd caught her, and in that moment, as his arms had closed about her, she had fallen hopelessly, instantly in love.

What girl wouldn't have lost her heart to a man as sexy and charismatic as James Benson? To a naïve six-teen-year-old, he was everything she'd ever dreamed about, and when he'd wrapped his strong arms around her she'd been in heaven, a state of bliss that she'd wanted to go on for ever and ever. She'd felt the warmth of him, his long, firmly muscled body next to hers, and as he'd steadied her and led her away to the refresh-ments tent, she'd felt that at last the world had granted her deepest heartfelt wish. He'd noticed her, he'd held her, and life couldn't get much better.

Except of course, it hadn't really been like that, had it? For James's part, he had simply been acting the host for his father's community endeavour, and it had been his role to make the contestants feel comfortable and at their ease. His natural charm had taken care of the rest.

She drew in a deep breath and tried to unscramble her brain. 'James is going to help with the renovation work,' she said now, breaking into the silence that had fallen between the two men.

'Ah, that's good. I'm glad you're getting some help.' Murray straightened, and perhaps he felt uncomfortable under James's dark scrutiny because he started towards the door. 'I'll leave you to it, then.' He glanced at the letter lying on the kitchen table. 'I wouldn't worry too much about that, if I were you.'

'No. Well, Sam is going to have to stop fighting and find some other way to solve his disputes.' She glanced at Sam, who responded with a look of benign inno-cence on his face.

Murray left and Sarah offered James coffee. 'We'll take it upstairs with us,' she suggested. 'I thought I'd make a start with the red paint in Sam's room.' She turned to the children. 'It means you'll have to share Rosie's room tonight,' she told Sam. 'Murray helped me to shift your bed in there earlier today,' she added.

Rosie's mouth opened in protest. 'Share with him? No way!' She placed her hands on her hips, taking a muti-nous pose, and Sarah's mouth made a downward quirk.

'It's only for a couple of nights, so that the smell of

paint can evaporate,' she said. 'Why don't you both go and call for the children next door? See if they want to play in the garden for a while, and after that you can go into the living room.'

Sam headed for the back door, quickly followed by Rosie, who was marshalling more arguments against sharing with her brother. 'You'd better keep your hands off my game pad,' she warned him, 'or you'll be sleeping on the landing.'

'See if I care.' The door swung shut behind them.

'They love each other really,' Sarah said. She frowned. 'At least, I think they do.'

James laughed. 'I guess we should get started on the room while we have the chance.'

'True. Who knows when things might erupt?'

All was peaceful, though, for the next hour or so, and Sarah found that she was beginning to relax in James's company. He worked on all three fireplaces, scrubbing hard to remove any rust and debris that had accumulated over the years, and then he cleaned everything down with a sponge and cloth.

'There shouldn't be any dust in the air to affect your paintwork,' he said as he worked with her in Sam's room. 'You're doing the far wall, so that's well away from here.'

They worked together in harmony, with music playing on the radio in the background, and every now and again they stopped to comment on a favourite tune or a particular melody.

'I danced to that music at Sam's christening,' Sarah commented some time later.

'It's a popular number even now.' He headed for the door. 'I'll go and wash my hands.'

She'd finished painting the wall by now, had tidied away brushes and roller, and was standing back to look at the result. It didn't look bad at all, and she'd actually managed to keep the paint off her hands and clothes. She rubbed moisturiser into her hands and turned around to study the fireplace.

James had applied a coat of red oxide to the heavy iron. At the weekend, he'd said, he would finish it off with the grate polish.

He came back from washing his hands in the bathroom to find her with a dreamy expression on her face. 'Sounds as though this tune has some special meaning for you,' he said, listening to the gentle rhythm of the music.

'I remember floating around the room feeling as though I was on a cloud.' She laughed. 'That was probably down to the wine that I had with the celebratory meal after the church service. And little Sam was so sweet, with his mop of black hair and his lovely blue-grey eyes that seemed to look deep into your soul. He was nine months old then, looking around and taking notice of everything, and I thought he was adorable... my half-brother, my family. I felt this huge surge of love for him.'

She closed her eyes, thinking about that moment, letting the music flow through her, over her and around her. 'The music stopped, and I looked at my stepmother. She was holding Sam in her arms and he was almost asleep. He had that soft, sleepy look that babies have, he was trying to stay awake and enjoy the fun, but his eyelids kept slowly closing, and Tracy was looking down at him with such love, such overwhelming happiness. And

I…' She broke off, the words catching in her throat. 'I thought, Why couldn't my mother love me like that?'

James slid his arms around her. 'Don't do this to yourself, Sarah. You don't know why she left, what went through her mind. You have to find a way to move on.'

'I know…but I don't know how…'

He held her close, his hand gently stroking the length of her spine, drawing her near to him so that their bodies meshed and her soft, feminine curves melted against the hard contours of his strong, masculine frame.

'You said it yourself, everything has happened so quickly of late. You lost your father and Tracy and you found yourself responsible for two young children. Then there was the move here, the new job. It's no wonder that you're feeling this way—your emotions are all over the place because now that you finally have time to breathe and take it all in, it's all coming home to you. You haven't had time to grieve properly.'

'I suppose you're right. It hadn't occurred to me.' She leaned against him, accepting the comfort he offered, drinking in the warmth of his body, taking refuge in the arms that circled her, keeping her close.

He kissed her lightly on the forehead, a kiss as soft as gossamer. She could barely feel it, and yet his touch seared her, its aftermath racing through her body like flame. 'I'm right,' he murmured, his voice deep and soothing, smoothing a path along her fractured nerves. 'All this will pass, and you'll get your life back together, you'll see. You've done so well to come this far.'

She wanted him to kiss her again, to hold her and kiss her on the lips, her throat, along the creamy expanse of her shoulders. He could make everything all right again. He was the only one who could do it. She laid her palm lightly against his chest. Her whole body trembled with longing, even as she knew it couldn't happen.

She'd been here before, yearning for his kisses, wanting him, only the memory of that time still haunted her dreams. She'd been seventeen, and she'd learned that the family was to move to Devon to start a new life. A new life away from James. That was how she'd thought of it, and she'd dreaded going away and leaving him behind. He had been all she'd had in the world. Her father and Tracy had been wrapped up in one another and she had simply been an outsider, looking in. How was she going to let him know how much she wanted him?

Just a few drinks, that's all it had taken, an opened bottle of wine in the fridge…no one would notice that she'd helped herself. Her father would think Tracy had drunk it, and Tracy would imagine her husband had finished it off.

It was pure Dutch courage. It was what she'd needed to give her the confidence to go and find James and show him that he needed her as much as she needed him.

And the clothes, of course…they were important, they had to be just right, extra-special. She had to look her best. And that was where her bridesmaid's dress came in, the one she'd worn to her father's wedding. It was the perfect creation for her, an off-the-shoulder cream dress in a filmy, soft material that clung to her curves and draped itself gently around her ankles. How could he resist her? Surely he would want her, and he would show her once and for all that she was the only woman in the world for him?

All she had to do was go to him, find him in his

apartment in the big country house. It was late autumn and he was home for Christmas, celebrating the beginning of his second year as a foundation doctor. She set off along the quiet, country lane to walk the half-mile to the estate.

James always left the side door unlocked until late at night, so it was easy to gain entrance to the north wing of the house. He was so startled, his eyes widening as she walked—no, sashayed—into his sitting room. Heady from the wine she'd drunk, she'd put her arms around him, letting her fingers trail through the silken hair at his nape, and she pressed her body close to his, her breasts softening against his chest. She lifted her face for his kiss. He had to want her. She wanted him, needed him desperately...

But there it all went wrong. His hands went around her in an involuntary motion, smoothing along the length of her spine, his palm coming to rest lightly on the curve of her hip. Then he sucked in his breath and his fingers gently circled her wrists, drawing her arms down from his neck, away from him.

She was stunned. This wasn't what she expected. This shouldn't be happening.

'I'm sorry, Sarah,' he said. 'I can't do this. You should go home. Come on, let me see you back to the house.' And he took off his jacket and wrapped it around her, taking her out of the room, out into the darkness of the night. The moon silvered the path, lighting their way, and she felt sick at heart. He didn't want her. He had rejected her, and she had made an almighty fool of herself. How could she face him ever again?

'Are you all right, Sarah?' The softly spoken words took her by surprise, and it was a moment before she realised that she was back in the present day, and they were standing in Sam's room, with the smell of paint filling the air and the music on the radio winding down to a soft murmur.

'I… Yes, I'm fine.' She eased herself away from him, her fingertips trailing across his shirtfront as she stepped back, putting distance between them. 'You're right,' she said huskily, 'these last few months have been an emotional roller-coaster. I'm probably overwrought and not thinking as clearly as I might.'

'Maybe you need to spend some time relaxing, instead of working on the house,' he suggested. 'A day on the beach, perhaps, or a visit to the village spring fayre. The change might do you a world of good.'

She nodded. 'I'm sure you're right. I'll have to sort something out.'

He smiled, looking at her a little oddly, as though he was trying to fathom what was going on in her head.

But she was safe enough, wasn't she? He couldn't possibly know what she'd been thinking, how close those memories had encroached on the here and now. Could he?

CHAPTER FOUR

'WILL you be coming along to the village's spring fayre?' James was writing up his patient's notes on the computer, but he looked up as Sarah came over to the desk.

'Um, when is it?'

He laughed. 'You're telling me you haven't seen all the notices posted up around the village?'

'I'm afraid I haven't.' She had the grace to look shamefaced. 'When I'm home I tend to dash about here and there, and the only things that tend to filter through to me are what to make for dinner, how did the laundry bin get full so quickly, and if Sam's managing to stay out of trouble.'

His mouth made a crooked line. 'Like I said, you need a break.'

'Yeah. Don't we all?' She bent her head so that he wouldn't see her reaction to his comment. That's what he'd told her last night, that she needed a break, and a wave of heat ran through her as she thought about it. She didn't want to recall those tender moments when she had been wrapped in his arms, but despite her misgivings the memory of that embrace had haunted her ever since. It had brought with it so many searing emotions, recollections of that earlier time when he had held her close. It was difficult enough seeing him every day, working with him, without being reminded of the foolish crush she'd had on him for all those long years.

To hide her discomfort, she began searching through the lab reports in the wire tray. 'So tell me about the fayre. I suppose I ought to support it if it's to do with the village.'

'It's tomorrow, from ten in the morning. Any money that's collected will go towards the fund for the new swimming pool—we want to build it in the grounds of the village school, so that all the local children will get the chance to learn how to swim from an early age. Being surrounded by the sea, as we are, it's really important that we keep them safe, but at the moment they have to go into the nearest town if they want to learn, and that's quite a drive for most villagers.'

She nodded. 'I see your point. It sounds like a really good cause. How's the fund doing?'

He smiled. 'Pretty well. I'm pleased with how things are going. We're almost there, and if the spring fayre brings in a goodly amount we should soon be able to start work on the pool.' He sat back in his chair, watching her, completely relaxed, his long legs stretched out in front of him. How could he be so laid back when she was distracted simply from being near him?

He was waiting for her answer and when she stayed silent he said, 'So, what do you say? Are you up for it?'

'Uh…yes, okay. I expect Rosie and Sam will enjoy a day out.'

'Good.' His mouth curved with satisfaction. 'I'll come and collect you, if you like, at—what time? Would around midday suit you?'

'Um, thanks, that will be absolutely fine.' He was only offering to do that so that he could show her the way, wasn't he? He didn't have any deep-seated interest in her, other than as a colleague, so there was nothing for her to read into his suggestion, was there? He was good with everyone at work, helping them out whenever they had problems. Why would she be any different? A peculiar frisson of dismay crept through her at the thought, but she hastily pushed it away.

Anyway, wasn't one rejection enough for her? Why would she even entertain the idea of getting involved with him outside work? It didn't count that he was helping her with the house—he'd probably taken one look at it and made up his mind that she needed all the help she could get.

'Ought I to contribute something to the stalls?' She pursed her lips, trying to decide what she might take along. 'Some groceries, perhaps, or a cake? I could make a fruit cake and ice it. Rosie's really keen on baking these days and Sam's always up for joining in.'

He seemed to be quite taken with that suggestion. 'A cake sounds like a good idea,' he said cheerfully. 'We could have a guess the weight of the cake competition.'

She nodded, giving it some thought. 'That would certainly bring in some more money. It means I'll have to make a cake that looks fairly scrumptious if it's going to end up as a prize.' A niggling doubt crept in and she added in a rueful tone, 'Perhaps I should have had a bit more practice at cake decoration.' Then a thought struck her and her eyes narrowed on him. 'You're giving this whole thing the big sell—are you on the organising committee or something?'

'Uh…you could say that. The fayre's being held in

the grounds of my house, and I've had quite a say in what's being included. And of course we have to make provision for all kinds of weather, so part of the house will be opened up as well.'

'Oh, I see.' She frowned. How would he come by the land that would be needed for such an enterprise? 'Going on past experience, an event like that could take up a big area…but you told me you weren't living on the family estate any more, didn't you? So how is it possible for you to do it?'

'You're right. I moved out some time ago. But I inherited a property from my great-grandparents—well, strictly speaking, my brother and I both shared the inheritance, but I bought out his half. He was happy for me to do that.'

'Even though he has a wife and children? Wouldn't he have welcomed the chance to have a property of his own instead of sharing with your parents?'

'Jonathan's comfortable staying on the family estate. There's plenty of room for them all there, and they have a separate wing to themselves. He acts as manager of the estate for my parents, so it's really convenient for him to be living on site.'

'I imagine it would be.' She hadn't reckoned on this, and it took some getting used to, discovering that James had not moved to an ordinary detached property, as she'd imagined, but instead he'd inherited another grand house. It just went to show that there was still this huge divide between them and perhaps she ought to have realised that his wealthy background would always be a part of him.

Giving herself a moment to absorb all this, she

glanced at the paper in her hand and then frowned as she read through Nicola Carter's test results.

'Is something wrong?'

'Not wrong…a bit worrying, perhaps. I have the results here for Mrs Carter, the patient who collapsed after the road accident with bruising to the liver. From the looks of these lab-test results, she has a secondary adrenal insufficiency. Both the ACTH and the cortisol levels are low.'

His expression was thoughtful. 'We'd better do an MRI scan to see if anything's going on with the pituitary gland. In the meantime, we'll go ahead with steroid treatment and see how she responds to that.'

'I'll see to it. I'm going to look in on Rachel, too, to see how she's doing. Hopefully, she's over the worst as far as the drug abuse goes, and the alcohol should be out of her system by now, so I might be able to talk to her, and maybe find out if she needs counselling of some sort.'

'They all need counselling when they get into that state,' he said in a dry tone. 'It wasn't an unusual situation for her, by all accounts. Her blood-alcohol level was sky high, and drug-taking has been a common thing for her.'

'Well, I'll do what I can for her in the meantime. Are we going to move her on to a medical ward?'

'Yes, and Mrs Carter, too, as soon as we have the results of the scan.'

Sarah nodded, and hurried away to set things in motion. She was relieved to be able to put some distance between James and herself. It was more difficult for her than she had expected, working with him. It had shocked her to the core to relive all those old humiliating feelings last night, when she'd been in his arms. What must he think of her? And yet he'd said nothing, either then or now…and he'd certainly never commented on her immature, futile attempt at seduction when she was in her teens. It was hard to know whether that made things better or worse.

The rest of the day passed quickly, with a flurry of emergencies being brought into A and E after a traffic accident and a near-drowning off the coast at Land's End. They brought their patient, an eleven-year-old boy, back from the brink of death, and Sarah couldn't help thinking that James was right about the need for swimming lessons. The sea could be a dangerous place for the unwary.

Rachel was able to sit up in bed by now, and the endotracheal tube had been removed so that she was breathing unaided, but she looked pale and unhappy when Sarah went to see her. Her long brown hair was lank and her hazel eyes were dull and lacking in any kind of interest in her surroundings.

'Hello, Rachel,' Sarah greeted her. 'How are you feeling today?'

'Tired. My chest hurts… I'm a bit breathless.'

Sarah nodded, and checked the heart and respirations monitor. 'It's an after-effect of the Ecstasy you took,' she explained. 'You've had some problems with your heart rhythm, but things are beginning to settle down. That would have been worrying enough on its own, but the alcohol added even more complications. It does seem as though you've set yourself on a bit of a downward spiral. I'd like to think we could help you to get your life back on course. Maybe we could talk about anything that's bothering you.'

'There's no point.' The girl turned her head away.

'There's a lot of point, surely? Your friends have been to see you, I hear. They're obviously very worried about you.'

Rachel didn't react, apart from a slight movement of her shoulders, as though she could scarcely find the energy to respond. Sarah said softly, 'Is there anyone we can contact for you—your parents, for instance? I saw from your notes that you're living in a flat, so I presume you left the family home a while ago.'

Rachel shook her head. 'There's no one.'

'I'm sorry.' Sarah frowned. 'Do you want to tell me about it? Did something happen to your parents?'

'No. Not really. We were always arguing, it was a bad atmosphere, and I decided it would be better if I moved out. My brother left a couple of years ago, and I thought I'd do the same.'

'Do you keep in touch with your brother?'

'Not lately. I used to see Harry every now and again, but since I left home last year I haven't heard from him. He was sharing a house with a friend, but he's not there any more.'

'But you used to get on well together?'

Rachel nodded. She closed her eyes, and Sarah could see that even this short conversation had been too much for her. If they could find this brother, perhaps he could do something to lift his sister out of this self-destructive pattern of behaviour. 'I'll leave you to get some rest,' she said quietly. 'Try to drink plenty of fluids—I see your friends have left you some orange squash. The nurses will keep your water jug topped up. Just ask them if you need any help while you're not able to get out of bed.'

After work, Sarah picked up the children from

Murray's house and took them into town to buy football boots for Sam and new shoes for Rosie. 'I think we'll pick up some ingredients for sugar paste and some food colouring, while we're about it,' she told them.

'Why? Are we making cakes?' Rosie asked. 'We did sugar paste at school and made all these little flowers. They were lovely. And you can eat them, too.'

'Well, just one cake,' Sarah explained, 'for the village fayre. We'll make it after we've had our evening meal. And then tomorrow, when it's completely cool, we'll have a go at icing it.' It meant she would be spending what was left of the evening searching the internet for tips on how to decorate cakes but, then, it was all in a good cause.

'There we are… I think that's turned out pretty well, don't you?' she said later that evening, as she took the rich fruit cake from the oven and slid it onto a rack.

'It looks yummy,' Rosie commented, admiring the luscious, deep golden brown cake.

'And it smells good,' Sam agreed. He pulled a face. 'But I think we ought to be able to keep it after the fayre and eat it.'

'Mmm. Sorry about that.' Sarah smiled. 'But whoever guesses the weight gets to win it and take it home.'

His expression brightened. 'We'll just weigh it, then,' he said, licking his lips in anticipation.

'Away with you! That would be cheating.' She laughed. 'Anyway, I'm sure there'll be lots more goodies for you to try when we go to the fayre tomorrow.'

The next day, Sarah was up early, anxious to ice the cake before James arrived to take them over to his house. She was a little bit apprehensive, thinking about the day ahead, being with James away from work, and the only way she could counter those feelings was to keep busy. She covered the cake with a layer of marzipan and then spread the white icing over the top and sides.

It had been a long, long while since she had spent a day out with James, and it was one thing to do that on neutral territory, but somehow the prospect of being with him on his home ground was a different thing altogether. It was far too intimate a setting, and not at all what she had envisaged when she'd made up her mind to keep things on a professional basis between them. She gave a rueful smile. Her plans in that regard had probably been scuppered from the outset, what with having lunch with him and with him helping her to renovate the house. Hadn't it always been that way in her dealings with James? Whatever she decided, life had a way of turning everything upside down.

'What are we going to do?' Rosie asked, yawning as she came into the kitchen some time later. She blinked, trying to accustom her eyes to the sunshine that filtered into the kitchen through the slats in the blinds at the window. 'Are we going to cover it with icing sugar flowers, or ribbons and bows? Or both?' She looked at the collection of decorative materials that Sarah had set out on the pine table.

'I'm not sure yet,' Sarah said. 'We'll have to think about it while we have breakfast.'

'I think we should do a water picture, if it's to get money for the pool,' Sam announced, coming to join them at the table. He was still dressed in his pyjamas, and his shoulders slumped as though he would much rather be snuggled up in bed but hadn't wanted to miss out on anything.

'That's actually quite a good idea,' Rosie said in a surprised tone. She looked at her brother as though she didn't quite know him. 'It'll be good to have a swimming pool at the school. Everyone will be able to have lessons, or practise, won't they?' Then she frowned. 'Mum taught us how to swim when we were small. It was fun, and we used to go to the pool every week. She said we were her little water nymphs.' Her grey eyes clouded momentarily and Sam's expression dissolved into sudden anguish.

Sarah sucked in a silent breath. 'Maybe we should make this a special cake, then,' she suggested, thinking quickly. 'We could do a design to show we're thinking of your mother, with a garden pond, perhaps, and two water nymphs sitting on flower petals nearby. What do you think?'

'Oh, yes, that'd be brilliant.' Sam was smiling now, and Rosie had a thoughtful look about her.

'We should have a blue colour for the pond,' she said, 'and there should be some water lilies on it. You'll need green sugar paste for those, and white and yellow for the flowers.' She inspected the bottles of food colouring that were set out on the table. 'And then some bigger flowers for the water nymphs to sit on.'

'Or they could be in trees, with little houses in them.' Sam was looking pleased with himself, excited about the project. 'And there could be a frog on the pond and a boy fishing.'

'That sounds lovely, but let's not get too carried away,' Sarah laughed. 'The simpler the better, I think. After all, we only have a few hours before James comes to pick us up, and I'm not exactly used to doing this sort of thing.'

* * *

By the time James arrived at midday, they were just about ready, with the children dressed and raring to go and Sarah putting the finishing touches to her make-up. She was wearing dark blue jeans and a smooth-fitting cotton top, and she'd pinned her hair up into a loose topknot.

'Hi. Are you all set?' James asked. He gave her an admiring glance and then relieved her of the holdall she was carrying and tested the weight with his hand. 'Heavens, what have you packed in here? We're going for an afternoon out, not a week's trekking expedition.' He grinned.

'It's just a few extras—an emergency first-aid kit and clothes in case the weather turns to rain, or one or other of the children manages to fall into a mud pile or some such.'

He laughed. 'That's hardly likely to happen, is it?'

She sent Sam a surreptitious look. 'Don't you believe it,' she whispered. 'I still haven't recovered from taking them to the zoo last month.'

'That wasn't my fault,' Sam put in with a frown. There was obviously nothing wrong with his hearing. 'I didn't start it. I was looking at the monkeys and Rosie got fed up waiting and pushed me out of the way.'

'Did not!' Rosie let out a shriek of indignation. 'I was trying to get by him.'

'Did too. And so I pushed her back and then we got into a fight and we both ended up rolling down the slope. Wasn't my fault it had been raining and the ground was all messy.'

Sarah groaned. 'Oh, please…don't remind me.'

James looked puzzled. 'I take it things got a bit out of hand?'

She nodded. 'As they do quite often.' She studied him briefly. 'You seem surprised. But you must know how these things are…you're used to children, aren't you? You said your brother had a boy and a girl.'

'Yes, but they're only one and two years old.' He gave her a doubtful look. 'There are never any problems with them…not that I can see, anyway.'

'Oh, dear.' She gave him a sympathetic look. 'I can see this is all new to you. For myself, I've watched Rosie and Sam growing up, and I have friends whose offspring are always up to something or other, so nothing much surprises me any more where children are concerned. You've been well and truly sheltered, haven't you, living the bachelor lifestyle these last few years?'

'I suppose I have.' He smiled as they walked out to his car, a sporty, silver streak of mouth-watering beauty. It had a soft top, and the hood was down to leave the occupants free to enjoy the sunshine and fresh breeze. 'Hop in the back, you two,' he said to the children, tossing the holdall into the boot. He glanced at Sarah. 'Is that the cake you're carrying? Do you want me to put it in here along with the holdall?'

'I think I'd rather keep it with me,' she said, guarding the cake tin as though it was something precious, not to be let out of her sight. 'After all the work we've put into it, I want to be sure we get it there in one piece.'

'I can't wait to see it. Do I get to have a peek now?'

'Okay.' She carefully prised the lid off the tin. 'You won't be able to see the sides this way. Rosie and Sam decided we needed pale green fronds all the way round, to represent reeds.'

He looked into the tin and gave a low whistle of appreciation.

'So, you like it?' she asked.

'I certainly do. That's a real work of art. If I won it, I wouldn't be able to bring myself to cut into it.' He glanced at her, his gaze full of admiration. 'What a brilliant idea, to have a water theme. I love those little water nymphs.'

She nodded. 'That came from Sam. He's quite a deep thinker, underneath it all. And both of the children helped, especially with the flowers and leaves.' She'd made the wings for the water nymphs herself, lovely gossamer creations made from golden spun sugar strands.

'I can see why you want to keep it safe,' he said, waiting as she carefully replaced the lid on the tin. He held open the car door for her as she slid into the passenger seat. 'You're amazing…definitely a woman of hidden talents.'

She mumbled something incoherent in return and he gave her a quizzical look as he slid behind the wheel of the car. As if he'd ever wanted to explore those talents. The thought came to her unbidden, and she swiftly pushed it away. She had to keep her mind off that track. The past was done with, finished, and it was high time she acknowledged that, if only for her own peace of mind.

He followed the coast road for a while, and then turned off down a winding country lane. At first there were houses clustered together but these gradually became more and more isolated until finally they came to what must have been a large farmhouse at one time. James took them along a wide driveway, bordered on either side by manicured lawns, where stalls were set out. Some displayed goods for sale, while others offered games to be played and prizes to be won.

'Here we are,' he said, pulling up in front of the house and cutting the engine. 'This is my place.'

'Wow.' Sam was impressed. He jumped out of the car and stared up at the wide frontage of the two-storey building. 'Do you live here all by yourself?'

'I do. But a lady comes from the village to clean up for me a couple of days a week. She does a bit of cooking, too, because she's afraid I might starve to death, left to my own devices.'

Rosie frowned. 'Would you really? Starve, I mean?' She was obviously worried by that. 'You could always put stuff in the microwave, you know. It's easy to do that. That's what my mum used to do when we all wanted different things.'

'That's what I do, too, sometimes.' He smiled at her. 'You should come and see my kitchen. I've just had it re-modelled, and there's a microwave and a tabletop slow-cooker in there, as well as a built-in oven—all kinds of equipment that I still have to learn to use.'

'You should ask Sarah to help you out,' Rosie suggested helpfully. 'She's had to learn how to do all sorts of cooking 'cos she says we're not allowed to eat rubbish. We have to grow and be strong and healthy.'

Sam flexed his muscles. 'I've been eating lots,' he said. 'I'm going to get big so's I can beat Ricky Morton.' He began to jab at the air with his fists, like a boxer.

Sarah raised her eyes heavenwards. 'What did I say about no fighting?' she reminded him.

'Yeah, well…if he comes at me, I'll be ready for him.' He made another lunge with his arm.

Sarah looked once more at the house as they started

to walk towards the stalls. It was built of mellow, sand-coloured stone, and there were lots of Georgian-style windows, with an entrance porch at the mid-point. Jasmine rambled around and over the porch canopy, its waxy, star-shaped white flowers adding a purity and delicate beauty to the archway. The walls were covered in part with dark green ivy, lending the house an old-world charm. 'It's lovely,' she said, smiling appreciatively.

'I'm glad you like it.' James looked fondly at his home, set against a backdrop of mature trees and colourful shrubs. 'It's always had a special place in my heart—not just because of the house, though it is beautiful, but because my grandparents lived here before they bought the house where my parents live now. There are so many memories locked up in this place that I couldn't bear to see the house go onto the open market. It belongs within the family.'

There was a far-away look in his eyes. 'My brother and I used to come here on visits, and we had our own rooms when we stayed over.' He winced. 'After my grandparents left, it was let out as apartments for holidaymakers for a number of years. It's taken a while but it's good to have it restored to a family home once more.'

She nodded, understanding how he must feel. 'And to think I worry about my small renovations,' she said with a laugh. 'I couldn't even begin to tackle something like this.'

'Can we go on the bouncy castle?' Rosie asked, looking eagerly towards where children were jumping and squealing with delight. 'I can see Frances from school, and her brother, Tom. He's in Sam's class.'

'Yes, that's okay. We'll be looking at the stalls over here when you've finished.'

The children hurried away. 'We could put your cake on the table next to where the raffle is being drawn,' James suggested. 'One of the helpers made up a "Guess the weight" chart, so there's nothing else that needs to be done.'

'All right.' They put the cake in pride of place on the table, and straight away a small crowd formed, oohing and aahing over it.

'It's already looking as though that will be a money-spinner,' James said. 'Perhaps Rosie was right…you could give me a few tips on how to cook.' He slid an arm around her waist as they walked away, drawing her close to him and setting up a tingling response in her that rippled through her from head to toe.

'I'd be happy to do that, though I can't see you spending much time in the kitchen, state-of-the-art equipment or not,' she answered, trying to ignore the heat that was spreading through her. 'You're far more likely to drop by Martha's shop for doughnuts and sticky buns.' She looked him over, lean and muscled in chinos and T-shirt, with not an ounce of fat to spare. 'Heaven knows how you manage to stay so fit looking.'

He grinned. 'It must be all that hands-on exercise I get in A and E that does it. It certainly seems to work for you, anyway.' His glance shimmered over her, and Sarah felt a small glow start up inside her. At least he wasn't calling her skinny any more.

'I don't think that's just down to the work at the hospital. There are two energetic youngsters who have a big hand in keeping me on my toes.'

'True.' They wandered around the stalls for a while,

trying their hands at spinning the wheel to win a soft toy, and knocking down skittles for a bag of sweets. Rosie and Sam came to join them after a while, playing hoopla and firing water pistols at toy ducks to see if they could knock them off the stand. Then the children sat for a few minutes while their faces were painted and they were transformed into a glittery princess and a fiery tiger.

'You look fantastic,' Sarah told them, and James nodded in agreement.

'But we came here with Rosie and Sam,' he said with a puzzled frown. 'Any idea where they've gone?'

Rosie giggled.

They spent some time at the barbecue, munching on succulent chicken and rice, kebabs and salad. Then Rosie and Sam wandered over to one of the toy stalls, keen to spend some of their pocket money on new treasures. They came back a few minutes later, eager to grab Sarah's attention.

'Can we go round with Frances and Tom for a bit?'

'There are pony rides round the back of the house,' Sam added, 'and we want to have a go. Their mum says it's all right. She said we could meet up with you in the refreshments tent at four o'clock, if that's all right with you.' He pointed towards Frances's mother in the distance, who mouthed carefully and gesticulated that she would look after them.

Sarah nodded and mouthed 'Thank you' in return. She'd met and talked with Kate Johnson on several occasions and knew she would carefully watch over them. 'Okay. That's fine with me. If you need us before then, we'll be out here somewhere, looking at the stalls.'

'Or maybe we'll be in the house,' James put in. 'I thought I might show Sarah around.'

'Okay.' The children ran off to join their friends, and James took Sarah's arm, guiding her towards the tombola table. 'Let me buy you some tickets,' he said. 'I'm sure you'd love to win a basket of fruit, wouldn't you?'

'I certainly would,' she said, eyeing the basket that had pride of place amongst the beans, sauces and pickles. Instead, she ended up with a jar of strawberry jam. 'That's an excellent jam,' she said, looking closely at the jar. 'I love it, but Sam will pick out all the strawberries and put them to one side.'

'Tut-tut…' James smiled, his mouth crooking attractively. 'That's sacrilege.' They reached the coconut shy, and he took careful aim with a wooden ball, hitting the target full on.

A minute or so later he weighed the coconut in his hand and said in a droll tone, 'I don't even like coconut…and have you ever tried to open up one of these things?'

She chuckled. 'I dare say a hammer and chisel would come in pretty handy.' She walked with him to the plant stall, picking out a selection of plants for her small garden. 'I don't have a lot of room out back,' she told him, 'but I thought I could brighten the borders with begonias and marigolds. And I love antirrhinums, so I have to find a spot for those.' She gazed into the distance, looking at his beautifully landscaped gardens, where flowering shrubs added swathes of colour to the front of the house. There were low-spreading berberis with an abundance of orangey-yellow flowers, magnificent cotoneasters and attractive yellow cytisus.

'I'll carry these for you,' James said, helping to place

her purchases in a plastic plant tray. He wedged the coconut in one corner. 'Perhaps we should drop these off at the house, and I'll give you the grand tour?'

'That sounds good to me.' She smiled at him, and realised that she had enjoyed these last few hours. Away from work, relieved of responsibilities for an hour or two, she'd been able to relax, and she discovered that being with him was fun. They talked, shared anecdotes, and took pleasure in the simple things of life. Perhaps she was living dangerously, being this close to him, watching him smile as he looked around and saw how everyone was making the most of their day out, but for the moment she was glad to cast her anxieties to one side.

'I've had quite some time to make the changes here,' he said as he led the way into the house. Some of the rooms had been opened up to the visitors to the fayre, and French doors were open to allow easy access. There were cake stalls in here, and a table set up with a tea urn and cups and saucers. A few tables and chairs had been laid out so that people could take a few minutes to sit and chat over a cup of tea, with cake or scones, or even appetising sandwiches cut into small squares.

'Let's go through to the rooms that aren't being used for the fayre,' James suggested, taking her through an archway into a spacious hall. He'd taken the precaution of labelling the doors in here with signs saying 'Private'. They went into a large room, filled with light from a number of tall windows along one side. 'I use this as a study,' he said. 'If I need to keep up with the latest medical research, I come in here to sit at the desk and use the computer. Or if I want to read or listen to music, I have everything I need in here.'

'You certainly have a lot of books,' Sarah remarked, looking around. Bookshelves lined one wall, filled with an assortment of reading material, from medical and scientific volumes to travel books and a collection of the latest bestsellers. There was an armchair by the open fireplace, cosy and inviting, with well-stuffed cushions and a footstool close by. 'I could curl up in here for a week, just reading the murder mysteries you have on this shelf alone.' She trailed a finger over the spine of one novel, her eyes shining. 'I love anything by this writer,' she said. 'I've read everything he's ever published.'

'You're welcome to drop by any time and make yourself at home,' he offered, his grey glance moving over her like the lick of flame. 'I'd be more than happy to have you spend time here.'

Heat filled her cheeks. Was this how he managed to charm all the women at work? She was more than tempted to take him up on his offer, but a cautious inner voice warned her that it could only lead to trouble.

'Seriously, if you want to borrow any of the books, that's fine, just help yourself.' He smiled at her. 'I might have known you'd have a taste for the more exciting, edge-of-the-seat kind of writing. That daredevil, always-up-for-a-challenge girl has never really gone away, has she?'

'Oh, I wouldn't say that. I've learned that there are other kinds of challenge, like medicine, for example, that can be just as stimulating.'

'Yes, you're right.' He nodded, becoming serious once more. 'I think I've always wanted to be a doctor deep down, especially since I realised that you can make a difference by stepping in when someone's seriously ill or suffering from life-threatening trauma. I wanted to be first on the scene, with the ability to save lives—but you need to have a good team working with you. That's why I try to get the best of both worlds, by working in the hospital and outside with the air ambulance. It makes for a good balance, and stops the work from becoming mundane.'

'Yes, I'm with you there.'

They wandered from room to room, and it became clear that he had an eye for what was elegant and uncluttered. Everywhere was tastefully furnished, with colours that reflected nature, soft greens, pale gold and shades of russet. There were period pieces here and there—a couple of Hepplewhite chairs and a Georgian inlaid card table in the study, and a grandfather clock and oak settle in the sitting room.

The floorboards here were covered with luxurious oriental rugs and there was a wood-burning stove to provide warmth on chilly evenings.

The kitchen was just as he had said, completely fitted out with modern equipment, all discreetly blended with natural oak cupboards and marble worktops, and an island bar where you could sit and enjoy a cup of coffee while watching TV on a pull-down screen. At one end of the room there was a table and chairs next to the window that overlooked the landscaped garden. On another wall there was an antique oak dresser displaying beautiful hand-painted crockery.

'Mmm…you have everything you could possibly want in here,' she said. 'It's a dream kitchen. It would be a crime not to whip up some delicious meals in here.'

'I suppose so…though I've learned I can get by quite happily on take-away food, especially since the Chinese restaurant set up in the village a few months ago. They do a fantastic chop suey and egg fried rice.'

'Oh, don't!' she said on a soft sigh. 'I've eaten lunch, but I could still work my way through chop suey, chow mein and sweet and sour chicken. They're my absolute favourites.'

He chuckled. 'Perhaps we'd better move on from the kitchen. I'll show you upstairs.'

He led the way, showing her onto a wide landing, where several doors led off in various directions. 'There are four bedrooms, all with their own en suites,' he told her. They walked from one to the other, and Sarah was impressed by each one in turn.

'What do you think?' he asked. 'I've done them out in pale, restful colours, and carpeted them so that they're quiet and comfortable. I know some people don't like carpets, but I tend to wander about in bare feet first thing in the morning, and having wool underfoot seems to make life so much more relaxing.'

'I think they're just perfect. Especially this master bedroom.' She could imagine him padding about in here, bare-chested, yawning and stretching as he looked out of his window onto the garden below. This room was filled with his presence…everything in here reflected his calm, understated vitality. It was something she'd always admired in him, that effortless way he had of moving, all that latent energy waiting to be unleashed. And now…now she began to feel hot and bothered, overwhelmed by a sudden rush of hormonal feverish-ness. A pulse started to throb at the base of her throat and her chest felt tight.

'Are you all right?' He moved closer to her, search-ing her face, a small frown indenting his brow, and for once she couldn't hide the flush of heat that swept along her cheekbones. Small beads of perspiration broke out on her forehead.

'I'm fine. A bit hot, that's all,' she said huskily. 'Perhaps we should go.'

He shook his head. 'Sit down for a while. You look as though you're going to faint or something.' He waved a hand towards the bed. 'I'll open a window.'

'No, I'll be fine, really. There's no need for you to do that. Perhaps the salad dressing I had earlier was a little salty. I should have had something to drink.'

'I'll get you some water. But you need to sit down,' he insisted, taking her gently by the arm and leading her over to the bed. 'In fact, maybe you should lie down for a while.' He felt her forehead with the back of his hand. 'You're really very hot.'

'I'm… It's nothing, really…' Her voice faded, and suddenly as James moved away from the bed it seemed like a good idea if she were to lie back for a while. Perhaps he was right after all. Maybe it wasn't hormones that were troubling her. She'd rushed about yesterday evening, seeing to the children, preparing the cake and studying cake decoration late into the night. And then from early this morning she'd been on the go, sorting the laundry, doing the chores and icing the masterpiece. And there'd been the notes she'd had to finish for her internet article. She'd been working to a deadline…

Her eyelids were heavy. It wouldn't hurt to close them for a second or two, would it? She heard him moving about in the bathroom, that gloriously cool room with the bathroom suite that gleamed palely and the ceramic tiled walls that reflected exquisite good taste. Her

mouth was dry, and she could feel heat rising along the
column of her throat. It felt damp to the touch.

There was something attached to her arm. She
looked at it in vague disbelief. A blood-pressure monitor? James was taking her blood pressure?

'What are you doing?' she said, frowning, a head-
ache starting at her temples.

'Your blood pressure's way too high,' James murmured, releasing the cuff from around her arm. 'No
wonder you felt strange. Here, drink this.' He slid a
hand behind her shoulders and gently raised her to a
sitting position. With his other hand, he held a glass to
her lips and she felt the cold drops of water trickle into
her mouth.

She drank thirstily, and when she had finished he
carefully laid her down again.

'You should get some rest,' he said, giving her a concerned look. 'I think you've probably been overdoing
things lately. With that, and the move from Devon to
Cornwall, and taking on the care of the children, you've
had a lot to take on board. Your body's telling you to
slow down, take time to breathe.'

She tried to sit up. 'The children,' she said. 'I should
go and take over from Kate.'

'No. I'll see to it. You stay here. Try to get some
sleep. There's nothing to bother you here, no one to
worry about. I'll see to everything.'

'I'm so sorry,' she muttered. 'I can't believe this is
happening. It has been such a lovely afternoon.'

'It still is,' he said, his mouth tilting at the corners.
He laid a hand lightly on her shoulder, and she thought
for a moment that he was going to brush her cheek with
his hand, but then he brought his fingers down to her

cotton top and he slowly began to undo the buttons at her throat.

'I… You…' She tried to protest, but the words wouldn't come out, and she simply stared at him, wide eyed, her lips parting a fraction.

'There's no need for you to panic,' he said. 'I'm not trying to take advantage of you. I'm only undoing the first few buttons to cool you down. There's nothing for you to worry about.'

'No?'

It was a query, and he answered with a smile. 'Any other time, maybe it might have been different…but right now I want to look after you,' he said. 'You'll be safe here, I promise. Close your eyes and get some sleep.'

Any other time… Her mind did a strange kind of flip as she absorbed that, but then caution overtook her once more. 'The children…' she said, her voice slurring as weariness overcame her. 'You don't know how to…'

'They'll be fine. I'll let them loose on my DVD collection. And when they're tired of that, we'll make supper.'

'All right.' She closed her eyes and let herself sink into the soft, cushioning duvet. 'Thanks.'

She didn't know what was happening to her but it was sheer bliss to simply lie here and do nothing, to let the healing power of sleep overtake her.

Her mind drifted, oblivion taking over. She thought she felt him move closer, lean down and brush her forehead with a kiss that was as soft as a cotton-wool cloud.

But he wouldn't do that, of course. She must be dreaming.

CHAPTER FIVE

SARAH slowly opened her eyes. She wasn't sure what had woken her, but the room was dark, and for a while she lay there, trying to recall where she was and what had happened. The last thing she remembered as she'd drifted away had been the heavenly feel of the mattress beneath her, as though she was being enveloped in softness. Later, she'd stirred, feeling a chill in the air, but soon afterwards there had been the sensation of something floaty being draped over her, and she'd sunk back into a blissful, deep sleep.

Now she tried to sit up, her eyes becoming accustomed to the shadows and the faint glow of moonlight that seeped into the room through the curtains.

'I didn't mean to disturb you,' James said softly, his voice deep and reassuringly calm. He switched on the bedside lamp, and a pool of golden light shimmered around her. 'I saw that you were a bit restless, so I made some hot chocolate.'

'Oh, thank you, that was thoughtful of you,' she murmured, still drowsy. She frowned. 'What time is it? How can it be dark? Surely I haven't slept for all that long?'

He placed a tray on the bedside table and sat down

on the edge of the wide bed. 'It's around ten o'clock. Once you settled down, you were well away.'

'Oh, no… I can hardly believe it. How could I have done that?' It suddenly struck her that she was supposed to be looking after the children, and she sat up straight in a panic. 'The children…'

'They're fine. They're fast asleep in the guest rooms. I told them they could sleep in their underwear for to-night.'

'But… Oh, this is awful. I let them down. I should go to them…'

He laid a hand on her shoulder and gently pressed her back against the pillows. 'You don't have to go any-where. I explained to them that you were very, very tired and that you needed to rest. Of course, they wouldn't take my word for it and they insisted on coming up here to see you. Once they knew you hadn't been kid-napped or whisked away anywhere, they were fine. They watched a DVD and then we made sandwiches and popcorn.'

'You had popcorn in your kitchen?' She sent him a doubtful look and he grinned, handing her a mug of hot chocolate.

'Drink that. It'll help you settle for the night. The popcorn was Sam's. He bought a bag from the food stall and Rosie showed us how to heat it up in the mi-crowave. I had no idea you could do that with corn.'

Her mouth curved. 'Well, I guess we learn something new every day.' She sipped the creamy chocolate and sighed with contentment. 'This is delicious.' Then she frowned. 'I really should get them home.'

'No, you don't have to do that.' He shook his head. 'It would be a shame to wake them.'

She chewed at her lower lip. 'We've been a lot of trouble to you, disturbing your peace. You probably had plans for this evening.'

'I didn't, beyond finishing off the fireplaces at your house.' He laughed. 'How sad is that?'

'Oh, enormously sad, for a man in his prime.' She laughed with him. 'Seriously, though, thanks for taking care of Sam and Rosie. It can't have been easy for you if you're not used to children.'

'It was okay.' A small line etched its way into his brow. 'They never stop, do they, kids? You think you have them settled, that everything's sorted, and they come up with something you never thought of…like "Can we sleep in a tent in the garden?" That was Sam. And "Why don't we make a spaghetti Bolognese?" That was Rosie. "You only need mince and tomato puree and herbs," she said, "and spaghetti, of course." Which would have been fine, seeing that I had some herbs in the kitchen.'

'And the rest of the ingredients?'

'Unfortunately, no.' He shook his head, his mouth making a wry shape. 'She doesn't have a very high opinion of my culinary efforts, I'm afraid.'

She smiled, swallowing more of the chocolate, before looking at him curiously. 'Did you ever think about having a family of your own? I mean, seeing your brother settled with his wife and children, did you think you might want to do that some time?'

'Some time, maybe, with the right woman.' His gaze rested on her intently for a moment or two, his gaze dark and unreadable, then he shrugged awkwardly and appeared to give the matter some thought. 'I've been too busy, up to now, with one thing and another, working my way up the career ladder. There have been a lot of specialist exams, different hospital jobs along the way. A wife and family probably wouldn't have fitted in too well with all that.'

'I suppose not.' Was that the reason he hadn't wanted to get more deeply involved with any of the women he had dated? From what she'd heard back at the hospital, there were more than a couple of women who mourned the fact that he hadn't wanted more than a light-hearted romance. She put down the mug.

His glance trailed over her, lingering on the burnished chestnut of her hair that framed the pale oval of her face, before he let it glide over the silken smoothness of her arms. 'What about you? I'd have expected someone to have snatched you up by now.'

She shifted a little under his dark-eyed scrutiny. She was still dressed in jeans and cotton top, but her buttons were undone, exposing the creamy swell of her breasts, and the light from the lamp added a soft sheen to her bare arms. She was covered with a light duvet, and now she pulled this up around her. 'I don't think I'm settling-down material, I'm afraid. I have this problem believing in happy ever after.'

'Ah…yes.' There was a regretful note in his voice. 'I can see how you might feel that way. When your mother went away, she left you with a scar that refuses to heal, didn't she?'

She glanced at him briefly from under her lashes. Her mother hadn't been the only one to do that to her, although the pain he'd caused her had been done unknowingly. 'Something like that.'

'But you've had boyfriends?' He was looking at her intently, a faint glitter in his eyes.

She nodded. 'Some.' She wasn't going to enlarge on that. Either they'd become too keen and she had ended the relationships, or they just hadn't gelled with her. Anyway, there was only one man she'd ever really wanted and he'd made it pretty clear years ago that he didn't want her.

James laid his hand over hers. 'You should get some sleep,' he said. 'It'll do you the world of good to rest and rid yourself of your cares for a while. I'll look in on the children, but I don't think you need have any worries on that score.'

'But this is your room… I'm in your bed.' She tried to sit upright once more but the duvet hindered her, wrapping itself around her.

'Mmm…' His mouth quirked wickedly and there was a gleam in his eyes as his gaze shimmered over her. 'I'd be more than happy to join you…breathtakingly happy, in fact…but I've a feeling that would be a big mistake. You're vulnerable right now, and you'd probably hate me in the morning.'

She drew in a sharp breath, her eyes widening. Was he really, actually saying that he wanted her? She made a second attempt to sit up.

He gently urged her back down, laying his hands on her shoulders in such a way that stirred up a fever inside her. 'Relax,' he said. 'I'll be in the room next door. If there's anything you need, just call out.'

The mere thought of doing that made her heart begin to throb heavily in her chest, banging against her rib-cage. Should she wind her arms around him and tell him just how much she wanted to keep him close? What if she were to call out for him in the night and wait for him to come to her? Would he reject her this time, as he had done once before? Undoubtedly not, from the looks of things…but dared she risk everything in doing that?

But then he stood up, looking down at her for a moment or two before heading towards the door. She gave a soft sigh of relief mingled with regret. She wasn't thinking straight. How could she even imagine how it would be to lose herself in him…this man who couldn't commit?

After he'd gone, she switched off the lamp and lay down, snuggling under the warmth of the duvet. Her body ached with longing for what might have been.

In the morning, after a deep sleep, she woke feeling renewed, refreshed and full of energy. When she drew back the curtains, it was to a bright day with the sun making the colours of nature even more vivid than usual. She opened the bedroom window, breathing in the crisp, fresh air, and if she listened carefully, she was sure she could hear the sea in the distance, dashing against the rocks. James had a truly wonderful home, in a perfect setting.

She showered quickly, washing her hair, and then wrapped herself in a clean, white towelling robe that she found in the airing cupboard. She'd washed her underwear and cotton top, and left them on the heated towel rail to dry. They wouldn't need ironing, and within an hour or two they should be ready for her to put back on. There was a hairdryer in a drawer in the bedroom, and she sat for a few minutes at the dressing table, blow-drying her long hair.

James was in the room next door, he'd said, so she sought out the other two guest rooms and looked in on the children. They were both fast asleep, Rosie, pink cheeked, her arms flung out on the duvet, Sam curled up under his covers, with only his nose peeping out.

She smiled, and quietly left them, making her way downstairs. To her surprise, James was in the kitchen.

'I didn't realise you were up,' she said. 'I thought it was early.'

'It is.' His gaze seemed transfixed on her for a moment, and she wondered belatedly if it had been a mistake to come downstairs wearing just a towelling robe. It fitted to just below her knees, but there was still a good expanse of her legs showing. She pulled the robe a little more closely around her.

'I hope you don't mind. I showered and washed my clothes through.'

His gaze wandered over her hair, the rich chestnut tresses spilling over her shoulders in a silken swathe. 'No…uh…um…' He seemed to be having trouble with his voice, and he cleared his throat. 'Not at all. I… uh… I'm an early riser. And I thought I'd make a start on breakfast. I'm sure you must be hungry, after you missed out on supper.'

'I'm starving,' she admitted.

'Good. You'll be able to tuck in, then.' He seemed to have recovered from whatever was bothering him and waved her to a chair. 'Sit down. There's some fresh tea in the pot. And while you're relaxed, I'll take your blood pressure again.'

'Oh, there's really no need for you to do that,' she protested. 'I'm absolutely fine. Having those few hours of sleep did me a world of good.'

'Even so, I just want to be sure.' He fetched a blood-pressure monitor from a cupboard and began to wrap the cuff around her arm.

'How many of these things do you have secreted about the place?' she teased.

'Just one.' A smile hovered on his lips. 'You were pretty much in a state of collapse yesterday, so I dashed down here to grab this machine.' The monitor beeped and he checked the reading. 'That's great,' he said. 'Back to normal. Like I said, it must have happened because you'd been overdoing things.'

'I knew it would be all right.' She gave a rueful smile. 'Anyway, it wouldn't go down too well if a doctor couldn't stand up to a little pressure, would it?'

'There are different kinds of stress,' he pointed out, putting the monitor back in the cupboard. 'As I said before, you haven't really had time to come to terms with your father's death, as well as the worry of having to sell his house and find somewhere for you and the children to live. You can't manage on an adrenaline rush for ever. Sooner or later something has to give, and perhaps being able to relax for once led to meltdown.'

'I suppose you could be right.' She poured tea for both of them. 'I'll help you with breakfast. What were you planning on having?'

'I hadn't worked that out yet.' He looked in the fridge. 'I've plenty of eggs, fresh tomatoes, mushrooms, and there's some bacon and gammon, too.'

'How about I whip up an omelette while you make toast?'

He nodded. 'Sounds perfect to me. We'll make a great team.'

He fished pans out of the cupboard and laid slices of bread on the grill pan. 'Is there anything else you need?'

'A whisk? A simple hand-held one will do.'

He frowned, searching through the cutlery drawer

until with a flourish he triumphantly produced one. 'One whisk.'

'And a bowl to mix the eggs in.'

'I can do bowls.' He produced a selection and she chose one of them.

'Thanks. I'm all set now. Do you want to put plates to warm?'

They worked in harmony for the next few minutes, and the kitchen soon became filled with the appetising smell of cooked bacon and golden fried mushrooms.

Rosie and Sam appeared as James was buttering toast and setting it out on plates at the table. 'You're just in time,' he said. 'Grub's up.'

'I'm not eating grubs.' Sam pulled a face, and James looked nonplussed for a moment or two.

'Are you sure?' he teased. 'I heard they were really good for you.'

Rosie laughed. 'There are no grubs,' she told Sam. 'It's your favourite—bacon and mushrooms and omelette.' She sniffed the air appreciatively.

'So that's one more dish I've learned to cook,' James said, and Rosie nodded.

'That makes two, then, if you add popcorn to the list.' Rosie gave him a serene smile as she dipped her fork into the fluffy egg, leaving the others to dissolve into laughter.

After breakfast the children went to play in the garden, where they discovered an old swing and a rope ladder tied to a tree. There was a tyre, too, suspended from the sturdy branch of an apple tree, and Sam took to it with relish.

'They seem to be having a good time,' Sarah said happily, watching them through the kitchen window.

'Were those things put up when your grandparents lived here?'

James nodded, coming to stand beside her. His long body brushed against hers, and the warmth coming from him permeated through her towelling robe, bringing a flush of heat to her cheeks. 'My brother and I used to spend hours out there. We had a great time. My grandfather knew how boys needed to burn off energy with lots of outdoor activities, so he made sure we had our very own adventure playground. I renewed the ropes and kept everything as it was because I thought maybe Jonathan's children would enjoy them some day.'

'I'm sure they will. It was thoughtful of you to do that.' She smiled at him. He'd taken a lot of care in renovating this house and making it into a home, and it showed his love of family in the way he'd kept this playground for his niece and nephew. This house and its garden were made for family life, but would they ever be given over to that? Would there come a time when James decided he wanted a wife and children of his own? A small frisson of alarm rippled through her at the thought. How could she bear it if James were to set up home with another woman?

'What is it?' He gave her a quizzical look.

'Nothing...' She faltered. 'I wondered... I don't think I'll ever settle into a relationship. Too much can go wrong, and I'm just not up to coping with that. But it's a shame, because I was thinking that I'd like children of my own one day. I have Sam and Rosie to care for, of course, and they'll always be precious to me, but I would still have liked to have a baby, or babies, at some point.' She sighed. 'Anyway, it wouldn't work—Sam and Rosie wouldn't understand, would they? I'd hate them to feel that they were being pushed out.' She gazed at him, her green eyes troubled.

Perhaps there was something in her expression that tugged at him, because he quickly put his arms around her and drew her close. 'Is that how it felt for you, when your father married again and started a second family?' Her silky hair hung loose about her shoulders, and now he brushed away glossy tendrils that had fallen across her cheek, hiding her face.

'I don't know. I'm not sure quite how I felt about things at the time.' All she could think about just now was that it was really good to be in his arms. He made her feel warm and safe, as though he truly understood and cared about her. 'I loved them from the first…but somehow I began to feel that I was in the way, intruding on their family life. It wasn't anything that was said or done, but I felt a bit like an outsider, looking in. I don't ever want Rosie and Sam to feel like that.'

'I'm sure they won't.' His voice was gentle and re-assuring. 'They think the world of you, and they know how much you love them. I can see it in the way they talk to you and the way they act around you. It says a lot that they're confident enough to make friends and go out there and enjoy being children. Things could have been very different if you hadn't taken on the respon-sibility of looking after them.'

'Maybe. I want them to be happy.'

He gazed down at her. 'And what do you want for yourself? Don't you deserve a shot at happiness, too? You've worked really hard to get this far—it's no won-der you collapsed yesterday. Perhaps it's time to start thinking about what you want out of life.'

'I have what I want.' It was true. Right now, she was

blissfully content simply to be wrapped up in his embrace. She could kid herself that she was cosseted, cherished almost, as his fingers splayed out over her spine and his other hand rested warmly on the curve of her hip. It didn't matter that he was simply comforting her, offering to share her burden.

'Do you?'

She lifted her face to him, and was immediately lost in the intensity of his gaze. 'For now, anyway.'

He shook his head, frowning as though he was battling with himself over something. She couldn't tell what he was thinking. But after a moment or two it seemed to pass, and now flame shimmered in the depths of his eyes and a smile hovered on his lips—lips that were just a breath away from hers. He lowered his head, and heat surged in her as she realised what he was about to do. Her heart lurched inside her chest, and then his lips touched hers, soft and compelling, achingly sweet, leaving a trail of fire in their wake.

A pulse began to throb in her throat, and she wanted to lean into him, to let her soft curves mesh with his hard body, but most of all she wanted him to kiss her again, to want her, to need her and take all she had to offer. She hardly dared believe that he might truly want her. Shakily, she ran her hands up over his chest, curving them around his shoulders and gently kneading the muscular contours with the tips of her fingers.

He sucked in his breath, and then a ragged, shuddery sigh escaped him. His hands moved over her, shaping her, moulding her to him and tracing a path as though he would learn every dip and hollow and commit it to memory. His mouth came down on hers, crushing the softness of her lips, tasting, exploring, and growing ever more passionate as she hungrily returned his kisses. She clung to him, wanting this moment to go on and on.

Then, with shocking suddenness, the kitchen door clattered open and the electric tension in the air was shattered, lost in time as they broke apart and turned to see what had caused the interruption.

'Rosie won't let me go on the swing.' Sam's chin jutted with indignation. 'She's been on it for ages. You have to tell her that it's my turn.' Thankfully, he was so het up about his grievance that he didn't notice there was anything at all wrong with either of them.

Sarah was breathing deeply, trying hard to slow the heavy, thudding beat of her heart. She was in a state of shock, overcome by the realisation that for a while she'd forgotten completely where she was and how she should behave. What was she doing, getting herself involved with James? How many times had she told herself that she must steer clear of any entanglement with him? Was she determined to set herself up for more hurt?

'Tell her she has five more minutes,' she said, pulling in a deep breath and finding her voice, 'and then you must swap over. I'll let you know when the time's up.'

'Wha-a-t? That's not fair!' Clearly, he wasn't happy with the five-minutes rule, but Sarah was in no mood for a drawn-out discussion.

'You heard what I said.'

Sam went out again, muttering to himself, and a moment later they heard him shout triumphantly, 'Five minutes, then you've gotta give me a go or you're in big trouble. Sarah says so.'

James looked at her. He was frowning, and she guessed he was as troubled as she was. 'Sarah, I…'

'It's all right.' She shook her head. 'It's just as well he

came in. We were both carried away there for a while. It's been a strange couple of days. I don't think either of us is thinking straight.'

His expression was sober. 'I don't want to hurt you, or cause you any more problems. The truth is I wasn't thinking at all.'

'No...well, it doesn't matter.' Perhaps he'd discovered that she wasn't a skinny teenager any more, and being a red-blooded male he'd been carried away with the heat of the moment. It hadn't meant anything to him...nothing of any importance, at any rate...and that was why he'd said he didn't want to hurt her. 'Let's forget it happened, shall we?' She was giving him a get-out clause.

'Okay. If you say so.' His voice was ragged.

He took them home a couple of hours later, and spent time finishing off the fireplaces with the black grate polish, while Sarah caught up on chores and Rosie and Sam went to play with the children next door.

'I'll have a go at sanding the floorboards downstairs another time, if you like,' he offered when she went to admire his handiwork a little later. The fireplaces looked magnificent, as good as new, and she really appreciated the work he had done.

'You've done a great job,' she said. 'I can't ask you to do any more. I've already asked too much of you. And I don't want you to feel obliged to help me out. I can manage, I'm sure. It takes time, that's all.'

'It's not a problem. Like I said, I'm interested in renovation...it's good to see a property fulfil its potential, and these floors are basically sound. They need a bit of care, that's all. And I have a machine that will do the job in no time at all.'

She smiled. 'Okay, then. Thanks. For everything.'

He nodded. 'I'd better go.' His grey gaze slanted over her. 'I'll see you at work tomorrow.'

'At the air ambulance station, yes.' She looked forward to those days that were spent out of the hospital, attending to on-the-spot emergencies. They weren't good for anyone unfortunate enough to be involved in an accident, or to be taken ill suddenly, of course, but from a professional point of view it was good to know that they could give immediate lifesaving help in that first all-important golden hour.

She went with him to the door and watched him slide into the driver's seat of his car. He hadn't made any attempt to touch her since Sam had burst into his kitchen, and while she was glad of that, she was sad about it, too. She was mixed up inside, emotionally vulnerable, and at a loss to know how to deal with her feelings.

James didn't appear to be having any problems on that score. Kissing her had been a momentary lapse and now he was back to his normal self, confident, energetic and ready to move on. It would take her a little longer to get there.

In the morning, she was at the air ambulance base when the first call came in. 'Okay, it looks as though we're on our own on this one,' Tom, the pilot, said. 'James is still attending an incident that came in an hour ago. It was only a couple of miles away, so he took the rapid-response car. The paramedics wanted a doctor on the scene.'

'Do you think you can handle this without him?' the co-pilot asked as they scrambled for the helicopter. 'An ambulance is on its way to the scene, but apparently it's been held up.' Alex frowned, running a hand through his wavy, brown hair. His hazel eyes were concerned.

'I'll be absolutely fine, Alex,' she said quickly. 'You don't have to worry. I won't let anyone down.'

'Sorry, Doc.' Tom looked embarrassed. 'Alex worries about all the new people who join the crew. It's not meant to be a personal criticism—but we were hoping James would be back before we took off.'

They were airborne within a couple of minutes, and Sarah concentrated on finding out all she could about the incident they were about to attend.

'It's a ten-year-old boy who has fallen down a mine shaft,' Alex told her. 'An old copper mine, apparently. They're dotted all around the area. Trouble was, they were closed down decades ago, and when they were abandoned the entrances to the shafts were covered with timber and soil. I think, over the years, the timbers have begun to rot, and every now and again they cave in.'

'That's awful,' Sarah said, her heart going out to the child who had unwittingly been swallowed up into a deep chasm in the ground. 'I can't believe that no one's taken responsibility for them.' She thought about the child lying at the bottom of the shaft, cold and most likely wet, too. He was the same age as Sam. 'Are his parents at the mine, do we know?'

Alex shook his head. 'He was with his older brother when it happened. The police have been trying to find his parents, but they're not at home.'

They flew over heath, covered with mauve heather and yellow gorse, and soon the helicopter landed in a safe area close by the mine. Police and fire crew were already there, and Sarah was beginning to see why Alex might have been worried about her working on this ven-

ture. Someone would have to go down into that mine
shaft to rescue the child. It was more than likely he was
badly injured after such a fall, and was probably suffering from broken limbs—if he was still alive. That new
anxiety struck her forcibly.

'Has he been talking?' she asked one of the fire crew.
'Has anyone been able to speak to him?'

'He's said a few words…nothing much, nothing in-
telligible, anyway.'

That could mean he was semi-conscious, making it
all the more important that he have medical attention
as soon as possible. 'I can see you have the winch in
place. I'll need to get into a harness to go down to him.
Will you help me with that?'

'Are you sure you're up to it?' The man gave her a
doubtful look. 'It can be dangerous going down into
these shafts. There could be loose timbers, rock falls—
perhaps it would be better if you gave instructions to
one of our crew. He'll tell you how the boy is doing,
and you could maybe tell him how to go on from there.'

She shook her head. 'I can't see that working. Your
fireman might not be able to take precautions against
spinal or pelvic injury, and I doubt he'll know how to
give injections or set up a fluid line. You need a medic
down there.' She started to walk towards the winch.
'Will you help me get set up?'

Reluctantly, he did as she asked. The harness was
designed to fit snugly around the person, and there were
lots of buckles to be fastened and checked. It was im-
perative that everything be fixed in place so as to be
perfectly secure.

'What's going on here?'

Sarah had started to climb into the harness when

James's voice cracked through the air like a whip. She looked up at him, startled to see his face etched in taut lines, his mouth flat, compressed.

'I'm going down into the shaft to look after the boy,' she said. 'His name's Ross. He's fallen about twenty feet into a cavern and might be semi-conscious.' She gave him a brief smile. 'I'm glad you made it here after all.'

'So am I. Step out of the harness, please, Sarah. I'll go down in your place.'

She stared at him in disbelief. 'But I'm all ready to go.'

'Not any more. This is way too risky for you.'

Affronted, she tilted her chin, and said firmly, 'For you, too, I'd have thought. I've had a lot of rock-climbing experience. I'm quite prepared to go down there and see to the boy. I don't see it as a problem.'

'You may not, but I'm afraid I do. Rock climbing is not the same as caving or potholing, and I have experience in both of those, so I'll go in your place. Step out of the way, Sarah, please.'

Everything in her told her that she must stand her ground, but she was all too conscious of time passing while they argued, with danger to the boy increasing with every minute. Neither did she want to create a scene in front of the police and fire crew, so she said in a low, exasperated voice, 'What gives you the right to stop me?'

'Seniority.'

She gave him a furious glare and finally stood to one side, leaving him to get into the harness. How could he do this to her? What had possessed him to play the seniority card like that, when she was perfectly capable of going down that shaft?

He had his medical kit with him, and she handed him a torch. 'It'll be pitch black in there,' she said.

'I know. Thanks.'

All she could do now was watch and wait while James descended the shaft, followed by one of the fire crew. It was galling to have to stand there and do nothing.

After several minutes a stretcher was lowered down, and more time passed before James indicated that they were ready to come back up. The firemen began to winch up the stretcher, and slowly hauled the boy to safety.

'How's he doing?' Sarah asked as soon as James came to the surface. She was still smarting at his treatment of her, but her focus had to be on the child.

'He has rib and pelvis fractures,' he answered quietly. 'He's not doing too well at all, I'm afraid. I think there must be massive internal bleeding. His blood pressure is falling and his heart rate's rapid.' James hesitated briefly, and she could see that he was acutely disturbed by this young boy's condition. Now that the child had been brought to the surface, he set about finding intravenous access and began to put in a fluid line to help resuscitate him. 'I'm worried that he might go into shock, so we have to get him to hospital as soon as possible. I've given him painkillers and stabilised the fracture with a pelvic sling, so that should compress the area and stop some of the bleeding.'

Sarah knelt down beside the stretcher. 'He's struggling to breathe,' she said in an urgent, low voice, glancing at James. The boy was being given oxygen through a mask, but it obviously wasn't sufficient to help him. 'His condition's deteriorating rapidly.' She studied the rise and fall of his chest and said quickly, 'Something's not right. There's a segment of his ribcage that's not moving in tune with the rest.' She frowned. 'There must be several rib fractures—part of the ribcage has broken and become detached.'

He winced. He had the fluid line in place now. 'A flail chest,' he said in a low tone. 'I suspected as much, but it was too dark down there to see properly.'

Sarah quickly examined the boy, who was lying motionless but groaning in pain. 'I know this must be uncomfortable for you, Ross,' she said softly, 'but we'll look after you and help you to feel better. It won't be too long before we have you in hospital.'

She turned back to James. 'His windpipe has deviated to one side and his neck veins are distended. One of the ribs must have pierced his lung.' This was more bad news. It meant that air was collecting in the pleural cavity and had nowhere to escape. As it built up, it was disrupting other organs and tissues. 'We have to act quickly.' If they didn't act promptly to do something about it, the child could go into cardiac arrest and they might lose him.

He nodded. 'I'm on it.' He reached for equipment from his medical pack and then carefully injected anaesthetic between the boy's ribs. Then he made an incision in the chest wall and slid a catheter in place. There was a satisfying hiss as trapped air escaped, and Sarah sealed off the end of the tube in a water-filled bottle that acted as a one-way valve.

'Okay, I've taped the tube in place.' He glanced at

her. 'I'll stabilise the flail segment with a gauze pad and then we can be on our way.'

'Good.' She didn't say any more. She was too annoyed with him to speak to him about anything other than work, and her only concern at that moment was that Ross needed to be transported to the hospital in a matter of minutes. By the time he was there, perhaps his parents would have been located and would be in time to visit him and reassure him before he went to Theatre for lifesaving surgery.

They loaded Ross into the bay of the helicopter and within a couple of minutes they were on their way. The ambulance still had not arrived, and Alex told her it had been held up by a road-traffic accident that had happened while they'd been on their way to the mine. She absorbed the news with a sombre expression. Without medical intervention, it was doubtful Ross would have been alive by the time the paramedics arrived. This way, he at least had a chance of survival.

Once they were at the hospital they handed Ross over to the trauma team, who whisked him away. His parents were there, waiting for him, and Sarah breathed a faint sigh of relief as his anxious mother hurried forward to hold his hand.

She walked back to the helicopter without looking at James. She held her head high, ready to deal with Tom's and Alex's comments. They were all too aware that James had set her to one side like a spare part.

Strangely, though, they were quiet on the subject. Were they on her side? Or did they think that, as a woman, she shouldn't be taking on such risks? It was such an old-fashioned viewpoint.

James had no such inhibitions. 'I was horrified when

I saw you getting ready to go down into that mine,' he said as they took their seats on the helicopter. 'All I could think about was the danger you were putting yourself in.'

'You didn't seem to have any qualms about going down,' she answered in a terse voice. 'And from the looks of things, you didn't come out of it unscathed.' Now that she had the chance to look at him properly, she saw that he had a deep gash on his forehead, hidden for the most part by an unruly lock of dark hair. There was a graze on his hand, too, she noticed, when he pulled on the seat belt and fastened it in place. 'If I'd been allowed to do my job and go down, I would have accepted injuries as one of the hazards.'

'And that's okay, is it, to risk your life in the course of the job?'

Her eyes widened in astonishment. 'Why on earth should that be all right for you and not for me?' she demanded.

'I'm not the one with a family to care for,' he said bluntly. 'I shudder to think what might have happened to you. What do you imagine will happen to Sam and Rosie if you're injured or worse? How will they react if anything bad happens to you? Who will look after them? Haven't they suffered enough? Surely you can't think purely of yourself now, if you really mean to act as a permanent guardian to them?'

She was stunned by what he said. It was true she hadn't thought beyond helping the boy, but what would he have her do? This was her job, and if he weren't around, wouldn't she do the same again?

He was right about Rosie and Sam, though. If she was serious about taking care of them, she had to rethink her priorities. It troubled her deeply, thinking about that. Perhaps, on the face of it, he'd had good reason to step in and take over, but the intrusion still needled her. He'd pulled rank, and that annoyed her intensely.

CHAPTER SIX

'How is Ross doing?' Sarah asked the specialist nurse in charge of the paediatric intensive care unit. 'The poor child was in a really bad way yesterday. I couldn't bring myself to start work without coming here to check up on him first.'

'He's still in a critical condition, I'm afraid.' The nurse gave her a sympathetic smile. 'It was dreadful, what happened to him. His parents have been beside themselves with worry and I've had to send them down to the cafeteria to take a break. Otherwise, I don't think they would have eaten since yesterday.' She frowned. 'I doubt he would have survived if it hadn't been for you and Dr Benson. But the good news is he had surgery on his pelvis yesterday, almost immediately after you brought him into A and E. Mr Norris managed to stop the bleeding, but of course the lad had lost a lot of blood already.'

Sarah nodded and looked down at the white-faced child lying in the hospital bed. There were drips and tubes taped in place so that he could receive lifesaving fluids, oxygen and medication, and where his broken pelvis had been treated there were post-operative surgical drains.

His blood pressure was still low and his heart rate fluctuated as she watched the monitors.

'On top of everything else, he was dreadfully cold when he arrived here,' the nurse told her. 'We were all very worried about him.'

'I know you're taking good care of him,' Sarah told her. 'We can't do anything more but wait now to see what happens.'

'Mmm. He doesn't look very strong to start with, does he?' The nurse gave Ross one last look before excusing herself to go and see to another patient.

Sarah stood by the bedside for a while longer. 'You have to get better, Ross,' she urged. 'Be strong. You can do it.'

There was a movement beside her, and she looked around to see that James had come to join her. She might have known that he would come to see how the boy was getting on. They were in tune when it came to how they felt about their patients. She checked him out surreptitiously and, as ever, when he was at work, he was immaculately dressed in a dark grey suit, with the jacket open, showing a pristine shirt and soft blue-grey tie.

'You're obviously worried about him,' he said, 'but from what I heard, the surgery went well, and they've done X-rays of his chest to show that the chest tube is in the right place. They're giving him strong painkilling medication at the moment, so hopefully his breathing will be more comfortable.'

'Yes, it looks as though they're doing everything they can for him.' Her expression was rueful. 'I can't help feeling particularly involved with this young lad. Looking at him, it feels as though time's going backwards.' She sighed, thinking of what had happened some time ago. 'It was a boy like Ross that caused me to take up medicine in the first place.'

'Really?' He studied her thoughtfully, his dark brows lifting a fraction in query. 'What happened?'

'I was on a rock-climbing weekend with Murray when we heard a shout. A moment later we saw a boy come tumbling down the cliff face near where we were. I think he must have climbed over the safety fence then lost his footing and slipped over the edge. We called out the emergency services, and started to go back down the cliff to where he had landed on an outcrop.'

Even now, it was distressing to think back to that worrying time. 'He'd broken his arm, and his foot was at a weird angle to his leg. Murray used dressing pads from his emergency first-aid kit to stem the bleeding, and we splinted his limbs as best we could using tape from the pack. I was glad we were there for him because he would have been terrified if he'd been on his own. At least we were able to comfort and reassure him, otherwise I don't know how long he would have lain there before anyone found him.'

'It was a good thing you knew what to do.'

She winced. 'It was Murray who knew what to do. He'd done a first-aid course because as a climber he was worried about these sorts of situations cropping up. It made me think seriously about doing a course myself, but in the end I decided to go in for medicine instead.'

He smiled. 'There's a huge amount of difference between those two choices. For what it's worth, I think you made a good decision.'

'Yes.' She gave a wry smile. 'Contrary to popular

opinion, I did manage to make one or two back then.'
She said it in a droll tone, and he sent her a quick glance.

'I'll hazard a guess that you're still annoyed over
what happened yesterday. Would I be right?'

'You could say that.' She flashed him a sparking
glance. 'Annoyed is such a mild word, don't you think?'
She moved away from the bedside. 'You undermined
me in public and stopped me from doing my job. You
were way out of line.'

'I did what I thought was right.'

'Of course you did.' Her mouth made a flat line.
'Anyway, I don't want to talk about that now. I'm a few
minutes early and I want to go and look through the lab
results before I start my shift on A and E.'

'I'll come with you.'

'Fine.' She didn't say any more, and responded to his
conversation with brief one-word answers. The more
she thought about it, the more she resented his actions.

Once they were in the A and E unit, she went over
to the central desk and looked through the wire tray
for lab and radiology reports. 'There's an update here
on Nicola Carter,' she told him, glancing through the
patient's file. 'It's no wonder she suffered an adrenal
crisis. The radiologist's report says she has a tumour
on the pituitary gland.'

His mouth made a downward turn. 'We'd better get
the endocrinologist to take a look at her,' he said. 'Let's
go and bring these scans up on the computer.'

They went into the annexe, and brought up the patient's notes on screen, but Gemma, the triage nurse,
came looking for them a moment later. 'There's someone asking to see you, Sarah. He says he's Rachel

Veasey's brother, Harry. I've shown him to the relatives' waiting room.'

'Oh, brilliant. Thanks, Gemma. I'm glad we managed to find him.'

'You're welcome.' Gemma walked away, in a hurry to see to incoming patients.

'How did that come about?' James asked with a frown. 'This is the girl who collapsed through drink and drugs, isn't it? I thought she didn't have any family.'

'She told me she had a brother, and her friends said they thought he was living in a village in Somerset, so I tried to track him down. I thought he might be on the electoral register, and when I looked I found there weren't that many Veaseys listed, so I took a chance and contacted one of them. I wrote to him.' Her mouth curved with pleasure. 'It seems I might have been lucky and managed to find the right person.'

'You went to a lot of trouble to get in touch with him.' He studied her curiously. 'Is this because you feel the need to bring families together?'

'I suppose it must be. I think Rachel needs someone from her family to care about her. There was a void, and I wanted to fill it.'

'Because you can't fill the void in your own life?'

She pulled in a deep breath. His calm, penetrating assessment shocked her. 'Maybe.' She shrugged awkwardly. 'I know you don't think it's a good idea, but I've never given up on finding my mother. I want to know why she walked out, and the question keeps eating away at me. I feel as though I can't move on until I have an answer. I can't settle. I can't get my life in order.' She ran a hand through her hair. 'The card I had from her last Christmas was postmarked London, but I just don't seem to be able to track her down.'

'It would surely be easier for her to get in touch with you? She probably doesn't want to be found—I can't help thinking you're laying yourself open for trouble if you insist on looking for her.'

'That's as may be. I'm still determined to try.'

He smiled wryly. 'I guessed that might be the case.' He was pensive for a moment or two. 'It's possible she could have remarried, I suppose. Maybe you need to get in touch with the General Register Office and see if you can track down a marriage using her maiden name. Hopefully, that will give you her new name.'

She blinked, looking at him in stunned surprise. 'Oh, wow! You're right, of course. Why on earth didn't I think of that?'

He smiled, his head tilting slightly to one side as he studied her. 'Perhaps because you're too close to the problem?'

'Yes, I see that.' Her green eyes were wide, shimmering with a sudden film of joyful tears. 'Thanks, James,' she said huskily. She was so overwhelmed by the significance of this new idea that she wrapped her arms around him and gave him a hug. 'I absolutely forgive you for everything. You're a genius.' She lifted her face to him, ready to plant a swift kiss on his cheek, but at that moment he turned his head and their lips met in a soft collision. She heard his sharp intake of breath, and tension sparked like a flash of wildfire between them.

There was an instant of complete stillness and then, with a muffled groan, he pulled her to him, covering her mouth with his. He kissed her hard, a deep, fervent kiss that caught her off balance so that she clung to him, revelling in this exhilarating, heat-filled moment.

Almost as soon as it had begun, though, it was over. James lifted his head and held her at arm's length as though he needed space but was reluctant to let her go completely. The air between them was thick with unbidden yearning. His breathing was ragged, coming in short bursts, and Sarah stared at him, her whole body feverish from that brief, close encounter.

His features were taut, and his eyes were dark and troubled. 'I shouldn't have done that,' he said in a roughened voice. 'I mustn't do that. I'm your boss. You're on a probationary three months and it isn't right. It isn't a professional way for me to behave. I'm sorry.'

Sarah's throat was suddenly dry and she swallowed carefully. 'It was my fault. You shouldn't blame yourself. I was carried away by the heat of the moment, thinking I might be able to get in touch with my mother after all this time. I shouldn't have flung myself at you.' The ethics of the situation didn't seem relevant to her—after all, she was a qualified doctor, not a student in training, but it obviously bothered James, and she wasn't going to try to persuade him otherwise. Perhaps he was looking for an excuse to keep away from her. She had no real idea what made him tick as far as she was concerned. Maybe he was as confused as she was.

He released his hold on her and she moved away from him, not knowing what else to do or what to say. 'I'll…I'll go and talk to Harry, and then I'd better see who Gemma has lined up waiting for me.'

'Okay.'

She made a hurried escape. Her heart was still thudding from the intensity of that kiss, but the whole episode puzzled her. What did James really feel for her? He clearly wanted her, but was it just a whim, a passing fancy, a fleeting passion? The whole thing was bewildering.

She spoke to Harry for a few minutes and then took him to Rachel's ward. The young girl was still thin and pale looking, and she was very tired, probably as a result of the irregular heart rhythm she was suffering as a result of her use of Ecstasy. Sarah checked her notes, satisfying herself that everything was being done to help her to recover.

'Harry?' Rachel's face lit up with pleasure. 'You're here… I didn't think… Oh, I'm so glad to see you.'

'Me, too.' Harry pulled up a chair and sat down at his sister's bedside, and Sarah decided it was time to leave the two of them to talk to one another in private.

'I'll be in A and E if you need me,' she told Harry. She wrote her phone number down on a scrap of paper and handed it to him. 'Here's my number in case you want to talk to me or if there's anything I can do to help your sister.'

He thanked her, and she went back to the emergency department, feeling lighter at heart now that Rachel had someone dear to her close by.

'There's a girl waiting to be seen in the treatment room,' Gemma told her a minute or so later. 'She's twenty years old. A friend called the ambulance. Apparently she passed out a couple of times and was out of it for a while. The paramedics said her blood pressure and pulse were both low. She just had a breakup with her boyfriend, so the friend thinks it might be something to do with that…an emotional reaction.'

'I'll look at her and see if we can find out what's happening. Thanks, Gemma.' Sarah went to the treatment room and introduced herself to the young woman who was waiting for her there. She was a pretty girl, blonde with blue eyes and a slender, shapely figure. She told Sarah that her friend had gone to get them both a coffee from the machine.

'Okay, Ann-Marie, do you want to tell me what happened?'

'I collapsed,' the girl told her. She was pale, and her eyes were red rimmed as though she'd been crying. 'I felt really strange all at once, and it was as though I couldn't breathe. I was dizzy and light-headed.'

'Did you have breakfast this morning?'

'Yes, I had a bowl of cereal.'

Sarah smiled. 'That's good. You're not watching your weight, or anything like that?'

Ann-Marie shook her head. 'No, not at all.'

'So, did anything happen just before you started to feel this way—a bang on the head or has something out of the ordinary happened recently?'

This met with another shake of the head, but Ann-Marie added huskily, 'I had a text from my boyfriend. He wants us to break up…says things aren't working out.' Tears welled up in her eyes and she sniffed and dabbed at them with a tissue. 'It upset me, and after that I started to feel strange. It was as though everything drained out of me.' She hesitated. 'It's not the first time I've fainted, though…so I'm not really sure if it's the break-up that made me ill.'

'It must be distressing for you, but try not to upset yourself.' Sarah brought her stethoscope from her pocket. 'I'll examine you, if I may, and see if we can find out what's wrong.'

The examination didn't reveal anything untoward, but Sarah said quietly, 'That all seems to be okay, but I think we'll admit you to our observation ward so that we can run some tests and keep an eye on you for a while. I'll ask the nurse to set up an ECG to monitor your heart rate and exclude any problems there.'

She made the arrangements and went to see the rest of the patients on her list. Some time later, when she was treating a man suffering from an asthma attack, James came to find her and drew her to one side.

'Keep him on the nebulised salbutamol for the time being,' she told the nurse, 'and let me know if there's any change in his condition.' She left the room with James.

'Is something wrong?' she asked. She saw he had Ann-Marie's file in his hand.

'Gemma tells me you've admitted this woman to the observation ward,' he said. 'We've quite a high number of admissions already and I'm wondering if it's really necessary to keep her here. After all, her symptoms are probably something her GP could deal with... they could even have a purely emotional basis. Perhaps she's overwrought and not coping too well with her love life. That's not strictly something we should be dealing with here.'

'That's all possibly true, but something's bothering me. I have an instinct about her.' Sarah was on the defensive. 'She said it had happened before, and I want to get to the bottom of it. She was in a state of collapse when the paramedics picked her up, and I'd sooner we were on hand to deal with the situation if it happens again.'

'All right. But if she's stable in the morning, you should send her home with a letter for her GP.'

She nodded. 'I will.' At least he hadn't overridden her decision, and she was glad about that. She might be wrong about Ann-Marie, but it was a case of better safe than sorry as far as she was concerned.

James glanced at her as she started to walk back towards the treatment room. 'If it's all right with you, I could come round to your place to start on the floors after work today. I know you're always busy with one thing and another, but I won't get in your way. I've hunted through the mountains of stuff in the outbuildings and found the sanding machine, so it should make fairly light work of them.'

'You don't need to do that,' she said quickly. After what kept happening between them, perhaps it would be for the best if she avoided any more contact with him outside work. Going on as they were was surely like playing with fire? Sooner or later, she'd find her fingers were burned.

'I know that, but I'd like to get to work on them. It's very satisfying, seeing things restored to their former glory. Will you be at home?'

'Yes.' She frowned, searching for excuses. She didn't want to be blunt and tell him to stay away, but everything in her was telling her she needed to steer clear of him away from work. 'I'll be very busy, though, working on the internet article for next week's topic. And I promised Rosie and Sam I'd take them to the local library to choose some books. So, you see, you could be making a wasted journey and I don't want to put you out. You really don't need to worry. I'll get around to doing the floors myself some time. My priority right now is to get the roof repaired, and I've made an appointment for a roofing company to send some-one round.'

'Yes, I can see that's important. It might not be too big a job, though. Let's hope so, anyway.' He didn't say any more, and she hoped he'd taken the hint. It was a re-lief. It would surely be far better if they kept their work and private lives separate from now on.

The rest of the day flew by as she dealt with a steady stream of patients and by the time she went home and picked up the children from Murray's house, she was more than ready for a break. Sam was unusually sub-dued, she noticed, but Murray didn't have any clue what that was all about.

'He hasn't said anything to me, except that he has to get some information together for a school project. He's supposed to present it to the class some time next week and he hasn't made a start yet, apparently.'

Sarah's expression was rueful. 'Perhaps it's just as well we're making a trip to the library, then. With any luck he might find something there to inspire him.'

They arrived back at the house some time later, armed with several colourful books, and Sarah began to prepare supper while the children disappeared into their rooms. Murray came round to collect a book she'd picked up for him, and she invited him to stay and eat with them.

'It's nothing much, just a casserole. I put all the in-gredients together this morning and set the automatic timer, so it should be ready any time now.'

'It smells wonderful,' Murray said, sniffing the air, and when she served up the meal a short time later, they all ate appreciatively.

Sam was still morose, not saying very much, and Sarah tried to wheedle out of him what was wrong, while she stacked crockery in the dishwasher, but it was no use. He wasn't talking.

Then the doorbell rang and Murray went to answer it. He came back a moment later, saying, 'You have a visitor.'

She looked up, and was startled to see James standing next to him. 'James? I hadn't expected— So you decided to come after all?'

'I did. After all, you didn't expressly tell me not to come.' He glanced at Murray and then looked back at Sarah. 'I hope I'm not intruding on anything. I can always leave.'

'No...no, not at all. You're welcome to stay.'

'I'd better be going, anyway,' Murray said. 'Thanks for the meal, Sarah. It was delicious. I'll return the favour some time.'

'I'm glad you enjoyed it.' She went with him to the kitchen door, waving him off.

'You and he must spend quite a bit of time together, with him living next door,' James said speculatively, his dark eyes narrowed. 'You seem to get along very well with one another.'

'We do.' She looked at him fleetingly, not wanting to dwell too long on his powerfully masculine frame, made all the more impressive by the clothes he was wearing. Dark jeans moulded themselves to his strong, muscular legs, and a T-shirt hugged the contours of his chest. 'I see you've brought the sanding machine with you,' she said. 'You must mean business.'

'If that's all right with you?'

'I... Yes, of course. I haven't cleared any of the furniture out, though. I was pretty sure you wouldn't be coming.'

'That's not a problem. I'll see to it.'

Rosie had stayed quiet so far, but now she looked carefully at the machine. 'What's that for?' she asked.

'It's for getting all the old dirt and sealant off the wooden floorboards so that they come up looking clean and new,' James told her. 'Then, when that's done, they can be sealed again with polyurethane to give them a fine sheen.'

'That'll be good,' she said approvingly. 'They look old and grotty now, don't they?' She smiled. 'I can help you move the furniture if you like. Do you think you might start with the dining room?'

'That sounds like a good idea, though I don't want you hurting yourself moving furniture.' He glanced at Sarah. 'Is it all right with you if I start in the dining room? What do you think?'

'Yes, that's okay.' She glanced at Sam, conscious of how quiet he was being. 'Perhaps you'd like to help us get the furniture out of the room, Sam?'

Sam lifted his shoulders but didn't make any attempt to answer, and James said in a sympathetic tone, 'Are you all right, Sam? You're not saying very much, and that's not like you at all. Is everything okay?'

Sam pressed his lips together and seemed to be thinking hard about something. Then he looked at Sarah and said, 'If you're doing the floors, does that mean we're staying here, or are you making the house look good so you can sell it?'

'Heavens, where did that thought come from?' She looked at him in surprise. 'What makes you think we would be leaving? Is that what's been troubling you these last few hours?'

'Ricky Morton says we're not a proper family—you're not our mum, he says, and we don't have a dad. And he says if you get fed up of looking after us we won't have anybody and we'll have to go into care. Then you can sell the house and get somewhere just for you.'

Sarah reeled back from that as though she'd been kicked in the stomach. It took her breath away momentarily and she struggled to get herself together again. 'That's an awful lot of guesswork from Ricky,' she said at last. She was still shocked and flummoxed by Sam's innocent outburst. 'Why on earth would I get fed up with looking after you?' Sarah hugged him close to her, shocked that he could even think such a thing. Rosie came and huddled next to her and she put a protective arm around each of them.

'It seems to me Ricky's saying an awful lot of things that he doesn't really understand,' she said carefully. 'He's wrong. Perhaps he has problems of his own that make him think that way, but it isn't going to happen. I'll always want to take care of you.'

Sam gazed up at her, his expression earnest and pleading at the same time. 'Do you promise?'

'I promise, Sam. I love both of you, and we can be a family, the three of us. There are lots of families where there's only one parent.' She looked at James and saw that he was frowning. 'Isn't that true, James?' she said, willing him to back her up in this.

'It is,' he responded, 'and things often work out very well for them.' He hesitated for a moment, and then went down on his haunches by the children and said carefully, 'I think you're very lucky to have Sarah taking care of you. She's changed her life so that the three of you can be together. And as to making the house look good, she's doing it because she can see it's a solid house with big rooms and she wants it to be perfect for you.'

Sam slowly nodded. 'I was scared. Mum and Dad went away, and I don't want Sarah to do the same.'

'I don't ever want to go away,' Sarah told him softly, bending to kiss him lightly on the forehead. She hugged them both tight. 'Everything I'm doing, I'm doing for both of you.'

'And that means making a start on the dining-room floor,' James said, standing up. 'Do I have some helpers?'

'Sarah and I can move the chairs,' Rosie decided, already on her way out of the kitchen.

'Can I have a go with the sander?' Sam wanted to know.

Some half an hour later James was ready to make a start, and after Sam made a few forays with the machine alongside the wall where the cupboards used to stand, the children disappeared upstairs to play in their rooms. There was half an hour left before bedtime and Sarah advised them to make the most of it. Two minutes later an argument erupted between them as Sam tried to muscle in on Rosie's computer game, and Sarah had to go and sort things out.

She came downstairs a short time later and made coffee. 'It was difficult earlier,' she said, offering James a cup, 'finding the right thing to say to Sam. I know they worry, and I do what I can to reassure them, but I can't promise them that everything will go smoothly. You were right about me taking risks going down the mine shaft, but I didn't want to admit it. Sometimes, when it's called for, we have to do what we think is the right thing. And it seemed that way to me at the time. If I had to choose between taking a chance on saving that boy's life or doing nothing, I'd take a chance, without even thinking about it. It doesn't mean I don't care about Rosie and Sam.'

He swallowed some of the hot liquid and set his cup down on the mantelpiece. 'I know that. The truth is, when I saw you getting ready to be lowered down into that pit, I was shocked at the thought of what might happen to you. It overrode my better judgement, if you like. If it had been anyone else, I'd probably have suggested that I go down into the mine alongside him or her, but with you, somehow, it's different. Perhaps I was wrong, but I can't say that I wouldn't do exactly the same thing if those circumstances arose again.'

Her jaw dropped a fraction. He'd done it because he cared about her and hadn't wanted to see her heading into danger. Her heart made a tentative leap within her chest. He cared about her and wanted to keep her safe. That was more than she could ever have hoped for. Even so, for her own sake, she knew she mustn't read too much into it.

She gave a rueful smile. 'I have to make choices and face the consequences, and I have to do it on my own. You're a caring, thoughtful person, but it isn't right that you should have to worry about my wellbeing.'

His mouth twisted. 'I don't think it works quite that way.'

'No?' She sent him a quizzical glance. 'I accept I have responsibilities now. I have to look out for Rosie and Sam, and I'm doing it the best way I can. I'm really glad you backed me up earlier…it helped a lot. It made me feel better, and I could see the children were reassured, too.'

'I'm pleased about that, too.' He frowned. 'It's difficult looking after children, isn't it? They can be quite a handful. It's not just a question of sorting out fights at school, or stopping them from rolling about in mud at the zoo…there are all these undercurrents going on as well, not to mention the everyday problems of getting them to where they need to be and keeping them from laying into one another.' He brooded on that for a few seconds. 'It must have been difficult for you…but you seem to have the perfect temperament for it.'

'I don't know about that. I've not really had a choice.' She sipped her coffee, watching him over the rim of her cup. 'I've had to learn how to do things. I'm still learning.'

'Yeah.' He smiled and reached for the sanding machine. 'It's a hard lesson, but you seem to be handling it pretty well. I'm amazed by the way you've got to grips with everything and turned your life around. You should be proud of yourself.'

He started up the sander and set to work, and Sarah stood by, watching him for a while, enjoying the way he moved, at one with the machine, making calm, steady inroads into the years of accumulated grime that had discoloured the wooden floorboards. Then she wandered away, going back into the kitchen and switching on her computer so that she could start work on her internet article.

Her fingers hovered aimlessly over the keyboard. James obviously felt something for her, or why would he be looking out for her? And he wanted her…when she was in his arms his kisses left her in no doubt of that.

Despite his misgivings, she was certain he wanted more, and this time she wasn't a naïve seventeen-year-old. She was a woman, and if she pushed things, she was pretty sure his resolve would melt like snow in the sunshine.

But that didn't mean he was ready for anything other than a heady affair, did it? And even if he was, how could they ever have a future together when she was so uncertain about the steadfastness of relationships? Hadn't her own mother abandoned her? Why should James be any different? She couldn't bear it if one day he chose to turn his back on her.

CHAPTER SEVEN

'Hey, look at you! You're doing really well, young Ross. It's great to see you out and about. Last time I saw you, you were flat on your back in Intensive Care.' James gave the boy a beaming smile, watching as his mother pushed him in a wheelchair into the emergency department. She came to a halt by the central desk, and James exchanged a few words with her before turning his attention back to her son. 'You're looking so much better than you did a few days ago,' he said, raising his hand, palm open. 'High five?'

Ross slapped hands with him, grinning from ear to ear. 'I wanted to say thank you for getting me out of the mine,' he said. 'I was really scared, and I didn't think anyone would come to get me.'

James nodded. 'I can imagine how you must have felt down there. It was pitch black and you were in a lot of pain. But luckily for you, your brother sounded the alarm…so we came and found you as soon as we heard.' James looked him over. 'How are you feeling?'

'I'm okay.' Ross made a small frown. 'They give me tablets for the pain, and someone comes to help me exercise my legs. I can walk a bit on crutches, but the nurse says it might take a few weeks before I'm back on my feet properly.'

'Yes, it can take a while, but you're out of bed and on the mend, and that's very good. I'm really pleased to see you up and about. Well done.'

'Yeah. I can't wait to get back home and see my mates.'

Sarah watched the interchange from the other side of the desk, where she was looking through her patients' notes on the computer. For all James had implied he didn't understand children too well, he seemed to be learning fast. He was naturally compassionate and it came across in his dealings with them.

It was plain to see that the child was still troubled by his experience, and clearly he was still in some pain, but, as James had pointed out, he was on the mend, and that was great news to hear. Ross's mother was smiling, happy to see her child lively and animated once more. They left A and E a few minutes later, with James promising to go and visit Ross on his ward.

'It's wonderful to see things turn out so well,' she said, and he nodded.

'That's the thing with children...they pick up so quickly. Perhaps it's because they're eager to get on with their lives, and they have so many things going on to distract them from their troubles.'

He came around the desk to look at the computer screen. 'This is Nicola Carter's file...so you're still keeping track of her?'

Sarah nodded. 'Some patients come into the emergency unit, get treated and then they're on their way, but with others it's not quite so simple. I want to know what happens to them after they leave us...like Ross, for instance. Technically, he's no longer our concern, but neither of us can resist checking to see how he's doing, can we?'

He laughed. 'True. So what's happening with Nicola? She was waiting for an appointment with the endocrinologist, last I heard.'

'She's already seen him and he arranged for her to have surgery to remove the tumour. He told her it was stopping the pituitary gland from functioning properly and that was why she collapsed and needed to be given steroid treatment. She'll be going to Theatre later today.' She frowned. 'I hope she'll be all right. She has a husband and three children, and they're all very worried about her.'

'I'm not surprised. Any surgery can be worrying, but for most people brain surgery's a frightening thing to contemplate. Let's hope the neurosurgeon manages to leave the pituitary gland intact. That way, it can start to produce the right amount of hormones and she at least has a chance of getting her life back.'

'From what I heard, he's new to the team...a youngish man, not very communicative.'

'Surgeons can be like that.' He gave a wry smile. 'They don't need to have much of a bedside manner when their patients are unconscious on a slab in Theatre, do they?'

Sarah had opened her mouth to answer him when Gemma came hurrying towards her. 'There's a problem with the patient you admitted to the observation ward—Ann-Marie Yates. Her boyfriend has just been in to see her and she's very upset, and now she's unwell again.' She shook her head. 'It's such a shame. Things started off all right. She's been fine since she was admitted, and we disconnected all the monitoring equipment as soon as we knew she was to be discharged this morning. She was getting ready to go home with her friend—apparently they share a flat—and then he walked in and they started to argue. And soon after he left, she collapsed again.'

'Oh, dear. She's not having too great a time, is she? Get her back onto all the monitoring equipment straight away and I'll come along and see her.'

'Okay. Thanks.' Gemma swivelled around, her sleek, black hair swishing as she hurried away.

James frowned, and Sarah jumped in before he had a chance to speak. 'I know you want me to refer her to her GP, but I still think we should investigate each episode thoroughly just in case there's something else going on.'

'I agree with you.' He said it in a calm, even tone, and she looked at him in surprise.

'You do?'

'You're an excellent doctor, Sarah. You've proved to me over these last few weeks that you're extremely competent, and the least I can do is go with your instincts. I'll come along with you to see how she is.'

She hadn't expected anything like that, but she was extraordinarily pleased and a little glow started up inside her. 'Okay. Thanks.' She led the way to the observation ward and arrived at Ann-Marie's bedside in time to see her struggling for breath and lying back against her pillows in a state of exhaustion.

'Hello, Ann-Marie,' Sarah greeted her. 'I can see you're unwell again. What seems to be the problem?'

'My chest hurts,' the girl whispered on a breathless note. 'I can't...breathe... I...'

'That's all right. Try not to worry. We'll give you

something to help you feel more comfortable,' Sarah said in a reassuring tone.

'I'm...dizzy... I...' Ann-Marie's voice trailed off, her words becoming a jumble of incoherent sound.

'Let's get her some oxygen,' James said to Gemma, who had just finished taking the girl's blood pressure.

Gemma nodded and quickly went to fit a face mask over Ann-Marie's nose and mouth. 'Relax, and try to take deep breaths,' she told her.

'Her blood pressure's very low, and her heart rate is forty beats a minute and dropping,' Sarah said in a quiet voice. 'This isn't a straightforward emotional upset.'

'I think you're right.' James was studying the readout from the ECG machine. 'Her heart rate is way too low. We'd better put in an intravenous line and get ready to give her atropine. That should stimulate more output.'

Sarah was already seeing to that, but a short time later it was clear that the atropine wasn't working. Ann-Marie's heart rate had dropped even further and was at a dangerous level. 'We need the defibrillator on hand,' she told Gemma. 'I'm going to give her an epinephrine infusion, but if that doesn't work, we'll have no choice but to try transcutaneous pacing.'

It was a worrying situation. The electrical impulses in Ann-Marie's heart weren't stimulating the heart muscles to contract and pump blood around her body, and if her heart rate dropped any further she could soon go into cardiac arrest.

Sarah set up the infusion and they waited to see what would happen, but after some time James shook his head. 'There's no change and we can't waste time trying any other medication while she's in this state. There's only one thing for it...we'll have to go ahead with the transcutaneous pacing after all.' He started to prepare sedative and painkilling medication while Sarah did her best to explain to their patient what they were about to do.

She couldn't be sure Ann-Marie was fully aware of what was going on around her, but she persisted in her efforts, saying, 'You might find this procedure a bit unpleasant, but we'll give you medication to help you feel more comfortable.'

James was already applying pads to the girl's chest and back, and Sarah started to set the controls on the machine. 'Okay, here we go. I'm starting the electrical impulses, low to begin with and increasing in strength until we have the rhythm we're looking for.'

'What's happening to her?' A man's voice cut into the tense silence of the room a minute or so later. 'Ann-Marie…'

Sarah glanced at him. He was in his early twenties, she guessed, tall, with unruly dark hair and anguished grey eyes.

'You'll have to stand back, sir,' Gemma said firmly. 'She's very poorly, and we need to get her condition stabilised before you can talk to her.'

'M-Marcus…?' Ann-Marie's voice was weak, but it was clear that she was coming round from her dazed state. Her blood oxygen level was improving as her heart began to beat a little faster, and a short time later Sarah stopped the machine from emitting any more shocks.

'We have a normal rhythm,' she announced, relieved that the procedure had worked.

'Ann-Marie, I'm sorry,' the young man said. 'I'm

here. I couldn't stay away. I was stupid… I thought… I thought you were seeing someone else.'

Gemma intervened once more. 'She needs to rest,' she told him. 'If you want to stay with her, you have to be quiet.'

He nodded, gulping back what he had been about to say. He hesitated. 'I'll just hold her hand…is that okay?' He looked around the room and Sarah nodded.

'If there's any sign that her treatment is being undermined, you'll be asked to leave,' she said. 'Am I making myself clear?'

Marcus nodded. 'As crystal. I won't do anything to upset her, I promise.'

Ann-Marie pulled the oxygen mask to one side and looked anxiously at James. 'Will I need to have that done again?' she asked in a breathless voice. 'What's happening to me?'

'It's possible,' he told her, 'but now we know what's happening we'll try to give you medication to regulate your heartbeat and avoid the necessity for such drastic treatment. From the looks of things, your heart's electrical system isn't working properly, so you might need to have a pacemaker fitted at some point in the near future.'

'Oh. I see.' She was struggling to take this in, but she glanced up at Marcus for reassurance. He gently squeezed her hand.

'In the meantime,' James said with a smile, 'we'll make arrangements for you to see a specialist. You don't need to worry about it. You'll be well looked after.'

'Thank you.'

Ann-Marie closed her eyes briefly, and Marcus pulled up a seat alongside the bed, continuing to hold her hand. 'How could you believe I'd go off with any-one else?' she muttered under her breath.

'I think we can leave her in Gemma's care for now,' Sarah said, her mouth curving as she sent James a quick glance. She finished writing up the medication chart and handed it to the nurse. 'Thanks for your help, Gemma.'

She walked back to A and E with James. 'Aren't you glad I didn't send her home yesterday?' she said with a crooked smile.

His mouth quirked. 'Rub it in, why don't you?' Then he sobered and said thoughtfully, 'I dare say I'd have come to the same conclusion as you if I'd examined her and taken a history. It goes to show you should trust your team.'

'Am I one of your team?' she asked softly. 'I'm still on probation, aren't I?'

'I think we both know what the outcome of that will be, don't we?' He smiled. 'Your job's safe, so you can relax as far as your future here is concerned.'

'I'm glad.' She gave a soft, shuddery sigh. 'It's a re-lief to know that you have faith in me.'

His gaze burned into her. 'I do, Sarah.'

Her green eyes glimmered as she returned his gaze. 'I'm just thankful one of my biggest worries has been taken away. I want to be able to tell the children their future is secure.'

James nodded and keyed in the security code to un-lock the door to the emergency department. 'I've been thinking about that...especially about young Sam's wor-ries. A lot's happened to him and Rosie in these last few months and maybe they both need a little more reassur-ance. It might help if we all spent some time together this weekend. What do you think? We could go down to the beach—try to get Rosie and Sam used to going down there once more. I know they have trouble with that...Rosie told me. Between us, though, we should be able to cope with any problems that come up.'

'You're making it hard for me to refuse when you put it like that,' she said.

'Do you want to refuse?' He sent her an oblique glance, looking at her keenly as though her response was all-important.

'No...not at all. An afternoon on the beach sounds like a great idea.' The idea of spending an afternoon with him was suddenly enormously attractive, and her heart made an excited leap inside her chest. She had to remind herself that he was only doing this for the children.

'Good. I'll come to your place around lunchtime on Saturday. It'll be good to spend time together. We could perhaps start off by having something to eat at the local inn?'

'I think that would be lovely.' Inside, she was bubbling with anticipation. 'I'll look forward to it.'

By the time Saturday came around, Rosie and Sam were eager to be off. Sam swivelled around in his seat by the computer. 'Will we be going in James's sports car?' he wanted to know. 'I wish I could drive it. It's well good.' He started to turn an imaginary steering-wheel with his hands and made brumming sounds like an engine roaring off into the distance.

'I expect so. The inn is a couple of miles from here, so I doubt we'll be walking.' She frowned, glancing around the room. Rosie was rummaging through a hold-all on the dining-room table, anxious to make sure that all the preparations were in hand, but Sam was being his usual self, oblivious to any need to do anything other than play his game.

'Are you two about ready?' she asked, fetching coats from the hall cloakroom. 'Come away from that computer, Sam. You need to find your beach shoes if you're going on the sand—I don't want you ruining your best trainers. Make sure you put them in your bag. And find your swimming stuff.'

'Aw…can't you do it for me?' Sam protested. 'I'm in the middle of this war game. We're holed up in a cave in the mountains and the rebels are coming after us.'

'No, I can't. James will be here in a few minutes and I still have to go and look in the shed for buckets and spades. You can put your swim trunks on under your clothes. Save the game and play it later, or I might have to switch you off at the wall socket.' She came over to the computer table and let her hand hover over the plug.

'Spoilsport,' Sam complained. 'I'm nearly up to level ten…another few minutes and I'll have cracked it.'

'Crack it some other time.' Sarah waited while he saved the game and then she switched off the computer. 'Rosie, put a couple of bottles of pop into the backpack for me, will you, please? We're bound to need a drink down on the beach.'

'Okay.' Rosie went to do as she asked, and Sarah followed her into the kitchen, on her way to the back door.

'Are you all right about this afternoon's trip?' she asked. 'We don't need to stay for too long if it bothers you, but I thought it would be nice for you to have the chance to splash in the sea for a bit and maybe play ball with Sam on the beach.'

'I think so. I don't know.' Rosie looked up at her, a

variety of expressions flitting across her face. 'I feel a bit peculiar inside.' She slid bottles and tumblers into the bag and glanced at Sarah. 'It'll be different, though, going with James. I like him. He showed me how to set up my new dance game when he came to do the fireplace in my room, and when I was cross with Sam for being a nuisance, he took him away and helped him with his war game.'

'Yes, I've noticed he's good at finding solutions to things.' James didn't make a big song or dance about anything, but somehow or other he managed to smooth the path whenever there was a problem.

She went out to the shed and rummaged around for a bit. It was full of stuff from the children's former family home in Devon, as well as bits and pieces that Sarah had brought with her.

A few minutes later she went back to the kitchen with her hands full of buckets, spades, plastic sieves and a large beach ball. She was startled to see James standing by the table, talking to Rosie. As she entered the room his glance skimmed over her.

'You look great,' he said, his eyes lighting up, and her cheeks flushed under his avid scrutiny. She was wearing jeans that clung where they touched and a simple, short-sleeved top that outlined her curves. He was equally casually dressed, in dark jeans and a T-shirt. 'Rosie let me in,' he said. 'She told me you were almost ready, but apparently we're waiting for Sam to find his shoes.'

'Except he's upstairs playing on his game pad,' Rosie commented drily. 'Shall I go and tell him to hurry up?'

'Better not, or there's bound to be a fight. You could find some tissues and put them in my handbag, if you like.' Sarah smiled. 'I'll go and see what Sam's up to in a minute when I've found a home for these buckets and spades.'

'I'll put them in the boot,' James murmured. He grinned, looking at the bags and accumulated paraphernalia. 'Are you sure you haven't forgotten anything... folding table, portable gas stove, water canisters?'

'Oh, very funny,' she retorted, flicking him a pert glance as they went out to his car. The top was down, reflecting the warmth of the summer's day. The sky was blue, with no clouds in sight, and the air was fresh and clean. 'Like I said before, you've no idea how much preparation goes into a trip where children are involved.'

'Obviously not. Though we are only going for the afternoon, you know.' There was a glint in his eye as he gave her a sidelong look. 'Unless, of course, you wanted to make a weekend of it. It's not beyond the realms of possibility that we could go for longer...there's a lovely Smugglers' Inn along the coast where they do rooms.'

There was a hint of devilishness in his voice, sparking her pulses into a throbbing beat. He wasn't being serious, of course, but even so, she had to take a moment or two to calm herself down before answering him.

She carefully arranged the buckets and spades to one side of the car's boot. Then she looked at him, raising finely shaped eyebrows. 'It isn't going to happen. I'm not seventeen years old any more, you know. I hope I've a little more sense than to go throwing myself at you as I did back then.'

'No? Are you absolutely sure about that?' He was teasing her now, with laughter in his eyes and a roguish smile playing around his mouth.

'Definitely not. That was a big mistake. I can't think

what came over me…and it certainly won't happen again.' She went hot all over, thinking about how she'd pressed her soft curves up against him and wound her arms around his neck. Her green eyes narrowed on him. 'Besides, I seem to remember you saying something recently about keeping things on a professional footing between us.'

'Hmm.' His mouth made a downward turn. 'I guess I've been fooling myself about that all along. I must have had a change of heart somewhere along the way. Perhaps seeing you in total command of yourself in A and E over these last few weeks has made me realise I should never have insisted on the three-month trial period in the first place. I was being over-cautious.'

'I'm glad you think so.' She moved away from the car as Rosie came out with the bags. 'Sweetheart, you should have left those for me,' she said in consternation, seeing her struggle with the weight.

James took the bags from Rosie and loaded them into the car. 'You did well to manage these,' he said. 'I was just telling Sarah she's packed everything bar the kitchen sink.'

Rosie chuckled. 'She wants to make sure everything is just right. I think she would have packed a hamper, but you said we were going out for lunch, didn't you?'

'I certainly did.' He glanced at the expensive watch on his wrist. 'And I think we should be getting on our way. Is there any chance of dragging your brother out of game paradise, do you think?'

Rosie shook her head. 'I don't think so. He doesn't even listen after he's loaded it up.'

'Uh-huh…we'll see about that.' Sarah went to fetch him, and within a minute or two they were all installed

inside the car and were on their way. The children were
hungry and already debating what there might be to eat,
and Sarah admitted that it had been a long time since
breakfast for her, too.

'I had a slice of toast before the children were up, and
ate it while I skimmed my emails and read through my
letters. They were a bit disappointing really, just bills
and a printed estimate for the roof repairs.'

'Were you looking for something more?' James drove
along the coast road, and Sarah leaned back in her seat,
enjoying the feel of the breeze riffling her hair. The
children were absorbed in watching the gulls circle the
bay and trying to count how many boats were moored
in the harbour.

'I was hoping there might be something from my
mother.' She winced. 'I checked the marriages for the
postmarked area over the last few years, and there
weren't all that many with my surname and my mother's first name. So I followed them up, and I think I've
found her.'

James shot her a quick glance. 'That must have come
as a bit of a shock after all this time. Did you find an
address?'

She nodded. 'Yes. I wrote to her, and I've been waiting to hear ever since. I gave her my email address and
my phone number.' She sighed. 'There's been nothing so far. I keep kidding myself that she might be on
holiday, or that I have the wrong person, but I suppose
I have to accept that the truth is she probably doesn't
want to know.'

'I'm sorry.' He clasped her hand in his briefly, keeping one hand on the steering-wheel. 'I'm not convinced
that getting to know her again is such a good idea, any-

way. As time's gone by you've been gradually getting your life back together, and I can't help thinking that if she turns up you'll find yourself drawn into an emotional whirlpool all over again.'

'It was never going to be easy, was it? Anyway, from the looks of things, it probably won't come about.'

They drove on for a while, until they came to an attractive, seventeenth-century inn, set back from the road. James parked the car and Sarah took a moment to look around at the white-painted building. It had lots of sash windows and there were hanging baskets at the front, filled with red geraniums and bright petunias. Wooden tables and chairs were set out on the forecourt, each group with its own red umbrella, and there were stone tubs dotted about, laden with flamboyant, crimson begonias and trailing foliage.

'Have you been here before?' James asked, and she shook her head.

'No, I haven't, but if the outside is anything to go by, it's lovely.'

'I asked the landlord to reserve a table for us by a window,' he said, shepherding the children out of the car and along the path. 'We can eat and look out at the sea at the same time, and if Sam and Rosie are finished before us, they can go to the play area at the back of the pub. We'll be able to see them from where we're sitting.'

'That's great.' She sent him an approving glance. 'It sounds as though you've thought it all out.'

He nodded. 'I want you to have a good time and be able to relax for a while.'

'Thanks.'

They went inside, and Sarah admired the low, wooden beams and the huge fireplace filled with logs.

There was wooden bench seating on two sides, made comfortable with luxurious padded upholstery, and tables and chairs were grouped in cosy, recessed areas brightened with the golden glow of wall lamps. There was some raised decking, and their table was on one of these sections, by a tall, wide window that allowed daylight to pour into the room and gave them a beautiful sea view.

'Seafood's the specialty here,' James explained, handing her a menu, 'but there are all sorts of other dishes for you to choose from.'

'I want the chicken nuggets,' Sam decided, with the speed of lightning.

'As if you ever eat anything else.' Rosie studied the menu for a little longer. 'Could I have gammon and fries, please?' she asked.

'Of course, whatever you like.' James looked at Sarah, his dark brow lifting in query. 'What would you like?'

'I'll have the sea bass,' she said with a smile. 'They say it's cooked with lemon, ginger and honey. Yum… it sounds delicious.'

'It is. I can recommend it.'

James chose the same, and they spent a pleasant hour enjoying the good food and looking out over the coastline, watching the waves roll gently into the bay. They talked about all sorts of things—the times when Sarah had been learning how to climb rocks, and her job in Devon when she'd gone out and about with the ambulance service. James told her about his efforts to do up the house he'd inherited, and of his visits home, when he helped his brother with the running of the farm estate.

'The orchards are massive, aren't they?' Sarah commented. 'I remember when I worked there in the summer holidays there were tons of apples to be picked. And you would come round with scrumpy cider for all the workers when we were on our lunch breaks.'

'Mmm... Technically, you weren't supposed to have it. It was pretty lethal stuff. But I think I gave you just a taster and made up the difference with orange juice.'

She laughed. 'Yes, I remember that now. I was so cross at the time.'

'You were cross about a lot of things back then.'

'Why were you cross?' Rosie asked, and Sarah gave a small start. She had forgotten the children might be listening in.

'It was because my mother had gone away,' she said quietly. 'I thought she should have stayed.'

Rosie frowned. 'Why would that make you cross? Our mother went away, but we were sad about it, not cross.'

Sarah took a moment to think how she should answer that. 'Yes, of course, that's understandable. But your mother didn't have a choice. Mine did. She chose to go away. She didn't want to stay.'

Sam's gaze was troubled. He reached out and patted her hand. 'It's all right, Sarah. We're here for you now.'

Sarah's eyes misted over at his innocent, sweet gesture of compassion. She blinked hard and swallowed against the lump that had formed in her throat. 'That's good to know, Sam,' she said huskily. 'I'm glad I have you and Rosie.'

James sucked in a deep breath. 'What more could anyone ask?' He smiled at the children and then glanced at the debris of crockery that littered the table. 'Except maybe for lots of ice cream and strawberry sundaes...'

'Yay...I'll have one of those!' Sam exclaimed. 'Can I?'

James nodded. 'They do them with fresh strawberries.'

'Yummy, scrummy, scrumptious,' Rosie said happily. 'They're my favourites.'

'Mine, too.' James gave their order to the waitress, and then glanced at Sarah. 'Are you okay?' he asked in a low voice. He reached for her hand, and folded it within his own.

'I'm fine.' She nodded. Rosie and Sam were busy colouring in the pictures on the printed sheets of paper that the waitress had given them and weren't taking any notice of what she and James were doing. 'I'm glad they feel the three of us belong together. Little gestures like that make it all worthwhile somehow, don't they?'

'They do.'

The children finished their desserts and Sarah sent them out to play on the climbing apparatus for a while. She and James took a few more leisurely minutes to drink their coffee, and turned the conversation to good food and wine.

When Sam and Rosie tired of the small adventure playground outside, they gathered up the baggage from the boot and headed down a winding path towards the beach. Here there were smooth stretches of sand broken up by rocks and boulders scattered around the base of the cliffs, and the children headed over to the rock pools with whoops of delight.

'Did we bring the fishing nets?' Sam asked, and Sarah had to shake her head.

'Sorry, we didn't.'

'You can use the small buckets to scoop things up,' James said. 'Here, let me help.' James walked alongside

Sam, looking in the pools left behind by the tide, searching for crabs and other small crustaceans, while Rosie stayed with Sarah, picking up shells and examining patches of seaweed that had been washed up by the sea.

Later, the children slipped off their outer clothes and ran into the sea in their swimming gear, splashing in the shallows as the waves broke on the shore, before venturing further out and jumping with the bigger waves that came along. 'That's far enough,' Sarah told them. 'Stay close by the shore.' She and James rolled up their jeans and went into the water with them, laughing as an unexpected wave drenched them from the knees down.

James slid an arm around her waist and helped her run back to the shore as another wave threatened to overtake them. Still laughing, they dropped on to the sand, looking out over the sea to where the children played.

James was still holding her, and Sarah was content to lean back against him, folded into the crook of his arm. It seemed so natural to be with him this way, and as the sun warmed her bare arms and dried out her jeans, she thought how good it would be if the afternoon could go on for ever.

It couldn't, of course. As time went by, a breeze blew up, and Rosie and Sam were getting cold and ready to scramble out of their wet things and into their dry clothes. Sarah covered them in beach towels and helped them to get dressed, and then they all trooped back to the car.

'That was terrific,' Rosie said, settling back in her seat and lifting her face to the gentle wind as James drove them home.

'Especially the rock pools and the ice creams,' Sam

added. 'The crabs were well good. I saw ten. Wait till I tell Ricky. He'll want to come as well next time. Can we bring him with us one day?'

'I expect so.' Sarah lifted her brows as she turned in her seat to look at him. 'Does that mean you're best friends now?'

'Yeah.' Sam didn't volunteer any more than that. He drew his game pad out of his pocket and concentrated on the screen.

Sarah smiled. 'I guess I shouldn't have worried,' she murmured, and James chuckled.

'I guess not.'

They arrived home a few minutes later and the children disappeared into their bedrooms. Sarah flicked the switch on the coffee percolator and started to set out mugs for her and James.

'I had a great time this afternoon,' she said, smiling at him as he came to stand beside her.

'So did I.' He wrapped his arms around her, drawing her to him and lowering his head so that his forehead lightly touched hers. 'It was good to hold you, out there on the beach, but I wanted to do so much more than that.'

'You did?' She looked up at him, her green eyes questioning. She trailed her hand lightly up across his chest, her fingers coming to rest on his powerful biceps.

'Oh, yes,' he said, his voice becoming rough edged, his lips hovering close to hers. 'I've tried so hard to keep my distance from you...physically, at least...these last few weeks, to avoid touching you or getting too close to you, but I'm fighting a losing battle. I know how much you worry about getting involved, but whenever

I'm near you I want to kiss you and hold you and show you just how much I want you.'

'I'm glad,' she whispered. 'I want you, too.'

His body reacted instantly, as though she'd delivered him an electric shock. His hands pressed her to him, tugging her even closer than before and she gloried in the feel of him, in the way their bodies fused, one into the other, her soft curves blending with his taut, muscular frame. Her fingertips slid upwards into the silky hair at the nape of his neck, and she clung to him, loving the way his arms encircled her. His thighs moved against hers and his hands began to make a slow detour over her body, worshipping each and every rounded contour.

A shuddery sigh escaped her as his hand tenderly cupped her breast, and he covered her mouth with his, cutting off the soft groan that formed in her throat.

Hunger surged in her, raging through her body like a firestorm, and as he lovingly caressed her she realised, through the haze that filled her head, that he must feel the same way. His heart was pounding, so much so that she could feel the thunderous beat of it against her breasts, and the knowledge filled her with a heady, tingling exhilaration. He wanted her every bit as much as she wanted him.

'I need you, Sarah,' he said huskily. 'I'm glad you're not seventeen any more. I don't know how I can go on without you...' His heated gaze swept over her, burning in its intensity, and he kissed her again, his hands roaming over the swell of her hips and easing her against him until pleasure built up in her and threatened to spill over in wave after wave of heady, tantalising desire.

'I want...' She started to say something, to tell him how much she wanted him, too, but something disrupted the heightened tension in the atmosphere, piercing it as though it was a pocket of hot gas that had built up and was ready to explode.

'What was that?' James suddenly became still, frowning as he, too, sought to find out where the disturbance was coming from.

They heard hissing, popping and bubbling sounds that were coming from behind them, and Sarah said in a bemused voice, 'It's the percolator.' She looked at James. 'I'd forgotten all about it.'

'Me, too.' He reluctantly eased himself away from her so that he could turn it off, and would have reached for her once again if it hadn't been for Rosie coming into the kitchen at that moment.

'Can I use the laptop?' she asked Sarah. 'I want to see if my friends from Devon are on line, but Sam's on the other computer.'

Sarah pulled in a deep breath, trying to get back to something like normality. She sent James a quick, sorrowful look. The mood had been broken, and they couldn't get back to where they'd been. He inclined his head briefly, sadly. Perhaps he felt it, too.

With the change in atmosphere, along came a niggling doubt. James hadn't wanted her all those years ago. Why did he want her now? Were his feelings purely a physical response?

'Yes, that's okay.'

Rosie sat down by the table and ran her fingers over the keyboard. There was a tinkling sound, and she said, 'Oh, you have some emails. They've just come in.' She glanced up at Sarah, her grey eyes wide. 'I think there's one you've been waiting for. The heading says, "Getting in touch".'

'Uh... I...' Sarah felt winded all at once, and a little dizzy. Her head was still up in the clouds somewhere from being with James, and now this had come at her, out of the blue.

She couldn't think what to do, and it was James who said quietly, 'I think you'd better sit down and read it, don't you? I'll see to the coffee.'

She floundered for a moment or two and then managed to find her voice. 'Okay, thanks.'

Rosie smiled. 'I'll come back in a couple of minutes, shall I? I'll go and text my friend from school while I'm waiting.'

'Yes, that's a good idea. I won't be long.' Sarah sat down and opened up the email. It was short, just a few lines, and she read through it quickly. Then she frowned and stared at the screen, not knowing what to think.

'What's wrong?' James asked, his expression guarded as he slid a mug of coffee towards her.

'I... Nothing, really. I mean, she's got back to me... my mother...which is what I wanted after all.'

'But? There is a but.'

'I'm not sure.' She read the email once more.

'Doesn't she want to meet up with you, is that the problem?'

'No. I mean, yes...she wants to see me. She's suggesting that I go over to London and have lunch with her some time at a local restaurant. She doesn't have a lot of time to spare, she says.' She looked up at him. 'That's okay, I suppose, isn't it?'

It wasn't quite what she'd expected. Maybe she'd been hoping for something with a little more warmth, an expression of joy at being able to link up with her after all this time. Not this cool, brief invitation to lunch as though she was a mere acquaintance who'd happened to drop her a line. She was her daughter, but she might as well have been a stranger. Sadness clouded her eyes. It was like being abandoned all over again. Was she really so undeserving of love?

James looked at her with concern, and he put his mug of coffee down on to the worktop next to him. 'You're asking me if it's okay? I don't know, Sarah. My instincts tell me it isn't, and from the look on your face, you feel the same way. Is that all she says? After all this time it doesn't feel as though it's enough. Not by any means.'

Sarah pressed her lips together. 'Well, she wants us to get together, and that's what I wanted after all. Only...I think I'd expected something more.'

A muscle flicked in his jaw. 'Of course you did. She walked out on you, her only child. She's made no effort to find you through all these years, and now she can't even be bothered to go to the trouble of coming here to see you? I'm sorry to be blunt, but at the very least she might have suggested you stay over at her place for a couple of days.'

'Perhaps she's afraid we won't get on. Or maybe she has a family of her own now.'

'And you aren't her family? Who has the better claim?'

'Even so...'

Exasperated, he came over to her. 'May I read what she has to say?'

'Of course.' She nodded and turned the laptop around so that he could see the screen.

A second or two later he sucked in his breath. 'Sarah, please tell me you're not going to dignify that by agreeing to go and have lunch with her. That's the chilliest invitation I've read in a long time. There's not even an expression of regret for what she did. You deserve so much better than that.'

She ran the tip of her tongue lightly over her lips. 'It might not be such a bad idea to go and see her. At least it would be a start.' He made a stifled sound, and she added, 'I'm not sure what I'm going to do yet. I have to think about it.'

'What is there to think about?' His voice was terse, reflecting the anger in his expression. 'She has the nerve to say that she's busy and can't spare you much time. She has a business to run…an online business, for heaven's sake, selling handbags and fashion accessories. How difficult can that be? Doesn't she know you're a doctor, working weekends sometimes, out on call at other times too? Did you tell her that?'

'Yes, I did. I told her quite a bit about myself and about my father and the children. I was sort of hoping she'd tell me more about herself.'

'The woman is selfish, Sarah. Always has been, always will be. Perhaps you should face up to the fact that she isn't going to change. When are you going to realise that you can't let her ruin your life any longer?'

'Like I said, I have to think about this.'

He shook his head, as though he was trying to rid himself of the whole idea. 'I almost wish she had never answered your letter. This is going to stir everything up all over again, isn't it? You were doing so well, getting yourself back on track, and now she's going to drag you down into her cold, self-centred world once more. She'll destroy you, and make you feel worthless all over again. Hasn't she already started the process with that wretched little note? I can see how badly it has affected you.'

He moved restlessly. 'I'd hoped there might be a chance for us…for you and me to get together, for us to be a couple. But you'll never settle to that, will you? Oh, it might be all right for a while, but there will always be doubt at the back of your mind, won't there? The worry that you'll be abandoned all over again?' He looked into her eyes, his gaze searing her. 'You know I want you, Sarah. Do you think we have any kind of a future together?'

Her lips parted as she tried to answer him. She'd waited so long to hear him say that they were a couple, that they would be together… Of course she knew he wanted her. He'd made that clear over the last few weeks, the way he'd been there for her, cared for her. But he was right, there was always a niggling doubt in the back of her mind that things would not work out for them. How could he love her, and want to be with her for ever? Had he ever mentioned love? And what of the other women, from the hospital and other walks of life, who'd set their hearts on him and had had their hopes and dreams dashed? Was she to become another one of them?

'James, you have to understand, it's hard for me to trust, to put my faith in anyone. I've been badly hurt, and I don't know how to put that behind me. I try, but something always gets in the way. I don't know how to change. You said once that being abandoned was like a scar on my mind, and maybe you were right— perhaps it has damaged me for ever.'

He sighed heavily. 'Then I guess I have my answer,

don't I?' He turned away from her, picking up his car keys from the worktop. 'There's no hope for us.'

'James…'

'I'm sorry. I have to go. I can't do this any more. I have feelings too, you know.' He was already striding towards the door. 'I need to get some air and maybe drive around for a bit. You must do what you think right where your mother is concerned.'

He walked out, and Sarah sat at the table for a while after he had gone. What had been a wonderful day had turned to ashes, and for the moment she didn't have any idea how to deal with the aftermath. She stared into space, wishing with all her heart that James had stayed, that she'd been able to give him the answer he wanted.

'James has gone. You were arguing with him, weren't you? I heard you.' Rosie was shocked, and there was disbelief in her voice. 'How could you let him go like that?'

'We weren't arguing, Rosie. We were just…'

'You were. I heard you. Your voices were loud and he was angry.' Her face crumpled. 'Now it's all gone wrong.'

Sarah stood up, seeing the distress in Rosie's face. 'Rosie,' she said gently, putting an arm around the small girl, 'it wasn't an argument, not really. We just don't agree on some things, that's all. Sometimes grown-ups have differences of opinion. It's all right to do that.'

'No, it isn't,' Rosie sobbed. 'I like James. I wanted him to stay. We could have been a family, and now it's all ruined.'

Sarah hugged her, shocked by all those expectations that had been slowly simmering beneath the surface. She glanced across the room and saw Sam standing in the doorway. 'Did you feel that way, too?' she asked quietly, and he nodded, white faced.

'I wanted him to stay as well.'

'I'm sorry.' She held out an arm to him and he came into her embrace. They were echoing her own thoughts, but right now there wasn't a thing she could do about it.

Her mother's leaving had always been at the heart of her problems, making her uncertain, insecure and feeling unloved…unlovable. James had been dealing with that for some time, and now he'd decided enough was enough. He'd gone, and things might never again be the same between them. She couldn't bear it.

CHAPTER EIGHT

SARAH's pager went off, alerting her to an incoming emergency, and she winced inwardly. She was looking after a man who had suffered an angina attack and she really didn't want to leave him right now. He was frightened, fearful of the pain and desperately worried about what was happening to him.

'The nitroglycerin spray will help relieve the pain,' she told him. 'It widens the blood vessels and helps the heart pump blood around your body more easily. Just try to breathe slowly and evenly, and it should soon start to pass.'

She glanced at the nurse who was assisting her, and said in a quiet voice, 'I have to go and attend to another emergency. Will you stay with him and make sure that he's comfortable?' She reached for the medication chart and made some notes. 'I've written up his medication, but if there are any problems, call the registrar. He's due to take over from me in half an hour.'

The nurse nodded. 'I'll take care of him.' She held the oxygen mask to the man's face. 'Take it nice and slowly. Deep breaths. That's right. That's fine. You're doing really well.'

Sarah glanced at the ECG printout and saw that the

attack was receding. 'You're in good hands,' she told her patient. 'You should feel better very soon.'

She hurried away, heading for the resuscitation room, and found herself walking swiftly alongside James. Her heart seemed to clamp into a tight knot inside her. She'd hardly had a chance to speak to him all day, and it looked as though they were still going to be tied up with work now, when it was nearly the end of her shift. There was so much she needed to say to him but here at work their conversation was muted, constricted by their surroundings, by work and the constant bustle of colleagues all around them.

'It looks as though we've both been paged for the same case,' he said with a frown.

'Yes. Do you know what it's all about?'

He shook his head. 'I was dealing with an appendicitis case—it's been non-stop all day.'

'You're right. I didn't even get to stop for lunch.'

'It goes like that sometimes.'

'Yes.' She sent him a quick glance. 'I tried to phone you yesterday, but all I got was your messaging service telling me you'd been called out to the hospital. It looks as though the rush started yesterday for you.'

'I had to come in to do some emergency surgery.' He pushed open the door to the resuscitation room and Gemma hurried to update them on the situation.

'This is Lucy Myers. She gave birth to a baby girl about eight hours ago. She was sent home as normal, but she became unwell and started to bleed heavily so her husband turned the car around and brought her straight here to A and E.'

'And the husband is…where?' James glanced around as he went to introduce himself to the young woman.

'In the relatives' room with the baby.'

'Okay.'

Lucy was already connected up to the monitors via various pads and electrodes, and it was plain to see from the readings that she was in a bad way. She was being given oxygen through a face mask but appeared not to be aware of her surroundings.

'She complained of dizziness and feeling faint,' Gemma said, 'and she's suffering from palpitations. It's hard to estimate how much blood she's lost, but from her condition it's a fair amount, I'd say.'

James spoke quietly to their patient, trying to calm her down and let her know that she would be safe. It was difficult to know how much she was able to take in, because the loss of blood was having a system-wide effect on her. 'I'm going to take some blood from your arm so that we can see if there's anything to pinpoint what might be causing this,' he said. 'But you had a prolonged labour, from what the records tell me, and that can sometimes lead to problems like this.'

Sarah made a careful examination and gently palpated the woman's abdomen. 'It looks as though the uterus isn't contracting as it should,' she murmured. Usually, after the placenta came away, there would be some bleeding, which would gradually stop as the womb contracted and compressed the blood vessels.

James relayed that information to Lucy. 'I'm going to put in an intravenous line so that we can give you fluids to help make up for what you've lost, and at the same time give you medication to help make the uterus contract,' he said.

Lucy didn't say anything. She was conscious, but

too exhausted and debilitated to take any notice of what was going on.

'She's not responding too well, is she?' Sarah remarked softly. 'I've been massaging the uterus, but it hasn't helped to stimulate the contractions.'

'No.' James checked the monitors. 'Her heart rate's far too high. I'll give her oxytocin and see if that starts things off.' He turned to Gemma. 'Alert Obstetrics and Gynaecology, will you, please, Gemma? They need to be aware of what's going on.'

'Will do. Do you want me to have Theatre on standby, too?'

He nodded. 'That would be for the best. I'm hoping it won't come to that, but it's possible she'll need surgery to stop the bleeding.' He frowned. 'You'd better talk to the husband about the possibility—he might have to sign the necessary consents if his wife isn't up to it.'

'Okay.'

James gave Lucy the medication through the intravenous catheter, and then he and Sarah stood back away from the bed for a while, waiting to see if her vital signs improved.

Sarah stretched, easing her aching muscles. It had been a long day.

James glanced at her. 'Are you okay?'

'I'm fine.' He seemed calm and relaxed, and there was no sign of any tension in his manner towards her. She wanted to talk to him about what had happened between them on Saturday afternoon, but this was hardly the place to do that. Instead, she kept to safe ground, talking about their work. 'I checked on Nicola Carter this morning,' she told him. 'Apparently the tumour was benign.'

James smiled. 'Yes, I read her notes. That must be a great relief for her family.'

'I imagine so.'

'What's happening with the girl you were worried about? Rachel, the one who had a bad reaction with Ecstasy?'

'She's doing much better. Her heart rhythm has settled down, and it's possible she'll be discharged soon.'

'To go back to her old lifestyle?'

Sarah shook her head. 'I don't think so. Her brother put her in touch with her parents, and from what I heard they all had a heart to heart and managed to sort things out. I think she'll be going back home to live with them.'

'That's good.' His gaze swept over her. 'At least somebody's family has been put back together again.'

'It goes to show that it's possible sometimes.' She lifted her chin. 'It all comes down to both parties making an effort to meet each other halfway.'

'Yeah, maybe.' He checked the monitors once more and went to carefully examine Lucy. 'The uterus is still soft and relaxed, and there are no contractions,' he said, under his breath. 'We'll try one more medication and if that doesn't start things off, there's nothing else for it—she'll have to go up to Theatre for surgery to clamp the blood vessels.'

'What are you going to use? Methylergonovine?'

'Yes. It might mean she won't be able to breastfeed for a few days, because it could pass into the milk, but I don't see that we have a choice.' James was already preparing the intravenous injection.

Once the injection had been given, they waited once again for it to take effect. 'Perhaps her husband could come in now?' Sarah suggested in a low voice. 'If this works, it would be good for her to see him and the baby…it might help with the bonding process. She had a long, exhausting labour, and then she collapsed, so she's had very little time to hold her baby. The midwife said she wasn't able to hold her for more than a minute or two because she was so weak.'

James frowned. 'So why was she discharged after only a few hours?'

'They had no beds and a couple of emergencies came in. I don't think they had much of a choice, once her temperature and blood pressure were okay.'

His expression was sombre. 'The days are gone when new mothers would at least stay in hospital overnight.'

He went over to the bed and examined Lucy once more. 'The uterus is contracting,' he told Sarah. 'It looks as though her condition's about to stabilise.'

Lucy gave a low moan and stirred briefly. Then her eyelids flickered open.

'Hey,' he said softly, 'you're back with us. That's terrific. Are you okay, Lucy? How are you feeling?' The monitors showed that her blood oxygen level was up and her heart rate was gradually coming down to a more normal level.

Lucy nodded, pushing the oxygen mask to one side. 'I'm okay,' she said in a thin, tired voice. 'What happened to me? I feel wiped out.' Then, anxiously, 'Where's my baby?'

Sarah smiled. It was great that she was asking after her newborn infant. 'She's on her way. Your husband is looking after her. The nurse has gone to fetch them.'

The husband arrived in Resus a few minutes later, armed with a fresh, warm bottle of milk formula for the baby. 'I think she's hungry,' he said, looking down at the squalling infant in his arms. 'She's been asleep all this time, and then she suddenly woke up and all hell was let loose. She has a good pair of lungs on her and that's no mistake.' He smiled at his wife, and went to stand beside her. 'The nurse went to fetch the milk for me.'

Lucy held out her arms for the baby, and he carefully lowered the crying infant down to her. She snuggled her close in the crook of her arm and tested the milk for heat against the back of her hand. Then she gently eased the teat into the infant's mouth and there was instant peace in the room, with only soft sucking and gurgling sounds coming from the contented baby.

Sarah watched them, a tender smile on her lips. There was a hint of sadness in her expression too, though, and James looked at her curiously and murmured, 'It's good to see them together like that, isn't it? We'll let her recover for a while and then admit her to the observation ward.'

She nodded, but didn't say anything. They started to walk out of the room. Their job here was finished, and she could go home now, secure in the knowledge that their patient was out of the woods.

He asked quietly, 'Is something bothering you?'

'Not really. But I can't help wondering how my mother felt when she held me for the first time. Perhaps she never experienced that glow of motherhood. For her, having a baby might have been a burden, something that she felt she had to do to please her husband.'

His brows shot up. 'What makes you think that? Have you spoken to her about it?'

'We've exchanged a few emails. She says she never wanted children. She wanted to have a career, but my father was keen for them to start a family, so she went along with it.'

'Good grief.' His expression was bemused. 'I'm surprised she would admit to something like that.'

She gave a faint smile. 'I had pretty much the same thought, but I'd asked her to be honest with me, so I suppose I can't complain. Anyway, I'm going home now, so I'll be able to see if she has anything else to say.' She glanced at him as she reached for her purse from a locked cupboard behind the central desk. 'Will you be going off duty soon?'

'In about half an hour.' He caught hold of her arm as she would have walked away, gently circling it with his fingers. 'Sarah, I was wrong the other day when I suggested you shouldn't go and see her. It's not up to me to say what you should or shouldn't do. You have to do what you think is best. I just don't want to see you hurt.'

'I know. I understood that.'

'I'm glad.'

He might have said more, but Gemma called him to go and look at a patient, and Sarah made her way out of the department and set off for home. She was sad because her mother had turned out to be not quite what she'd expected, but at least she was in touch with her now, and gradually they would begin to get to know one another.

Now that she was over the initial shock of making contact, she'd realised that what bothered her most of all was not how she and her mother would go on but the state of her relationship with James. When he'd walked out on Saturday, she'd been lost, as though she'd been cast adrift.

She collected the children from Murray's house, and

took them home to give them tea and biscuits to stave off the hunger pangs while she prepared the evening meal.

'Don't go eating too many, Sam,' she warned as he went to dip his hand in the biscuit barrel for the third time. 'I know it's been quite a while since lunchtime, but it's important that you eat all your dinner.'

'What are we having?'

'Beef risotto.'

'No problem. I love it.'

'Even so...' She replaced the lid on the biscuit tin as his fingers began to stray once more. 'You've had enough for now.'

'Can I fry the onions?' Rosie asked. 'I know how to do them until they're golden brown.'

'Okay.' Sarah smiled. Inside, she was aching a little for all that might have been, but Rosie and Sam kept her from thinking too hard about that. Whenever she was in danger of sinking into thoughts of James and how things could ever work out the way she wanted, one or other of them demanded her attention. 'Let's see, we need onions, mince, a little garlic...'

'Tomatoes and peas,' Rosie added.

'Yes, you're right.' She checked the items off one by one as she placed them on the kitchen table. 'I think that's about everything, don't you?'

'It won't be any good without the rice,' Sam said, frowning. 'Whoever heard of risotto without the rice?'

Sarah laughed. 'It's a good job you're here to keep me on course, isn't it?'

He gave them both a smug smile, and then went off to his bedroom to play for a while.

Some twenty minutes later the appetising smell of

risotto filled the kitchen. 'We'll give it another fifteen minutes or so,' Sarah said. 'That'll give you time to do some colouring or—' She broke off as the doorbell sounded. 'It can't be Murray,' she said with a frown. 'He said he was going out this evening to have dinner with his girlfriend.'

She went to the front door and found James waiting in the porch. 'Oh…hello,' she said, her heart giving a small leap inside her chest, a smile curving her mouth. 'I thought…well, it's good to see you.' She waved him into the hallway, but he stopped, standing still and sniffing the air approvingly.

'Something smells really good,' he said. He looked uncomfortable. 'I didn't mean to barge in on you when you were about to sit down to your meal.'

'That's okay. You can stay and eat with us. We made plenty.'

He followed her as she walked towards the kitchen, and Sarah glanced up as she saw Sam flit across the landing upstairs. 'Hi, James,' he said, and then disappeared into his room once more.

Rosie greeted him with a sweet smile. 'Hi,' she said. She stared at him for a while and then added, 'I was afraid you might not come here again.'

'Oh, why's that?' James frowned.

Rosie's shoulders did a strange little wiggle. 'Because you and Sarah had an argument last time.'

'No…no…' He glanced at Sarah, his expression sombre. 'That was just a bit of a difference of opinion, that's all.'

'That's what Sarah said.' Smiling happily, she went to join her brother upstairs.

Sarah listened for a moment or two, waiting for them

to start arguing, but nothing happened, and she turned to James. 'I'm really glad you came,' she said. 'I was miserable when you went away. I wanted to see you again, to talk to you properly, without worrying about being at work with people all around.'

He came over to her and took her in his arms. 'I was thinking exactly the same thing. I thought I should stay away, but I can't. I need to be here with you.'

'You're not still cross about my mother getting in touch?'

His mouth flattened. 'That was the least of my worries. But I think I was afraid that you would always be living in your mother's shadow, worrying about why she didn't care enough to stay, and it seemed such a waste. All these years you've been scared that there was no future for you, that you wouldn't have a family of your own because in the back of your mind you felt you didn't deserve it. You have to know that you can enjoy these things the same as everyone else. Your mother didn't reject you—she rejected the idea of motherhood. It doesn't mean that you're unlovable.'

'I think I'm beginning to realise that.' She pressed her lips together briefly. 'I don't know what I was hoping for…to find some reason that turned her against me and my father, I suppose. But it wasn't that after all. It was simply that she never wanted a family. She wanted a career and freedom to do as she pleased without being tied down. And one day it all became too much for her, so she left to go and live her life the way she'd always wanted to.'

He ran his hand lightly down her arm. 'I'm sorry. Have you decided what you're going to do? Will you go and see her?'

'Maybe, one day, but not for some time. I thought it would be better to take things slowly. We can exchange emails, photos, get to know one another that way, and then perhaps we can talk on the phone at some point. I'm still not sure quite how I feel, but somehow it's as though a weight's been lifted off me. I really thought there was something wrong with me, and that she'd walked away from me…but now I know that she's the one with the problem. It's made me look at things in a whole new light. It made me think that I was wrong in believing none of my relationships could ever work out.' She looked up at him. 'I mean, I was wrong in thinking things would never work between you and me.'

He exhaled slowly. 'I'm glad you've come to realise that. I was hoping you would see things that way, but I didn't think it was possible.' His arms circled her, wrapping her in his warm embrace. 'I care about you so much, Sarah. I want you to know how I feel about you, but I needed you to know that things can be good between us. Everything doesn't have to turn sour.'

She lifted her face to him, her eyes troubled. 'I know you want me, but I don't really understand what you feel for me. You didn't want me when I was a teenager… you turned me away then…so what's changed? Why is now any different? I'm still the same person—a little curvier perhaps, not so impulsive and reckless, but basically I'm still me.'

'Ah, Sarah…' He bent his head and dropped a kiss on her startled mouth. 'I always wanted you. It took every ounce of willpower I had to turn you away that night. But I had to do it. You were so young and vulnerable, so confused… After your mother left, you put on this tough exterior, but I knew it wasn't for real, you were a young girl crying out for attention, and I couldn't take advantage of you. I wanted you more than anything, but I knew you'd hate me the next day, perhaps for always.'

He frowned. 'Besides, I had to go away to work. It wasn't as though I could stay close by. You had your future ahead of you. I knew you had to get rid of the demons that were driving you before you could settle to any kind of relationship.' He gave a rueful smile. 'I just didn't think it would take this long.'

She stared at him in bewilderment. 'You're saying that you wanted me back then? That you've wanted me all along?'

'More than that. I love you, Sarah. I couldn't let you know. I didn't want you to fling yourself into a relationship with me then realise you'd made a mistake and blame me later. I wanted you to be sure of your feelings. I love you and I'll always be here for you. That's why I've never been able to settle into a relationship with anyone else. You're the only woman I've ever loved. I'll never leave you, you need to know that, but do you think you can conquer your doubts?'

Joy welled up inside her. She lifted her arms, wrapping them around him, and lifted her face for his kiss. 'I've always loved you,' she said. 'I never had any doubts about that. I was afraid you wouldn't be able to love me in return.' She made a choking little laugh. 'I was such a pain back then. I think I wanted to do my worst to prove to myself that no one could possibly love me.'

'It didn't work,' he said. 'It just made me want to protect you all the more.' He kissed her tenderly, brushing his lips over hers, trailing kisses over her cheek and along the smooth column of her throat. 'I love you and I want to spend the rest of my life with you.'

Her eyes widened. 'Do you really mean it?'

'I do.' He gently stroked her cheek, gazing down at her. 'Will you marry me, Sarah?'

She smiled up at him. 'Yes, please. It's what I want more than anything.' But then her expression sobered as she thought of something else that might be a stumbling block to mar their happiness. 'You realise, don't you, that it means you'll be taking on not only me but Rosie and Sam as well?'

'Oh, I think I can cope with that,' he said confidently, swooping to kiss her once more. 'We'll be a family, you, me, Rosie and Sam. You won't need to worry about anything.'

She snuggled against him, wrapped securely, satisfyingly in his arms, and for the next few minutes they were lost in one another, oblivious to everything around them. Sarah sighed happily. It was exhilarating, being held this way, having him kiss her and show her just how much he loved her. She wanted this moment to go on for ever and ever.

EPILOGUE

'ARE you ready? Do you have everything you need? Something old, something new…?' Sarah's mother fussed around her, adjusting the folds of Sarah's ivory silk wedding gown and carefully draping the lace edged veil over her bare shoulders. 'Oh, you look so beautiful. I just can't believe… I never imagined I would see this day.' She wiped away a tear with the edge of her white handkerchief.

'Something old…' Sarah fingered the silver necklace she was wearing. Her father had given it to her when she had been a bridesmaid at his wedding, and she had treasured it ever since. 'Something new…' She smiled. 'James bought me these earrings to wear.' She turned her head this way and that, to show them off.

'They're lovely, absolutely exquisite.' Her mother's eyes were misting over once more.

They were diamond droplets, with an emerald at their core. 'To match your beautiful eyes,' James had said, and Sarah's mouth curved at the memory. 'Something borrowed, something blue…that's how the saying goes, isn't it?' She glanced down at the white silk ribbon that tied her bouquet of pink roses and fragrant orchids. 'I'll give this back to you later. I understand how much it means to you.' She hadn't understood the significance at first, but when her mother had explained that it was the ribbon from Sarah's christening gown, tears had come to her eyes. After all that had happened, her mother hadn't been able to part with this one tender memento of her baby girl.

Her mother nodded. 'I'll have new memories to treasure after this, though, won't I?' A line creased her brow. 'Can you ever forgive me, Sarah? Getting to know you all over again, and seeing you with James and Rosie and Sam has made me realise how badly I've behaved and just how much I've been missing. I'm so proud of you.'

'I forgive you,' Sarah said softly. On this day, of all days, she was thinking only of the future...of the wonderful, love-filled life that she was going to share with James.

Her mother sighed heavily, the breath catching in her throat. 'Thank you. It's more than I dared expect.' She frowned as a car drew up outside and there was a knock at the door. 'Oh, the taxi's here... I have to go.' Her voice rose in agitation. 'Where are Sam and Rosie? They have to come with me.'

'It's all right, we're here, we're ready,' Rosie said, coming into the sitting room. 'Murray was showing us pictures of the seaside where he's taking us for the next two weeks—him and his girlfriend. I like her, she's fun...and there are caves and rock pools and lots and lots of sand.'

'It'll be well good,' Sam joined in. 'He says we can go on sail boats and try out body surfing and stuff.'

'I think you'll have a great time,' Sarah said. 'But you'd better phone me every day, or else,' she warned.

Rosie laughed. 'We will.' She gave a twirl, showing off her pink silk dress and letting the skirts billow out around her. 'Do I look all right?'

'You look stunning, as pretty as a picture.' Sarah turned to Sam. 'And you make a wonderful pageboy, Sam. You're so smart in your suit, and I love that silk waistcoat. Do you think you can keep it clean until after the ceremony?'

He gave her a nonchalant smile. 'Of course.'

Sarah saw them out to the waiting taxi and waved them off. In just a few short minutes she would be setting off herself in the wedding car, with Murray by her side to do the traditional 'giving away' of the bride.

She was suddenly overcome by nerves. Would James like the way she looked? What was he thinking right now? This was the biggest commitment either of them would ever make, and she wanted everything to be over with so that she could be with him, just the two of them for a short while, to start their new life together.

Some twenty minutes later she stood in the stone archway by the church door, calmly waiting while Murray, looking splendid in a morning suit, chivvied the children into their places behind her. Everything would be all right. She remembered the love token that James had given her to pin to the inside of her dress. It was a small silver hoop that held a trio of tiny charms— a carriage to represent their journey together through life, a silver horseshoe for luck, and the something blue—a sapphire heart, to show the love that he would always have for her.

The wedding march sounded out, cutting into her reverie, and she took Murray's arm, walking slowly down the aisle towards the man she was to marry.

James turned to look at her as she approached. His lips parted in stunned surprise, his eyes widening as he gazed at her, and then he smiled. At the same time the sun shone through the stained-glass windows of the church, lighting up the altar and the gleaming silver candlesticks and spreading its warm rays over the flowers that decorated the pedestals.

He came to stand beside her. 'You look sensational,' he whispered, clasping her hand in his, his grasp firm and assured. 'I love you.'

The vicar stepped forward. 'Dearly Beloved,' he said, 'we are gathered here today…' And the service began. Sarah glanced at James from time to time, and each time he responded, looking into her eyes, showing her all the love that was in his heart.

'With this ring, I thee wed.' James slid the gold ring onto the third finger of her left hand, and Sarah felt a lump rise in her throat. This ring bound them together for all time. It was what James had promised when he'd slipped the diamond engagement ring on her finger just a few short weeks ago, and now this simple act in the wedding service completed that promise.

He held her hand as he walked with her down the aisle a few minutes later, and they stepped out into the sunshine, to be greeted by cheering friends and family, who showered them with confetti and clamoured for him to kiss the bride.

He took her in his arms and obliged cheerfully, kissing her with a thoroughness that took her breath away and pleased the onlookers enormously. 'My lovely wife,' he said, some time later. 'I feel as though I've waited for this moment for an eternity. I can't believe how lucky I am.' His gaze travelled over her. 'From this day forward,' he murmured, quoting from the wedding service, 'I'll always be here for you, Sarah. Don't ever doubt it.'

'I won't,' she said softly. 'We'll be together, for ever.'

And then he kissed her again, to the great delight of the photographer and everyone around.

* * * * *

Special Offers

Every month we put together collections and longer reads written by your favourite authors.

Here are some of next month's highlights— and don't miss our fabulous discount online!

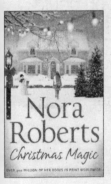

On sale 5th October

On sale 5th October

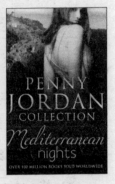

On sale 5th October

Save 20% on all Special Releases

The World of Mills & Boon®

There's a Mills & Boon® series that's perfect for you. We publish ten series and, with new titles every month, you never have to wait long for your favourite to come along.

Blaze.

Scorching hot, sexy reads
4 new stories every month

By Request

Relive the romance with the best of the best
9 new stories every month

Cherish™

Romance to melt the heart every time
12 new stories every month

Desire™

Passionate and dramatic love stories
8 new stories every month